LOAD BEARING

A Novel

JANE HARTSOCK

ISBN - 13: 9798991612500

Cover design by: Sortilèges: Evening dress, de Beer (1922) fashion illustration in high resolution by George Barber.

Library of Congress Control number: 2018675309

Printed in the United States of America

Content Warning: This novel contains explicit descriptions of suicide, discussions of child abuse, mental illness, and substances use disorder, and frank depictions of consensual sex.

❀ Formatted with Vellum

For Hal, Greyson, and Julia

PROLOGUE

"It's a very historic home," Debbie said, knowing full well the kind of work "historic" was doing in that sentence. Her eyes danced back and forth expectantly, taking in the couple standing before her—the man, who was clearly the decision-maker, and the woman who eagerly sought his decision. One tired, sideways glance from the man told her he was not inclined toward euphemisms.

As a realtor, Debbie had seen just about everything and prided herself on being an astute judge of character, a skill that had served her well in her long career. The husband, Michael Korman—apologies, Dr. Michael Korman—was a chemical engineer, an MD, PhD relocating from Boston to Indianapolis to work at Rue McMillian, the pharmaceutical giant that served as one of the few industries in Indiana to survive the twentieth century. Debbie had accepted the referral from "Rue", as it was called, to assist Dr. Korman and his wife in finding a new home. Dr. Korman was scheduled to begin his new position by the end of the next month. If the couple bought this house, it was unlikely, given its current condition, that he would start that position from this address, but that wasn't Debbie's concern.

The wife, a tall, willowy thing named Hannah, stood next to her husband in the gravel horseshoe in front of the house, a toddler propped on her hip. The couple appeared somewhat mismatched. Dr. Korman carried an air of pervasive disinterest, though it was hard to tell whether that disinterest related solely to this house or whether it extended to all areas of his life, his wife included. Debbie had only been working with the Kormans for four days, but in that time, she'd never seen Dr. Korman express a single strong emotion, nothing beyond an elevated discomfort, which he exuded presently as he stared straight ahead at the yellow bricks and lead-paned windows before him.

Hannah, in contrast, radiated a refined elegance. A bit older than the ubiquitous social media influencers—now in her early thirties—she evoked the pages of Vogue or Vanity Fair with gray-blue eyes set above the kind of cheekbones Debbie recognized as a prerequisite for glossy magazine pages. Her height—shoulder-to-shoulder with her husband even in flats—suggested she could have had a career beyond either social media or print. Debbie looked at the little girl squirming in Hannah's arms and thought it fortunate the child tended, at least at this early stage, to favor her mother.

"I don't get it," Dr. Korman said.

Debbie wasn't sure whether he'd spoken to her or to his wife, but it didn't surprise her that he didn't "get it." She thought probably much escaped Dr. Korman. Obviously successful in the research-and-development arm of the pharmaceutical industry—or his budget for relocation would have been more modest—he'd checked his phone no fewer than six times since the couple had stepped out of their Range Rover five minutes before.

As Debbie waited for clarification as to from whom Dr. Korman sought an answer, the couple's daughter babbled a protest at being held, and Hannah set her down on the ground.

"It's not safe for Molly," Dr. Korman said as the little girl toddled along the gravel driveway.

"Well, we wouldn't move in right away, Michael." Hannah gazed ahead at the house. She had a gentle way about her, even while arguing.

"Why would I buy a house we can't live in?"

"I don't think it would take long to get it up and running," Debbie added—a comment that inspired yet another tired, sideways glance from Dr. Korman. His patience had worn thin.

"I just want to understand," he began in the tone of someone intent on making sure others understood. "I'm expected to spend over a million dollars on a fixer-upper that we cannot even live in. Is that the ask?" He'd directed the question to Hannah, but she didn't answer. Up ahead, their daughter turned back, seeking reassurance for her continued exploration.

"This house would cost upwards of ten million dollars in Boston," Hannah offered as if reciting an interesting piece of trivia.

"We're not in Boston. We're in Indianapolis. And this house would be condemned in Boston."

"Not condemned, Michael. It's not that far gone," Hannah said, her voice calm, fluid, like still water being poured into fine crystal.

"What's the story here?" Michael asked, ignoring his wife and directing his question to Debbie. "Why is this place such a dump?"

"The owner died in 2014, and none of the children were interested in living in the house. So, they sold it to a developer who was going to flip it—" Debbie began.

"Flip a mansion?" Michael repeated, incredulous.

"Maybe 'flip' isn't exactly the right word," Debbie said. "The previous owner had been only the second owner to live in the house, and it required considerable updating. But the location is quite desirable—"

"I don't know about that," Michael interrupted again. "As I understand it, if you want a luxury home in Indiana, you buy in Carmel." He'd pronounced the suburb incorrectly, accenting the second syllable.

"The luxury home market in Carmel certainly has some remarkable properties," Debbie said, pronouncing the town's name correctly.

"All new construction, though," Hannah said, her eyes on the toddler.

"There are some older properties in Carmel," Debbie countered. "But you're correct that the overwhelming majority of the luxury market was built after 1990 and none from this era, pre-Great Depression."

"It's been empty then for nearly ten years," Michael observed, returning to the earlier comment about the death of the owner.

"Not quite empty. Fritz Brothers did spend a good six months on renovations in 2017, and when we go inside, you'll see they made some headway. But no one has lived in it since 2014."

"So, what happened? Why didn't they finish the work?" Michael asked.

"They got in a fight," Hannah volunteered. She'd already had this conversation with Debbie over the phone prior to requesting to see the house "in-person."

"One sued the other," Debbie said.

"Over this house?" Michael asked.

"No," Debbie said. "Over some projects in a neighborhood called Meridian-Kessler. They violated a neighborhood building code and couldn't sell the properties. At the end of it, there were liens and cross-liens and foreclosures and ultimately a bankruptcy."

Dr. Korman pouted his lower lip, impressed with the saga, and quipped, "Guessing Thanksgiving's pretty awkward in their family." No one laughed, but he seemed unconcerned that his joke had fallen flat.

Hannah began to walk toward the front steps, following her daughter, and the momentum toward the house prompted Debbie.

"Should we go inside?"

Dr. Korman shrugged—the most agreeable gesture he'd yet offered.

The front of the house greeted them with a set of three stone steps, leading to a small portico surrounded by an elaborately carved stone railing and baluster. Stone—probably limestone, given this was Indiana—trimmed the oversized, arched entryway of the house. The iron head of a wolf emerged from a large, forged iron plate affixed to the door, a heavy black iron knocker in its mouth.

"Imposing," Dr. Korman said as he lifted the ring of the knocker with his index finger.

A lockbox hung around the handle of the thumb latch, and Debbie pulled the key, opening the door with a little assistance from her shoulder. She hadn't shown the house very many times and never to someone who'd expressed a sincere interest in purchasing it. But upon opening the door, she adjusted her voice as the couple and their young daughter stepped into the foyer.

"The house was built in 1926 by Hoosier architect Andrew Decker. He purchased this land and all of the surrounding land in 1921 from a farmer—this was all farmland before that. The original farmhouse is on the other side of the neighborhood, if you're curious. Decker designed this house and each of the other fourteen original houses built in the neighborhood between 1922 and 1929."

"What happened in 1929?" Hannah asked.

"The Great Depression," Dr. Korman answered, not attempting to hide his disappointment in his wife's apparent ignorance of basic U.S. history.

"Of course. I just didn't know if there'd been something specific to him."

Debbie wasn't sure whether Hannah had offered this as an attempt to cover her gaffe or whether she really imagined some personal tragedy had befallen the man. Undoubtedly, there were tragedies in 1929 other than the Great Depression.

"I'd guess as an architect, the Great Depression felt pretty specific to him," Dr. Korman said.

"As you can see, much of the original woodwork, tile, and fixtures remain," Debbie continued, thinking it best to focus on the attributes of the house.

Hannah, who had picked Molly up and had the child once again perched on her hip, gazed down at the stone tile floor of the foyer, then up, pirouetting slowly to follow the line of an intricately carved U-shaped staircase extending over the front door to the second floor.

"The home offers nine thousand square feet of living space across two floors. There are eight bedrooms and six full baths on the second floor." Debbie walked into the center of the foyer. "There's also a partially finished third floor that comprises the servants' quarters with four more bedrooms and a bathroom not included in the square footage. To the left, you'll find the formal living room. That fireplace is original, as are the pocket doors to the study there and all of the woodwork throughout." At this, she offered a flourish of her hand, sweeping it up toward the crown moulding and around the living room.

Hannah walked farther into the living room, and Debbie and Dr. Korman followed closely behind.

"What's in there?" Hannah asked, tilting her head toward the arched doorway at the far end of the living room.

"That's the music room," Debbie said, smiling widely. So few houses had a true music room these days. "The piano in there is a concert grand, and it comes with the house. Do either of you play?"

"No," Dr. Korman said, stepping briefly into the room. "And that's not a concert grand."

"Well, a grand anyway," Debbie offered amiably as he returned to the living room.

"What do we do about all this stuff?" he asked, referring to the haphazardly placed furniture, random bric-a-brac, and stacks of books and magazines that filled nearly every free space in the living room.

"Well, I suppose you can do whatever you want with it," Debbie said. "As you know, you take possession as-is, and that includes the contents of the house. Fritz Brothers sold some of the possessions in an attempt to cover their losses from the bankruptcy, but much of what you have in here is the furniture of the first two owners, and that's true throughout the home."

"Jesus," Dr. Korman hissed, opening the drawer of a table next to a large green velvet sofa. "How is there dust inside a drawer?"

"Probably from the construction," Debbie said. "Here, let's head over to the other side of the house."

As Debbie walked the couple back across the foyer, passing an empty solarium that extended off the back of the house, she heard both Dr. Korman and his wife suck in their breath. She assumed Dr. Korman did so as he took in the absolute devastation of that side of the house, while Hannah saw only its potential.

"The kitchen has been demo'd and partially framed out. You can see the footprint of a really quite luxurious space here—a blank slate waiting for ideas," Debbie said. Hannah smiled; Dr. Korman did not. "A laundry room is just beyond that doorway, then there's a food pantry." She quickly opened and closed a door that left the kitchen with a decidedly musty odor. "The butler's pantry is here, leading back into the dining room. Fritz was smart enough to leave most of this alone, so these are all the original built-ins and counters."

Dr. Korman consulted his phone. Again.

"Should we head upstairs?" Debbie nearly sang the invitation.

"No," Dr. Korman offered at the exact moment Hannah purred a "Yes."

"Fine," Dr. Korman acquiesced.

The second floor of the house offered the eight bedrooms Debbie had described but, consistent with houses built in the 1920s, contained little in the way of closet space. The six bathrooms that had been promised were of the one-sink, one-toilet, one-bathtub variety, luxurious for the time, but hardly luxury-grade in the twenty-first century. Additionally, the bedrooms over the kitchen and dining room amounted to relatively modest guest quarters—small chambers suited to party attendees overserved during the roaring twenties, who required a place to sober up until they could find their way home.

"The home comes with Fritz Brothers' blueprints, which significantly alter the layout of this second floor," Debbie said as Dr. Korman and Hannah continued down the second-floor hall, opening and closing doors along the corridor. Of the six bathrooms, all but one stood in some state of demolition. "I'm guessing Fritz Brothers intended to complete the kitchen and bathrooms as the first phase of their renovation and didn't get much further than that. Four of the bathrooms still have the original tile, though, and three still have the original cast iron tubs."

Back on the landing overlooking the foyer, Dr. Korman strode toward the stairs. He'd decided the tour was over.

"You're not interested in seeing the servants' quarters?" Debbie asked. Honestly, she was disappointed. The house had been listed for years, first by Fritz Brothers, then by Dennis Fritz himself, then by an investor who purchased the mortgage from the bank, and now by the county. While she'd earn less commission than if she pushed the Kormans further into the budget they could afford, to be the agent who finally sold this home would be a feather in her cap.

"I think we've seen all we need to see here," Dr. Korman stated definitively, continuing his progress toward the foyer.

"Think how close you'd be to work," Hannah offered, doing Debbie's job for her.

"It's the only thing we'd be close to. Is there even a grocery store around here?" Dr. Korman complained.

Debbie tried to appear neutral as she speculated silently on whether Dr. Korman regularly did any of the grocery shopping in his marriage.

"You can't have it both ways, Michael," Hannah said evenly. "You can't have a home that is secluded on a large lot in a residential area and be surrounded by grocery stores and movie theaters."

Debbie suspected Hannah didn't work outside the home, but if her interests extended to real estate sales, she had a knack for it.

"You should keep in mind, too, that it's much easier to get around Indianapolis than it is to get around Boston," Debbie added. She didn't actually know if this was true. She'd never been to Boston. She'd been to Chicago and to New York. Boston probably wasn't much different. "My favorite grocery store is in Broad Ripple, which isn't too far from here." She tried to sound casual amid the rising tension between the couple. "I usually do my weekly shopping there after my exercise class on Sunday morning. My exercise studio is almost next door."

"Studio? What kinds of classes do they have?" Hannah asked, bouncing Molly over to her other hip. Molly put her head down on her mother's shoulder. Must be nap time.

"Barre. Cycle. HIIT. Yoga. A little of everything," Debbie replied.

"That would be nice," Hannah said softly.

"Finally get the last of that baby weight off," Dr. Korman added, swiping an index finger across the screen of his phone.

Debbie hadn't taken him for an intentionally cruel man and initially questioned whether he might not have realized he made the comment aloud. However, no apology for the remark followed, and Hannah fell silent. Her gaze dropped to the runner on the stairs. Her hand rubbed circles on the center of Molly's back as the child's eyes became weighted.

Debbie had seen couples like this before. She was familiar with the marital assemblage of a wealthy man and a beautiful, younger woman.

A woman who, Debbie assumed, thought herself entitled to the leisure and luxury afforded by such a man. And now, a few years and one baby later, she was learning the hard truth of that old cliché: When you marry for money, you earn every penny.

CHAPTER 1

Michael liked it when Hannah was on top. She knew this. It left his hands free to hold her waist, which he was doing now, and to caress her breasts, which he'd been doing before. She loved this, being wanted. He reached for her, his hand curving around the back of her neck, persuading a kiss. As she leaned toward him, she could see the outline of her torso, the slope of her shoulders, the slight incline of her head in the lacquered finish of the headboard. Not their headboard. It came with the fully furnished bungalow they'd rented in a neighborhood not far from the Decker house. Their furniture—most of it anyway—sat in storage, awaiting the completion of the renovation, which hadn't yet started. The bed was a queen-sized sleigh, a poor substitute for their California king with the upholstered headboard.

In these moments—with him reaching for her—Hannah was struck by the unlikely occurrence of their ever having met, much less married. But he'd found her, and she was grateful to have been found, even if it was behind the bar of the Sheraton Hotel in Columbia, South Carolina.

That had been eight years ago, now. He'd come into town for a friend's wedding and had just returned from the rehearsal dinner, late, probably close to midnight. He'd ordered a Jack and Coke, planning to sit at the bar, sip his drink, and catch up on emails. But when Hannah handed him the cocktail, he made a joke about not drinking on the job, and as he tucked his phone into his blazer pocket, Hannah commented casually, "That's the idear."

"Idear," Michael repeated. "Are you from up north?"

Hannah responded with the abridged edition of her biography. A practiced summary, it allowed her to avoid the bits about the spiral fracture of the humerus when she was twelve, the pediatrician who wouldn't allow her to leave the hospital, and her mother sobbing in the emergency department when the social worker advised that the Department of Child and Family Services had been notified.

"I grew up in Clover," she said. "But I'm originally from Worcester, Mass." Two sentences that summarized the whole of her life. But it was enough, and she could tell he wasn't really interested in where she was from.

He explained that he hailed from Boston, had completed all of his education there—undergraduate, graduate, professional, and doctoral. He worked for a pharmaceutical company developing drugs that treated people for everything from Alzheimer's to Zika. All of this sounded fascinating to Hannah whose options for adult life had been more limited.

She spent the rest of that evening walking back and forth between the occasional hotel customer who ordered a drink and Michael, who for two hours and for reasons obvious enough to Hannah, stayed and talked until she had to inform him the bar was closing, and they said good-night. She'd never expected to see him again, but the next night, after the wedding, he returned, and they resumed their conversation. When the bar closed, he invited her to his room for a drink. She recalled the way he'd deflated ever-so-slightly when she stepped down from behind the bar, still eye to eye with him. But his disappointment seemed to be offset by his open admiration for the length of her legs, emerging as they had from a tight, black skirt.

"You are the most incredible woman I've ever seen," Michael said as Hannah arched back against his hands, her silhouette fading with her distance from the headboard. The late evening light crept into the room around the drapes and divided the ceiling above her—one half silver, the other black.

He'd said those exact same words that first night, too, and she recalled the warmth that surrounded her at such generous superlatives. She didn't tell him—then or since—that on more than one occasion, she'd accepted the invitation to a guest's room at the end of a long evening. The hotel beds provided more comfort than her own, and the sex was usually nice. She assumed she must have been quite different than the women he'd slept with before, though she never asked, and he didn't seem especially keen to disclose. After that first night together, he drove her to her apartment so she could shower, change, and accompany him to a brunch at the bride's family home. It seemed that at least a couple of people there recognized her from the hotel, but no one said anything. A week after he'd returned to Boston, he called and asked her to move in with him. Shortly after that, they were engaged. She was twenty-four. He was forty.

I'm not twenty-four anymore, she thought as she reached forward again, leveraging her palm flat against the headboard, seeking more depth with each movement of her hips.

"Oh my god, I fucking love you," Michael said, the words slurring with the effort of his restraint.

The time when she would have believed that seemed to reside just beyond her field of vision, like the watercolor shadow of her body in the headboard and the silver lake of moonlight on the ceiling. But she could recall a time, vaguely, when her life so vastly out-measured her expectations, she almost couldn't believe it belonged to her. The first one or two years of their marriage, Michael seemed nothing short of astonished she was his. He'd arrive home from work in the evenings with his eyes wide and his cheeks flushed ready to consume her as if she were the most expensive dessert on a menu that had always exceeded his budget. It had taken some time before she saw that she'd become little more than an accessory; maybe she'd always been one. Like the degrees on his wall, like the bonuses on his salary, he'd earned her. Or some woman like her. And it all became just another of the many wounds she carried.

"Hannah. God," he stuttered. And in a single movement—perhaps slightly more awkward given the smaller dimensions of the sleigh bed —he rolled her beneath him and brought one of her legs over his shoulder.

"These legs," he breathed, running a hand along the outside of her thigh, reminding her of the way his eyes had dragged up her legs as they stood under the bright lights of the elevator bay that first night.

"There," she encouraged, running her hands up his arms to his back. "Like that."

He accepted her instruction, and the growing crescendo brought her back to the present. It didn't take long before she felt the heat swell and radiate out from the center of her body as she reached the edge and tumbled over, taking him with her.

"I love it when you look at me like that," he said, collapsing onto the bed beside her.

His voice suggested he wasn't fully present. And she wasn't looking at him; her eyes were closed. She knew what he really meant was that he loved the way she looked. Still, that was a kind of love—in its own way. Hannah pulled the covers over her chest, examining the ceiling once again as Michael drifted off to sleep.

Far away, somewhere on the east coast, Hannah's mother slept. Or Hannah hoped she did. When Hannah left Boston, she'd called her mother to let her know she was moving to Indianapolis with Michael. But the last number she had was disconnected, and when Hannah drove to the last address she had, a young man answered the door, stating that he'd been renting the property for the past six months and didn't know the prior occupants. He also didn't know whether a man had been residing there prior, as well, and so Hannah had no sense really of whether her mother was alive or dead, whether she was safe or not, whether her father, Jack, was there with her, or whether he slept on a bunk in a jail as he was known to do from time to time. But Hannah hoped her mother was asleep right now. She hoped she was somewhere safe. And with that thought, Hannah closed her own eyes and drifted off to sleep.

FOR HER FIRST day in the Decker house, Hannah planned to inventory, room by room, the work required. She'd be interviewing three contractors and hoped to give them some idea of her expectations, her vision. As she drove up the gravel driveway to the house, she felt a pronounced apprehension; the weight of potential failure loomed before her as the home rose out of the debris of overgrown hedges, decomposing fall leaves, and the increasingly pervasive gray of Indiana's approaching winter.

The Decker house was only the second thing Hannah had ever asked Michael for. Molly had been the first, and she'd been genuinely surprised when he simply said, "No. I don't want children." He'd left no room in the response for discussion or negotiation. Or what Hannah wanted. It had never occurred to her that a man wouldn't want children, but Michael made his position painstakingly clear on that point: he liked the freedom they had without children; he didn't want to be fifty and chasing around a grade-schooler; he liked their relationship as it was; and he worried what pregnancy might do to Hannah's health. Michael eventually relented, and Hannah welcomed Molly Elizabeth Korman into their family.

He'd relented on the house too, though not without a fight.

Hannah couldn't explain why she wanted the Decker house so badly. Michael had originally been completely uninterested in the project of finding a home in Indianapolis and had turned the work of doing so over to Hannah and "Whoever is in charge of the relocation at Rue McMillian." This had turned out to be Debbie, though Hannah had already perused the online listings of available homes. Although she modified her search parameters, changing the maximum or minimum cost of the house, the school district, its age, the minimum number of bedrooms or square footage, the Decker house always appeared in the listing until Hannah finally clicked on it and saw that it was both beautiful and damaged. And she loved it.

Hannah loved the yellow bricks rising out of the overgrown grass, the carved limestone arches surrounding the doors and leaded windows, the terra cotta pipes stretching up from the stately chimneys along the roofline, the row of dormers peeking out of the gray slate roof. She loved the way her mind expanded and bent as she clicked through photographs of the solarium, the study, the living room packed with the refuse of some other family's life, the stained walls of the dining room, and the cracking plaster of the owners' suite. Finally, she loved that the listing warned the potential buyer that they would be taking possession of the property "as-is," which she thought meant she necessarily would be taking possession of the property as it had been and as it could be again.

She parked the Range Rover in the horseshoe directly in front of the stone steps she'd walked up just two months before. As she stepped out, she exhaled a breath, the vapor just barely visible, and steadied herself for the work that lay ahead. She fumbled with the keys at the front door, but eventually succeeded in getting herself and Molly into the foyer. The house was cool, and with no electricity yet, she'd have to dress more warmly going forward.

Hannah set Molly down on the floor and immediately realized that tackling the house with a toddler would be even more difficult than she'd anticipated, and she'd anticipated it would be pretty difficult. Molly wanted to walk only to the most dangerous parts of the house— staircases, the exposed wires of an outlet, the open ductwork of a floor register. Hannah picked her up and returned to the Range Rover pulling a pack-n-play along with a blanket and a small selection of Duplo blocks from the trunk. She set the enclosure up in the living room and placed Molly in it with a quick kiss to her strawberry-blonde head before pulling a pack of Post-it notes from her purse and beginning her work in earnest.

"Well, how should we do this?" Hannah asked aloud, speaking to both her daughter and, she felt, to the house itself. As she surveyed the living room, she determined it would be easier to tag the items she intended to keep over those that could be hauled away. In the end, this amounted to: one area rug, a green velvet couch, two mahogany end tables, and a sideboard. Five items in a room that seemed to hold thousands.

She opened the pocket doors to the study. Her work there was even simpler. The large bankers-style desk in the center of the room, along with the enormous red, blue, and yellow area rug beneath it could stay. Everything else had to go. She turned her attention to the bookcases that shared the wall with the living room and flanked a large fireplace, and her thoughts turned to her grandmother.

Moving in with her grandparents had been a strange transition for Hannah. Not just the culture shock of South Carolina after life in New England, but the difference between a world of constant noise, yelling, and violence, and one of perpetual silence. Her grandparents, always thoughtful and generous, were, one might say, reserved. While not inclined toward displays of rage, for which Hannah was more grateful than she could express, they weren't really inclined toward displays of anything much at all.

Hannah's grandmother, Annis Kemp, had been a librarian before she retired and had brought the etiquette of the library into her own home, insisting that it be clean, orderly, and quiet. A single television had occupied her grandparents' living room, used for the sole purpose of watching the evening news—local and national. The television was then turned off before the shows most of Hannah's classmates enjoyed —shows with laugh tracks and quick-witted teens who lived with their parents in two-story homes. Teens who wore clothes from Abercrombie and Hollister, whose broken bones were the result of football and soccer injuries that healed over the twenty-two-minute span of a single episode, not over four months of seventh grade.

Perhaps not surprisingly, Annis was a reader. With the television turned off, she'd open whatever paperback topped her bookstack while Robert dozed next to her, his shoulder slowly slumping as evening became night, until it rested lightly against his wife's. Hannah quickly adopted her grandmother's practice of evening reading. She kept it up even after she left their house, acquiring a rather eclectic library drawn predominantly from the hotel's lost and found.

"No one ever comes back for the things they leave behind at a hotel," Hannah once told her brother, Mason. Seven years her senior, she'd survived not quite one year in the house with her father after Mason turned eighteen and Jack rather violently evicted him from their home. But Mason had visited Hannah regularly after that, including at the hotel where she'd shown him the large canvas laundry bin that held those items the hotel's patrons abandoned.

"Really, this should just be called The Lost," she'd joked.

"I don't know. Looks like you found it," Mason had replied as he checked the size of a plaid Brooks Brothers oxford.

Hannah might have been tempted to keep some of the Decker house books, too, but as she scanned the shelves, her mind was drawn to the stacks of their boxes in storage. Between herself and Michael, plenty of paperbacks would eventually fill these shelves. She'd call the Central Library to gauge their interest in this collection.

Hannah glanced back at the pack-n-play in the living room where Molly happily mouthed a red Duplo block as her mother placed the yellow tags on the handful of ostensibly random objects.

"Hellooo," a voice called out from the foyer.

Hannah jolted, then called back, "In here," recognizing the voice as Debbie's.

Debbie walked into the living room as Hannah emerged from the study, her Post-it notes in hand.

"Getting started already, I see," Debbie observed.

"I have the Fire Dawgs coming tomorrow," Hannah explained, identifying a group of firefighters who made extra money by running a rent-a-dumpster service. For an extra fee, they would do the hauling, too.

Debbie carried a large basket wrapped in cellophane, which Hannah took from her hands, examining its little jars of jam, hard sausages, crackers, and cheese.

"Just a little thank you for using our services in the purchase of your new home," Debbie said in the practiced manner of someone who'd already uttered the phrase more than a few times.

"Thank you. How thoughtful," Hannah said, setting the basket on the sideboard. She playfully placed a Post-it on the basket. "Keep," she chirped pleasantly.

Debbie stood beside Molly, who'd taken an interest in her, and Debbie allowed her to hold her thumbs while jumping in the pack-n-play.

"I think you've made a friend, Molly." Hannah smiled at her daughter, who smiled at Debbie.

Debbie freed a hand from Molly and reached into her large shoulder bag. "These are the blueprints Fritz Brothers drew up. They detail changes to both the kitchen and the second floor." She handed Hannah a long, black plastic tube and Hannah placed it next to the gift basket on the sideboard.

"So, what's your plan, if you don't mind me asking?" Debbie prompted as Hannah stuck a Post-it on top of the blueprints.

"Well," Hannah said, resting her hands on her hips and looking around the room, "I'd like to get the first floor finished so we can move in, and then we can live down here while they're working on the second and third floors. They'll have to update the plumbing, electric, and HVAC first, though. I'm assuming the walls are plaster and lath, which will make it tricky to put in central air and heat."

At the word "lath," Debbie's gaze, which had been slowly arching across the room, stopped abruptly and fixated on Hannah. Hannah felt an appraisal taking place—toe to crown—that she knew well but had never completely acclimated to.

"I can't believe no one ever bothered to put in heat and air," Hannah said, trying to pull Debbie's attention back to the conversation. "I guess they would have had to update the knob and tube to do it, so maybe they just decided against all of it."

Debbie turned, her body fully facing Hannah as if she'd intended to say something, then reconsidered. "Only two owners," she finally commented somewhat absently.

"I'm sorry?" Hannah asked.

"There were only the two owners—the original owners and their daughter. She probably was just used to the house the way it was and didn't see any reason to change it."

"She?" Hannah asked. For some reason, she'd always imagined the second owner had been a man. Maybe it was the beige recliner so prominently featured in the listing photographs of the living room. Or the three decades of Sports Illustrated magazines that welcomed her when she toured the house.

"Yes. Margaret Decker. Well, Margaret Moore. She was married."

"Huh," Hannah mused. "Do you know anything else about the house?"

"No. Sorry. Just that it was originally the crown jewel of the neighborhood. It's set up on this hill so that it overlooks the rest of the houses on the loop below. I get the feeling the architect must've been kind of egotistical building the neighborhood—and his house—that way."

"Maybe so," Hannah said. She knew a little something about egotistical men.

"Hey, you know what?" Debbie began. "You should do one of those reno-blogs while you're working on this."

"Reno-blog?" Hannah asked.

Molly began to fuss in the pack-n-play, and Hannah glanced at her watch. Nearly lunch time. She picked Molly up, bouncing her, and she calmed a bit, though Hannah sensed this was only a temporary reprieve from her fussing.

"Yeah. Like that French chateau on Instagram. That couple photographs the before-and-after and sometimes adds little stories about their renovation. You could do something like that. You might even get sponsors."

"Interesting." Hannah didn't have much interest in sponsors or the notoriety that it sounded like this French chateau had. But she'd already planned to document the renovation, and a blog might be a good way for her grandfather and Mason to see her progress. Molly might be interested in it when she got older, too.

Molly began to twist in Hannah's arms. She wouldn't be delayed for lunch much longer.

"I could make some recommendations for sitters," Debbie said, eyeing the little girl.

"That's okay. I like having her with me," Hannah said. "I think we're going to head home for lunch. Would you like to join us?"

"Oh, I'd love to, but I have a showing at noon. Another time," Debbie replied as the two women headed toward the front door.

While walking down the front steps toward their cars, Hannah recalled a comment Debbie made when she'd shown them the house.

"Hey, what's that little exercise studio you were talking about that's by the grocery store in Broad Ripple?" Hannah fastened Molly into her car seat and handed her a pouch of applesauce she pulled from her diaper bag.

"Why? Are you interested in joining?"

"I might be. Do they have childcare?" Even before having Molly, Hannah had avoided gyms. They made her feel exposed and vulnerable in the large, cavernous weight and exercise rooms, mirrors on every vertical surface. But a smaller space with just a few classes might be nice. Far preferable to the online workout programs she'd been using.

"For some classes they do. I'll text you the info, and you can see if you might be interested. If you do take a class there, make sure you tell them I referred you. That way, you can have one free class before you decide whether you'd like to join."

"Okay. I will," Hannah promised. Then she closed the door of the Range Rover and led Debbie down the gravel driveway and through the wrought iron, deco wings of the Decker house gates.

※

"THE FIRST ONE'S FREE. Isn't that what drug dealers say?" Michael teased as he sat down to eat dinner with Hannah and Molly.

"I wouldn't know," Hannah replied coolly, passing him the salad bowl.

"Well, I don't have any objection to you joining a fitness studio. How's the house?" he asked.

"It was nice to finally get inside," Hannah said as she cut a meatball into thumbnail-sized pieces for Molly. "I went through the first floor today and sorted through what has to be thrown out and what we can keep."

"There are things you want to keep?" Michael asked.

"Definitely," Hannah said, a little breathless at the thought of the beautiful sideboard and the desk in the study. She hadn't even gotten up to the second and third floors yet.

"When do the contractors come?" Michael asked.

"Tomorrow."

"Do you need me to be there?" he asked between bites.

"I don't think so. They're going to email their quotes, so you can look at those and call them if you have questions."

Michael nodded. Evidently a reasonable enough plan, it required a minimal amount of effort on his part, which Hannah imagined probably made it distinctly sensible in his estimation.

"Did you get out into the neighborhood at all?" he asked.

Hannah tonged some salad onto her plate. "Just a little bit," she said. "I took Molly for a walk around the loop after lunch, but it was kind of damp, so I didn't want to keep her out for too long. Didn't want her to catch a cold."

"That's not how you catch a cold," Michael said, not quite under his breath.

"How do you catch a cold?" Hannah asked, confused by the comment.

"You're exposed to a virus that's transmitted from someone who's a carrier of the virus. Jesus, we just had a pandemic. Did people learn nothing?"

"Don't swear around Molly," Hannah said sharply. "Anyway, I did take a walk around the neighborhood, and I love it. It's split into two parts. A southern loop and a northern loop. The southern loop is the older part of the neighborhood. It has the houses Decker built before the Depression. Then, building didn't pick up again until the 1950s."

"Makes sense," Michael said, twirling some pasta with his fork.

"Yeah. So then, the northern part of the neighborhood is all 1980s construction, split-levels and whatnot. I like it. Lots of other people out walking, too. Well, not lots. But several. I met a history professor from the university. He teaches the history of medicine. He has a Rottweiler, and she looked very intimidating, but she was so friendly. Her name is Gertie, which is a weird name for a dog, don't you think? Anyway, she loved Molly. I think we're really going to like it here—there."

Michael examined her, a quizzical expression on his face. "I think this is the most excited I've seen you about anything in quite some time."

She shrugged, not sure whether he thoroughly approved of her enthusiasm. Though, he was right; she almost percolated with happiness.

CHAPTER 2

Fritz Brothers had left the second floor of the Decker house in moderately better shape than the first. Although they had partially demolished all six of the bathrooms—and fully renovated precisely none of them—the bedrooms were relatively well preserved, albeit within the decade in which they'd last been decorated. Sorting through the bedrooms wouldn't be nearly as time-consuming as the first floor had been. Molly proved to be an asset in this project as well, happily affixing Post-its to those things her mother designated—and a few she did not.

The Fire Dawgs arrived late that morning, quoted Hannah a fair sum, and began hauling old magazines, buckets of paint, and box fans out the door to the giant green dumpster they'd parked in front of the house. They were mid-haul when Dan Milston of Milston & Leake Construction arrived. With the front door wide open already, he beckoned Hannah with a loud hello from the foyer, and she trotted down the stairs with Molly, eager to meet the first of the contractors.

"Dan Milston," the man said, holding out his hand. He looked to be just a little younger than Michael, wearing a pair of dockers and a zip-up cardigan with Milston & Leake Construction embroidered on the breast.

"Hi. I'm Hannah Korman," she said, hefting Molly just a little higher on her hip as she accepted the man's hand. "Where would you like to start?"

"What do you mean?" he asked.

"Do you want me to show you around? Tell you what we're looking for?" Hannah asked.

"Oh, no ma'am. There's no reason for you to do that. I got your email, and you got your hands full. I can find my way. I'll call for you when I'm done, and we can go over any questions I have then." He held a leather-bound folder in his hand, which he opened to reveal a new, clean notepad. Reaching under his cardigan, he retrieved a ball-point pen, and clicked the end, ready to take notes.

"Okay," Hannah said, hesitating. "I guess I'll leave you to it."

Dan nodded his agreement and began a slow progression toward the kitchen-end of the house. The Fire Dawgs were still coming in and out of the front door, in and out of the living room, up and down from the second floor. Hannah was disappointed that Dan seemed not to have much use for her despite the preparation she'd put into the meeting. Still, she found the emerging chaos exciting, an indication that the project finally had momentum, and she and Molly returned to their work upstairs.

Two hours later, she heard Dan once again calling for her from the foyer. She picked up Molly, who was none too pleased about being removed from the Post-its collage she'd been making on the wall of one of the guest rooms. She let out an angry squawk as Hannah traded her a teething biscuit for the Post-its. Reluctantly accepting the consolation prize, Molly regarded her mother skeptically as she waited to see how all this would play out, clearly displeased by its progress thus far.

"I think I've got most of what I need to put a quote together for you. Just a few questions as I finish up," Dan said, meeting Hannah and Molly in the foyer.

Hannah tried to get a look at his notepad. At least a third of the pages curled over the back of the leather folder, but Dan's handwriting comprised a script decipherable only to him. Hannah couldn't even make out the numbers.

"In your email, you said something about already having blue-prints?" Dan asked.

"Oh, yes. From the contractors. The plan for the kitchen side and the second floor. We'd like to just use those plans." She jogged quickly into the living room and pulled the tube off the sideboard.

Dan took it from her and immediately opened it, laying the blueprints out on the floor of the foyer and squatting down next to them. He examined the plans carefully before looking up at her. He had a friendly face, kind. Weathered, too, like he'd spent quite a bit of time out in the sun, which Hannah imagined he probably had in his line of work. His hair was thinning up on top, which she could see as he squatted next to her.

"It's a big house, I'm sure you know that, so it's a big project. I'll start at the top and go down." Hannah nodded as Dan adopted an air of rehearsed exposition. "Looks like most of your roof is holding up okay, which is kind of incredible considering how long this place has been empty. But each of your chimneys needs tuck-pointing, and they need new caps. There have been some leaks in the roof—nothing huge —but we'll have to repair those areas and replace the damaged plaster with sheetrock. The configuration here of the master suite should be fairly straight forward. We'll have to keep this wall here," he pointed, "it's load bearing, and over here in the guest quarters, this one's load bearing, too, so we could move those, but it's easier if we don't."

He continued on, talking Hannah through her own house, detailing the major structural changes. After moving through each room, Dan would add a staccato, "patch, prime, paint."

With each itemization of work required, Hannah felt herself sinking lower and lower until both of them finally reached the base-ment of the house. At this point, Dan stood and rolled up the blueprints, placing them back in the tube.

"You want to finish that basement?" he asked as he handed her the tube.

"No. I can't think of any reason to do that," Hannah said almost to herself. From the look on Dan's face, she was prepared to hear that there wasn't any reason to do *any* of the work.

"You been down there?" he asked.

"No." It was simple, really. The basement scared Hannah. She'd opened the door once, seen the wood slat staircase extending into the dark abyss below, and closed the door right back up.

"Okay. Well, it's not in great shape," Dan said, his voice carrying a warning. Hannah knew something about basements, about foundations. If yours was "not in great shape" your whole house was "not in great shape."

"If you're not interested in finishing it, that makes it easier. We can tuckpoint the brick and treat it with a waterproofing agent. The bigger issue is that almost all your pipes down there are galvanized, which means probably all of the pipes in the house need to be replaced. Your electric is knob and tube, that all has to come out, and I'm assuming you want central heat and air. So, we'd have to install that as well." He looked at her then, a conspicuous assessment to determine whether she fully grasped what he'd told her.

She did. What he'd told her was that the house hadn't truly been updated in nearly one hundred years. It had wiring that would prevent her from getting homeowners insurance; it had pipes lined with lead; it had no air conditioning, despite Indiana summers routinely marked by day after day of ninety-plus-degree heat. The house was heated—where it was at all—with steam heat and fireplaces. It wasn't an exaggeration to suggest the best course of action would be to tear the house down and start over. The excitement that had existed only minutes before evaporated as Hannah realized that Dan really anticipated only one acceptable response, and by failing to suggest that he be contracted to level the house, she wasn't giving it.

"A little about our company," he continued, suddenly pivoting. "I'm the general contractor. I'll be here most days. We work only with licensed, bonded, and insured subs, but we will sub out for the roof, the plumbing, and the HVAC. We'll do all the demo, construction, and electric ourselves. We require twenty percent up front and then usually what folks like to do for a project this size is set up an escrow, and we pull from that at intervals."

"Okay," Hannah said. She thought she caught most of what had been said, as well as quite a lot that had not. "How long do you think it will take to finish?"

"Hmm." Dan bit his lip and looked around the room. "I'd say a good eight months. Maybe a year if we get into the walls and find any surprises. Which I'm assuming we will in a house this old."

"Oh. Wow," Hannah said, adding an inevitable lease renewal to her growing anxiety. "Would it be possible for you to focus on the first floor, and then we could move in while you worked on the second and third floors?"

The answer, judging from Dan's stunned expression, was not a simple, "No," but "Oh my god, what an incredibly stupid idea."

"I wouldn't advise it," he said, his words less of an indictment than his face.

"I see. Well, thank you for your time," Hannah said, concluding the conversation in the manner she recalled from her observations of her grandfather. They shook hands again, and Dan saw his way out.

Not more than an hour later, the second contractor arrived. Driving up in a large, white pickup with the words "White Fences, LLC" emblazoned along the doors, Hannah couldn't help but be impressed by the three identically dressed men who stepped out of the cab. Each introduced himself as he entered the house, and Hannah returned the courtesy. Having learned from Dan, and with Molly requiring her attention anyway, Hannah left them to their work.

As the three men traipsed off between the two-by-fours framing the kitchen, Hannah walked through the living room, marveling at how large the space felt now emptied of its former contents. An enormous bay window looked out at the haggard, untended front lawn, and the room appeared to hold more light than it had even the day before, though not enough to get them through the end of the day. Time would have to be spent wisely until electricity could be installed.

Hannah crossed the threshold into the study, standing just inside the doorway. The large desk floated, solitary, in the center of the room, unaccompanied but for the rug beneath and the shelves full of old books opposite. Molly ambled over to a set of French doors that opened to a small terrace and placed her hands flat against the panes of glass, pressing her nose to the window. The doors were closed now, too cold and damp to have them open. When spring came, Hannah would place a patio set out there, open the doors wide, and let the breeze flow across the room as she imagined it once had years ago.

"Ow-well," Molly said, interrupting Hannah's thoughts and pointing across the lawn. Hannah walked over to the doors, standing beside her daughter and followed her line of sight. Sure enough, a large gray and brown owl perched in a tree at the far end of the yard.

Elsewhere in the house, Hannah could hear the heavy steps and faint voices of the three men, who would surely tell her that everything in her house from the basement to the roof required repair or replacement. They would hint, as Dan had, that it would be cheaper to tear the house down and start over. The land was what was really valuable, the way it presided over the neighborhood from its perch on the hill. She should just start over.

❦

IT HAD TAKEN Hannah most of the morning to go through the second floor, but still much less time than had been required of the living room and study downstairs. She'd designated a handful of abandoned furnishings that remained relatively stylish and in good shape, including a couple of landscape paintings, and three celadon vases that she wished to keep.

By late afternoon, Hannah slumped. Fatigue from physical work and disappointment from the lackluster responses of the two earlier contractors had slowed her movements to nearly a crawl when she heard one of the firefighters call for her from the foot of the stairs.

"I think another contractor's here," he yelled up to her.

Hannah tapped the face of her watch and noted the time. "Oh shoot," she hissed, realizing the contractor was right on time, and she hadn't been at the door to let him in.

"Let's go, Molly," she said, walking quickly down the stairs, reaching the foyer nearly breathless.

The man awaiting her looked to be approaching sixty or so. He wore a light green golf shirt that had the appearance of having been washed and dried more than a handful of times—"boiled and baked" was the phrase her grandmother used to describe her grandfather's method of doing his laundry. A brown leather belt held a pair of ill-fitting jeans in place, and gray hair peeked out from under an Indianapolis Indians baseball cap.

"Gary Cummins, ma'am," he said, holding out a hand.

"Hannah Korman," she said. Molly held her hand out, too—she'd gotten the hang of this.

Gary laughed and shook the little girl's hand. "Who do we have here?" he asked.

"This is Molly."

"Well, hello, Molly. You look like you're about the same age as my Cora."

"She'll be two in January."

"Yep," Gary said. "Cora will be two next month. It's a fun age. I don't know what they mean by 'terrible twos'. This is when you can actually talk to them." It seemed Gary had opinions on the matter.

"Is Cora your only daughter?" Hannah asked.

"Granddaughter," Gary corrected. "She's my only *grandchild*. So far," he added. "You must have your hands full, though, watching this little one and trying to get a project of this size off the ground."

"She's a pretty good baby. Makes it easy on me."

"I'm sure she is, but this is a lot to manage." He allowed an exaggerated survey of the foyer to underscore his point before broaching a discussion of the project itself. "Well, Mrs. Korman, why don't you tell me what you have in mind for this old place."

"Please, call me Hannah."

"Okay, Hannah. I take it you hope to live here someday?"

"I do," Hannah said matter-of-factly.

"Well, let's see how we can make that happen for you."

Hannah showed Gary the blueprints and explained that she mostly wanted to keep what Fritz Brothers had drawn up. Gary said that seemed like a fine plan but proposed that the kitchen might be slightly reconfigured beyond what the blueprints showed to add a family room. He could do this by moving the laundry room to the second floor, which he pointed out would be more convenient anyway with all the laundry Molly would generate. Hannah liked that idea very much.

As they headed for the staircase to discuss plans for the second floor, Gary dragged a hand across the wall.

"Yeah, that's what I thought," he said, pausing at the foot of the stairs.

"What?" Hannah asked.

"This isn't plaster. It's river-sand mortar," he said.

"I'm sorry. It's what?"

"Mortar. It's a little trickier to work with. But..." he trailed off. "You know what? Let's start with the basement. Do you mind?"

Hannah tamped down her fears of that dark space and offered a "Not at all." This might be more efficient anyway given that the last two contractors had waited until after evaluating the basement to tell her, in so many words, what a hopeless mess the Decker house was. Might as well get that out of the way on the front end.

As Gary, Hannah, and Molly walked down the stairs to the basement, Gary paused.

"See here?" he said, aiming a yellow and black flashlight at a small crack between the wall of the basement and the floor of the room above. "Not lath," he said. "Diamond cut steel."

"Steel?"

"It's not a house; it's a fortress." He laughed with something that almost resembled affection. "Basically, this entire neighborhood could crumble to the ground, but this house isn't going anywhere. Decker built this thing to last."

"Does that mean you can't renovate it?" Hannah asked, bracing for even more bad news.

"Oh no. We can still run wires through here. The pipes are a little trickier, and I'm sorry to say, Mr. Decker, we're going to have to cut into some of your walls to get the ductwork installed, but we can still do the job. You will need a diamond tipped drill bit if you ever want to hang anything on these walls, though."

Hannah thought she could manage that. She also thought she liked that Gary had apologized to the architect for the anticipated damage to "his" walls.

"Why was he so worried about the house falling apart?" Hannah asked, wondering if Gary knew as much about the architect as he did about the materials the architect had used.

"I don't have any idea. These materials were top of the line for fire-proofing at the time. So, maybe that's what he was thinking. He did plan to live here with his family. Had a wife and a little girl not much older than your Molly when he built this place."

"Margaret," Hannah volunteered.

"Margaret," Gary confirmed. "She always said they'd take her out of this house feet first, and I guess they did. I don't know why she was so hell-bent on living here after what happened, you know."

Hannah shook her head. She didn't know. As far as she knew, what had happened here amounted to two brothers who owned a construction company bankrupting their own business.

"Your realtor should have told you all of this." He shook his head and took a deep breath. "Mr. Decker killed himself. Right there in that study." Gary pointed in the direction of the study above them.

"What? Why?" Hannah asked, aghast.

"I mean, a lot of men did then," Gary said. "You're too young, but my dad, he remembered the Depression, would tell me stories about it when I was little. I'll tell you, this country tells that history like people just had to tighten their belts and be a little thrifty. Everyone seems to have forgotten how many people died. Starved to death, children abandoned at hospitals and orphanages, died of infections or worse." Hannah shivered at the notion of what might be worse than dying of an infection. "And the men. I know it's not popular to make like men and women are different or something, and there's no question women were suffering as they put their babies to bed with nothing but warm water in their bellies, but the men—they felt they were to blame for it all and some of them, they just couldn't take it. I guess Mr. Decker just couldn't take it."

"My God," Hannah said, feeling a sudden chill that spoke more of winter than early fall. The gleam of the diamond cut steel continued to reflect off Gary's flashlight, providing a convenient place for both of them to focus their attention.

"I'm sorry. I didn't mean to upset you," Gary said, breaking the long silence.

"No... It's okay. How do you know more about my house than I do?" Hannah asked with an uncomfortable laugh.

Gary chuffed and offered a tentative grin. "For more than thirty years, I've been renovating old houses in Indiana. Old houses come with stories," he said. "And there have been quite a few told about this place over the years."

"He lost his money, then? When the market crashed?" Hannah asked, as though to confine the death firmly within that history might somehow lessen the horror of it.

"Well, apparently not right away because he didn't kill himself till a few years later. 1933, if I remember correctly. But yeah. He sank his life's savings into this neighborhood, into this house. And it all just went up in smoke when the market crashed. No one could buy. All the construction stopped. Banks started calling in loans. And, as I always heard it as a boy, he sat down one afternoon at the desk in that study and shot himself."

"My God," Hannah said again. In her arms Molly had gone absolutely still, sensing that something of import was transpiring between the two adults in her company.

"Your realtor really should have told you this."

"Maybe she didn't know," Hannah said.

"Maybe," Gary said, though he didn't sound convinced.

"How did they keep the house if he was broke?" Hannah knew a little something about what happened if you couldn't pay your bills on time. "Didn't the bank come for the house?"

"Now, that I don't know," Gary said. "All I know is that Margaret lived here every day of her life. She eventually got married—to a nice man, too. Gerald Moore. And they had three kids who all grew up around here. I think one of them still lives in the area. But Margaret would not leave this house. I think she died on a hospital bed in that living room. Nothing was going to take her out of here. The irony, of course, was that none of her kids wanted it."

"Well," Hannah said, looking again at the glimmer of steel between the floor and the wall of the basement. "I want it."

CHAPTER 3

As Hannah walked up the stairs to the second floor of the gray stucco building that housed the exercise studio Debbie had told her about, she could hear the light voices of women and the low bass beat of music traveling down. Women passed her on their way out to the parking lot—one of the classes must have just let out. Her heart quickened as she approached the doorway. She dreaded meeting new people, and there wouldn't be a single person here that she knew. She'd hoped to take a class with Debbie—at least one familiar face in the crowd—but Debbie's schedule didn't overlap with the hours offered for childcare or with the Fire Dawgs, scheduled for another day at the Decker house later that morning.

"Hi. Welcome. I'm Susan. You must be Hannah," an airy voice said from behind a desk in the small reception area. The studio was compact, the entire space consisting of two exercise rooms, a play-room for children, and a single bathroom, with the reception area as the entry point for all four spaces.

"I am," Hannah said, weaving her way through the women, both coming and going.

"Welcome. We're so glad you could make it," Susan said. Hannah was struck by the sincerity of her voice. "Is this your daughter?"

"Yes. This is Molly," Hannah said as Molly put her head down on Hannah's shoulder, suddenly bashful.

"Hi Molly. I'm Susan," she sang, stepping out from behind the desk.

Susan stood a good six inches shorter than Hannah, a petite build with a narrow frame. Her long, nearly-black hair was pulled up half-heartedly into a ponytail, which made her large, round, brown eyes appear more prominent. She was older than Hannah, but it was hard to say by how much—five years, maybe. The age range in the studio ran the spectrum from those just out of high school to those whose gray hair implied a certain seniority. Susan sat somewhere in the middle.

"Oh! We spoke on the phone," Hannah said, connecting the dots.

"We did." Susan winked at Molly, trying to coax a smile from her. "Debbie's friend? You just moved here from Boston?"

Hannah could feel Molly turning her head toward Susan and suspected that she would get the smile she'd been seeking. "Yes. About a month ago."

"Okay, well, Jennifer is teaching this morning, and my daughter Gracie is babysitting in the playroom. So, get yourself settled. Class starts in ten. Let me know if you need anything." She strolled back to the desk, turning her attention to the computer there as Hannah dropped Molly off in the playroom. The allure of unfamiliar toys was sufficient to quell any protests Molly might have voiced, and Hannah made a quick getaway to the main exercise room.

In the studio, women organized themselves into two rows, setting down water bottles and hand towels to designate their workout space. Hannah had hoped to be in the back row, preferably in a corner, inconspicuous if not altogether invisible. But the back row evidently constituted rather desirable real estate, and Hannah was left with a spot in the center front of the room against the mirror.

Around her, she picked up on pieces of conversation between those who knew each other well, asking about jobs, children on various sports teams, vacation plans for fall break. Women who hadn't seen each other for a while hugged between exchanges about things going on around the city. But above all, what Hannah noticed, amid the Lycra and the sweatshirts and the light lilt of laughter, was the complete absence of men.

Hannah took a sip from her water bottle, and class started with a warmup that everyone already seemed to know. The flow required little in the way of cueing from Jennifer, who strolled between the two rows. A woman next to Hannah, roughly her own age with curly brown hair pulled up in something resembling a bun, leaned over as Hannah glanced around the room trying to mimic the movements of those around her.

"Back straight, spine aligned, you're lifting your knees, but you're using your abs to do it. It's not a march," she said with a friendly smile.

Jennifer, seeing the conversation, walked over to Hannah. "There you go," she encouraged. "You're getting it. Is it okay if I touch you?"

"Um... yes?" Hannah couldn't recall a time in her life when anyone had ever asked whether they could touch her before doing so. Jennifer placed one hand on the small of Hannah's back and the other on the front of her abdomen at her navel.

"These are working together every time your knee comes up. Can you feel that?" Jennifer asked.

Hannah nodded sensing this was the "right" answer, but she couldn't feel it. She didn't know what she was supposed to be feeling. What she felt was self-conscious, but when she looked in the mirror, she saw that she was the only person looking around the room. Everyone else focused either on Jennifer, who had returned to strolling between the rows, or on themselves making the most minute of adjustments in their posture, their pace, the angle of their leg as it rose and fell to the beat of the music.

"You'll get used to it eventually. It takes some time," the woman next to her said, smiling again. Hannah smiled back.

Class continued, and as Jennifer cued the room into a forearm plank, Hannah caught sight of the woman on the other side of her, the way the sweat dripped off her face onto the floor. Without disturbing her plank, the woman reached for a hand towel and placed it under her face catching the beads of sweat as they fell from her nose, her eyebrows, her chin.

The woman appeared ten years older than Hannah if she was a day, and she had an air about her, a singular focus that seemed to pull at Hannah even as it contained the woman within. Hannah knew she was supposed to use the mirror to check her alignment, ensure her hips tracked in line with her knees. But what she wanted to do was watch the woman next to her. Only with great effort did she pull her eyes away, and she was grateful when the woman spoke up between movements as it gave her a passable excuse to turn toward her again.

"If you're coming to Halloween, please text me to let me know. I need a final head count by Friday," she said over the music. Then she turned to Hannah. "You're new?"

"Yes," Hannah said, struggling to respond while also repeating the movements Jennifer demonstrated.

"You should come. You can get my phone number from Susan, or I can give it to you after class. I'm Kate Nielsen."

"Okay," Hannah said, forgetting to introduce herself. She felt unwieldy, gangly, the awkward, too-tall seventh-grader on her first day at the new school.

The class ended with five minutes of guided stretching during which Jennifer came around again, moving people's legs or hips to correct their positioning or deepen their stretch. As the class came to a close, Jennifer's enthusiastic voice decrescendoed into a meditation as everyone moved into "shavasana." Hannah knew the position from her online yoga classes: palms up, feet relaxed and falling open.

"Thank your body for being capable of this work this morning," Jennifer said as she strolled between the rows. This was Hannah's least favorite part of any exercise class—the corny things the instructors said at the end, the words of inspiration, the instructions to find the light inside you.

"And now," Jennifer continued, her voice breathy but even, "as we end our practice together this morning, take this time to reflect, allowing your body to relax, your feet to fall open. Bring your hands to your side, your palms facing up to the sky, open to possibilities. And if you feel that you are someplace safe, I invite you to close your eyes, breathing deeply, rising only when you are ready."

If you feel that you are someplace safe. No one had ever encouraged Hannah to evaluate whether she felt safe. Had they done so, for the overwhelming majority of her life, Hannah would have stated definitively that she did not. She would have said that she could not recall a single time in her life from her earliest memory, to her passing through the door of this studio an hour earlier, when she'd felt safe.

But as she lay between the woman throwing the Halloween party, and the woman with the mess of curls atop her head, Hannah turned her palms upward and closed her eyes.

❧

THE THIRD FLOOR of the Decker house opened into a single long corridor reached by way of a small "servants' staircase" that wound around through the second floor and down into the kitchen. Hannah had anticipated that the third floor would be dark—effectively an attic —but the dormers were unobstructed by the shadows of trees that hung closer to the ground, allowing the timid Indiana sun to filter in.

Debbie had been accurate in her description of the third floor as "offering" four bedrooms and an additional bathroom. But upon opening the doors of the bedrooms, Hannah found them entirely empty. The only things they held were dust and spiderwebs, though they held a fair amount of that. Even the small closets were empty save for the single built-in dresser in each.

"What do you think, Molly?" Hannah glanced down at her daughter and twirled her finger around a small strawberry-blonde curl of Molly's hair. Molly reached up and batted her mother's hand away, and Hannah chuckled lightly. She walked back out into the hallway between the north and south exposure, thinking maybe their work for the day had ended early and saw, at the end of the corridor, a small unassuming door leading to the unfinished portion of the attic.

"Should we go see what's behind door number three?" she asked Molly, whose face reflected a general indifference to the invitation.

Unfortunately, the handle was tightly locked and not amenable to the hopeful jostling Hannah attempted after realizing she'd left the ring of keys Debbie had given her on the first floor.

"Darn it," she said.

Returning to the door after carrying Molly down the two flights of stairs and back up, Hannah put her daughter down, taking a moment to catch her breath.

"The laundry room on the second floor is a good plan, Gary," she said aloud. Molly looked only confused by the comment.

It took no more than a few seconds for Hannah to identify the correct key and swing the door wide, revealing what was, in every conceivable sense of the word, a "storage" room.

"Dear God," Hannah gasped as she took in the unfinished half of the third floor.

"Dear Gawd," Molly echoed, her grin suggesting she anticipated this utterance might please her mother.

The space that stretched before them took the form of a chaos Hannah had not yet seen—not even in the living room. Furniture had been stacked into the room like an Ethan Allen Tetris puzzle—chairs on top of sofas backed against bookshelves, with tables, rugs, toys, paintings, lamps, ceiling fixtures, and bed frames all tucked in between. Wooden and leather trunks were shoved against the eves of the roofline, the slats of the underside of the roof leaving a distinctly dark and uninhabitable impression.

Hannah backed out of the room and closed the door.

"Let's go get lunch," she said, staring vacantly at the far end of the corridor.

❦

WITH MOLLY ON HER HIP, Hannah lugged the pack-n-play up to the third floor and assembled it in one of the north-facing bedrooms. They'd had lunch and a bathroom break at the bungalow, and with those small comforts of modern living, had returned to commence clearing out the attic.

"Nap time," she said to Molly, who stood in the pack-n-play rubbing the satin trim of her favorite blanket between her index finger and thumb. Hannah gave Molly a quick kiss, closed the door behind her, and headed back to her Tetris puzzle.

Before beginning her work, she took a quick picture of the room and texted it to Mason. Now in Montana working in construction, he'd get a kick out of something like this.

> Hannah: And you thought Grandpa was a packrat.

He wouldn't respond immediately. He never did, and she had work to do anyway.

With her tried and true Post-it-note-strategy, Hannah made admirable progress disassembling the wall of furniture. As she got through the first barricade of chairs and tables and what sadly proved to be empty trunks, she saw that, thankfully, the wall was longer than it was wide. Within forty minutes of work, a soft gray light from a window on the other side peeked through.

Having parted the furniture like some kind of art deco Red Sea, Hannah walked through the center to the far end of the attic. She peered out the window at the trees that lifted up from the ground along the hill on which the house sat, at the dark black asphalt of the neighborhood's loop below. She thought she saw Jeremy—the history professor she'd met a couple days before—and his dog, Gertie, walking slowly along the road. Absently she waved, then dropped her hand feeling silly—no reason for him to be looking up into the attic windows of the Decker house. It would be nice to have a friend in the neighborhood though, someone her own age. She wondered if he always took his walk at this time of day.

As she turned back to the semi-sorted furniture, she saw several stacked cardboard boxes lining the side of the attic. Unlabeled, she assumed they were cleaning supplies, or china if she was lucky. She was caught quite by surprise when she opened the first one and instead found photographs, some in albums, some still in their frames, some loose, the edges curled from exposure to the humidity of the unfinished portion of the attic.

Disregarding the thick layer of dust on the floor, Hannah knelt before the box and flipped through the pictures: a wedding album, color, too recent to be Margaret's, and with a distinct 1980s aesthetic. The people in the posed photographs had that strange appearance of being known to someone but not to the onlooker, not to Hannah. Somewhere in the large portrait of bride, groom, parents, grandparents, ring-bearer, flower girls—somewhere in there were Margaret and her children, but Hannah couldn't pick her out as between the two sets of joyful in-laws.

She set the album aside and picked through the loose photographs beneath, which helped to clarify the wedding picture. Margaret was the mother of the groom. Her son was "a good-looking boy," as Hannah's grandmother would have said. It was hard to tell his age from the photograph, but he shared his mother's piercing blue eyes, as well as the angular set of her jaw. Margaret's hair was an elegant silver, worn up in a French twist revealing the length of her neck. Hannah assumed her hair had been a bit darker than her son's chestnut color before it had grayed. Next to her, Mr. Moore smiled broadly.

At some point in the mid-eighties, Mr. Moore ceased to appear in the photographs, leaving Hannah to surmise that either death or divorce had excluded him from family gatherings. Predictably, all the photographs stopped in the early-2000s with the increasing reliance on digital photography and ultimately with Margaret's death.

Hannah closed the box and pushed it aside. She would reach out to Debbie on Monday for help tracking down the family to return the photographs. Surely, they hadn't intended to leave them behind. She then opened the second box and saw that it too contained photographs and that at least some attempt had been made to organize the boxes chronologically. The first box had started in the 1980s; the current box appeared to start in the 1950s, with Margaret's own wedding.

Although difficult to ascertain through the black-and-white photos, Hannah had been right that in her younger years, Margaret's hair had been a dark brown, appearing almost black as she stood with her groom on the steps of the church. The French twist, evidently her go-to for formal styling, served her well, accentuating the pearl choker around her neck and the delicate matching pearls hanging from each earlobe. Much as she had at her son's wedding, Margaret shone forth, absolutely jubilant, beaming radiantly at her husband, whose expression spoke of his utter disbelief at his good fortune.

As the years went by, the sepia tones of the 1960s began to creep in. The tailored lines of 1950s dresses and suits gave way to the eccentric patterns and exaggerated cuts of the late 1960s and '70s. Gary had been correct that the Moores had three children: two boys and a girl. And in contrast to what Hannah had imagined for a house that harbored a patriarch's suicide, the photographs depicted all the ordinary events of a happy, loving family. Again, Hannah set them aside, closing the box and vowing to ensure their safe return to the family captured in them.

Hannah checked her watch. She had about thirty minutes before she should wake Molly, or the length of her nap would disrupt her evening schedule. Besides, the light had already started to drop, and she needed to get back to the bungalow, use the restroom, and settle in for the evening. She had time to inventory the final box, though—or at least start on it. Somewhat predictably, it contained the pictures not of the Moores but of the Deckers with a gold framed black-and-white portrait of Andrew Decker as the first to greet her when she pulled back the cardboard flaps of the box.

When Hannah had previously imagined the architect, one-time owner, and resident of this house, she'd imagined someone wholly de-individualized, an anonymous face, malleable, appearing to be both "Andrew Decker" and no one in particular. At times, she'd imagined him to be vaguely similar to Michael—a serious man who did important things and had little time for nonsense. At other times, she'd imagined him like so many of the men she saw at the grocery store or gas station, amorphous German faces that matched names like Miller and Schuler and Decker.

The man who stared back at Hannah from the photograph in her hand, like his daughter, exuded joy. At what, Hannah could only guess. But he sat, one hip on the desk still in the study downstairs, one leg supporting his weight, his body facing the camera. His proportions, juxtaposed against those of the desk, indicated he'd been a tall man— the leg that supported his weight held a pronounced bend, the length of it markedly taller than the height of the desk. He wore a dark suit— black or navy, impossible to tell—over a white shirt and a tie, a vest buttoned neatly beneath his blazer. His hair nearly matched the dark color of his suit, and this wasn't the only trait that seemed also to have belonged to his daughter. The line of his jaw and the shape of his eyes would both eventually be passed on, like his house, to Margaret. And his eyes, they looked directly at the camera and consequently, through one hundred years, directly at Hannah. He seemed happy she'd found him, comfortable in her hands, his own hands folded neatly in his lap.

Suddenly, Hannah felt embarrassed, overcome with the sense that he knew she was staring at him. But she could not take her eyes from him, and she felt nothing short of grief at the fact there was no possibility—none—of them ever meeting.

Hannah's thoughts darkened as she wondered when the photograph was taken. How much time had passed between its relaxed happiness, and his family finding him dead of despair? She found her imagination wandering dark, morbid corridors as she thought about whether he was recognizable when he was found, or whether the angle of his jaw had been obliterated by the bullet, whether his thick, black hair, so neatly combed, had become matted and sticky with his blood. Had these penetrating eyes continued to view the world after his soul left it, or had he closed them before he took his life? And what earthly sum of money could possibly have been worth more than the life of this man?

Hannah turned the frame over, inspecting the black cardboard tile on the back. By the looks of it, the picture had sat on a desk or a shelf at one time, rather than hanging on a wall. Perhaps Mrs. Decker had placed this photograph of her husband on her vanity, glancing at it at intervals as she applied her lipstick or blush, brushed her hair, or spritzed her perfume.

Hannah pulled the tile from the back of the frame. A piece of old cardboard lay beneath, and she carefully removed that as well. A dull pencil noted a date: June 1929. The market would crash just four months later. He would be ruined. He had no idea what was coming. She brushed her finger over the date, her mind turning to the hand that had written it and how little time he had left on this earth from the moment this picture was taken. Strange to see him so light and happy.

"Mama!" Hannah heard Molly call from the bedroom down the hall. She checked her watch again. It was a little early, but far preferable to trying to wake Molly from sleep and then immediately putting her in the car to drive home.

"Coming, baby girl," Hannah called back. She quickly replaced the cardboard and tile in the frame, then gently placed Mr. Decker back in the box, closing the cardboard flaps over his face. She'd make every effort to ensure these pictures were returned to Mr. Decker's heirs, but they'd already been without them for some time. It wouldn't hurt if she took a day or two to sort through the remaining photographs. Just to see what was there.

❧

MICHAEL ARRIVED home that evening in an unexpectedly good mood. He wrapped Hannah in his arms and placed a kiss against her neck, backing her into the counter as she giggled at his enthusiasm.

"How would you like to go to London for a week?" he asked, tugging at the loops of her jeans, pulling her hips to his.

"When? What for?" Hannah asked, smiling. She'd never been to London. She'd never been to a lot of places.

"In July," Michael said. "They're sending me to the Basingstoke office for a week, but I thought I could stay for an extra week, and you could come, and we could spend it together."

"What would we do with Molly?" Hannah asked, her smile fading. A trip abroad sounded exciting, and she'd love to see London, but she'd love to see it as a family.

"My parents could come and stay with her," he suggested.

Hannah gave this some thought. Molly loved her grandparents, but Hannah wasn't sure a week with them was a great idea. She decided to keep her reservations to herself for the time being. July was an awfully long way off, and there were a lot of details of such a trip that could change in that amount of time.

"That sounds wonderful," she said, thinking it did sound mostly wonderful.

Michael had advanced his affections to include a purposeful hand under Hannah's shirt. It traveled slowly up the front of her body, and Hannah leaned into him as his thumb brushed across the thin lace that covered her breast, causing the flesh there to rise in response to his invitation.

"Tell me about our house," he invited, his lips finding hers and, as a practical matter, preventing her from speaking.

"I'll forward you the estimates when I get them," she said between kisses, omitting summary of the thinly veiled recommendation she'd already received from two of the three contractors.

"Mama," said a little voice at Hannah's leg.

"See, that's why we need a week in London alone," Michael said, looking down at Molly, who'd extended her arms to her mother.

"Pick you up? Pick you up?" the little girl said.

"Does she think she can pick you up?" Michael asked, laughing as Hannah bent over and lifted Molly into her arms.

"No. She's just repeating it the way she hears it. When I say, 'Want me to pick you up?' That's what she's saying," Hannah explained. She loved this frequent refrain. It was one of her favorite things that Molly said, and she'd be sad when Molly finally figured out that she was "you" and thus "you" was "me."

"Nobody picks up Mommy except Daddy," Michael said playfully, turning to Hannah. "Let's make sure she goes to bed on time tonight." He offered a final meaningful tug at Hannah's belt loops.

CHAPTER 4

Hannah's phone buzzed on the bedside table next to her. She set down her book and picked it up.

Mason: WTF? Where are you? What is that?

It had been two full days since she'd sent the picture of the Decker house attic. She shook her head, allowing an affectionate grin at his delayed, if exuberant, response.

Hannah: Attic storage room. Indy house.

Mason: Did you send to Grandpa?

Hannah: Yes. No response.

Mason: He probably can't see images on his Nokia.

Hannah: LOL! Where are you?

Mason: MT. Still. Fishing today.

Hannah: Catch anything?

Mason: No. Too many tourists stomping around.

Hannah: What are you doing now?

Mason: Trying to eat dinner but my sister keeps texting me.

Hannah: LOL! Jerk.

Mason:

She smiled into the phone at his emoji reference to her nickname —Hannah Banana—and knew the conversation had drawn to a close. It would be several days, maybe a week before she heard from him again.

Hannah: 🩶

She didn't wait for a response; there wouldn't be one. She set the phone back on her bedside table and smiled fondly at the mountain-shaped keychain she used as the pull on her lamp—his wedding present sent to her eight years ago along with his regrets. There had been a total of four people on her half of the guest list: Mason, her grandparents, and her mother. She hadn't expected her grandparents to attend. She thought it possible they'd never left South Carolina in their lives, and the wedding was in Mexico. She'd hoped her mother would at least RSVP her regrets but wasn't surprised when she didn't. She'd been disappointed that Mason couldn't attend—he couldn't take that much time off work—but the keychain from Yellowstone National Park came with an invitation for her to visit in what he described as the most beautiful place on earth.

Unexpectedly, Michael's parents had also declined to attend, stating "that kind of travel" was far too much at their age. Hannah thought other factors might have weighed into their decision as well. When she and Michael planned the wedding, she had no money for a dress, or flowers, or a formal reception hall. But Michael had been relatively unperturbed by her circumstances and suggested the wedding in Mexico. Hannah considered that to be the most extraordinarily opulent wedding she could imagine—a ceremony on a tropical beach followed by a honeymoon in a suite that opened onto a private pool and a view of the ocean.

"Were those the quotes?"

Hannah turned her attention from her thoughts of her brother to see Michael lying next to her, his book resting atop the covers.

"No," she said, finding she required some time to reorient herself. "No. It was Mason."

"How's he doing?" Michael asked, sitting up a little straighter in bed.

"Same. Still in Montana."

It had been more than three years since she'd seen him—since before Molly was born. He'd stayed with her and Michael in Boston during that visit as he helped their mother move out of her apartment with Hannah's father. Again. They all knew the pattern. Mason, Hannah, and their mother would enjoy the short respite, relish something that vaguely resembled a family, then their mother and Jack would reconcile and move in together again. And their mother would disappear from their lives. Again.

"We should ask him to come renovate the house," Michael suggested. A grin spread across his face.

"I think it's a more-than-one-person job." Hannah picked up her book and opened to the page she'd left off before Mason texted.

"It was a joke, Hannah. I know it'll take more than one person to renovate that house."

Hannah offered a single-syllable laugh that only succeeded in emphasizing that she'd missed his attempt at humor.

"How's work?" she asked in order to move Michael away from the topic of what exactly the contractors had intimated needed to be done.

"Excellent," Michael said, his face brightening again. "It looks like the Basingstoke trip is going to be kind of a big deal." He rolled to his side, resting on his hip. "They're thinking of moving the manufacturing of a new drug for SMA over there."

"What's SMA?" Hannah asked.

"It's a genetic disease. Pediatric. Usually lethal," he said. "Very sad," he added, though he didn't sound very sad.

"Why do they want to move the manufacturing there?" She set her book on her lap once again.

"PR. The NHS—the UK's health system—is saying they won't cover the drug because it's too expensive. This lowers the cost marginally, but it also creates jobs there, so a you-scratch-my-back-I'll-scratch-yours approach to getting the NHS to cover the drug."

"Interesting," Hannah commented. "Are we still going in July?"

"Oh yes. And maybe for longer than we originally planned."

"How long?" Hannah asked, thinking about where Molly would be during all of this.

"Not sure yet. I'll let you know when I know more," he said and dragged a finger down the length of her bare arm. Hannah offered him a tightlipped smile as he gazed at her hopefully.

"Hey. Before I forget. A woman at that exercise studio—"

"You went?" Michael interrupted.

"Yes. Earlier this week. I told you about it. Anyway, a woman in one of my classes—"

"How was it? Did you like the classes? Do you think you'll stick with it? Something like that would be good for you."

"Michael," Hannah said, frustrated with the interruptions.

"What?" Completely oblivious.

"One of the women is having a Halloween party and she invited us—"

"I won't know anyone," Michael said, abruptly shifting to rest his back against the headboard and raising his book to his face.

"I go to parties all the time where I don't know anyone when it's for your work. This is a good way for us to meet people out in the city," Hannah argued.

"What's her name?" Michael asked.

"Kate."

"Kate what?"

"I... I can't remember," Hannah admitted.

"So, you don't even know her."

Hannah sighed.

"What?"

"I'm trying to get to know her," Hannah said.

Michael looked at her, his brow furrowed. "It's not going to be a bunch of jazzercisers, is it?" he groaned.

"Probably not since the studio doesn't teach jazzercise classes. But it's fine if you don't want to go. Molly and I will go without you." She heard herself, her terse response. It hardly even sounded like her, more like she'd borrowed the voice from someone and merely tried it on for size.

Michael clearly noticed it, too, and seemed to freeze in mid-frame. Hannah set her book down on the bedside table, turned out her light, and rolled onto her side, her back to Michael.

"If it means that much to you, we can go," he said, his voice softening.

"I'm going either way. I'd love it if you came with me," Hannah said.

Michael didn't reply, but he turned out his light as well. Hannah heard him patting down his pillow and tossing and turning behind her until he grew quiet. Eventually, she heard his breathing, heavy but not quite a snore. She lay in the dark for some time, listening to the pounding of her own heartbeat, hoping it hadn't been loud enough for Michael to hear before he'd fallen asleep.

❧

HIGH INTENSITY INTERVAL TRAINING, but all the women pronounced it "hit." When Hannah arrived at the studio at 7:00 a.m., Susan greeted her with that same unexpected sincerity.

"Rob's teaching this morning," she said as Hannah dropped Molly off in the playroom. "Have a good class."

In the studio, Kate already occupied the same spot she had last time, and Hannah took her place next to her, setting her water bottle and towel against the mirror.

"You're back," Kate said as if she'd been waiting.

"I am," Hannah said shyly.

"Okay, that's enough chit-chat," Rob said to the room as he adjusted a playlist on his phone and connected it to the overhead sound system.

Hannah faced the mirror ready to begin.

"Deep breath in, everyone," Rob began, standing in the center of the room. "Exhale." Hannah did as she was told. "As we begin our practice today, as we think about the work we're going to do over the next forty-five minutes, let's start by setting our intention for this class. For me, I am, as usual, dedicating this class to absolutely fucking no one. Now let's get to work."

Hannah liked Rob.

❧

"Do you think you'll be able to make it to the Halloween party?" Kate asked Hannah as they all gathered their belongings from the cubbies outside the exercise room.

"I'd like to. It's Saturday?"

"Yes. Here, give me your cell phone number, and I'll text you the info."

Hannah obliged and received a quick bounce back with a text.

> Kate: This is Kate Nielsen from Studio BR.

Hannah smiled as she saw the message come through, followed quickly by a link to an Evite.

"You're new to Indy?" Kate asked.

"Yes. We moved here about a month ago."

"How do you like it?" Kate was stuffing her feet into a pair of boots, her words coming out with some effort as a result.

"It seems fine," Hannah said amiably.

"You work outside the home?"

"No. Do you?" For a former bartender, Hannah thought she should be better at these kinds of cold-conversations, but she agonized through each exchange as if it were the first time she'd ever talked to someone she didn't know.

"Yes. I teach history at the university west of here, just east of the river."

"Oh! We live over there," Hannah said. "Or we do for now. We're renting until our house is renovated."

"Where's your house?" Kate asked, as she pulled her coat on and zipped it up.

"In Hyde Park. West of the river." Hannah began putting on her own coat.

"One of my colleagues lives over there. Jeremy Linden. Have you run into him?" Kate asked, lifting her head. She had hair the color of the mahogany end tables in the living room at the Decker house and green eyes, almost the same celadon hue as the three pottery vases that Hannah had tagged as "keeping."

"Oh, yes," Hannah said. "With the Rottweiler. Yes. Just once. We just bought the house in September, and I haven't gotten a chance to get out much into the neighborhood. We just started renovating it this week." Hannah was aware that she had not just started renovating it; she had, at best, just started preparing for the eventual renovation. But she wanted to impress Kate and "preparing" didn't strike her as especially impressive.

Hannah could hear Molly in the playroom. She'd heard Hannah's voice and was growing impatient for her mother to come and collect her.

"Cool. Well, don't forget to RSVP," Kate said, as she started toward the door. She waved one final time over her shoulder before disappearing down the staircase.

❦

"NICE DRESS!" Michael whistled as Hannah entered the living room. She received the compliment with a diminutive curtsy and a flirtatious wink. It was a great dress—a sleeveless, peacock-blue silk with beadwork decorating a navy lace overlay. Hannah's hair was too long for the cute flapper bobs she knew would have been worn with such a dress, so she opted instead for a loose, off-center bun, worn low at her neck. She added a decorative hair comb tucked in just above.

"Where's your costume?" she asked, evaluating her husband's blue jeans and sweater. "I thought you were going as Indiana Jones. That was a good idea for a costume."

"I changed my mind, and the invitation doesn't say costumes are required," Michael protested, reaching for their coats from the closet.

"Fair enough." Hannah couldn't help her disappointment. As if sensing her displeasure, Molly pulled the hood of her costume up over her head, her little honeybee antennae bouncing from side to side as she toddled over to her mother.

"Pick you up? Pick you up?" she said.

"It's pick me up," Michael corrected.

Molly only looked at him, confused as Hannah pulled her into her arms, and they headed toward the door to leave for Kate's.

Kate's house, explained Michael as they circled her block looking for parking, was "typical" of the homes in Meridian-Kessler—the neighborhood that had been the eventual downfall of Fritz Brothers, LLC. An enormous Tudor that had undergone an expansion at some point with a large addition placed on the back, it had been built right around the time of the Decker house and the other original Hyde Park homes Andrew Decker designed. Michael commented that if he'd been more familiar with the area, he probably would have requested to see some listings, as several of his co-workers lived there.

Michael parked among the many cars that lined the curb, requiring the three of them to walk some distance to reach Kate's house. Hannah's pulse quickened as they approached the walkway that led to the front door. The lights were bright, shining through every window along the front of the grand home, and Hannah could see Kate in the dining room flitting about, calling back to someone behind her or in another room. Hannah steeled herself, closed her eyes, breathing in, breathing out. And then they arrived at the door.

"Hello!" Kate said, swinging the door wide before either Michael or Hannah could ring the bell.

"Hello," Molly said with equal enthusiasm.

"Come on in. Let me get your coats." Kate took Michael's coat from him, then helped Hannah peel out of hers.

"Oh my god! Great dress, flapper girl," she gushed, as she led them into a sea of Marvel superheroes, circus animals, Harry Potter characters, a leprechaun, and the more traditional Halloween ghosts and ghouls. Kate had opted for Star Wars with a Bo-Katan Kryze costume. The exaggerated silver armor suggested a strength Hannah had seen from Kate at the exercise studio.

Hannah introduced Michael just in time for a well-appointed Jedi to enter the foyer, throwing an arm around Kate's waist.

"I was wondering where you went," the Jedi said, kissing Kate on the cheek.

"Steve, this is Hannah and Michael Korman," Kate said.

"Nice to meet you," Steve said, seeming to mean it. "Kate tells me you're both from Boston."

"Yes," Michael said at the same time Hannah offered a tentative, "Sort of."

"And you must be Molly," Steve said to the little honeybee in Hannah's arms.

Molly reached a hand up and bobbed an antenna, seeming to say, *See what I can do?*

"That's quite a little costume you've got there." Steve received a shy smile in gratitude for his compliment. "Come on. Let's get you both a drink and some snacks."

From the number of people present, the decor, the caterers milling about replenishing trays of hors d'oeuvres, and the bartenders stationed in the dining room, Hannah saw that the Nielsens' Halloween party was not merely a gathering, not a get-together, hardly even a party. It was a full-blown occasion. Judging from some of the elaborate costumes, attendees planned for this party months in advance.

"Help yourself to snacks. We hired a couple babysitters from the university and have kids' activities in the basement. You can take Molly down there if you'd like, and she'll have plenty to do for the evening," Kate said as they began walking toward the kitchen.

"Kate! Steve!" someone called from the kitchen.

"Be right back," Kate said, jogging ahead of Hannah and Michael with Steve close behind her.

"Hey, there's Sam!" Michael said, waving to a man on the other side of the living room. Sam waved back and held up a finger indicating he'd be there shortly, but Michael was already making his way through the other guests toward him, which left Hannah, as she'd feared, standing alone in a crowd of people she didn't know.

In an instant, Hannah was thrown back to those first days of middle school after moving to live with her grandparents. She'd had the fleeting flirtation with popularity that often accompanies "new kid" status, particularly as it existed in the small town of Clover, South Carolina where very little happened and rarely was it "new." But the sheen of "new" quickly gave way to the stain of "different" as Hannah stumbled over explanations for the cast on her arm, the absence of her parents, and her strange *Wostah* accent. Even in Indiana, Hannah was aware that no consonant in the English language holds more power than an 'R'.

Staring out across the costumed heads of Kate's friends, neighbors, and colleagues, panic began to rise in Hannah's chest. She pushed it down by deciding Molly must be hungry, so she assembled a selection of hors d'oeuvres on a plate in the dining room and returned to the foyer where she and Molly sat on the stairs and ate.

In the dim light of the foyer, with the dissonant choir of guests' voices in the background, Hannah felt trapped. She'd insisted on going to this party, and now she couldn't wait to leave. She weighed her options. How long did she have to stay to be polite? How long before she could pull Michael away from whoever this Sam person was and return home without admitting defeat?

"Overstimulated?" came a voice from above. She looked up to see Charlie Chaplin walking down the stairs behind her.

"I'm not one for big crowds," Hannah said, a touch more curtly than she'd intended.

"Well, you're at the wrong party then," he said, coming around beside her. As she got a better look under the bowler hat and mustache, she saw that it was Jeremy from her neighborhood. "Don't feel bad. I had to hide upstairs for a minute to get away, too," he added.

"Oh my gosh, I didn't recognize you," Hannah said, disarming herself as she realized she'd met the man before.

"How do you know Kate?" he asked.

"We work out at the same exercise studio," she explained.

Jeremy took a seat on the stairs next to Molly. "Great dress. Goes perfect with the house."

Hannah beamed; that was exactly what she'd been aiming for.

"And I see you are accompanied by a honeybee. How are you?"

Molly responded by once again encouraging a little bob of the black bulb on top of her head, which inspired a chuckle from Jeremy.

"I think Kate has games and stuff for the kids in the basement," he said.

"I don't know where the basement is," Hannah replied. "Kate got pulled away before she could show me."

"Oh. I can show you." Jeremy rose to his feet and offered his hand to assist Hannah as she stood from the stairs. He led them through the foyer, around the corner, and back into the kitchen. An inconspicuous door opened into a stairwell down to a large family room with a television and seating area, where children were already running around, building towers of blocks, playing with Legos, Barbies, and other toys.

"Holy night," Hannah breathed, stepping from the last step onto the floor of a basement that seemed to run nearly the entire footprint of the house.

"Hi! Ohmigod I love your dress. Write your name and your daughter's name down on this sheet with preferred contact, and if we need you, we'll text you." The sentences were offered in the manner of a single thought expelled from a young woman in a Butler University sweatshirt.

"Hi, Dr. Linden," the student said. "I like your costume. Who are you?" Hannah thought she saw a hint of pink come into the young woman's cheeks as she addressed Jeremy.

"Charlie Chaplin," Jeremy said, turning his feet out at first position.

The young woman stared back at him blankly.

"Charlie Chaplin," he said again. "The silent movie star. Arguably, the most important figure in the history of film? No? Nothing?"

"Sorry. I don't know who that is," the young woman said.

Jeremy hummed his disappointment before turning to Hannah who was putting a squirming Molly down on the floor. "Do you know who Charlie Chaplin is?" he asked.

"Yes. My grandmother loves him. I grew up on his movies. My favorite is *City Lights*."

"Oh, that's a good one," he agreed.

Hannah added her contact information and name to a clipboard and waved a "good-bye" to Molly, who toddled over to a play kitchen set.

"Good to see you again, Chelsey," Jeremy said with some formality, then headed with Hannah back up the stairs.

At the top of the stairs, as she opened the door, Hannah was nearly run over by her husband, who appeared prepared to bound down not having realized anyone was in his way.

"Jesus Christ," he exclaimed, startled to find Hannah behind the door staring back at him. "Where have you been? I've been texting you for the past twenty minutes." The scold in his voice was unmistakable, and Hannah shrank back.

"I—My phone is in my coat. My dress doesn't have pockets," she stammered. "Michael, this is Jeremy Linden, the history professor from our neighborhood I told you about." She hoped the introduction would redirect Michael, and it appeared to do the trick as she and Jeremy stepped out of the stairwell back into the kitchen. Michael adjusted his demeanor and shook the costumed professor's hand.

"It's nice to meet a neighbor," Michael said. "You're a professor there at Butler?"

"I am. I teach History of Medicine," he said as the trio walked through the kitchen into the dining room.

"Very nice. I'm in R&D at Rue," Michael said, offering his position as though it were its own valuable currency.

They reached the table of hors d'oeuvres.

"Is that what brought you both here?" Jeremy asked.

Hannah popped a cube of cheddar cheese into her mouth. "It's Hannah Banana!" a voice called out before Michael could answer Jeremy's question. Hannah turned to see Rob and the woman with the curly hair from the studio approaching. To hear Rob use the nickname Mason had given her made her smile, if a bit wistfully.

The new round of introductions allowed Hannah to catch the other woman's name—Laura—and also stopped the flow of the conversation between Jeremy and Michael as people shook hands and exchanged what-do-you-dos, and where-do-you-lives, and where-are-you-froms. The group settled into conversation, and Hannah felt the anxiety of the earlier evening dissipate as she found herself surrounded by friends.

❧

"THAT HISTORY PROFESSOR from the university wasn't very impressive. I guess it's true what they say about education here. Probably should send Molly back east for college."

Michael hadn't specified, but Hannah didn't have to ask which history professor he meant. "College is a long way off for Molly," she said, feeling sad at even the thought of her daughter leaving home.

"Well, anyway, he didn't seem to know anything about gene therapy," Michael continued, sitting on the edge of the bed to pull off his socks.

"Why would he know about gene therapy? He's a *history* professor." Hannah was only half listening as she removed her bobby pins and earrings.

"History of *medicine*," Michael emphasized.

Hannah didn't respond.

"And what's the point of knowing the past if it doesn't help you understand the present?"

"Hmm," Hannah murmured, neither agreeing nor disagreeing as she stepped into her pajama bottoms and traded her bra for a t-shirt.

"Also, what was with his costume? Who comes to a costume party dressed as Hitler?"

"What?" Hannah spun around, unable to contain her shock. "He wasn't Hitler. He was Charlie Chaplin. Why on earth would you think he was Hitler?"

"Because of the mustache. He was wearing a Hitler mustache," Michael argued.

Hannah struggled to imagine how Michael could have possibly drawn Hitler out of a costume that included an ill-fitting black suit, a bowler hat, and a cane. As she stared at Michael in disbelief, she saw it dawn on him as well. The eyebrows and the mustache were "Hitleresque" but nothing else.

"That was the plot in one of Chaplin's movies," she said, her voice calm and even. "*The Great Dictator*. He played two characters—a Jewish Barber and the Dictator. They were mistaken for each other. Because of the mustache."

"Well, it was still a weird costume. He couldn't pull it off. He's too tall to be Chaplin."

"He's too tall to be Hitler," Hannah replied, distracted with her bobby pins.

She felt it immediately, the way the very atmosphere in the room seemed to shift, as if an ordinary and predictable current that had always moved west to east suddenly, inexplicably shifted north to south. Michael blinked at her from the other side of the bed, evidently caught in the vortex.

"I think you have a little crush on that history professor," he said with a palpable calculation.

"I do not," Hannah said.

"Ahh. The lady doth protest too much, methinks," he said, a smirk curling the corners of his mouth.

"I do not have a crush on our neighbor," Hannah said, her face hot with embarrassment and anger, the tears stinging behind her eyes. Did it seem like she had a crush on Jeremy? Had she done something? Said something? Would Jeremy think she had a crush on him?

"Oh, calm down. I'm just joking," Michael said, coming around to her side of the bed and wrapping his arms around her waist. She didn't return the gesture, not even after he added a kiss.

"Hannah," he said. "Come on. It was just a joke. Of course you don't have a crush on... see? I can't even remember his name."

Hannah almost volunteered the name but reconsidered. Best she pretend she couldn't remember it either.

CHAPTER 5

On Monday, Hannah received quotes from two of the three contractors she'd consulted on the Decker house. She already had a strong preference for Gary but decided to review the quotes from Milston & Leake and White Fences, as well. She'd imagined the famed low-ball, mid-range, and outrageously high quotes, and had hoped that Gary would be the mid-range estimate—the one everyone knows you're supposed to go with. Instead, Dan Milston and the White Fences team came back to her a minuscule twenty-five hundred dollars apart on estimates that nearly matched the purchase price of the house. As she examined the numbers in black and white, her stomach made a sound she was glad only Molly was around to hear, and she momentarily reconsidered the wisdom of the sausage McMuffin she'd had on her way to the Decker house.

Six years spent as the veritable apprentice to her grandfather, and she'd never seen a figure so high. She'd reminded Michael of her experience repeatedly when arguing that they should purchase the Decker house. She knew about construction, she'd said. She could even do some of the work herself. He'd put his trust in her.

He would be livid.

But it was more than the "Total Cost Estimated" line on the last page of the PDFs. It seemed that in reaching that total, the two contractors had found every conceivable defect in the house and laid it out in the starkest, most unflattering light. Repairs were necessary to the roof, the chimney, nearly every window in the solarium, the sagging floor in the living room. Notes referenced the additional cost of insuring the project due to the hazardous materials "typical" of such houses—lead, mold, rot, mildew, asbestos. The quotes included the costs of PPE for the crew to protect them from the toxic substances potentially lurking in the house.

Moreover, permits might be hard or even impossible to obtain. The contractors "made no guarantee" the job could be completed. The estimates gave the impression they weren't estimates at all, but an itemization of reasons to abandon the project altogether. And nothing spoke louder than the inclusion of the alternative "Tear Down/Complete Demo" estimate that amounted to approximately ten percent of the total cost of renovation—something Hannah did not want to see and absolutely had not requested.

By mid-morning, Hannah sat despondent on the green velvet couch in the Decker house living room, Molly on a blanket at her feet. She stared blankly at the two quotes as if her continued review might miraculously rewrite the lines and reorganize the numbers on them. She could already imagine Michael, having put his trust in her after she assured him she "knew about these things", taking one look at the quotes and selecting the cheapest "tear down" option.

A knock at the door interrupted her catastrophizing, and she was pleased to see Gary on the front step. He planned to deliver his quote in person since Hannah had already indicated a preference for hiring him. However, if she'd been hoping for him to save her from the other two contractors, she would be disappointed. His quote included all of the same line items and totaled only a thousand dollars less than White Fences—technically the mid-range quote, but not by any meaningful sum.

"These guys are fair," Gary said as he reviewed the other two PDFs on Hannah's phone. "It's a huge house that essentially hasn't been touched in a hundred years. And then it was all but abandoned for ten. There are a lot of unknowns in a project like this. Heck the kitchen cabinets alone are going to run you a good forty-five thousand dollars. There's not a right angle in this place. No offense, Mr. Decker."

"I didn't ask them what it would cost to tear it down," Hannah bristled. "Your quote doesn't say to tear it down."

"Theirs doesn't either, really. It just lets you know it's an option. I didn't include it in mine because I figured it wasn't an option for you. I have a feeling you would put this place back together with your bare hands if you had to."

"At least I could make the cabinets," she scoffed. "Look at that—we've already knocked forty-five thousand off the estimate." She wore the sarcasm like an ill-fitting blouse.

"You can't make cabinets," Gary said tenderly. "It's harder than it looks."

"No, truly. I can make cabinets," she said. "My grandfather was a cabinetmaker, and he taught me how."

"No kidding?" Gary quipped. "Where?"

"South Carolina," she said, her voice carrying a note of nostalgia as she recalled the warmth of her grandfather's callused hands over her own, gently guiding her, teaching her his trade. By the time Hannah had graduated high school, people were joking that the only way to tell the difference between the work Robert had done and the work she had done was the faint scent of Sir Walter Raleigh tobacco that accompanied Robert's woodworking. She smiled and then felt the corners of her mouth draw back down as she reconnected with the present.

"You don't sound like you're from South Carolina."

"I moved there in middle school," she explained in spectacularly incomplete fashion.

"I see," Gary said quietly. "Well, if you want to make the cabinets, I think that'd be nice. If you decide to stick with the project, I can set my workshop up in the garage, and you're welcome to use my tools in there to make anything you want."

"Thanks," Hannah said, glancing at Gary.

The whole conversation was irrelevant. Michael had hated the house since she'd first showed it to him in their living room in Boston. He'd be thrilled that two of the contractors had provided him an "out." Hannah stared across the living room at the green tile that surrounded the fireplace, imaging it reduced to rubble. The whole house would be leveled by Thanksgiving. She felt a tear slip from her eye and roll down her cheek, and she lifted the back of her hand, trying to brush it away before Gary noticed.

"Mrs. Korman. Hannah. If I might make a suggestion," Gary began. "I'm not sure what made you decide to buy this house. It sounds like your realtor didn't tell you at least a couple of things she really should have. But I think you should take a day or two to make a decision. Is this your house, or isn't it? Like Margaret. That woman decided this was her house, and nothing and no one was going to keep her from it. This might not be your house. And it's okay if it isn't. But each of these quotes will still be here on Wednesday, including mine. You call me then, and you let me know what you've decided."

Hannah wiped another tear with the back of her hand. Molly had stopped playing and looked up at her mother.

"It's okay, sweetie. I'm just having a blue day," she said, but Molly didn't return to her toys. She continued to glance back and forth between her mother and Gary, regarding them both with apprehension, even fear. Gary rose from the couch and gathered his notepad, the paper copy of his estimate, and his messenger bag.

"One more thing, Mrs. Korman—I mean, Hannah."

"Yes?" she said, her sadness giving way to a vacant emptiness.

"It's one thing if the issue is the money. If you don't have the money for this project, the project is over. But if you're thinking you don't have the guts for it, or that it's not worth the money, or that it's a silly project, or it's not actually possible to drag this house into the twenty-first century? Well. You need to let those thoughts go. The house is worth it. And the project is possible. And I know Dan and Rich are telling you to tear it down and just start over, but I would consider it an honor to work with you to renovate this place. It's worth it."

Hannah sniffed, new tears forming at the corners of her eyes. She nodded and got up from the couch, walked Gary to the door, and closed it firmly behind him.

A STRANGE BURST of warm weather moved in almost overnight, contrasting sharply with the cold, dreary atmosphere that had marked the previous two weeks. Hannah had her coat zipped up to her chin, but it was too much, and she was perspiring beneath as she pushed Molly's stroller for a second time around Hyde Park's south loop. She could tell from Molly's legs that her daughter was fighting sleep.

They'd had lunch and a bathroom break at the bungalow and returned to the Decker house, though Hannah wasn't sure why. Her time would have been better spent calling Debbie and asking her to find a house in Meridian-Kessler. Michael had liked that neighborhood. His colleague Sam lived there and for whatever reason, Michael hadn't been able to stop talking about how that was where they, too, should have moved. That Debbie hadn't shown them a house in that area, and that Hannah hadn't included one in her own search, was a serious misstep in Michael's calculation.

"Hannah," a voice called, interrupting her self-scolding.

She turned to see Jeremy and his Rottweiler, Gertie, jogging her way. The dog looked exceptionally unhappy about the pace they were keeping, and Hannah slowed, waiting for them to catch up. She gave a friendly scratch under Gertie's collar as Jeremy fell in step with Hannah and Molly.

"Trying to get her down for a nap?" Jeremy asked, his voice low.

"*Trying* would be the operative word," Hannah said, some bitterness still lingering after the first half of her day.

"Everything okay?"

"Yeah. I don't think we're going to be able to renovate the Decker house," she said.

"What?" He turned his whole body to her, as if he truly couldn't believe it.

Hannah saw him without Halloween makeup, without the rushed conversation she'd had when she'd first met him. He stood two or three inches taller than she. His hair, now without bowler hat, was a rich brown, darker than Michael's even before he'd started to gray, but Jeremy wore it longer, subtle waves that he combed back out of his face and that somehow cooperated in staying put. His eyes were the color of Swiss milk chocolate, and Hannah recalled the flush in the cheeks of the student at Kate's house when she'd spoken to "Dr. Linden." He probably got that a lot.

He raised his brows, his eyes growing wide, and Hannah realized he was waiting for her response.

"Hmm? What? Oh," she stumbled. "Yeah, we got the quotes from the contractors, and they're recommending we just tear it down. It's too big a project."

Gertie tugged Jeremy over to a pile of brown leaves, and he waited while she nudged them with her nose before making a modest offering on top of them.

"Wow. Man. I'm sorry to hear that. For some reason, I just really thought you and that house sort of went together," he said, rejoining her at the stroller.

"It was probably the Halloween costume." She laughed lightly, as if that party had been years ago and not a short forty-eight hours earlier.

"That was a great costume."

"Yours too," she said.

"I don't know about that. I think your husband thought I was Hitler," he said.

"Oh yeah? What makes you say that?" she asked and suppressed a knowing smile.

"He ended our conversation by saying something about the French Resistance. I can't remember what it was. It was kind of an obscure reference, and my area isn't World War II."

Hannah chuckled to herself.

"Anyway. I don't think he was the only one. I think it was because of the mustache, like in—"

"*The Great Dictator*," they both said together.

"Exactly," Jeremy said, laughing. He quieted himself, eyeing the back of Molly's stroller. "It drove me crazy a few years ago when everyone was sharing that speech at the end when the barber finally talks. I mean, I love that speech, but..."

"It's not the best part of the movie," Hannah said, agreeing with him.

"What do you think is the best part?" Jeremy asked.

"When the barber first returns to the ghetto from the hospital, and he hasn't seen how things have changed under the dictator. And he thinks it's insane; there's no way any of it makes sense. And you're like, 'Oh, right. If you hadn't had time to get used to it, you'd never tolerate it.'"

"Yep. That's it." Jeremy tried in vain to move Gertie away from the stroller, both to prevent her from bothering Molly and to keep himself from tripping over her. He succeeded in the former.

"Hey, shouldn't you be at work? Teaching or something?" Hannah asked.

"I teach on Tuesdays, Thursdays, and Fridays," he said. "I work from home on Mondays and Wednesdays—write, prep my lectures for class, walk my dog, bother my neighbors with pedantic conversations about silent films."

Hannah laughed, and it seemed that in the span of about four minutes her entire mood had changed.

"*The Great Dictator* was a talkie," she said as she continued to slowly push the stroller forward.

❧

"WHY WOULD WE TEAR IT DOWN?" Michael asked, looking over the screen of his laptop. He sounded personally offended by the suggestion.

Hannah had finally worked up the nerve to forward the quotes, and he had all three PDFs pulled up, clicking back and forth between them. Molly stood against the coffee table, stacking magazines one on top of another. Behind her, an elaborate—and probably very expensive—activity table gathered dust. Michael's parents had bought it for her half-birthday—something Hannah didn't know people actually celebrated. They would be disappointed that she preferred a stack of *The New Yorker* magazines to the plastic amusement park they'd thoughtfully selected.

"You look really upset about this," Michael observed. "Why are you so upset? We got this. *I* got this."

Hannah blinked back her surprise. She had absolutely expected Michael to take one look at the estimates, chastise her for the "mess" she'd gotten them both into, and tell her to figure out how to get rid of the house. That he viewed the "Total Cost Estimated" barely remark-able enough to merit pausing his episode of *Jack Ryan* couldn't have caught Hannah more by surprise.

"I guess... I mean, I knew it would be a big project, but I didn't know it would be this big. And I don't know what to make of the... tone of the estimates, I guess. The suggestion that we tear it down—I wasn't sure how you'd react." She pulled the sleeves of her shirt down over her hands, curling her fingers around the cuffs.

Michael shrugged. "There's no tone here; it's just a construction estimate. It's a big house. You should know that better than anyone. You like this Gary guy?" he asked, moving on with a stroke of his finger on the mouse.

"Yeah. He seemed to know the most about the house, and he seemed like he'd be easy to work with," Hannah said.

"Well, he's right in the middle of the other two, so I don't have any objection to you using him. I'd like to meet him before he gets started. Can you arrange a good time for us to talk?"

"Sure," Hannah replied, thoroughly stunned. She could feel the sting behind her eyes, the tears of relief just waiting to be acknowl-edged. She sniffed, as if that might persuade them to stay put.

"Hey," Michael said, tipping his head to the side. He pulled her hand from the sleeve of her shirt and took it in his. "Hey, everything's okay. The house is going to be great."

"Yeah," Hannah said, thinking maybe she believed him. "Yeah. Okay."

"Just set up that meeting with Gary so he can get started." Michael released Hannah's hand and picked up the remote. *Jack Ryan* awaited.

"Thanks, Michael," Hannah said.

"You're welcome, babe," he said quickly, as he un-paused the show, and the characters on the television sprang back to life.

CHAPTER 6

Gary scheduled construction on the Decker house to commence the first week of December. This would allow time to obtain permits, retain subcontractors, and finalize plans with Michael and Hannah.

"I don't want thirteen calls a day at work asking whether we should go with eggshell- or ecru-colored trim," Michael said when he met with Gary and Hannah in the foyer of the Decker house. That request suited Hannah just fine, as she suspected Michael didn't know the difference between the two colors anyway.

Hannah's request leaned in quite another direction. She wanted as much of the original features preserved as possible while bringing the house into this millennium. She noted a preference for distinct, defined spaces, in contrast to "open concept" floor plans. To the extent the layout of the house would be altered, she wanted to retain as much of the original character as possible. Any doors that could be repurposed should be. Any woodwork or crown moulding should be reused in the remodeled portions of the house. Built-in bookcases, china cabinets, cupboards, and the like should be preserved if at all possible, as new wiring, new pipes, and new ductwork were installed behind them.

"Speaking of cabinets," Hannah said as they all stood in what would one day be the kitchen. "I'd very much like to make the kitchen cabinets when the time comes. I know I was kind of joking when I said that last week, but it would make me feel good to contribute something."

"I think that's a fine idea," Gary said, sounding quite pleased.

"She's the real deal," Michael said as if Gary had suggested some skepticism, which he had not. "Her family's been woodworkers for generations." He sounded proud, and Hannah beamed under his recognition of her talents.

"Well, I'd like to see a sample of your work, but other than that, I'll just put in the order for the wood, and when we're ready, you can start the work."

So, it was decided that Michael wouldn't be bothered with constant updates and questions and requests concerning the construction on the house, and Hannah wouldn't find the constant updates and questions and requests concerning the construction of the house to be a bother. Gary promised to begin the process of securing permits immediately, agreeing with the other two contractors that there could potentially be some challenges in obtaining them. Then, he and Michael shook hands, leaving Hannah and Molly to continue their preparations for the renovation.

After Gary and Michael left, Hannah decided to continue her efforts in the attic. She pretended her purpose was purely utilitarian, sorting through furniture and magazines, plant stands and empty trunks. But her activities took a very different form as soon as she set up a play space for Molly under one of the dormers. Estimating that she had about an hour until Molly tired of the toys she'd brought with her, Hannah sat down in front of the third box of photographs and pulled back its flaps, finding Andrew Decker staring back at her from June of 1929. She picked up the photograph and set it to the side, face up, thinking she might like Andrew's company while she investigated the remainder of the box.

Significantly fewer photographs hid within this box than in the prior two. Hannah attributed this to the fact that so many of the photographs were framed and so took up quite a lot of space. She also appreciated that fewer photographs were taken of people in the first quarter of the twentieth century and thought about the thousands of pictures people took now with the ease of phone cameras. She felt confident there were more pictures of Molly's first year of life than of the entire span of Andrew Decker's. As she stole a sideways glance at him perched on the side of his desk, she thought that was a real shame.

Hannah pulled the next photo out of the box and found herself further back in time. No more than a teen, there was no mistaking Andrew, his eyes so uniquely belonging to him even as a young man. He sat on a curb in front of a white picket fence, flanked by two similar-appearing boys only slightly smaller than himself, and a young girl, maybe nine or ten years old.

Siblings, Hannah thought.

Judging from the picture, Andrew had been the oldest of four: three boys and a girl, all of them so obviously of the same family she could have picked them out as a family from a box overflowing with photographs of strangers. Their hair the same obsidian shade, a similarity of their eyes, some individuality in the shapes of their faces, the proportions of their lips and noses.

Her fingers next landed on a large, framed family portrait, which carried her forward in time and provided her first real look at the woman she assumed was Mrs. Decker, a woman who absolutely exuded 1920s glamor. Andrew's wife wore her hair cut short, bobbed and waved as was the style then. Light—either from a window or a strategically placed lamp—shone through the waves, her hair turning to corn-silk in a halo around her head. Her chin tilted down, allowing her to gaze up at the camera coquettishly from under her lashes. On her left hand, she wore a modest wedding band, but on her right, a large square stone, easily the size of her thumbnail, decorated her ring finger. Emerald, ruby, onyx, it was impossible to say from the black-and-white photo, but the ring was a piece, worn for one reason only—to impress.

Andrew stood to her side with one hand resting on the back of his wife's chair, the other tucked casually in his pocket. Margaret, maybe five years old, her ankles crossed, her feet dangling a few inches above the floor, sat on a bench in front of her father.

"Now that is a family portrait," Hannah said aloud, to whom, she wasn't sure. She set the picture down on the floor.

The size of the photograph in its frame had obscured the treasures beneath it. Loose black-and-white photographs that depicted the informal events of the Decker family—Easter, Christmas, Thanksgiving, a first day of school for Margaret, a portrait of Mrs. Decker taken in the image of a Hollywood starlet, the edges soft, her face taking on a porcelain quality. The pictures of Andrew showed a man so positively of this world, Hannah had trouble reconciling his present absence from it. There were photographs of Andrew at his desk working, sitting with his wife in the solarium and on the terrace of this house, standing on a barren plot of land, perhaps in this neighborhood. Some included men Hannah could only assume were business partners— dressed in dapper suits, never making another appearance in the documented record of his life.

Hannah gathered the photographs, loose as they were, into something of a stack and pushed them to a corner of the box. As the contents became more organized under her hand, two remaining objects occupied her complete attention. The first was a brown, leather-bound album. Upon opening it, she found herself a guest at the Deckers' wedding, the event memorialized in calligraphy at the front of the album:

> *Andrew Lawrence Decker*
> *Eleanor Alice Dailey*
> *19 June 1920*

The first page of the album presented the first official portrait of the new couple and depicted a wedding that had been a formal affair by any measure. Andrew wore a black tuxedo, Eleanor next to him in a cloud of white silk and lace, one square-toed, white slipper peeking out from under her dress. Hannah leafed through the pages, noting the photographs of family, wedding attendants, the couple during the ceremony. She set the album to the side, atop the family portrait.

If the wedding album had satisfied a specific curiosity, the remaining photograph left Hannah feeling an emptiness she hadn't been prepared for. The final framed photograph in the box showed Andrew holding Margaret, no older than Molly, in what appeared to be a home office or study, though not one in the Decker house. Margaret sat high against her father's ribs, her head even with his as he beamed openly at her. An unplanned photograph that had been held worthy of framing by someone. Andrew wore his shirtsleeves rolled up just under his elbows and he was—for once—without a blazer, even though his shirt was pressed and fitted neatly into his trousers. His hair fell to the side of his face, relaxed, rather than carefully combed back in the conscientious style he wore in other photographs.

As Hannah continued examining the picture, something caught in her throat. Not just that the picture strayed from her general association of that time period with stern faces, posing primarily for portraits, and not just that Andrew seemed somehow unassembled, even his collar undone. What caught her breath was how absolutely taken Andrew was with his daughter. The creases at the corners of his eyes announced the depth of his amusement at the little girl, and the definition of muscle in his forearm evoked an imminent or recent embrace, as if he'd picked his daughter up just to hug her and tell her he loved her, and it was that precise moment the camera had captured.

Of the hundreds of pictures of Molly she had on her phone and in her "cloud", Hannah knew not a single one of them resembled a moment like this—Michael so adoring of his daughter that his eyes nearly closed with the intensity of his joy at her.

"He loved her," Hannah whispered, pouring over every detail, the curve of his smile, Margaret's returned adoration as she faced her father. She could almost hear the child giggle through the image, through the glass, through the century between them.

Hannah sank back, sitting on her feet. She felt committed to returning the boxes. She couldn't imagine anyone would intentionally discard three whole boxes of family photographs, and even though Debbie had been clear that everything in the house ran with the house when it sold "as is," Hannah felt strongly that returning the items was simply the right thing to do. But as she considered further, she thought perhaps it would be possible for her to make a copy of some of the photographs first—the picture of Andrew from his study, the one of him with Margaret. That way, she could return the originals to the family, yet still have a picture or two of the architect of her home. It might be an interesting keepsake to display on a bookshelf or a desk or... somewhere.

She turned back toward Molly's play area under the dormer. She seemed happy enough, though she'd soon grow restless. Hannah carefully arranged the framed pictures in the box, setting the photograph from 1929 on top and the wedding album next to it. She then closed the flaps of the box, carefully placing a Post-it on top of each, and began the task of disassembling what little remained of the wall of furniture.

❧

AFTER LUNCH, Hannah resolved to address whatever was left of the home's garage. Situated behind the house, the garage was a detached three-car structure that, based on the exterior, Hannah felt less than optimistic could be salvaged. Half of the roof sagged down against broken rafters, pieces of which lay on its cluttered floor. And with one of the doors missing entirely, the interior had been exposed to every element and animal central Indiana had to offer. Much too dangerous for Molly, there would be no establishing a safe corner for her there. So, Hannah took the stroller from the back of the Range Rover, snuggled Molly in with a quilt, and set out on their laps around the south loop of the neighborhood in the hopes that Molly would nap.

The warm spell had brought the sun with it, and Hannah closed her eyes turning her face upward as she walked slowly along the empty road of her new neighborhood. The White River ran just to the east of Hyde Park, and she'd seen some evidence that wildlife regularly traveled up the steep ravine that led down to the water. A small, two-lane road traced the edge of that ravine and separated the east-most end of neighborhood from the river. But deer, ducks, opossums, foxes, raccoons, and coyotes still found their way into the yards of Hyde Park's residents. It occurred to Hannah that given the perch of the Decker house, the solarium on the back had once looked north at nothing but forest, and the population of creatures journeying up from the river to the Decker house must have been even more impressive.

Hannah's reverie was interrupted by something poking at the back of her knee, and she looked down to see a very different creature from those who left their paw-prints in the mud of her backyard.

"Hello there, Gertie-dog," she said.

Molly popped her head around the side of the stroller and waved. Hannah followed the line of a retractable leash back to Jeremy, who ambled toward them.

"Looks like we take our walks at the same time," Hannah said, her voice hushed as she tried not to disturb Molly.

"After lunch. It's a good time for a walk," Jeremy replied, tripping over Gertie, who refused to walk a straight line in front of him. "Damnit, Gert," he muttered, regaining his balance.

Hannah muffled her snickering as he finally fell into step next to them.

"How'd you come up with a name like Gertie for a dog?" Hannah asked. She estimated the large black-and-brown dog likely weighed in around one-hundred-fifty pounds and more resembled the canine version of a linebacker than the diminutive "little old lady" she pictured when she heard the name *Gertie*.

"I was dating a literature professor when I first moved here, and we got her together during COVID. I think the dog was supposed to be a test. One we failed, as you can plainly see. Anyway, she's named after Gertrude Stein." His perfunctory response did not invite further discussion about the literature professor, but the dog seemed fair game.

"Who's Gertrude Stein?" Hannah asked, reluctantly betraying the gaps in her knowledge to the professor.

"She's a writer from the early twentieth century," Jeremy said. "A modernist."

Hannah nodded, not knowing really what a modernist was.

"She was a fan of Chaplin, too," Jeremy commented.

"Hey. You're a historian," Hannah said as if it had just dawned on her.

"I am indeed. I have the exorbitant student loans and meager salary to prove it."

"If I wanted to know more about the architect of my house, how could I find that out?" she asked.

"I thought you were selling it."

"No. I talked to Michael, and we think it's a good investment." This wasn't exactly how that conversation had gone, but close enough for purposes of the present one.

"Decker," Jeremy said, his voice suggesting he just barely recalled the name. "Do you know his first name?"

"Andrew," Hannah said.

"Well, if you were one of my students, I'd ask you what your research question is. What do you want to know about him?" Jeremy asked.

Everything, Hannah thought.

"What do you know about him?" she probed instead.

"I mean... nothing. I know that he was an architect who built a few of the houses in this neighborhood—not mine—and that he built that house." He lifted his chin in the direction behind them where the Decker house sat sequestered behind a thick growth of trees. "I've never understood why this neighborhood isn't named after him. Why is it Hyde Park?"

"Hyde was the last name of the farmer he bought the land from," Hannah explained.

"Well, see. You already know more about him than I do. You might be able to find some of his blueprints at the Indiana Historical Society. He's probably too obscure to be on Wikipedia. And I tell my students to stay away from Wikipedia anyway," he said with a chuckle. Hannah didn't get the joke.

"He shot himself in that house," she volunteered abruptly. "In 1933."

"Because of the Depression?"

Hannah had expected Jeremy to respond with shock, but he was almost nonchalant about it. No big deal. Just a man sitting down at the desk in his study one day and shooting himself in the head.

"That's what Gary said. The Depression wiped him out."

"Who's Gary?" Jeremy asked.

"Our contractor."

"Oh. Well, I guess that makes sense," he mused. "If he was building residential properties during the late-1920s, he probably had a ton of money tied up in loans that were suddenly called in at the exact same time people stopped buying homes. He would've been ruined."

It made Hannah sad to hear this—that Andrew's suicide "made sense."

"How did he keep the house?" she asked.

"What do you mean?"

"The last person to live in the house was his daughter. She lived there her whole life. How come the bank didn't take that house?"

"That sounds like your research question," Jeremy said.

Molly's legs had stopped swinging in the stroller, the first sign that sleep approached. Gertie stopped suddenly—and for no earthly reason—causing Jeremy to trip over her once again.

"Damnit, dog," he said, again.

Hannah giggled under her breath, then asked, "Did you ever know her?"

"The daughter?" Jeremy asked.

"Yes. Margaret Decker. Well, Moore. She married a man named Gerald Moore. But I think he died in the 1980s."

"No. I just moved to Indy a few years ago. And then the pandemic happened, and I really didn't get to meet very many people. I feel like I'm just getting back out into the world in the last few months."

"She died in 2014, so you missed her by several years."

"Well, now I don't feel like such a bad neighbor," he said with an affable grin.

They'd nearly completed their lap around the neighborhood, bringing Hannah back to the large wrought iron gates that marked the end of the driveway.

"I'd start with Ancestry and Newspapers.com if you want to know more about Decker," Jeremy said as they paused in front of the gates. "I'd stay pretty local. That house is impressive, but a guy who built fifteen houses in Indianapolis before going belly up during the Great Depression isn't likely to show up in The New York Times, you know?"

Hannah thanked him for the suggestion and for the company on the walk, patted Gertie on the head, and headed for the garage.

The garage itself took less time than she'd imagined. All told, she used one Post-it—on a single cardboard box containing five cardboard tubes, which sat in the back under a workbench. Cursory inspection suggested they contained more Fritz Brothers blueprints. Hoping they might include a plan for the third floor, Hannah brought them with her into the house and placed them in the living room on the sideboard with the blueprints Debbie had delivered. Everything else in the garage could go. As for the garage itself, it was as if it had heard the contractors the week before: best to just tear it down and start over.

❧

HANNAH HAD no real reason to be at the Decker house during the three weeks prior to construction, but she found herself continually called back to it. She developed a pattern of sorts, beginning her days with an exercise class, followed by coffee with Kate or Laura or both. Subsequently, she'd make a trip to the house—just to ensure the safety of its contents, confirming no unexpected injury from wind, rain, or the increasing cold. On those days when Jeremy wasn't teaching, he and Gertie would join Hannah and Molly on their after-lunch walk. Then, she'd return to the bungalow, where she organized the remainder of the afternoon around Molly's nap and Michael's return home from work.

On each of those mornings, though, Hannah would climb the main staircase of the Decker house, looking down at her hand as it trailed along the rich, polished wood of the banister, and she would puzzle over the strange fact of her hand touching what Andrew also once had touched. On some days, she might stand in the master bedroom, imagining the space reconfigured per the specifications of Fritz Brothers' blueprints, but her mind quickly drifted to Andrew and the intimate moments of his life spent there. He'd straightened his tie in a mirror over a dresser. He'd crouched to pull Margaret up into his arms as she meandered into her parents' bedroom. He'd stood at the bay window, as Hannah sometimes did, gazing at the trees outside and the neighborhood beyond.

And every visit to the house, sometimes consciously, sometimes not, she journeyed up to the third floor and down the hall to the small, locked door at the end that held "storage"—those items the Fire

Dawgs hadn't disposed of. She'd unlock the door, go to the cardboard box—the third one—and lift back the flaps, peering down at Andrew Decker, who always smiled back at her, his hands folded neatly, his wedding band barely visible.

As Hannah became more familiar with the photograph, noticing the smaller details of it—a strand of hair just out of place, the crease of his pants at the bend of his knee and the fold of his waist—she began to see his eyes as not merely friendly. They were—depending on the angle she held the picture—almost inviting. Sometimes she pulled out the picture of Andrew with Margaret. Sometimes she sifted through the deck of loose photos, noticing a detail of one or another that had previously escaped her.

But always, at some point, she'd realize that far too many minutes had passed, and she had to part with him. And she'd replace the photographs carefully in the box and leave the room, locking the door carefully behind her.

CHAPTER 7

"How's your research going?" Jeremy asked as he and Gertie, and Hannah and Molly completed their first lap around the neighborhood. Gertie had settled in beside Molly as was her practice, and Molly extended a hand out of the stroller lightly resting on Gertie's back as was her practice.

"I actually haven't started it yet," Hannah admitted. "I've been so focused on getting the construction going, I haven't had a chance to look into any of that."

"When does construction start?" Jeremy asked.

"Gary says Monday." Hannah looked up at the sky, a tacit acknowledgement that the weather might complicate the project getting off the ground at the beginning of winter, and Jeremy pulled his scarf up a little closer to his ears—a gesture of understanding. "His team's over there dropping off supplies today."

"That's got to be exciting."

"I know I should be excited, but really, I'm just so nervous. What if they can't do it? What if the house is too far gone?"

"That doesn't sound very likely," Jeremy said. "The sorts of things that hold up a renovation like that are things you're already planning to do—plumbing, electric, HVAC."

"That's probably true. Hey, which of these houses is yours?" Hannah asked, changing the subject in the equivalent of a hard-right at full speed.

"It's up ahead." He pointed in a direction that could aptly be described as "up ahead."

"Which one?"

As they continued walking, Jeremy pointed to a yellow Cape Cod style cottage with blue shutters. Modest but cozy, the house had a well-manicured garden that spanned the front. A light dusting of snow frosted the dirt, which grew nothing at present.

"Do you garden?" Hannah asked.

"In the summer," he specified. "Not much time to garden during the school year, and not much reason to. You?"

"No. I can't keep a cactus alive. I could kill dirt," she said without a hint of false modesty, but Jeremy just tucked his face further into his scarf, muffling a laugh.

"Well, you'll probably have your hands full enough with that house without adding gardening to the mix."

Hannah nodded, looking up the hill toward the yellow stone edifice where she could just barely make out the movements of Gary's crew unloading materials from their trucks in preparation for their Monday start.

❧

HANNAH TYPED her search terms into her laptop: Andrew Decker, Indianapolis, Architect. On the floor, Molly clicked and clacked her Magna-Tiles together, engrossed in her own construction project. The walk with Jeremy had reminded Hannah of her research question: Why didn't the bank foreclose on the Decker house?

She'd accessed both *Ancestry* and *Newspapers.com* but found each required an account and a subscription fee. She thought about subscribing to one or both of the services but reconsidered. Even the rather modest fees seemed to imply a commitment to her project that she wasn't entirely comfortable with, as if paying to learn about the architect betrayed an interest in him that she wasn't sure she cared to admit. Not even to herself.

On the other hand, the local newspaper, *The Indianapolis Times*, made some of its archives publicly accessible, and an uncomplicated internet search quickly returned a couple of articles concerning Andrew Decker's death.

> **Indianapolis Times, January 13, 1933: Indianapolis Architect Commits Suicide.** The body of local architect and real estate developer Andrew L. Decker, 43, was found in his study yesterday afternoon by his young daughter Margaret. The cause of death is an apparent self-inflicted gunshot wound to the head from Mr. Decker's .45 caliber revolver. Mr. Decker was the developer of the exclusive Hyde Park neighborhood on the Northwest side of Indianapolis and the sole architect of the fifteen existing homes built there, including Decker House. The body was sent to the coroner.

The brevity of the article surprised Hannah as did its placement on the third page of the paper. Had he fallen so far by 1933 that his suicide didn't constitute front page news? She recalled Jeremy's description of him: a local architect, who built fifteen houses before going belly up. Hannah winced at the callousness of that description, as if Andrew himself could hear it. She read the notice a second time looking for details she'd missed, but details were hard to come by in the four sentences provided. She noted his age—forty-three—which placed the photographs in the attic within an ascertainable chronology.

An obituary followed a few days later. Also relegated to the back pages, its length was at least minimally commensurate with what Hannah would have thought to be the architect's significance. A photograph accompanied the tribute, one not contained in the boxes she'd inventoried. It showed Andrew in profile, standing in the study behind a drafting table, eyes cast down, presumably focused on his latest design, one pencil in his hand, another between his teeth. He wore a vest and a tie, but no blazer, the sleeves of his white shirt rolled up just below his elbows as he examined his work.

It was an interesting choice, as Hannah thought about it, foregrounding his professional identity, rather than his personal. She wondered why Eleanor chose it. Or whether she even had. The paragraphs that accompanied it shed no light on that particular question.

Andrew L. Decker, eldest son of Dr. Henry (deceased) and Mrs. Ida Decker, was born in Bedford, Indiana on September 28, 1889, and died in his home on January 12, 1933, at the age of 43. He was united in marriage to Mrs. Eleanor (Dailey) Decker also of Bedford on June 19, 1920. To this union was born one child, a daughter, Margaret (9), who survives her father. Also, surviving are Mr. Decker's wife Eleanor, his sister Mary Margaret Decker, and his mother.

Mr. Decker graduated magna cum laude from Columbia University in New York where he studied architecture and engineering. He made his living in real estate development, first as an architect with the New York firm of Grisfield & Lyons and then with Matson Architecture & Design upon returning to Indiana following the World War. Mr. Decker founded his own firm, Decker Developers, Ltd., in 1921 and commenced work on the desirable Hyde Park neighborhood in 1922.

His death comes as a shock to his friends and family, who knew him to be a devoted husband and father and an honorable and principled businessman. He is sure to be missed by his numerous friends and family and particularly by his loving wife Eleanor and daughter Margaret, whom his sister Mary describes as "the very center of his universe and the light that guided his every step in this world."

His friends remain baffled by his sudden despair and death, recalling a man whose laughter was, at times, the only respite from these bleak days. Alas, even this bright torch was not immune to the darkness of the financial devastation that has befallen so many of his profession in recent years.

Mr. Decker is predeceased by his father Dr. Henry Decker, and by his two brothers, Joseph and Francis, who died in Italy during the World War.

A funeral will take place at Holy Rosary Catholic Church on January 16 at 9:00 a.m. Mr. Decker will be interred at St. Joseph's Cemetery in Indianapolis.

A life. A whole life summed up in six paragraphs. His whole life. Hannah sat into the cushions of the couch and scrolled back to the top of the obituary. She enlarged the photograph of Andrew Decker, finding herself present in the instant before it was taken, before he realized the camera was on him. She wondered what had followed. Had he looked up, the lines of concentration giving way to a smile? Was he pleased by the interruption, grateful for the company? Or had he chastised whoever had taken the photo for disturbing him, pulling him out of his work?

The image grew distorted as Hannah continued to enlarge it, tracing the shape of his ear as it curved imperfectly, a small bump along the upper edge, the line of his hair precisely trimmed and combed, his face giving forth only the faintest dark shadow of growth. She enlarged the photograph again. His lips—so blurry, they hardly resembled lips at all. She reached a finger up to the screen, tracing the lower bow, the slight shadow cast by the arch of his lower lip.

"What is that?"

Hannah jumped at the sound of Michael's voice behind her, and the computer flipped off her lap, landing on the area rug at her feet. Startled by the noise, Molly turned her face up to the ceiling, opened her mouth, and bellowed.

Hannah picked up the laptop and set it on the couch, closing the lid as she did so, obscuring the image from Michael's view, then went to comfort Molly.

"Jesus," Michael mumbled under his breath.

"Sorry," Hannah said as she lifted Molly into her arms.

Molly's startle subsided, the tears short-lived. She recovered far more quickly than her mother, who worried that the trembling of her arms made her not an entirely safe berth for her daughter.

"I was just looking at something on Instagram," Hannah sputtered as Michael's confusion—and something that resembled disapproval—remained. "Dinner's almost ready."

Michael looked at her askance, his brow descending over his eyes. Then he shrugged and wandered back to his office with his messenger bag. Hannah exhaled as the tension leaked from the living room and her heart rate slowly returned to normal.

❧

KATE HAD SAVED a place for Hannah between Laura and herself—a spot in the front of the room, by the mirrors. As Hannah entered the studio, and the voices of the other women enveloped her, she was glad she'd pulled herself from the warmth of her bed and made the trek to Broad Ripple.

"...no, it's better than I thought it would be," Laura said as Hannah walked into the room and set her water bottle down against the mirror.

"How high were your expectations?" Rob asked, flipping through playlists, trying to find something appropriately up-tempo.

"Profoundly low," Laura admitted. "But it was actually interesting."

"I'm sure she used a ghostwriter," Kate said over the music pulsing from the speakers.

Hannah couldn't follow the conversation and didn't want to interrupt to ask what book they were talking about.

"Are you sure she didn't just copy and paste Michelle's book and try to pass it off as her own?" Rob asked, one eyebrow arched with skepticism. Kate exploded into laughter next to Hannah.

"I just want to know which Melania it's the autobiography of," Kate said to more laughter.

"There are not multiple Melanias. That's a conspiracy theory, Kate!" Laura scolded.

"It's my *favorite* conspiracy theory," Kate exclaimed.

"Well, anyway, it was actually good. You should read it," Laura said with an air of authority.

"I'm not going to read it. I'd rather read the installation instructions for my microwave."

"She has redeeming qualities. Everyone does."

"I challenge Kate to say something nice about Melania," Rob said and rested his elbow on an equipment shelf. Class would not proceed until Kate complied.

"Fine," Kate said. She placed her hands on her hips, cleared her throat, and looked at Rob, radiating defiance. "I liked her coat on inauguration day."

Rob and Laura groaned.

"How do you even remember that?" another woman asked from the back of the room.

"Because I actually liked it. It was a pretty shade of blue and had an interesting collar," Kate specified.

Rob rolled his eyes good-naturedly and increased the volume on the music signaling the start of class. Hannah took a deep breath and faced the mirror. She had no real opinion on Melania Trump other than her sympathy for the beautiful wives of powerful men—women whose entire identities could be reduced to nothing more than the vestigial organs of their husband's power. Hannah thought about Eleanor Decker, the beautiful wife of the famous—well, at least locally known and respected—architect. She thought about his obituary, which referenced Mrs. Decker only in passing: Mr. Decker's "loving wife." She thought about the reference to Margaret as the center of Mr. Decker's universe, Mrs. Decker grammatically excluded from even that hallowed realm.

The quote struck her as strange though, coming not from Mrs. Decker herself, but from Andrew's sister. Conceivably, Mrs. Decker had been too distraught to provide a quote, but her conspicuous absence began to weigh on Hannah more heavily as the class progressed, as the synthesized beats of Rob's music propelled her body in the short bursts of effort that defined the class.

Her absence. Omitted? Overlooked as so many women were at that time? Or erased, the consequence of someone's intentional efforts to expunge her?

She saw it then, in her mind's eye. Or rather, didn't see it. Not a single photograph of Eleanor after her husband's death. No portrait, no spontaneous picture of her in the kitchen, at Thanksgiving, at Margaret's wedding, with her grandchildren. Mary, Andrew's sister, appeared throughout the second box and some of the third. But Eleanor. It was as though she had ceased to exist, vanishing with her husband's death.

❧

"Hannah! What are you doing here?" Jason, one of Gary's men, had come from the kitchen upon hearing the front door close.

Hannah hadn't been inside the house since the first day work had started. On that day, she'd introduced herself and Molly to Gary's team and brought coffee and donuts for the crew, who openly pledged her their love and devotion. She'd then taken one last walk through the house before reconciling herself to her temporary separation from it.

This morning, however, Hannah had driven from her exercise

class directly to the Decker house, stopping only to get Molly a croissant at a coffee shop along the way. She wanted to confirm something, and although Gary had told her that the first month of work on the house would likely be the most chaotic, her curiosity couldn't wait.

As soon as she entered the foyer, though, she understood Gary's warning, as well as Jason's subdued alarm at seeing her with Molly in tow. The crew had only been at it for a week, but already the house held the ambient dust of walls that had been drilled, sawed, and sledgehammered away. Sections of the mortar were missing altogether revealing the dull silver of diamond-cut steel "lath" beneath. Tools and sawhorses lay about, and the crew had erected large standing lights attached to gas-powered generators—a necessity until the knob and tube wiring could be replaced with twenty-first century conduit and breakers.

"I need to check something up on the third floor," Hannah said, feeling oddly like she was trespassing in her own home.

"Up on the third floor?" Jason asked.

"Yes."

"Okay. Please be careful on your way up. We got cords and wires, and there's dust everywhere in here right now," he said, sounding genuinely concerned, his eyes focused more on Molly than Hannah. Hannah bobbed her head in acknowledgment before jogging up the stairs with Molly on her hip. This would have to be a fast trip; she hadn't brought anything for Molly to do.

In the storage room, Hannah sat Molly down on a blanket she'd grabbed from the car and handed the toddler her keys. The novelty of this "toy" would wear off quickly, but hopefully her investigation wouldn't take more than a few minutes.

She opened the box containing the photographs that began with Margaret's wedding. Flipping through the mid-century black-and-whites and their strange sunrise transition to color, Hannah's theory was confirmed: an older woman frequently appeared in many of the photographs, but it wasn't Eleanor—her hair too dark, her face lacking the soft, delicate contours of Eleanor Decker's face. As the years had passed, her dark hair became streaked with silver and by the time of the full-color-1960s, it had transitioned to a deep pewter, drawing out the near-navy color of her eyes.

This wasn't Eleanor; this was Mary. Hannah had missed these details before, missed the way the woman resembled Margaret in those traits shared not with her mother, but with her father. She had failed to recognize through the thin frame the two women had in common, that the woman at Margaret's side on her wedding day, at Thanksgivings, at Christmases, was too tall to have been the petite woman from the Deckers' wedding album.

Behind her, Molly had tired of the keys and began crawling around on the attic floor. Although the Fire Dawgs had successfully cleared out much of the furniture from the room, no one had actually cleaned it. The floorboards were dirty and rough, a potential source of splinters to the vulnerable hands of a child.

Hannah pushed the box aside leaving the flaps open and quickly slid over to the third box, opening it with some amount of urgency. She shook off the impulse to meet Andrew's gaze as his face emerged below the flaps of the box. Blinking back the compulsion to search the photograph for some new detail she'd missed before—a pastime of her prior visits to this room—she forced her hands down into the box to retrieve the wedding album.

She held the album up, her anxiety making her less careful than she'd been during her prior visits. She really only wanted to see the wedding portrait—the most complete image of Eleanor Decker—just to confirm the woman in the second box was not one and the same. It took less than a full second for her to be confident that it was not. Eleanor's hair was lighter, her skin paler, her frame more diminutive. And Eleanor did not appear in a single photograph that Hannah could find after her husband's death.

Hannah heard Molly scooting around on the floor behind her. She could dedicate no more time to this investigation. She closed the album, prepared to place it back in the box. Her fingers fumbled with the cover, a byproduct of her anxiety at the thought of being found leafing through photographs that didn't belong to her and which really had no business still being in her possession. An electricity—the sense of the finite time she could allot to the task—gave her less control over her hands, and she closed the cover with more force than she'd intended. Dust coughed out of the pages, and Hannah sneezed, altogether losing her grip on the small book, which fell to the ground next to her. She jumped at the sound of its clap against the floor.

Feeling self-conscious and foolish even in front of her daughter, she took a deep breath, steadied herself, and collected the album. As she lifted it back into the box, however, she saw the corner of a single sheet of paper poking out from between the last few pages. She initially worried she'd caused some damage to the album when she dropped it and carefully opened the cover expecting to see a crack in the spine or a torn page. Instead, she found in its back cover a small pocket holding two items: a letter, the edge of which had already presented itself, and a small prayer card, the image of St. Francis of Assisi on the front and his prayer on the back.

Even as someone not especially religious, Hannah knew the prayer: *Lord make me an instrument of your peace.* From her limited knowledge, she associated such cards with funerals, not weddings, leaving her questioning why the card would be stored in a wedding album. This confusion was, unfortunately, not to be mitigated by the letter itself. Hannah unfolded the single piece of paper to see a black penned script, but the words were illegible. Not only cursive, they appeared to be in another language and not one familiar to her. She'd taken Spanish in high school and knew enough French to be able to read at least a handful of words. But those words did not appear in this correspondence.

Hannah returned the album to the box and closed the lid, sliding it back against the wall. She then took the letter and the prayer card and tucked them into her coat pocket. She would ask Jeremy if he knew what language the letter had been written in or whether he knew anyone at the university who could translate it. A flutter of excitement ran through her at the thought of Andrew penning the letter, his hand in the gaslight, his forehead furrowed in concentration. She might be holding in her pocket his words, his thoughts, as they had actually existed at one point in time.

CHAPTER 8

When Hannah was about five years old, and Mason was about twelve, her father and their mother asked Mason to babysit while they went out for the evening. Hannah was too young at the time to have any sense of what was normal—either for couples broadly or for her father and mother more specifically. As adults, she and Mason could both recall periods like this, though. Times when Jack would pledge to try harder, to be better, when he would take their mother's hand and hold it while they watched TV, or would bring home flowers after work, or pat Hannah on the head while she ate breakfast, and the house would be quiet. Quiet for days or weeks or very occasionally a couple of months.

Seeming to relish the veneer of adulthood, Mason had made Hannah dinner, and the two watched a movie that their mother rented —such a special occasion—*The Sandlot*. When the movie ended, well after 9:00 p.m., their mother and Jack still had not returned. This left Mason to improvise, which he did by making himself and his sister coffee.

One taste of the bitter brew told Hannah they must have done something very wrong, but copious amounts of sugar and milk seemed to remedy the error, and Mason and Hannah sat at the kitchen table drinking their coffee and talking about what they wanted to do when they grew up. Hannah couldn't remember what either of them had said. What she did remember was that when Jack stumbled into the apartment with their mother just after 11:30, he was not amused to find his daughter and step-son still awake and fully caffeinated.

Attempts by their mother to calm Jack, to coax him back from the blistering scolding of Mason for his spectacular irresponsibility at giving a kindergartener coffee, from his description of Hannah as "a fucking retard" for drinking it, failed. Ultimately, the episode ended, at least for that evening, when Hannah, so terrified after the weeks of calm, wet herself, urinating through her pajamas onto the floor of the kitchen.

Jack had lunged for her then, with the well-worn refrain of such men: "If you're going to start crying, I'll give you something to cry about."

Mason, tall and nimble even at twelve, and quick too, had stuck out his foot, tripping his step-father, who careened forward, striking his forehead on the edge of the counter.

They all secretly hoped he was dead.

"You remember that, Hannah Banana? He was down for the fucking count," Mason said.

"Yeah, I remember," Hannah said into the phone, stirring her spoon around and around in her coffee, the tip of it singing against the bottom of the mug.

It had been weeks since she'd heard from him, but he'd called that morning to give her his new number. She'd grown accustomed to this unpredictability, transferring from one carrier to another, failing to pay bills and losing his phone number, breaking his phone and being unable to replace it immediately, resorting to "burners". But he had remained in Montana for years, probably longer than any other place he'd lived since they'd resided in Worcester together as kids. This, at least, made it easy to know when he was calling, even if the only clue was a consistent area code.

After confirming his new number, he'd asked her about the house. She filled him in on the construction, leaving out some of the treasures she'd found. When she'd told him she planned to head over to check on the work after she finished her coffee, Mason reminded her that she owed her affection for sweetened coffee to him.

"I remember," she said again, wishing in a way that she didn't.

He'd told the story the last time they'd gotten together, too. But, in the voice often adopted by those who have survived such childhoods, he'd performed it more than told it, forcing its horrifying shape to be reconfigured, molded into comedy. Dark comedy, but something to laugh at, nonetheless. And Hannah had laughed at it, at Mason's Looney Tunes sound effects added to his impression of Jack's head hitting the counter.

Later, she'd cried.

Who are you talking to? Michael mouthed as he walked into the kitchen, quickly organizing his materials for work. He paused briefly, looking at Hannah as she sat at the kitchen table.

Mason, she mouthed back.

"See you tonight," he whispered, and dropped his lips to her neck, to the flutter of her pulse there.

"Hey, Mason. I have to go. I need to talk to Michael before he leaves for work. Can I text you later?" Hannah asked, holding up her index finger to Michael – *Just a second.*

Hannah said good-bye to Mason and ended the call.

"What's up? I'm running late," Michael said.

"I wanted to ask when we're leaving for Boston. For Christmas. To visit your parents. I need to let the crew know." Hannah removed the spoon from her coffee and set it on the table.

In the time that Hannah and Michael had been a couple, they'd spent most Christmases with Michael's parents, and Hannah liked this tradition. She liked watching Michael's parents shower Molly with love. They had, she knew, little use for Hannah herself. But she'd given them something they wanted, something their own son had denied them and so ultimately, they had to concede that the marriage of their stubborn bachelor and only child to the bartender he met in South Carolina had inured very much to their benefit.

Michael placed a piece of junk mail from the counter on the spot beneath Hannah's spoon. "Do you think it's a good idea to leave the house when it's in the state it's in?" he asked as he dug through his messenger bag, trying to make room for his laptop. Hannah knew it wasn't really a request for her counsel. He was telling her they wouldn't be going to Boston for Christmas this year.

"Well, they won't be doing any work on it over Christmas," she countered.

"That's my point," Michael said, his words, indeed, feeling pointy as he headed for the living room. "Someone might break in while we're gone, and no one would know until after the New Year," he called back to her as he pulled his coat from the closet. He would wake Molly. Hannah got up from the table with her coffee and followed him.

"I could ask Jeremy to check on it for us," Hannah volunteered, lowering her voice not much above a whisper and hoping Michael would follow suit.

"Who's Jeremy?" Michael asked, not adjusting his own volume. Hannah regretted the suggestion immediately.

"The history professor who lives in the neighborhood. You met him at Kate's." There was no extricating herself now, and she could see Michael carefully choosing his next words. He'd pulled his coat over his arms, zipping it up the front, but he seemed to move in slow motion as he walked past her back toward the kitchen.

"I don't know that we know him well enough to ask for a favor like that. How would you even get ahold of him?" he asked, pausing at the kitchen table to pick up his messenger bag.

"I... I guess I don't know," Hannah replied even though she thought she probably could just knock on the door of the yellow Cape Cod with the blue shutters and the well-tended garden.

"Probably should just stay here, then," Michael said, and Hannah nodded, trying to hide her disappointment as Michael walked out of the kitchen to the garage.

✤

HANNAH KNOCKED LIGHTLY on the door. Too lightly, she knew. She wasn't sure she wanted anyone to answer. But Gertie heard the indecisive rap of her knuckles and, helpful as always, enthusiastically let her human know that someone had arrived.

"Be quiet!" Jeremy said. "Get back." His voice grew louder from behind the door, which he opened slowly, peering out, his face slowly breaking into recognition as he saw Hannah standing on the front step holding Molly's hand. He held Gertie by the collar and opened the door further.

"Hi," Hannah said.

Molly pulled free of Hannah's hand as she saw Gertie restrained by Jeremy and promptly invited herself into Jeremy's living room.

"Molly," Hannah called after her daughter.

"No, no. It's fine. Come on in. It's cold out there," Jeremy said, unable to finesse the awkwardness that accompanied the unexpected guests.

"Oh. Um... Okay... Thanks." Hannah hadn't expected the invitation into the house. She hadn't really thought much past the knock on the front door. In the next scene of her minimally rehearsed interaction, she pictured Jeremy in his light brown boots, a hat pulled down over the tops of his ears, his scarf tucked into the neck of his quilted black coat. But of course, that wasn't how she found him. As he stood back making room for Hannah and Molly to enter, he did so in a pair of blue jeans and a gray and blue Case Western Reserve t-shirt. Instead of boots, he wore a pair of thick, oatmeal-colored socks.

As he closed the door behind them, Molly toddled over to Gertie whose excitement at seeing her young friend could not be contained. The feeling was mutual, and Molly squealed with delight as Gertie nosed at her tummy, trying to encourage a few head pats.

The front door of Jeremy's house opened directly into his living room, and Hannah could see that she had interrupted him. The television was on and tuned to a game of cricket, though he'd muted the sound. Loose papers, pens, and highlighters covered a coffee table in front of the couch, all open and ready for use, with Jeremy's laptop resting on the papers. A stack of books sat tucked along the arm of the couch—one open, facing down against the cushion next to an indentation suggesting Jeremy's preferred sitting place.

"Are you grading papers?" Hannah asked, trying to sound both pleasant and knowledgeable. This was what professors did in their homes when they weren't teaching or taking walks with their neighbors. Or at least she assumed so based on things she'd heard Kate say.

"Writing," Jeremy said, and he ran an anxious hand through his hair, then rested it on his hip, looking with some remorse at the room behind him. "I... Sorry... I would have straightened up if I'd known..."

"Oh, no. I... I probably should have... well... I don't have your phone number so I couldn't call first. I should have waited for our walk." She winced immediately at her phrasing: *our walk.*

"Is everything okay?" Jeremy asked. He seemed to have caught the phrasing, too, but must have understood the importance of ignoring it. "Can I take your coat?" he asked formally, shifting into the etiquette the situation called for.

"Okay," Hannah said, and he hung it in a space under the stairs that served as a coat closet.

"Can I get you something to drink? I have coffee and... I have coffee."

"Coffee would be nice," Hannah said, unsure whether it was ruder to reject the hospitality or risk imposing by accepting it.

"Miss Molly, would you like to join us?" Jeremy asked. His attention to the toddler took some of the tension out of the room, though Molly probably preferred Gertie over the two adults in her company.

"Anana," Molly said, pointing at a fruit bowl as she cut past Jeremy and led him into his own kitchen. Hannah followed behind the two.

"I think that can be arranged," he said. "I'm sorry my kitchen is such a mess. My cleaning lady comes tomorrow." He chuckled. It was a joke, Hannah deduced; he didn't have a cleaning lady. Though, Hannah hadn't found his kitchen especially messy. It was simply used, the appearance of a kitchen someone regularly cooked and ate in. The counters were wiped clean, but a small stack of mail, a baseball cap, a toaster, and a coffee maker occupied the limited counter space, along with an empty bowl that Hannah presumed had held his breakfast. A bike rested against the wall next to the back door, but even that seemed in its assigned place, the helmet balancing on the seat.

Jeremy pulled out a plate and a knife and cut the banana, then placed it on the kitchen table for Molly. Hannah sat her on the chair, the edge of the table roughly even with the child's nose. Molly seemed unconcerned with the ratios of the furniture, scrambled to her knees on the chair, and enthusiastically shoved the pieces of banana into her mouth.

"I like your house," Hannah said, thinking she should say something to set Jeremy at ease.

"Thanks." Jeremy poured Hannah a mug of coffee. He grabbed a small bowl of sugar from the cupboard along with a Ziploc bag of creamers from the refrigerator and brought them to the table. "I like it. It must seem pretty modest next to what you're used to."

Hannah recognized the self-consciousness in his voice and saw herself, suddenly, through his eyes, understanding something about their past interactions that she hadn't before. The irony of it all froze her in place, and she stood in a frame, a single slice of her life pulled from the sequence of images that had come before it. Thirty-two years old, in jeans that cost more than a Friday night's worth of tips at the bar she'd tended in South Carolina, remodeling the largest house in the neighborhood.

"Oh. No, it's not like that," she started to say, then realized Jeremy likely could never understand. The etiquette that had saved them from the awkwardness of her interruption, the coffee she slowly stirred, her coat hanging in the closet under the stairs, it did not permit her to explain to him how it was that she'd learned to love her coffee with copious amounts of cream and sugar and how, because of that, his house was not "pretty modest" next to what she was used to.

"Thank you," she said, accepting the coffee and deciding to leave it at that.

Gertie joined them, waiting patiently next to Molly, no doubt hoping a piece of banana might come her way. If Molly's general eating habits were any indication, Gertie's patience would pay off. Jeremy sat down across from them, his mind seeming to operate on delay as he brushed some invisible crumbs off the table in front of him.

"I wanted to talk to you about a letter I found." She probably should have led with that, but the momentum from the door to the table had gotten the better of her. "I found it in the house. I think it's old. I think Andrew wrote it—"

"Decker? That's interesting." Jeremy's fidgeting quieted, and he seemed legitimately interested in Hannah's news.

"I can't read it though. It's not in English."

"What language do you think it's in?"

"I don't know. Not Spanish or French," Hannah said. "It's in my coat. In the left pocket."

Jeremy jogged to the closet and returned shortly having already opened the letter, examining the script.

"It's not *from* Decker; it's *to* him," he said as he walked back into the kitchen. "Looks like it's from his uncle." He glanced up vacantly as if he were standing in some space between the kitchen and whatever year the letter had been written in.

"You can read it?" Hannah asked.

"Yes," he mumbled into the pages in his hand. Then, as if he realized he wasn't really talking to her, he lifted his head and smiled. "It's in Italian," he said, holding the letter up as some sort of proof.

"What does it say?"

Jeremy sat back down at the table, still reading. He glanced at Molly, who grinned in return before handing a piece of banana to Gertie, giggling as the dog licked her palm.

"He told his uncle not to come to his wedding, it would appear," Jeremy said after taking a minute to review the letter.

"What? Why? Were they fighting?"

"Maybe? It's a strange letter. Give me a minute, and I can translate it for you." His eyes moved slowly across the page, and Hannah watched as his lips seemed to practice the shapes of the words he planned to speak.

"It's dated 7 June 1920.

"*Dear Andrew,*

I understand you will soon be married to Eleanor Dailey and that you have decided I am not to attend this celebration. I understand the difficulty of your position. There is no question we have had our disagreements over the years and been hesitant to seek or grant forgiveness from one another. I question whether it is reconciliation that is our obstacle, or whether maybe you think yourself so removed, so different from me that you are embarrassed to have me at your wedding to the daughter of the man who owns the quarry I once worked in. I hope this is not the case. In the event that it is, I offer you a prayer as you begin your marriage:

I pray that you grow in wisdom, the wisdom to know who you are, the wisdom to know who they are. You are not one of them, Andrew. You may think that because you went to their schools, speak their language, wear their clothes, and shake their hands, they count you among their numbers. They do not. She does not.

As you begin this new life, know that a new life does not make you a new person. Nor should you seek for it to. I would caution you to make sure that the person she marries is you and not some imagined man you think you should be for her sake.

With love,

Your Uncle Alessandro."

"Man," Jeremy exhaled, looking over the sheets of paper again. "That's a hell of a letter to get before your wedding."

Hannah took the pages back from him, her eyes following the indecipherable lines of faded black ink covering the yellowed paper. Her mind drifted to Mason and his wedding gift eight years earlier.

"So, it looks like Decker's uncle was a stonecutter. In the limestone quarries? You know about the quarries in Indiana?" he asked.

"No," Hannah said, feeling a bit like she'd shown up to class without studying for the exam.

"Yeah, I don't know a ton about it either. I wonder if Kate would know." He seemed to be talking to himself now, and although Jeremy's acknowledgement of the limits of his expertise provided some comfort to Hannah, she remained confused as to the larger point of what the actual disagreements between Andrew and his uncle had been.

"Kate's area's U.S. history, so this is more her wheelhouse than mine," he explained. "I can ask her about some of this tomorrow at work. Unless—are you going to see her before then?"

Hannah shook her head. Jeremy brushed the tips of his fingers over his lips, his gaze on nothing in particular.

"That would be complicated," he said finally. "I could imagine that would be complicated." He nodded evidently in agreement with the letter, or maybe just with himself. Certainly, Hannah agreed with him.

"He was embarrassed, you think? Andrew?" she asked. "He was ashamed of his family?" Hannah's eyes found a corner above one of the kitchen cabinets. The crown at the top of the cabinet had not been properly coped, and someone had tried to conceal the imperfections with caulk.

Jeremy fell silent, and Hannah could sense his gaze on her. Not like the agog staring of the men at the grocery store or the gas station. He was studying her.

"Well, maybe he was embarrassed of one of them," Jeremy said, and gestured toward the letter, indicating which one. "There's not a lot to go on—just one letter."

"His dad was a doctor," Hannah volunteered, thinking there might be some prestige in that bit of biography.

"He was? Here? In Indiana? What was his name?" Jeremy asked.

"Henry Decker," Hannah said. "I found Andrew's obituary online. His father was a doctor. And Andrew left home and went away to college and was an architect in New York before moving back to Indiana. His uncle couldn't have been surprised that he would—I don't know..." *Would marry someone like the woman in the photographs she'd seen,* Hannah thought, but kept that to herself.

"Why did he come back? Do you know?" Jeremy asked.

"He came back after World War I. Both of his brothers died in the war."

"Jesus. That's awful," Jeremy said. "Well, his father was a physician, but it sounds like his mother's family might have been stonecutters. So, this is his mother's brother writing to him. Decker's a German name anyway. Probably not too many Alessandro Deckers living in Indiana in the early 1920s."

"I guess," Hannah agreed.

Molly had grown bored of feeding Gertie and crawled off the chair to explore the kitchen.

"I should probably get going," Hannah said, as her daughter headed toward the very much not-baby-proofed cabinets.

"Can I keep that?" Jeremy reached for the letter again, but Hannah pulled it back just a quarter of an inch. "Not forever. I just want to show it to Kate tomorrow and see what she says about it."

Hannah looked at the letter and then at Jeremy.

"I promise I'll give it back when I'm done," he said. "Where did you say you found it again?"

"In the attic. I was cleaning," Hannah explained, leaving out that she had found so very much more than just a letter.

CHAPTER 9

"And then there was light," Gary said. He swept his arms wide and grinned with self-satisfaction at Hannah and Michael.

The light that Gary so enthusiastically announced came not from lamps and chandeliers, but from several large tripods with caged bulbs sitting atop and cords that ran only to a fraction of the first floor. Still, each light plugged into actual three-pronged, grounded outlets that further connected to a breaker box in the basement. The Decker house had been introduced, at long last, to the twenty-first century, even if the second and third floors, for the time being, remained shrouded.

"Oh my gosh, Gary," Hannah breathed. "This is just fantastic. You guys are doing such an amazing job." In her arms, Molly let loose a squawk. She wasn't used to standing around in the house. When she and her mother came to the Decker house, they said hellos to the workers and asked if they needed anything. Then they went up to the third floor where Molly played while Hannah arranged and rearranged the photographs in the third of the brown cardboard boxes in the storage room.

"I'm sorry. She's restless," Hannah said as Molly fought to get down.

"Looks like everything's coming along pretty well here," Michael said.

Hannah exhaled with relief to hear him say so. In their conversations at home, she'd been relatively circumspect about the progress on the house, honoring his request to be bothered only if his approval or checkbook were required. But she'd privately anguished, worrying that when the time came for comment, his would be derogatory, or worse. That he seemed pleased with how things were going far exceeded what Hannah had hoped for.

"Yeah. I have to say, I thought there might be more surprises, but the electricity and the plumbing are basically as expected," Gary replied with a shrug.

"I like the sound of that," Michael commented. "You still thinking eight months?"

"Yeah. I think that's a reasonable timeframe."

One of Gary's workers walked through the kitchen and offered a "Hi, Miss Molly." The attention temporarily settled the little girl, who smiled with affected bashfulness.

"Is that Hannah out there?" came another voice from farther back in the kitchen.

"Yeah," the man called back. "Gary's giving them an update."

"Making friends everywhere you go," Michael commented in the ambiguous manner of compliments that are not bestowed as such. Proving the point, albeit inadvertently, Jason ventured out from a back corner of the kitchen.

"Hi there, Mrs. Korman," Jason said pleasantly, adjusting his usual salutation upon seeing Michael. In his hands, he carried a cardboard box not unlike the boxes that held Andrew's photographs on the third floor. Hannah's stomach dropped at the thought that one of the contractors might have found the pictures and would ask if she wanted to keep them.

"We all made these for little Molly," Jason said instead, lifting the box. Hannah and Michael peered down into it to see a collection of wooden blocks—squares, rectangles, triangles, circles, half circles.

"Oh, how nice of you," Hannah said.

"It's just the old wood that was in the garage before we tore that down, and we thought Molly might like to play with them while you did your work in the attic. That way you don't have to keep lugging toys up and down the stairs," he said, smiling proudly.

Hannah's smile, however, promptly vanished. The blocks were a thoughtful, generous gift. But her face burned hot with the revelation of her "work in the attic."

"What are you working on in the attic?" Michael asked, with more disapproval than curiosity.

Jason, evidently sensing he'd inadvertently stepped into the middle of a conversation for which he was not equipped, put the box of blocks on the floor as Hannah stood Molly in front of them, much to her delight.

"Cleaning," Hannah said quickly, standing back up and feeling a vibration in her voice that she knew betrayed her nervousness.

"Fritz Brothers didn't put together a plan for the third floor, so Hannah's been giving some thought to how y'all might use that space," Gary added.

"What do you want to do with it?" Michael asked, this time sounding genuinely curious.

"I'd like to make it a kids' retreat. For Molly," Hannah began. The explanation seemed to satisfy Michael, who, to his credit, listened to Hannah's plans. "I thought there could be a playroom, and maybe a children's library with bookshelves, and a cozy reading space. And a study for when Molly gets older and has homework."

"It's a great idea," Gary agreed. "I'm going to pull in an architect we work with and have her rough out some sketches for you both to look at. That's a little down the road, though." He looked around the kitchen as if to draw their attention to why it might be "a little down the road."

"Sounds nice," Michael said.

"Do you like your blocks there, Molly?" Gary asked.

Molly gazed up from where she squatted next to the box. Then, seeing she had Gary's attention, she showed him—with great exactitude—how to remove the blocks one at a time and place them next to the box they'd arrived in. Squares in one stack, circles in another, rectangles in a third.

"I have to get back to work," Michael announced.

"Let me take these upstairs," Hannah said, indicating the blocks with a tip of her head. She crouched down and started putting them back into the box, and Molly promptly let her disagreement with that plan be known.

"Can you pick her up so I can do this?" Hannah asked Michael, who reluctantly complied, lifting Molly off the floor and setting her on his hip. In her father's arms, Molly turned her torso away from him, her shoulder against his, her hands in front of her chest as she watched Hannah ascend the stairs.

Hannah placed the wooden blocks in one of the south-facing bedrooms of the third floor and quickly checked the door to the supply room. Locked.

As Michael drove them around the loop on their way out of the neighborhood, Hannah saw Jeremy and Gertie on their after-lunch walk. Wednesday. He probably wondered where she was. She wondered if he'd gotten a chance to talk to Kate about the letter. He turned, his face shifting as he recognized the occupants of the car, and waved at Hannah.

"There's that history professor," Michael said, waving back.

❦

"ARE you going back to the house tomorrow?" Michael asked Hannah as he crawled into bed next to her.

"I thought I would. I usually try to get over there every day," she said, pausing the movie on her iPad.

"What are you watching?"

"*Breaking Away*," she said. "It's an Indiana movie."

"There are movies about Indiana?" he asked, setting his glasses on the bedside table.

"At least one, I guess," she said. "It's good. Or it is so far. It's about this kid and his friends who just graduated high school, and they live down in Bloomington, and their parents were cutters—"

"What-ers?" Michael asked, returning his attention to her.

"Cutters. Their dads all cut limestone in the quarries. Anyway, it takes place in the late 1970s, and the quarries are basically closed, and they don't have any jobs or futures really, and they're trying to figure out what to do with their lives, and—"

"Why don't they go to college? IU's right there," Michael asked, as he dragged a finger along the span of Hannah's arm that extended out of her short-sleeved t-shirt.

"I think they feel like they don't belong. Like they aren't the kind of kids who go to college, you know?" she said, staring at the stilled frame of the four young men in the movie.

"No. I don't know. They should go to college. The only industry in Bloomington is the university."

"I think that's maybe the point of the movie," Hannah murmured. She was only about forty-five minutes in. The movie might have been making other points, as well.

Turning to Michael, she could see him trying to decide whether to continue the debate. He apparently elected not to because he removed the iPad from her hands and set it on the floor next to the bed, careful not to touch the screen and accidentally restart the movie. He turned back toward her and kissed her exposed arm, which lay somewhat lifeless on top of the duvet, and she saw the way his eyes settled on her, moving over her, taking her in.

"I'm glad you're liking Indiana," he said, though he'd never asked whether she liked the state, and she'd never told him she did. He reached under the duvet and found the hem of her t-shirt, sliding his hand just under the edge so that his fingers traced the smooth flesh of her abdomen.

Hannah turned off the lamp next to the bed, plunging the room into darkness. As her eyes adjusted, she could make out only the vaguest form of her husband next to her, but she could picture him in her mind even with his features lost in the blackness—his brown hair, graying to taupe, his eyes intent, perceptive, and purposeful. She slid down under the covers and his hand travelled to her breast. His lips found hers as he slid his other hand around her waist pulling her closer to him.

"Touch me," he said, his voice hoarse with effort.

She slipped her fingers under the waistband of his flannel pajamas and found him hard against her hand, and she thought he must have been thinking about her, about this, all day for as ready as he was. As he moved against her hand, and his tongue explored her mouth, and his hands continued their work against her breasts, she thought, in the dark, here, without even enough moonlight to cast a shadow, in the dark, he could be anyone.

❧

THE SEX WAS GOOD. Very good. In the inked cave of their bedroom, she held him in her hands, and in her mouth, and in her body, and in each of those moments she saw a tall man with black hair and black eyes perched on the edge of his desk, a long leg extended for balance as he smiled at her. She saw him in profile, a pencil between his lips, another in his hand, deep in thought.

Michael made her pay for it, though. Not that he knew, exactly. How could he? But when she came, he lay still in bed for several minutes before he rolled to his side and said, "I think we need to reconnect. Focus on our marriage."

When she said nothing in response, he added, "I think we should find a preschool for Molly."

When she continued in silence, he explained, "It's not good for you to be around a toddler all day long."

And when this was met with still more silence, he spat out, "Clearly."

Hannah thought he knew, and he was punishing her.

CHAPTER 10

"I have to find a preschool for Molly," Hannah said to Laura and Kate. She opened a packet of sugar and tipped its contents into her mug.

The three women sat at their usual table in the small coffee shop just a couple of blocks from Kate's house. The hour of the day lent itself to a distinct bustle as people on their way to their offices dropped in to grab a cup of coffee, barely making a sound with their heads bent over their phones, getting a jump on emails and appointments. They offered brisk and perfunctory *thanks* before shuffling out to cars that would carry them through the arteries of city traffic into downtown. This demographic mixed with a younger, more casual clientele, who sipped coffee from large cream-colored ceramic mugs while sitting at the intentionally mismatched arrangement of small cafe tables, eyes focused on computers connected to the coffee shop's Wi-Fi.

Hannah, Laura, and Kate represented a smaller demographic out and about at 8:30 in the morning, all similarly clothed in stretch pants and sweatshirts, young children at their sides. The coffee shop, catering at least in part to this group of coffee drinkers, had arranged an area in the back corner of the shop where Molly and Laura's daughter Chloe, along with other children, occupied themselves with blocks, a small playhouse, and, naturally, a table with a set of toy coffee mugs.

"This sounds like it might not have been your idea," Laura said, getting straight to the point.

She was right, of course. Hannah had hoped he'd forgotten the comments, made them in haste, but Michael had re-approached the topic after consulting with his parents over the phone—the same conversation in which he'd informed them that he and Hannah would not be spending Christmas in Boston. Hannah, sitting on the couch next to Michael, had been privy to only one half of that conversation, but when it ended, Michael calmly and clearly explained to her that he'd started school in Boston at two and felt strongly that children should be around other children, so they were "socialized." As he had been. Recalling their strange encounter several nights earlier, Hannah thought the motivation might have been more layered than that.

"I've always thought you liked her home with you," Laura said. She picked through a small white container full of sweeteners, her preferred packet obviously missing. Kate grabbed a selection from another table, and Laura pulled out a yellow packet.

"I do, but she turns two next month and my husband thinks—and I do, too—that she should be around other kids. That it's not good for her to be home alone with me all day," Hannah said.

"You think that, too?" Laura said, not doing much to hide her skepticism.

"Well, I guess." Hannah looked over at Molly, who sat next to Chloe, both content in each other's company if not fully in each other's consciousness. Molly had moved on from the coffee set and now focused intently on a toy rotary phone—an anachronistic object she'd never use in real life, but that whirled and rolled and dinged when she twirled its dial.

"What are you looking for in a preschool?" Kate asked, tilting her head, her voice suggesting caution as she proceeded forward.

"I—I don't know. What should I be looking for?"

"Nothing," Laura volunteered with some bite. Kate slid a hand over ever so gently until the edge of her pinky touched the edge of Laura's pinky, and Laura quieted.

"Indianapolis doesn't really have the same—" Kate hesitated and brushed a lock of mahogany-colored hair away from her eyes "—resources that a city like Boston has. There aren't very many free-standing preschools here, and I don't think you'd be very happy at many of the daycares. The preschools are generally attached to K-through-eight schools, but they don't start until really two years before the child enters kindergarten. So, for Molly with a January birthday, she'll start kindergarten in three and a half years, which means she wouldn't start preschool until the fall after next fall, when she's three-turning-four." Kate relayed all of this in a measured voice, calm and comforting, as one might explain a complicated diagnosis to an anxious patient.

"What do parents who work do? What did you do?" Hannah asked as she realized she wasn't going to be able to comply with Michael's directive.

"I've stayed home with both of mine," Laura said, looking deliberately in Chloe's direction. "Jacob just started kindergarten this fall, but Chloe is still home with me."

"I did a nanny-share with another professor at Butler to cover my time on campus," Kate explained. She had one son in middle school and a daughter already in high school.

Hannah tried to remember what her mother had done with her when she was Molly's age, but she couldn't, and she could no longer ask. Maybe Mason would know. Although maybe it didn't matter. Whatever her mother had done, it probably fell far below Michael's standards. Or even her own.

"Are you okay, Hannah?" Laura asked, the edge in her voice replaced by concern.

"What?" Hannah asked. She'd heard the voice, but not the words.

"I just—I mean, I know we're just exercise friends. We don't know each other very well. But it seems like this is something you don't want to do," Laura said, trying to catch Hannah's eye.

"It sounds like it's something I can't do anyway. So…" Hannah trailed off, avoiding Laura's invitation to a deeper conversation.

"Hmm," Kate agreed. "Yes. I would tell Michael that unfortunately, preschool will have to wait for Molly. Though you probably should start looking now so you can get her registered and on any waitlists at the places you and Michael like."

Hannah was astute enough to know she'd been offered a specific solution to her specific problem, even if neither she nor the two women with her were speaking specifically about it. Laura glanced knowingly at Kate and bobbed her head, continuing to do so well beyond the point necessary to affirm agreement.

"Hey! Jeremy told me you're doing some research on your house," Kate said. Hannah was grateful for the change of subject, and Kate turned to Laura, adding, "Hannah bought that old house in Jeremy's neighborhood and is doing research with him on the architect."

"Not really research—" Hannah began.

"Jeremy Linden?" Laura interrupted, a smile tugging at the edges of her lips.

"Yes. He's my neighbor," Hannah explained. "Do you know him?"

"I wish he were my neighbor," Laura said, and took a sip of her coffee, looking over the rim at Kate, who returned her gaze with playful derision.

"What?" Laura objected. "Didn't he get his heart broken by some Lit professor last year? I bet he could use some comforting right now." She adopted a far-off, dreamy expression that could only have been intentionally contrived for the amusement of her companions.

"How do you even know that?" Kate asked. She rolled her eyes until they eventually landed on Hannah, who listened intently to the exchange.

"Small town, big buildings," Laura offered.

"What does that mean?" Hannah asked.

"It's a joke about how Indianapolis isn't really a big city," Kate said. "Everyone knows everyone's business. Though I don't know how you managed to keep tabs on Jeremy Linden's love life." Kate shook her head at Laura, raising an eyebrow in her direction.

"He's in that cycling club with Kevin," Laura explained, referring to her husband.

"Small town, big buildings," Kate agreed.

"Did he show you the letter?" Hannah asked.

"What letter?" Laura rested her elbows on the table, leaning forward with interest. "From the Lit professor?"

"No," Kate said. "This is about the architect again. The one who built Hannah's house."

Laura sat back in her chair, clearly disappointed.

"Yes. I haven't had a chance to dig into it yet. I want to. I love this kind of stuff. Seriously. But I might not be able to get to it until after the semester."

"Of course," Hannah said, taking a sip of her coffee. "I understand."

"If I can get to it earlier, I will. I promise," Kate said.

"It's not research. I'm just curious, and Jeremy said he thought you might know more than he would," Hannah said.

"Invariably," Kate said with a controlled grin. "Why don't we set up a coffee for after the New Year to talk about it?"

"Can I come?" Laura asked, her interest evidently renewed.

"Sure," Hannah said. Coffee with Kate, Jeremy, and Laura sounded lovely.

"You absolutely cannot," Kate said, shaking her head.

"You are not a true friend, Kate Nielsen," Laura said.

"I am your truest friend," Kate replied.

CHAPTER 11

"You going anywhere for Christmas?" Jeremy asked.

It was really becoming too cold for these walks. Even with Molly bundled in a snowsuit and her blankets tucked snuggly around her, her little nose still turned pink by the end of the second lap. But neither Jeremy nor Hannah seemed inclined to give in to the weather quite yet.

"When we lived in Boston, we always celebrated Christmas with Michael's family, but he doesn't want to leave the Decker house unattended for a week while it's still under construction. So, we're staying here," Hannah explained.

"Can't they come here?"

"No. They don't like to travel. They didn't even come to our wedding," Hannah said without thinking, promptly wishing she hadn't shared that detail of her nuptials.

"Where was your wedding?"

"Mexico. What are you doing for Christmas?" she asked quickly.

"I'll probably head to my mom and dad's."

"Probably?" Hannah ribbed. "I hope they're not too far away. It's a little late not to have tickets."

Jeremy chuckled. "They live in Cleveland. So, I can just drive there with Gertie, which makes it easy to wait till the last minute to make a decision."

"Is that what you usually do?" she asked. Next to her, she heard Jeremy shift, tucking his hands into his coat pockets despite his gloves.

"Well, when I was with Erika, we always just celebrated together. The two of us," he said, his eyes focused straight ahead. "Depending on what day of the week Christmas fell on, we might go visit her family or mine."

"Where is she now?" Hannah asked, unable to stifle her curiosity.

"If Instagram is any indication, she's in Virginia and quite happy to be so," he said. "Hey, you aren't on any social media." Hannah recognized the strategic shift away from an uncomfortable topic.

"Yeah. I don't have any interest in any of that. Honestly, it creeps me out, the idea of people following me or whatever it is people do on Instagram. That reminds me," Hannah said. "Kate and I touched base on the letter from Andrew's uncle. She wants to have coffee—the three of us—after the New Year. She sounded really busy."

"Grades are due," Jeremy said with a distinct lack of enthusiasm. "Although I already looked into a little of it. Kate will be a much better source on this stuff than I could be, but I was curious... and I was procrastinating on grading exams. Anyway, it sounds like Decker's mom's family came to Indiana right around the time about twenty Italians immigrated here to work in the quarries. Most of the European immigrants in Indiana at that time were German, like his dad, or descendants of Scottish immigrants who migrated up from Appalachia. But there were these little pockets of other immigrants, and the Italian cutters and carvers were one. That letter might actually be pretty valuable if it's from one of those original Italian quarry workers."

"Interesting," Hannah said. "So, his family were stonecutters? I didn't quite understand that from the letter. It seemed to conflict with the obituary."

"Not his whole family. I think his mother must have been one of the stonecutter's sisters. She'd probably have been the right age. So then, Decker's mother would have been Alessandro's sister," Jeremy explained. "And his dad was a doctor, but being a doctor at that time, particularly in Indiana, was a little different than it is now. Not quite as prestigious." Jeremy's tone suggested he enjoyed the intersection of the Decker family history with his own research interests. "But, you know, with all of that, Decker himself was in sort of a strange position. He's kind of half working class, half middle class, marrying into upper class. His father would've been, you know, respectable, and his mother would've been pulled into that respectability. But her brother wouldn't have been. He would've been, well, essentially an immigrant laborer. That might have played into the rift. Though that letter makes it sound like there was more than one issue between those two. It would explain the last paragraph, though—all the stuff about Decker pretending to be someone he wasn't."

"And I thought my life was complicated," Hannah breathed.

"Have you found out any other information about him?" Jeremy asked.

"Like what?" Hannah responded far more sharply than the situation called for. "Where on earth would I find out more information about him?"

Jeremy swiveled his head in her direction, and she caught a sidewise glimpse of him. Fine lines had emerged at the corners of his eyes, and he'd brought his lip between his teeth. He seemed utterly baffled at the direction the conversation had suddenly gone.

"Do you want to set up a time to meet after New Year's?" he asked.

"How did you learn Italian?" Hannah asked, ignoring the invitation. Her mood was souring, but she couldn't pinpoint the precise cause. All this business about Andrew's uncle being the wrong class to attend his nephew's wedding. The ease with which Jeremy had assigned each member of Andrew's family, and then Andrew himself, to some impenetrable stratum of the social hierarchy—it didn't sit well with her.

"It was my doctoral minor," Jeremy replied. Two well-defined creases emerged between his brows, joining the pleats at his eyes.

"I don't know what a doctoral minor is," Hannah said, her voice thick with frustration.

"It's just like an undergraduate minor, but you get it when you're getting your PhD. I wrote my dissertation on Vesalius, so it made sense to know Italian—"

"I don't know who Vesalius is," she said before he could complete the explanation. The handle of the stroller blurred before her and she felt, inexplicably, like she might begin to cry.

"It's okay. He's pretty niche. He was a sixteenth-century Italian anatomist. He changed the way medical students were taught anatomy during the Renaissance." He stopped beside her, and Hannah stopped with him. "I'm sorry, Hannah. Have I done something wrong?" he asked, his eyes fixed on every movement of her face.

"No," she said resolutely. "I think I'm just worried about Christmas." She started pushing the stroller again, leaving Jeremy no choice but to fall in line beside her, if for no other reason than to keep up with Gertie, who would not leave Molly's side.

"What did you study in college?" he asked after some time, and more than enough silence had passed.

"I didn't go to college," she said, her voice every bit as bitter as the winter wind that stung her face.

Jeremy stopped walking again, then had to jog to catch up when Hannah continued forward.

"What?" she asked defiantly as he came up alongside her.

"Nothing. I'm sorry... I didn't mean ... What did you do after high school?" he asked. His voice was light, curious, as if he expected a story —she might say she'd backpacked around Europe or volunteered for the Peace Corps. She picked up her pace trying to get back to the end of her driveway as quickly as possible.

"I worked in construction and waitressed, and then when I turned twenty-one, I started bartending at a hotel, which is where I met Michael."

"Oh," he said.

Hannah stole another glance at him from the corner of her eye. The lines between his brows were back. She didn't care for them.

"What did you study in college?" she asked, her phrasing mimicking his, but her voice carrying the hint of a taunt.

"History," he said, his tone allowing for the possibility that he himself might be confused about it, and Hannah closed her eyes against the embarrassment. He was a history professor. Of course he'd studied history.

"Hey," Hannah exclaimed as soon as she heard Mason's voice on the other end of the phone. She knew she was overdoing it on the cheerful tone, but she remained unsettled after her walk with Jeremy, sensing that she'd left him totally bewildered. She didn't know really what to do about that, as she felt more than a little bewildered herself.

"Hey you," he returned.

She could hear the sounds of construction in the background, sounds she was exceedingly familiar with. She liked the idea that, separated by thousands of miles, she and her brother lived their lives against the same soundtrack.

"Are you at work?" she asked, though she knew he was.

"Yeah, but I can take a break. What's up? How's the house? Everything going okay? Michael treating you okay? Where are you now?" Hannah heard the sounds of the worksite receding into the background and received the series of rapid-fire questions as both a desire for an update and her brother's absent way of stalling until he could find a quiet place to talk to her.

"I'm at the bungalow," she said. "Michael's still at work."

"How's Molly? I got your Christmas card. She looks just like you, Banana," he said.

"Yeah. Everyone says that. You doing okay?"

"Yeah. You know," he said, and she did know.

"I wanted to ask you," she began. It would be a short call; phone calls with Mason always were. "What did Mom do with me when I was a baby, and she went back to work? Like before I could go to school."

"I don't understand. What do you mean what did she do with you?"

Hannah could hear the *flitch-flitch* of a cigarette lighter followed by a long exhale as Mason took his first drag.

"Like, who watched me while she was at work?" she clarified.

"Man, that was a long time ago," he said with an audible exhale.

Hannah could picture him perfectly, standing with his phone to his ear, a cigarette in the other hand, his sandy blond hair in desperate need of a trim, tucked under a knit cap.

"Um. There was this old lady who lived across the hall from us, and she watched you a few times," he continued. "I think I watched you a lot, but then, I was in school so I guess I couldn't have been with you during the day. I think she was in and out of a lot of jobs, so she probably watched you when she wasn't working. Why? What's going on?"

"Michael wants Molly to go to preschool, but the preschools here are hard to figure out, and my friends Kate and Laura said Molly still has a couple years till she's old enough to go." Hannah fought to keep her voice steady—Mason didn't need her blubbering to him while he was at work.

"Oh. Well. Whatever Mom did is probably not something you'd want for Molly," Mason said. Hannah heard another exhale into the phone.

"Yeah. Probably not," she agreed.

"You hear from her lately?" Mason asked.

"No. I tried to track her down before we moved, but I couldn't find her. You?"

"She called me a few months ago and asked how I was doing. She's in Florida now. She said she wanted to come out here and visit, which would be cool. I have space for her. She said she left Jack. Again. I guess. I told her that was good because she's welcome to stay with me anytime, but if that motherfucker steps foot in Montana, I'll fucking kill him."

Hannah thought that while a lot of the men in her life were prone to bluster, Mason had probably said exactly those words to their mother. And meant them.

"Anyway, I called her back maybe a month after that, and the number was disconnected, so I'm assuming Jack is back," he laughed sardonically.

"You should come to Indianapolis," Hannah said, warmed by the thought of her brother seeing the work on the Decker house and playing with Molly.

"I don't have a car right now," he said. "But you know, these roads out here have two lanes. Some even have four." It wasn't quite an invitation, but she thought she got his meaning.

"Maybe this spring," she said hopefully. "I don't think Michael has ever been to Yellowstone. Maybe we could come out for a family vacation."

"You let me know, Banana. I can show you all around out here. It is just beautiful." She heard him exhale in what seemed an especially long breath and assumed he'd reached the end of his cigarette, which meant they'd reached the end of their conversation. "Hey, kiddo, I gotta get back to work," he said. "But it was good to hear from you."

"You too, Mason," she said, fighting again to steady her voice.

"Call me any time."

"Okay. I love you," she said.

"Yep," he said and ended the call.

Hannah slouched into the couch. Mason had been in Montana for close to ten years and technically, now that she lived in Indiana, she was closer to him than she'd been during that entire time. But the distance felt unnavigable. Their conversations were getting shorter. They were running out of things to talk about. The things they had in common were the kinds of things no one should have in common. The things they might talk about were unspeakable.

CHAPTER 12

That evening, Michael rhapsodized exuberantly through dinner about the developments with the Decker house, about how quickly things were moving along. He even attributed Gary's hiring to Hannah—her intuition about him had been right. Well done, there. But that night when he crawled into bed next to her and burrowed his lips into her shoulder, she pulled away. A second attempt received a similar response.

"What's the problem?" he asked.

"I'm just tired."

He rolled his eyes with a grunt and grabbed the book from his bedside table. This, of course, meant that his lamp remained on even after Hannah turned off her own, indicating her desire to go to sleep. But Michael continued to read for another thirty minutes or so such that he wasn't getting laid, and she wasn't getting sleep. At long last, he turned the light off, placing his book heavily on the table next to his head. Then he flipped and flopped, bouncing the mattress for another several minutes before finally settling on a position and falling asleep in it.

Sleep didn't come quite so easily for Hannah. When she finally gave in to the temptation and picked up her phone, the bold white numbers told her it was 2:o8 a.m. In the silvery darkness above her face, she saw the replay of her afternoon, heard her sharp voice with Jeremy and his confusion. She heard the distant, truncated conversation with Mason—their mother was in Florida. What on earth was she doing *there*?

Resigning herself to the fact she wasn't going to drift off to sleep, she crawled out of bed and sneaked to the living room. The letter she'd found, and Jeremy's translation of it, had distracted her from her original observation of Eleanor's absence from the photographs after Andrew's death—the very thing that had brought her to the Decker house earlier in the week.

She pulled her laptop from her bag and entered her search terms: *Eleanor Decker; Indianapolis; death*.

Indianapolis Times. January 14, 1935. BODY FOUND! The body of Eleanor (Dailey) Decker, 42, of Indianapolis was found this morning in a quarry in Bedford. Mrs. Decker went missing on January 12, 1935, two years to the day after her husband Andrew Decker's death. The suspected cause of death is drowning. Mrs. Decker's grief at the loss of her husband was well known to her family and friends. The body has been delivered to the coroner.

As she had with the articles concerning Andrew, Hannah read and re-read the notice of Eleanor's death. But there wasn't much to read, and the newspaper hadn't even bothered to provide a photograph of Eleanor to accompany the article. She searched the online archives further, thinking she might be able to find Eleanor's obituary as she'd found Andrew's, but no luck. Eleanor's death wasn't news. She reflected on the sequence of events unfolding before her. Eleanor's absence from the photographed chronology of her daughter's life was the result of her own death—an event so unremarkable it had barely been reported in the papers, and even Gary seemed unaware of it.

Hannah closed her eyes and imagined Eleanor, devastated at the loss of her husband, slipping into her own despondency, withdrawing further and further from her friends, from her daughter, until one dark evening on the two-year anniversary of his death, she'd gotten into her car, gone to her family's quarry, and drowned herself. Driven mad by grief, like some kind of Midwestern Ophelia.

Her thoughts shifted to Margaret. That poor girl. Andrew's sister must have stepped in to raise the child. Fortunate that she was able to do so. It clarified to some extent why Margaret had continued to live in the house after her parents' deaths. The house would have been hers at that point, and with the housing market in ruins and few financial resources of her own, Margaret wouldn't have had the ability to move. Hannah assumed that in 1935, Mary, a woman about whom Hannah knew almost nothing, but who evidently never married or had children of her own, also wouldn't have had the ability to buy a new home for herself and her orphaned niece.

As she thought about Jeremy's recitation of the few facts he'd managed to put together about Andrew, she recognized that one of the things that had upset her was the realization that she didn't even know what to ask. She had, she felt, let Andrew down, unable to ascertain even the most basic features of his life. Worse, Jeremy's sudden interest felt intrusive; the invitation to meet with Kate felt like an encroachment on some private matter belonging only to Hannah. Her eyes closed, and she rested her head against the soft curve of the back of the couch.

"Hey." Hannah heard Michael's voice behind her. It had lost its petulance from the night before. Worry. He was worried about her. "Are you sleeping on the couch?"

She prepared to say no, when she realized that she had indeed fallen asleep on the couch. At some point, her thoughts about Andrew, Margaret, Mary, Kate, Jeremy, all of those thoughts had taken on the shape of a dream. Her laptop lay closed and on the floor. She rested on her side, her head not on the back of the couch, but on one of the throw pillows. As she opened her eyes in response to Michael's voice, she saw that he'd moved, his face just inches from her own as he crouched next to her.

"What time is it?" she asked.

"Nearly 4:00," he said. "Come back to bed. I'm sorry for pouting." He took her hand in his, kissed it softly, and gently pulled her to her feet, guiding her to the bedroom where she found that sleep came more easily now that she had something that resembled a plan.

❧

THE RAINBOW OF LIGHTS BLURRED, their colors bleeding into one another as Hannah continued to stare at the Christmas tree. She preferred the multi-colored lights to strands of white and opted for an angel rather than a star on top. These decisions weren't necessarily intentional or even really conscious, and she hadn't realized they were preferences *per se*, until she and Michael were standing at Lowe's, their first year of marriage, and she'd reached for one set of lights as he reached for another.

"I like the colorful ones," she'd said. "They seem happier."

"Happier?" Michael had asked.

"And warm."

"Warm," he'd repeated as she placed a box of them into the cart.

"Yes."

"Well, we'll need more than one box." He picked two more off the shelf and added them to the cart.

"Thank you," she'd said.

"Thank you?"

They didn't really know each other, then. Not really. Not now either, she supposed, because he now knew she liked the multi-colored lights, and he continued to replace the strands yearly as one faulty bulb inevitably extinguished the entire strand. But he never asked why, and she never told him.

He just replaced the strands, all the same.

"What are you looking at?" Michael asked.

She thought he'd fallen asleep in the chair, and she'd muted the TV so that she could read in quiet. But the lack of noise must have awakened him just as it had lulled her into something of a trance.

She brought herself back to the present. "The lights," she said. "They look so happy."

"Happy lights," he said as if he found the notion amusing somehow.

"Do you know why I like the multi-colored ones?" she asked.

"I figured that's just what you had as a kid. Brought back happy memories." He looked around the seat of his chair, then the floor beneath it. Hannah handed him the remote; she'd taken it from his lap when she'd muted the TV.

"It is what we had as kids," she said. "But shouldn't that make me not like them?"

"Hmm? Why?" He flipped slowly through the recommended shows on Hulu.

"Because. Christmas wasn't always happy."

"What's the happiest Christmas you can remember?" He set the remote down on the arm of the chair and gave her his full attention.

She felt the tug of her lips as if the memory itself were pulling them into a smile. "I got a ten-speed. A really nice one. And Mason and I went out and rode our bikes together. There was no traffic because it was Christmas."

"Wasn't it cold? Boston in December?" Michael asked.

"This was in Clover."

"I don't think I realized he visited you so often," Michael said. His phone buzzed noisily on the table beside his chair. "Mom," he said, as he picked it up and accepted the call.

"I'm going to bed," Hannah whispered, rising from the couch.

Michael lifted his chin. "Okay," he whispered back.

She took a quick picture of the tree and texted it to her grandparents.

> Hannah: Merry Christmas! I love you both.

> Grandma: Love you too, baby girl. Merry Christmas.

CHAPTER 13

Andrew Moore lived north of Indianapolis, in Zionsville, one of the city's more desirable suburbs. While not as substantial as the Decker house, his home spoke to the success of the endocrinologist with its numerous gables, wide side driveway, and impeccably landscaped front lawn. A woman, who Hannah assumed was Dr. Moore's wife, answered the door and welcomed her into a large foyer smelling a bit aggressively of cinnamon and vanilla. A garland left over from Christmas wrapped around the banister of a large, curved staircase leading up to the second floor of the stately home. Beyond the foyer, Hannah could see the glow of a Christmas tree accompanied by the small details and festive decor of the season, which hadn't yet been packed away following the New Year.

"You must be Hannah," the woman said, smiling at both Hannah and Molly. "I'm Joyce. Come on in. Let me take your coats."

Hannah obliged and felt herself immediately at ease as Joyce ushered her past the staircase into a large, vaulted family room. "I'll get Andy for you."

Hannah felt a tinge of recognition at the name. It was the same electricity she'd felt when, shortly before Christmas, Debbie had given her the contact information for the only Moore child still residing in the Indianapolis area. He'd been named for his grandfather, she assumed.

"Can I get you something to drink?" Joyce asked.

"Oh, no, thank you," Hannah said.

Joyce disappeared into the house and returned a short time later with both Andrew—a distinguished-looking man approaching seventy—and a box of wooden tracks and trains for Molly to play with. Joyce smiled tightly as she set the box down in front of Molly and left Andrew and Hannah to their scheduled meeting.

Although Hannah had hoped she'd see in Andrew something beyond a shadow of his namesake, the man had only the slightest resemblance to his grandfather. Part of this, Hannah knew, was his age. Unlike his grandson, Andrew Decker had been frozen in time, never aging past his early forties. Still, as he settled into a navy-blue wingback chair, Andrew Moore appeared smaller in build. His hair had been a light brown, not the dark ebony of his mother and grandfather. His face bore little similarity to the face of the man who peered at Hannah from the black-and-white photographs in her attic, and as Hannah examined him more closely, it was evident it never had.

Hannah became aware that she was staring too intently as he cleared his throat purposefully.

"Thank you for meeting with me," she said.

"No problem. You found some pictures?" He shifted his eyes to Molly, whom he seemed to regard with distant affection.

"Oh. Yes," Hannah said, feeling self-conscious, realizing she'd made the man uncomfortable. "We're renovating the Decker house, and I found them in the attic."

"In the attic, eh?" he said as his brows furrowed together. "I thought Nancy went through the house and got everything."

Hannah assumed Nancy was his sister or another family member. The use of the word "everything" revealed that Andrew must not have followed up on Nancy's efforts since there was really no way to describe what had been removed from the house as "everything."

"They were in the storage room that's up on the third floor," she explained.

"Oh, I know that room," he said, coming alive. His eyes darted about her, no doubt looking for the photographs.

"Sorry. They're out in the car. There are three boxes," she said.

"Three boxes?" Andrew repeated as if he couldn't believe it.

"I wondered—" Hannah paused, the meeting already departing from her expectations. She'd hoped for a familiarity between them—she would know him, he would recognize her, and he'd begin regaling her with stories of the family of his youth as if they were sitting around a campfire on a late autumn evening. Instead, it seemed she'd interrupted him, pulled him away from something he'd been doing elsewhere in the house, and the conversation took on the form of a business negotiation—she was there to trade photographs for information.

"I wondered whether you could answer a few questions about the house for me," she said timidly.

"Questions?" His eyes narrowed; he was already suspicious.

"Um... well... I wanted to know more about the architect who built it. Your grandfather." She felt suddenly juvenile and thought about Kate and Jeremy and the specific questions they would have known to ask—questions precisely designed in such a way as to elevate their interests as scholarly, purely academic.

"What do you want to know?" Andrew asked, crossing an ankle on top of his knee.

"I don't know where to start," she said, smiling. Andrew remained stoic, and Hannah steeled her nerves. "There are some things about the house that are a little confusing to me."

Andrew stifled a guffaw. "I'll say."

She lifted her eyes to meet his and attempted another smile, flustered, but he declined to return anything resembling a friendly expression. "Yeah. So, I guess the first thing I don't understand is why the bank didn't foreclose on the house after Andrew... Mr. Decker... your grandfather died," she said, remembering what Jeremy had called her "research question."

"That's your first question?" he asked somewhat derisively.

"I... um... I don't really have a set order for them," Hannah admitted.

"Well, I can't help you with the answer to that one. I honestly never even thought about it. Though now that you mention it, that's why he shot himself. 1933. He had some deal fall through, I think. Worst year of the Depression."

Hannah hadn't known that was the worst year of the Depression, or that there even was a worst year. She thought of the Great Depression as a calamitous crash, tumbling into a devastating ravine in which the country remained, static, until World War II. Again, she regretted not waiting to meet with this man until after she'd met with Jeremy and Kate.

"But it's strange," she began, the register of her voice elevating just slightly with her nerves. "I mean, if things were so bad that he had to —" she could hardly say the words "—take his own life, wouldn't the bank have come for that house? How did your mom end up keeping it?"

Andrew remained quiet, his eyes narrowing subtly. On the floor at Hannah's feet, Molly was already growing tired of the wooden trains, and Hannah knew it wouldn't be long before her daughter demanded her attention.

"What's your interest in all of this?" Andrew asked, wearing his suspicion openly.

Hannah hadn't prepared an answer to that question, but explanations marched through her mind, nonetheless. "I guess I just think with a tragedy that great, I'd like to understand it better."

"I'm not sure anyone's ever going to understand it. I never did." He settled back further into his chair as if he'd made a decision about something, about her. He exhaled and tilted his head, a restrained smile finally breaking through. "They didn't tell you about it before you bought it, did they?"

Hannah could see that he'd worked out some part of her story, though she suspected it was incomplete. "They didn't," she said, thinking he wanted her to agree with him.

"I knew they'd do that. You technically don't have to disclose a suicide in the sale of a house. You have to disclose a murder, but not a suicide. And she killed herself too, you know. Did you know that? My grandmother. The both of them."

"Oh my gosh." Hannah said, unsure whether she should reveal her late-night googling.

"Yeah. I think the house was all Mom had left of them," he said. "She was nine when he died and just a couple years older when her mom died. I think she couldn't stand the thought of someone else moving in and, well, doing basically what Fritz Brother did. Tearing down walls and leaving it in ruins. She'd be really happy that a family has moved in. She'd like that." He had a momentum to him now, some thread he was ready to tug.

"I always thought the most interesting part was them," he went on. "As a couple. Mom didn't talk about them much, but I remember her saying they were a couple for the ages. His mom's family were cutters. You know about the cutters?" he said, interrupting himself.

"Some," Hannah replied.

"The cutters—stonecutters—they were really almost the bottom of the social hierarchy, and that was his mom's family. His dad was a doctor. Which is probably how he was able to go off to New York, for school. He went to Columbia."

"His obituary mentioned that," Hannah said, finding herself opening up to Andrew as he opened up to her.

"Kind of incredible when you think about it," he went on, pride filling his voice, his shoulders broadening as he continued. "First generation American. His dad's just this little country doctor, and he goes to an Ivy League university. And then he comes back home and marries the daughter of the owner of the quarry his own family is mining in. That might actually be how she kept the house. My grandmother's family had money, I think. Not like Carnegie money, but those quarries were pretty profitable back then. Though I don't really know what effect the Depression had on them. I'd assume it was substantial just like it was for every other industry. It honestly never occurred to me to ask Mom about it. They got out of that business in the seventies when I was still pretty young. I remember thinking in college that the house was basically a mansion. None of my friends had a house like that. But when you're growing up, you don't really notice those things. It's all just normal because that's what you're used to, you know?"

Hannah did know a little about that.

"Anyway, I guess there was some drama to that marriage. Her family wasn't happy about it. Or her father. Her mother—that would be my great-grandmother—she died when my grandmother was a child, or maybe even an infant. I'm not really sure. Anyway, as I understand it, my grandmother was smitten. And I can guess why. You've seen the pictures. He was a good-looking guy. Wish I'd gotten some of those genes."

Hannah blushed as her thoughts seemed to intersect with Andrew's.

"But the way Mom would talk about them, I mean, she was just a kid who loved her mom and dad, and there's no question he was her favorite person in the world, then. She had all kinds of stories about him taking her to job sites and to the quarry when he'd go there. He taught her to read, and she said they used to stay up late at night, and he'd be reading to her from Dickens or Twain." He stopped abruptly and looked up from where he'd been staring off toward the Christmas tree. "I'm sorry. I think I've gotten carried away."

"No. No, it's fine. It's very interesting," Hannah said. In truth, she could have listened to him talk all day as the images of Andrew Decker, beloved husband and father, materialized in her mind, coming to life with the descriptions of him layering upon what little she already knew.

"Yeah, well. I just hope my kids love us that much." He said this with a good-natured laugh, a contrast to what had become a rather somber story.

"Why didn't any of you want the house?" Hannah asked. "My realtor said that none of the kids wanted the house."

"Well, that's a little more complicated. Mom left it to all three of us, but I'm the only one still in town, so I'm the only one who could have lived in it. Except, I already have a house." He gestured around his family room, denoting his present residence. "I've been living in this house for thirty years. And if Joyce and I were going to move, it'd be to some place smaller. What are we going to do—a couple of empty-nesters—with a nine-thousand-square-foot mansion in Indianapolis?"

Hannah nodded. The decision had been a pragmatic one, then.

"Craig and Nancy were pretty upset about that. But, you know, if they wanted the house to stay in the family so badly, they should've moved here themselves. I think it's just not a very practical house. It was a blast to grow up in, even after we understood... you know... what had happened there. But... yeah... it just made more sense to sell it and split the proceeds. You like it there?" he asked fondly, as if checking in on an old friend.

"Yes. Well. We don't live there yet. We're still doing work on it."

"What kind of work are you doing?"

"Updating the plumbing, electric, HVAC and then painting and decor." She intentionally omitted that she, too, would be removing some walls.

"Maybe we'll come visit it when you finish. I mean if that's okay with you," he suggested.

"I'd like that," Hannah said honestly. Andrew grew quiet.

"Why don't I walk out with you and help you with those boxes from your car," he offered, and Hannah accepted that he'd said all he was going to say about Andrew Decker and the Decker house.

❧

"MICHAEL," Hannah called back from the living room. "Michael, there's a car in our driveway. Some enormous SUV."

Michael emerged from his office where he'd been ensconced all morning working on an SBAR for the Basingstoke project.

"They're here," he said, exhaling deeply as he often did when attempting to settle his nerves.

Hannah stood in front of the window, the sheer curtain pulled to the side as she peered out at the driveway. Michael came up alongside her, looking over her shoulder.

"Who's here?" she asked.

Michael's head snapped in her direction, his brows creasing together and his mouth curling up in disbelief. "My parents," he said, with an air of overt frustration.

"Your parents?" Hannah parroted.

As if the phrase had the power to summon them, a young man in a black suit stepped out of the SUV, opened the rear passenger door, and Gail Korman emerged.

"God, Hannah, we talked about this. You asked me if we were going to Boston for Christmas, I said no, you were upset about it, so were they, so I invited them here for Molly's birthday. Jesus, you sulked all through Christmas."

Hannah flipped through the events of the last several weeks, searching for a memory, a sliver of such a conversation, but could find none. Had he told her? She'd been awfully distracted, her mind occupied by Gary and Molly and Kate and Laura, and everything going on with the Decker house. It was conceivable. It was conceivable he'd said something, and she'd simply missed it.

"It must have slipped my mind," she said, watching as the trunk of the SUV glided up, and the chauffeur pulled out two large roller bags, setting them on the short walkway leading to the front door.

Michael left her side, heading out without his coat into the brisk winter air to help his parents bring their luggage in. Hannah watched as Gail placed a kiss on Michael's cheek, then used her thumb to rub away the lipstick she'd left behind. Michael's father, Ian, stepped out from the other side of the SUV and approached his son, shaking his hand energetically and clapping him on the back as they all approached the house.

"Hannah, dear," Gail said, stepping into the living room. She said the two words like they were one, like it was Hannah's full name—Hannahdear—and offered the same kiss-and-swipe she'd used with her son.

"Hi, Mom," Hannah said, stunned.

"Gummy!" Molly called out as she ran out from the kitchen.

"Oh my word!" Gail exclaimed, picking Molly up and hugging her close. "I can't believe how big you've gotten in just a few months. Hasn't she gotten so big, Ian?"

"Did you tip the driver, Dad?" Michael looked out the window at the suited man who remained in their driveway.

"Shit. Is he still out there?" Ian asked. "Can you handle that?" He lifted a brown leather wallet out of his coat and pulled a few bills from the billfold, thrusting them toward Michael.

"We tipped when we made the reservation," Gail said, between blowing raspberries on the backs of Molly's hands.

"Then what's he doing still out there?" Michael asked.

"Did you get the gifts from the trunk?" Gail asked of no one in particular, it seemed.

Ian didn't respond as he tucked his wallet back into his pocket.

Michael walked with pronounced aggravation back out to the SUV and returned with the assistance of the chauffeur, who appeared absolutely expressionless as he set four large boxes down on the floor inside the door and accepted the bills Michael handed to him.

"I'm going to have to order out for dinner," Hannah said, her mind moving over the logistics of the situation. Michael brushed past her, one roller bag in each hand as he made his way to the guest room.

"Order from Hollyhock Hill. They'll love it," he said over his shoulder.

"Did Michael not tell you we were coming?" Gail asked, her eyes wide as she followed the form of her son heading back to the guest room.

"We've had a lot going on with the other house," Michael said.

"Oh, the house!" Gail was now bouncing Molly. *A-one, a-two, a-three.* And Molly squealed with delight as her grandmother added a single deep bounce on three. "I cannot wait to see it."

"We'll do that tomorrow," Michael said, reemerging from the guest room. "It'll be dark soon, and you won't be able to see anything tonight."

"I'll go order dinner," Hannah said, walking back into the solitude of the kitchen, grateful for a task that removed her from the chaos of the living room. She happily volunteered to pick the food up as well.

Michael was right; they did love the meal. So perfectly Midwestern with pickled beets, fried chicken, green beans, and mashed potatoes.

"I was looking online and there's a museum at the Speedway," Ian said as they sat around the dining room table, plates still resting in front of them but the meal already behind them. "Is that something worth going to?"

"I honestly don't know, Dad. I can ask some friends from work." Michael picked up his phone and began texting.

"Put your phone down, dear," Gail instructed. "Not at the table."

Michael finished his text, then set the phone next to his plate. It immediately pinged, and he read the text without lifting it up.

"Yeah. Sam says it's good," he replied. "Recommends the NCAA museum, too."

"And the Children's Museum," Gail said. "Would you like that, Molly? If you went with Gummy and Pop to the Children's Museum?"

Molly smiled broadly as Hannah replied on her behalf. "That museum is incredible. We have a membership—"

"We do?" Michael asked, texting something back to Sam, using only his index fingers so as to allow the phone to remain on the table.

Gail's expression dropped as she regarded her son from beneath one sharply elevated eyebrow. "Does your daddy work too much?" she asked—ostensibly—Molly. Molly offered no opinion on that matter but lifted her hands to show her grandmother the striking purple color left by the pickled beets.

"Pur-ple," she said and grinned widely.

"Ian! Did you hear that? Do you know your colors, sweetheart?"

"She's very smart," Hannah said proudly.

"Things picking up at Rue?" Ian asked Michael. "How's Basingstoke?"

"Yeah, that project looks like it's going to be a lot more involved than we originally bargained for. I mean, in a good way, but it's a lot of work."

Hannah tried to catch Michael's eye from across the table. He'd been spending an increasing amount of time in his office, and when she'd asked, he'd offered her the same cursory explanation: *That project looks like it's going to be a lot more involved than we originally bargained for.*

"They paying you for that?" Ian asked. "Don't let them take advantage of you. They couldn't do this without you. You've got to get in there and make sure they know that—make sure they know *you* know that. They can't move you out to the bible belt and then pay you with kind words."

"Yeah, Dad. I know, I know. No one's taking advantage of me. And this isn't the bible belt."

"What is it? Is this the rust belt?" he looked to Gail for a response to his question, but she only shrugged.

"They call it the heartland," Hannah volunteered.

"Oh, that's lovely," Gail said, smiling at Hannah. "I do like that. The heartland."

"Dessert anyone?" Michael offered, rising from his chair. "There's apple crisp."

"I picked up some vanilla ice cream to go with it," Hannah added.

"Yeah, I'll have some of that," Ian said.

Hannah began collecting the dinner plates from the table, scraping the refuse of the meal onto one plate, and then stacking them expertly, piling the silverware on top. She rested two of the serving dishes along her forearm, then lifted the plates carrying the entire, intricately balanced collection out to the kitchen.

"I think this is going well," Hannah whispered, setting the plates next to the sink. "Don't you think? Everyone seems happy." She omitted mention that Michael did not seem happy.

"I'm sure he'll find some way to get in a dig," Michael said as he scooped ice cream into small bowls of apple crisp and handed them to Hannah, who delivered them to the table.

"Hannah," Gail said, her voice low and conspiratorial as Hannah took a seat at the table, Michael trailing behind her. "Now I know it's not polite to say so, but you just look amazing. Truly. I'll say it: I can't remember the last time I saw you looking so healthy. Is this from that gym you've been going to?"

"Thank you," Hannah said, struggling to conjure an appropriate response. "That's very nice of you to say."

"You've made some friends there, too, haven't you, Hannah?" Michael said, taking a bite of dessert.

"Yes. Kate and Laura," Hannah said.

"Kate's the Chair of History at Butler. Her husband's an attorney. Corporate litigation," Michael said.

"How nice," Gail said.

"Well, I think it's great that you're taking care of yourself, Hannah," Ian said with confidence. "I swear, these women who have a baby and then keep the weight like it's a non-refundable baby shower gift."

"Ian! What an absolutely horrible thing to say. What has gotten into you lately?" Gail scolded.

"There it is," Michael muttered.

"It's true, though. You didn't let that happen to you," Ian said, tipping his forehead in the direction of his wife.

"Not everyone has the privileges I had when Michael was young," Gail said, taking a delicate bite of the crisp.

"Maybe," Ian said and quickly moved on. "So tomorrow then, Michael. You show us the house and then we go to the Children's Museum and the NCAA."

"That's a lot for one day, Dad," Michael said.

"That's fine. We're here all week. We can spread it out."

"I can't take a whole week off of work. I took tomorrow off. But you guys don't need me for all of this," Michael said.

"Fair enough," Ian replied, pushing his dessert bowl back from the edge of the table. "Hannah can show us around."

"Sure," said Hannah agreeably. "I'd be happy to."

CHAPTER 14

"She's running late," Jeremy said as he walked into the kitchen. He held up his cell phone as evidence, though the screen was black, and Hannah guessed she wouldn't have been able to read the face of it from her distance in any case. He sat down at the kitchen table adjacent to her, his body maintaining a stiffness that she'd noticed as soon as she'd walked into his living room.

"Where's Molly?" he asked.

He hadn't been the only one to notice her absence; Gertie had displayed no small amount of confusion at Hannah's appearance without the small charge who usually accompanied her. Even as Hannah and Jeremy continued sitting at the table, Gertie seemed to observe every noise exterior to the house as if it signaled the arrival of her missing friend and would rise, approach the front door, wait for a short period of time, and return, flopping dejected at Jeremy's feet beneath the table.

"She's with her grandparents. They're in town for her birthday this week," Hannah explained.

"Oh, that's nice. I thought they didn't like to travel."

"They don't," Hannah replied. "But I guess they decided it was worth it when Michael told them we wouldn't be coming to Boston for Christmas."

"How long are they in town?" he asked, though there was no real reason for him to have any interest in the travel plans of her in-laws, and it seemed more probable he was just trying to fill the silence.

"Just till tomorrow. Then they fly back," she said, and the silence stretched out between them again.

Hannah noticed the creases of Jeremy's shirt—a light blue Oxford she assumed had been a Christmas gift newly unfolded from its box. He wore it tucked into a pair of gray flannel trousers. He'd been expecting company and had dressed for it.

"How was your Christm—" Hannah began just as Jeremy offered an unprompted, "I wanted to apologize for—"

"Go ahead," he invited.

"No. It's fine. You go," she returned.

"I just wanted to apologize for overstepping in your research before Christmas. I feel really bad about that. I should have asked before pulling Kate onto your project," he said, plucking a loose thread from his pants.

"You did ask," Hannah pointed out. "And it was a good idea to involve her. And I wouldn't say I'm doing research. I'm just curious. And if I were doing research, I wouldn't know how to do it, so—"

A knock at the front door served as both interruption and salvation, and Jeremy rose from his seat and opened it to his colleague. It was strange to see Kate in actual clothes. Dispossessed of her Lycra and sports bra, she wore a pair of navy-blue pants and a gray turtleneck sweater, her eyes more prominent with the accentuation of mascara and eye shadow.

"Happy New Year!" Kate announced. She handed her coat to Jeremy in a movement probably better suited to an interaction with the coat check attendant at a restaurant. Jeremy seemed not at all bothered at being treated like the hired help in his own home.

"Would you like something to drink?" he offered both of the women now sitting at his kitchen table. "I have coffee, Diet Coke, water, La Croix... I guess it's a tad early for wine..."

"Coffee, please," Kate said without hesitation.

"Same, please," Hannah added.

Jeremy pulled two mugs from the cabinet and poured coffee into them, delivering them to the table with cream and sugar.

"I take it black," Kate said, with a flit of her eyes to the sugar dish and bag of creamers.

"They're for Hannah," Jeremy said and resumed his seat at the table as Hannah poured a spoon full of sugar into her mug.

"So, let's talk about this house of yours," Kate began, addressing Hannah as she lifted the screen of her laptop and took a sip of her coffee.

"I did look into it just a little before Christmas," Jeremy said.

"I knew you wouldn't be able to help yourself," Kate said with a chuckle. "He's interesting, isn't he? Decker, I mean."

"I didn't get very far," Jeremy admitted. "Did you look into his uncle? I think he might've been a labor organizer."

"Well, that would go a long way to explaining some of the awkwardness at that wedding." Kate dropped her eyes to her computer screen, evidently consulting some source she had on the matter. "Here's what I've got so far. Decker's wife, Eleanor Dailey, she was the only daughter—the only child—of Walter Dailey. He owned Dailey Limestone down in Bedford, which was one of the original handful of limestone companies in the area. The first quarry, as you know, was Stinesville, which opened in 1827." She looked to Jeremy with this, evidently assuming it was something he would know. Jeremy said nothing to reveal whether, in fact, he did. "The Daileys opened their quarry in 1842 and by the time the 1920s rolled around, it was one of the five largest limestone operations in Indiana. Which, as a practical matter, made it one of the largest limestone companies in the world."

Hannah's eyebrows lifted as she received this information, and Kate took a sip of her coffee and continued. "You probably already know this, but Indiana limestone has been incredibly important to the construction of this country. It began to rise in popularity as a building material after the fires in Boston and Chicago in the 1870s. People realized, you know, stone doesn't burn the way wood does; maybe we should be building—especially residential buildings—with stone. I don't know what to say about the fact that this didn't dawn on folks until 1870."

Jeremy offered a chortle at this remark, and Hannah settled into her chair, sipping her coffee as Kate hit her stride.

"By the 1920s when the Deckers were married and building this neighborhood, more than ninety-five percent of the limestone used for building in the United States was coming from Indiana."

"Wow," Hannah breathed.

"Yeah. I mean, it's not as sexy as the gold rush or anywhere near as profitable as steel or oil, but it was plenty profitable, not to mention important. Biltmore is built with Indiana limestone. So is the Empire State Building, the Washington Monument, the state house in Harrisburg, Pennsylvania. I could go on. Basically, if you see limestone on a building anywhere in this country that was built between about 1880 and 1935, it is almost certainly limestone from Indiana."

Kate clicked a few strokes on her computer as she appeared to be switching documents and glanced up at Jeremy and Hannah, both of whom listened intently.

"Some of the original quarry owners back in the first half of the nineteenth century were sons of English aristocracy, so there was old money floating through the quarries, too. I don't know if Walter Dailey was part of that, but the time period is right. I still have more research to do on that. Then, as you might imagine, once that boom hit at the turn of the twentieth century, investors and businessmen came here from New York, Chicago, all over Europe, all trying to buy quarries or part ownership in them. There were consolidations and then individuals broke off, then re-merged. It was just, well, the wild Midwest," she said, clearly finding the comment clever.

"Dailey Limestone Limited—that's what the company was originally called—seems like maybe it was part of some of those consolidations, but honestly, it's pretty hard to trace that history. That's going to take some time. It looks like it was still relatively independent even through the mid-1920s. And I'd assume very profitable. There was a time when Indiana limestone revenues totaled about $300 million a year in today's dollars." She squinted her eyes at her computer screen as if trying to confirm the figures. "Jeremy tells me you managed to find out a little bit about Decker, too?" She directed this to Hannah, a twinkle in her eye. Hannah could see Kate was hooked, and she understood why.

"Yes. Andrew—he was the son of a physician, Henry Decker. In Bedford. And his mom's name was Ida, but I don't know her maiden name."

"Ida's a nickname. You don't know her full name?" Kate asked.

"Um, no. Sorry."

"It's fine. Continue," Kate said with a flip of her hand.

"Yes. Okay. He—Andrew—was born in 1889."

"That makes sense," Kate interrupted. "I mean, if we assume his mother was part of the Italian immigration that came here after the unification of Italy. You'd probably know more about that history than I would." She looked at Jeremy again.

"Not if it doesn't intersect with medicine," Jeremy returned.

"Well, anyway, I agree with you, Jeremy, that Decker's uncle was probably one of those twenty Italian stonecutters Dailey hired. I mean, he almost had to be. You think he was a labor organizer? That would make sense. The stonecutters did eventually form unions."

"Could've been. I only scratched the surface on that during winter break."

Kate turned to Hannah. "Do you know anything else about his family?"

"Um... He had two younger brothers and a younger sister. But his brothers died in World War One," Hannah said.

"Very good. Not that they died. Just that you've got a handle on his biography."

Hannah accepted the strange compliment as she began to see how Kate had already organized their respective responsibilities. Kate had researched the quarries and, consequently, the Daileys, including Eleanor. Jeremy might be able to translate family documents and could supply some information about Italian immigration to Indiana and perhaps to the United States, more broadly. But Kate looked to Hannah to supply information on Andrew Decker, himself—after all, she was now living in his home.

"So, Eleanor Dailey Decker is essentially the heir apparent to a pretty extensive quarry operation at what was the height of the limestone industry, 1922-1932. When did they marry?"

"1920," Hannah said. The neatly scripted names and date from the wedding album drifted through her mind.

"Yeah, they're right there in what local historians call 'The Decade of Dominance.' Anyway, her father has no one else to leave it to. It has got to be making serious money given the year. And she comes home saying she's going to marry the nephew of one of the cutters in the quarry."

"We were thinking—Jeremy and I—that all that might have been what caused the argument or falling out between Andrew and his uncle. That's why Andrew didn't want his uncle at his wedding," Hannah said.

"I don't know that I'm entirely convinced it was Decker who forbade him from coming. I could imagine Eleanor's family might've had some thoughts on that matter. Either way, it's a shitty thing to do, though I can't say I'm surprised given the time." She took another sip of coffee. "Not to mention this state."

"This state?" Hannah asked.

"I guess it's a little early for the Klan—1920," she said. "When did the KKK try to organize that march down in Evansville?" She seemed to be asking Jeremy, who now sat, lips parted, eyes wide.

"I'm sorry. What?" he asked, having as much trouble as Hannah at following Kate's rapid-fire procession of information.

Kate glanced between the two, waiting for either one to supply some explanation. When neither did, she continued. "There was an enormous amount of anti-immigrant sentiment in Indiana around this time. Not just in Indiana, really. Throughout the whole country."

"People keep describing him that way—" Hannah said.

"What people? What way?" Kate asked.

"Like he was this poor, immigrant kid. I don't think he was. I mean, he wasn't," Hannah argued, asserting her expertise if only on this one point. "He graduated from Columbia. He fought in World War One. He worked in New York City as an architect before he came back to Indiana. He wasn't even a kid. He was thirty-seven when he built the Decker house. Isn't that enough?"

"Isn't that enough?" Jeremy echoed, almost a whisper.

Kate glanced at him, and he quickly diverted his gaze to the top of the table.

"Yeah, I hear you," Kate said, a gentle smile directed to Hannah. "But I think we forget how hard those lines were to cross back then. Especially in this state. And even if Decker had managed to cross them, that doesn't mean his uncle had. You have to remember, the first time this country passed a law requiring a visa for entry was in 1924, and Italians were one of the groups that law targeted."

Hannah felt a familiar sour mood return and busied herself trying to negotiate with a hangnail on her thumb. Beside her, Jeremy's chair scooted against the tile of the floor as he brought his outstretched legs under him. From the corner of her eye, she thought she caught a brief look of discomfort passing over his face and wondered whether he understood something about how hard *those lines* were to cross even today.

"Well, anyway," Kate said, bringing the cadence of her seminar down. "It would have been a complicated relationship. Especially given the religious issues."

"Oh my," Hannah sighed, thinking there really could not be much more, though apparently there was. "What religious issues?"

"Well, she's Protestant. Definitely. But if his funeral was at Holy Rosary, and he's buried in St. Joseph's, and he's Italian, he's Catholic. And so, on top of everything else, that can't have made her family very happy."

"How is he buried in a Catholic cemetery if he died by suicide?" Jeremy asked somewhat suddenly. "Didn't the Church have rules against that back then?"

"A lot of that depended on the individual priest, whether he would look the other way," Kate said. "Maybe he did, here."

Hannah finished the last of her coffee, which had turned cold and tasted bitter and chalky against her tongue. The discussions around the complexities of Andrew's marriage, his relationship with his family, his position in society, hell, even where he was allowed to be buried— these things had bothered Hannah deeply for reasons which had initially eluded her but, after today, were embarrassingly plain.

"That's a lot to take in," Jeremy said, his thoughts apparently converging with Hannah's.

"Yeah," Kate agreed. "Look, it's the beginning of the semester, and I don't know how much time you both have, but I'd like to keep looking into this. I'm not sure where it'll go. Maybe nowhere. But do either of you have any objection to me doing a little more digging?"

Hannah and Jeremy shook their heads. Hannah thought she wouldn't mind doing a little more digging herself, though she wasn't quite sure how to go about that.

Sensing that the meeting was coming to a close, she thanked Kate and Jeremy for their time, for humoring her "silly curiosities." Kate quickly pointed out that none of it seemed silly to her, and she hoped Hannah would update her if she learned anything more about the Deckers.

With their meeting concluded, Jeremy walked Hannah to the door, asking if she planned to "be in the neighborhood" next week. She would be. She stood there for just a second too long, unsure how to part ways, the entryway itself seeming to call for exchanges that did not suit them. Ultimately, Hannah leaned forward and hugged Jeremy, a strange and uncomfortable embrace that he returned, patting her on the back before pulling away.

He then offered a tentative, "Okay then," before closing the door and presumably returning to the table where Kate sat, having made no qualms about the fact she wasn't yet ready to leave.

☙❦❧

"Hey," Hannah said, leaning against the frame of the office door.

Michael had been at his computer for most of the day, breaking only to take his parents to the airport, but otherwise isolated in his office for the rest of the Saturday. He swiveled his chair to face her, his eyes glassy from the amount of the day he'd spent staring at his computer screen.

"What's up?" he asked, raising his eyebrows in attention.

"I just thought I'd see how you're doing," she said. "Did your parents catch their flight okay?"

"I'm assuming they did. I haven't heard from them since I dropped them off." Michael rested a forearm on the desk as if he wanted to be able to spin as quickly as possible back to his laptop.

"Are you working on Basingstoke stuff?" she asked.

"Yeah. I'm really behind because of their visit. My dad just sucks my will to live. I'm basically going to have to make up an entire week of work over this weekend. Do you have anything fun planned for next week? Anything interesting happening at the house?" He tapped his fingers lightly on the top of the desk.

"Gary thought he might bring Cora by for a playdate with Molly," Hannah said.

"Who's Cora?"

"His grand-daughter. She turned two in November. I know you wanted Molly to be around some other children her own age."

"That's not really what I meant—" Michael started, but at the sound of her name, Molly ambled into the office before Michael could clarify. She stood in the center of the room, wearing a pair of red corduroy overalls with tiny sheep embroidered on the smock and glanced back and forth between her two parents.

"Is that one of the outfits my mom bought her?" Michael asked.

Hannah nodded. The outfit came with a white crocheted cardigan, but Hannah had taken that off for lunch and not put it back on her.

"It's cute," Michael said, his finger tapping increasing its tempo.

Molly seemed encouraged by this compliment and toddled over to her father, placing a hand on the top of his leg.

"Oh! She wants to sit on your lap," Hannah said. "Do you want Daddy to pick you up?" Hannah asked Molly, who lifted her arms up toward Michael. He reached down and brought her onto his lap.

"Stay right there," Hannah said. "Let me go get my phone. I want a picture of the two of you together."

She spun from the doorway, heading to the living room as Michael called after her, "Wait! Where are you going?"

It took just a minute to find her phone. When she returned to the office, however, Michael had already turned back to his computer, Molly was meandering over to a bookcase next to the window.

"What happened?" Hannah asked. "I wanted a picture."

"She started trying to play with the keyboard," Michael said over his shoulder. "Listen, Hannah, I know it's the weekend, but I have to get caught up. Can you close the door, please?"

"Of course," Hannah said, putting her phone in her back pocket. She picked Molly up before she could begin removing the binders from Michael's bookshelf, left the office, and closed the door behind her.

CHAPTER 15

When Jeremy and Gertie caught up with Hannah and Molly, they'd already completed their first lap around the neighborhood. Jeremy fell into step alongside them, and Molly's small, mittened hand extended out from her stroller to rest on Gertie's back. Hannah turned to him, offering an apprehensive smile.

"I thought maybe you weren't home," she said.

In truth, she'd worried that he was avoiding her. The way they'd parted at his door had left her with a strange sense of distance. She blamed herself for this, first for her terse response to his conversation before Christmas, then for her inability to navigate a socially adept good-bye when she left after their meeting with Kate.

"I was on a call," he said, pleasantly. If he felt any residual strangeness, he hid it well. "My sister is due in March and just found out she's having a boy."

"Oh! Congratulations... to her. Also, to you. What do you say to uncles?"

"Congratulations probably works. I wanted to give you this," he said, extending a folder.

With both hands on the stroller, Hannah had trouble taking it from him. She initially placed it on the umbrella of the stroller, but the wind threatened to blow it to the ground. She looked to the basket below the stroller, but crinkled her nose in disapproval of that location, damp from the winter slush that the wheels had spun up.

"I'll hold it till we get to your driveway," he offered.

"What is it?" she asked as he tucked the folder under his elbow.

"Newspaper articles. I asked our department librarian to pull everything he could find on Decker from the local papers. He got them to me yesterday. I gave Kate a set, too, but I've only skimmed them."

"Oh! Thank you," Hannah said.

Molly's hand slid off Gertie's back, falling against the armrest of the stroller. Gertie, persistent as always, nudged the little hand with her nose, but couldn't coax its slumbering owner to return it to her back.

"You gave a set to Kate? I had coffee with her and Laura Kramer this morning, and she didn't mention them," Hannah said.

"I forgot Laura Kramer's at that studio. I cycle with her husband," Jeremy said.

"She mentioned that," Hannah said with some control.

"God. Everyone goes there. Maybe I should sign up," Jeremy said, lowering his voice.

"I think you'd be very popular," Hannah said and then swallowed the remaining air in her mouth as she realized the words in her head had come tumbling out of her lips. "I just mean—There aren't—It's mostly just women. It's all women. Well, and Rob. But he's an instructor, so he doesn't count. And I think he's gay. But I don't know that. I shouldn't presume. And not that gay people don't count."

"We're at your driveway," Jeremy said, interrupting Hannah, who was doing a marvelous job stumbling over her uncomfortable narration of the client and instructor rosters at her exercise studio.

"Oh, right." She turned toward the house. A cheery yellow, it was a stark contrast against the gray January sky. Several trucks were visible from the road, and it was evident that work continued on the house.

"Do you want to see the progress they've made?" she asked.

"Sure," he said.

Hannah led Jeremy inside the house and parked Molly's stroller in the study against the far wall in front of the bookshelves. With the addition of electricity to the house, she'd been able to plug in a baby monitor along with a space heater—a large black cylinder that rotated in one direction, paused, then rotated back. Its consistent low hum did a reasonable job drowning out the construction noise that still dominated other corners of the house. She ushered Jeremy and a very confused Gertie out into the living room, closing the pocket doors of the study behind them, and sequestering Molly in at least some amount of solitude for her nap.

"Is that you, Hannah?" called one of the workers from the other half of the house. Hannah waited until she'd crossed the foyer into the kitchen to answer.

"Yeah, it's me. I brought a neighbor who wanted to see the work," she said, which was sort of true.

Jason met them in the kitchen, pausing, a silent exchange seeming to pass between the two men before Jason extended a hand in introduction. Jeremy attempted to return the gesture, but this was complicated by the folder he still held and by the dog leash that occupied his other hand. The two accomplished something resembling a half-wave, half-handshake, before Jason began with the update he usually provided to Hannah when she dropped by.

"The electric is continuing to come along. We've got nearly all of the first floor and some of the second done," Jason reported. "We haven't really started on the attic because the architect hasn't been able to come by and look at it yet. There just won't be any power going to those lines, and we can replace them when we finally get up there. We're waiting to do the owners' suite, too, until we move the walls."

Hannah saw Jeremy nodding along as if his agreement had been sought.

"The plumbing is taking a little more time, but we'll get there," Jason went on. "Gary's coming by later today with the HVAC guy to start roughing out the plans for the heating and A/C."

Gertie, tired from her walk, sat heavily on her haunches and slid her paws forward, lying down between Jeremy and Hannah.

"Your dog nice?" The question was directed to Jeremy.

"Oh yeah. She's a one-hundred-fifty-pound puppy. The most dangerous part of her is her tail," Jeremy said with a chuckle.

Jason reached down and patted Gertie on the head to test this out and was met immediately with a full roll of the dog onto her back, inviting belly-scratches, which Jason supplied.

"I'm going to show Jeremy the rest of the house," Hannah said as Jason stood back up.

"Sounds like a plan," he replied. Hannah thought she saw that same wordless exchange pass between the two men once more.

The tour didn't take long given the state of demolition of the house, with many of the rooms limiting them due to their "look from the doorway only" condition. But she enjoyed having someone to talk to about her plans, the expansion of the owners' suite, the consolidation of the multiple small guest rooms, the tile that could be salvaged from several of the bathrooms. On the third floor, she explained her idea for creating a suite for Molly to read and study and play, and all along the way, Jeremy offered a mused commentary of pleasant remarks: "That'll be really nice." "I would have loved that when I was a kid." "That's going to look great when it's finished."

They completed the tour descending a set of stairs to the kitchen where Jason had resumed work, pausing as the two of them cut through the kitchen back out to the foyer. True to Jeremy's warning, Gertie nearly knocked over a strategically positioned tripod light as she bumped her way through.

"Sorry about that," Jeremy said, quickly righting the light as Hannah took Gertie's leash from him.

As they crossed into the foyer, Jeremy took the folder from under his arm. "Where should I put this?" he asked.

"I'll take it," Hannah said, trading him the leash for the folder. "Do you want to read through some of this with me?"

"I flipped through some of it already, but sure," he said and followed Hannah into the living room where she set the folder on the sideboard, opening it flat.

The contents amounted to: one newspaper engagement announcement; a short article about Andrew Decker's return to Bedford from New York following World War I; the obituary of Dr. Henry Decker from 1929; the obituary of Mrs. Idalia Filannino Decker from 1934; and a handful of articles about the quarries, along with the articles concerning both Eleanor's and Andrew's deaths, which Hannah had already found on her own.

Jeremy reached over Hannah's arm for the obituary of Henry Decker, reading it to himself before offering a: "Yeah, that's what I figured."

"What did you figure?" Hannah asked.

Jeremy unclipped Gertie's leash, and she trotted over to a spot in front of the green velvet sofa where she promptly collapsed onto the rug, dropping her head and closing her eyes.

"His dad. Decker's dad. He was just a little country doctor. This was very common in Indiana—well, throughout the Midwest—at this time. See, says here he emigrated from Germany after completing his medical training there, and then he was a general practitioner in Bedford. Doctors then weren't like they are now. It was very informal here. It wouldn't have necessarily been prestigious to be a doctor or have a father who was one when Decker was growing up, though that's probably how he could afford to go to Columbia. I'll also say, if his father was educated in Germany, which he may have been, he would have been one of the better doctors in the area. Either way, his practice was in a small town mostly before the medical school here was even built."

Hannah listened attentively as Jeremy went on.

"These other articles look interesting." He spread them across the top of the sideboard. "What are these?" he asked, his attention suddenly drawn to the cardboard tubes resting against the back of the sideboard.

"Oh, I think those are more blueprints from Fritz Bothers—the developers who were working on the house back in 2017," Hannah said still focused on Henry Decker's obituary. "I found them in the garage under their work bench. They must have had their tools set up out there."

"I don't think so," Jeremy said. He lifted one of the tubes, examining it more closely. "They look older than that." He turned it over in his hands. "May I?" he asked, requesting to open the tube.

"Sure. I haven't bothered. I was going to wait for the architect who'll be working on the attic."

Jeremy removed the cardboard cap from the end of the tube and carefully pulled out its rolled contents. Laying it flat, he secured the four corners with his house keys, the dog leash, and two green vases.

"Oh, Hannah," he said, his voice melodic.

"What?" she asked. She felt his arm against hers through her coat as she came closer, trying to see. Without speaking, he pointed to the black inked signature along the bottom right hand of the blueprint.

"Hannah. These are Decker's. His blueprints."

Hannah leaned over and saw it, too. Slightly distorted and not perfectly preserved after unknown years in the garage, but the signature unmistakable:

Andrew L. Decker

"These are the plans he didn't build," Jeremy said after opening two of the five tubes.

The first contained three residential blueprints; the second contained what appeared to be an unfinished plan for an office or possibly an apartment building.

"Look at this one," he said, directing Hannah's attention to the apartment building.

Replacing the plans in the tubes, Jeremy stepped back. "I think you might have all of his unfinished blueprints here," he said, running a hand over the row of cardboard tubes, delicate, almost reverent. "You have to take these to the historical society. And you need to be very careful with them."

Hannah turned, examining his profile, his eyes wide as though he gazed upon treasure, and perhaps from the perspective of an historian, he did.

"What would the historical society do with them?" Hannah asked.

"I don't really know," Jeremy said. "But they sure as hell wouldn't end up on the floor of a garage again." He regarded the tubes a bit longer as if trying to determine what he should do with them.

"I'll keep them safe," Hannah promised.

"Yeah," he said, noncommittally.

Silence fell over the living room, the only sound coming from the construction taking place on the other side of the house. At some length, Jeremy patted the tubes again seemingly willing them to stay safe and said, "Listen, I'm going to head out. I still haven't finished preparing for my class tomorrow."

Gertie seemed to know departure was imminent and rose from the carpet.

Hannah walked Jeremy to the door, electing a well-executed wave of the hand and a friendly, "See you later," before returning to the living room and settling into the green velvet couch to review the rest of the newspaper articles the librarian had provided.

The articles had been arranged in the manila folder in chronological order, which struck Hannah as a very history-professor-kind-of-thing to do, and at the bottom of each article, the librarian had written the date and source from which the article had been printed.

The first article, a somber piece from *The Bedford Gazette*, dated February 22, 1919, reported the return of Andrew L. Decker to Indiana following the end of the World War. Although the article tried to couch the return of the Deckers' eldest child as a joyful homecoming, there was no avoiding the connection between Andrew's return and "the fragile health of Mrs. Henry Decker following the deaths of the two younger Decker boys in Italy."

The article recited many of the same accolades Andrew's obituary had highlighted, but commented further that "while the circumstances of Mr. Decker's return are overshadowed by the horrors of war and the tragedies of his brothers' deaths, the expertise he brings with him after his time in the employ of one of New York's most prestigious architecture firms is bound to inure to the benefit of our capital city to the north, where Mr. Decker has chosen to reside." The article further commented that Andrew had accepted a position with the firm of Matson Architecture & Design, Ltd., and would begin work there the following month.

A photograph of Andrew accompanied the article, small but no question it was him. An official portrait of the time, Andrew would have been in his late twenties based on the dates of the war and his return to Indiana. He wore his full military uniform, buttoned, pressed and with his cap upon his head, his expression stoic and at a slight angle. The photograph didn't reveal whether he'd yet laid eyes on the horrors the article mentioned almost in passing, or whether his brothers still lived as he gazed intently, as he almost assuredly had been directed by the photographer.

An engagement announcement next caught Hannah's attention—Andrew Lawrence Decker (30) to Eleanor Alice Dailey (26). The article confirmed the description of that relationship offered by Kate and Jeremy the previous week, describing Eleanor as the sole child of Walter and Lottie (deceased) Dailey, of Bedford, Indiana, but oddly omitting reference to Andrew's family, altogether. The announcement described Eleanor as having graduated from Indiana University in 1916, since which time she'd been working closely with her father "learning the operations of the trade that will one day pass to her." It struck Hannah as unusual that a woman should be so integrated into her father's business during this era. But she assumed that either Walter Dailey had been a surprisingly progressive man for the time—surely some had to exist, even in Indiana—or he'd reconciled himself to the fact he didn't have any other options and had to make do with the daughter God gave him.

"Maybe both," Hannah said aloud as she continued reading.

The article also detailed how the couple met. Having returned to Indiana from New York "where Mr. Decker completed his education and had been working for a firm in the city," Andrew had accepted a position with Matson, and found himself negotiating with Dailey Limestone, Ltd. for the purchase of their product and the expertise of their carvers to be used on the residential buildings Matson was constructing in the up-and-coming neighborhoods directly north of downtown. It was during these negotiations that "the established architect had cause to cross paths with the beautiful and tenacious daughter of Walter Dailey."

"Beautiful and tenacious," Hannah whispered into the room. She hadn't thought of Eleanor as especially "tenacious." In the photographs of her, she'd appeared delicate, refined, demure. But she was, evidently, tenacious. At least in the opinion of whoever had drafted the announcement of her engagement. The wedding was to take place on Saturday, June 19, 1920, at St. John's Episcopal Church in Bedford, Indiana.

Hannah looked at the notation at the bottom of the article, which provided the date—March 3, 1920—with an additional notation in a different handwriting, which she assumed was Jeremy's: "Pregnant?" The meaning unambiguous in light of the short length of the engagement. But Margaret had been born in 1923, so if Eleanor was pregnant in 1920, that pregnancy had not ultimately produced a child, nor would the subsequent marriage for more than two and a half years.

Finally, the librarian had included a handful of articles that outlined the consolidation of various quarries, their purchase and sale. These articles, totaling seven in number, showed a history of mergers followed by acrimonious dissolutions, rapid purchases of new land to be quarried, the short-lived establishment of a subsequent company, followed by another merger. Hannah couldn't follow their chronology, but Dailey Limestone, Ltd. featured in each of them.

She checked her phone. Molly slept soundly, but it was nearly time to wake her. She opened the pocket doors allowing the commotion of the house to filter into the study and took the folder to the desk, placing it in the center drawer. She had some awareness that her decision to place the articles in the desk reflected not only an attempt to secret them away from Michael, who she imagined would find her "research" at best uninteresting and at worst downright weird. The location also served as tacit recognition of a distinct relationship to the objects. The desk itself and its contents belonged to Andrew, both merely having come into Hannah's possession. She likewise moved the cardboard tubes with Andrew's blueprints into the study, placing them on top of the rows of books within the shelves.

Molly stirred in her stroller, not fully awake, and Hannah sat at the desk. The "desk chair" was a cold, gray metal folding chair in unfortunate condition. Of the many thoughts that passed through Hannah's mind as she pulled the chair in behind her, one included that she probably should buy a true desk chair for the room. The black "ergonomic" office chair Michael already owned was completely ill-suited to this room and to the desk that would be its companion.

The other thoughts that passed through her mind included the image of Andrew sitting on this very desk, one leg stretched out, slightly bent at the knee, supporting his weight as he smiled at the camera; the image of him in profile, contemplative, focused, standing at a drafting table, which long ago had been discarded—no sign of it anywhere in the house. By the arrangement of the study, it must have stood near the French doors looking out on the front lawn. Hannah recalled the way the light came through the glass and filtered in over Andrew giving the photograph the appearance of having been taken through the thinnest sheath of gauze.

Finally, Hannah couldn't stop herself from thinking, even as she sat at the desk itself, of Andrew's final moments there. Of his body slumped to the side in the chair that once had surely been there. Or had he fallen forward with the force of that fatal event?

These thoughts, she knew, should have inclined her to omit the desk from the salvation of her yellow Post-its, leaving it, like so many other things, to the fate of the Fire Dawgs. But they didn't, and as Hannah ran her fingers over the grains of oak, smoothing them as though they were the wayward strands of his tousled hair, she felt that her proximity to the desk was an act of comfort where one might expect revulsion. And she regretted only that she offered such comfort far too late.

CHAPTER 16

"Hey. What's the status of getting Molly into pre-school?" Michael asked as Hannah sat on the couch with her laptop on her thighs and Molly at her feet.

Hannah responded, relaying a summary of Indianapolis's early childhood education according to the script Kate had composed for her—a paragraph she'd rehearsed no fewer than twenty times in anticipation of this very question.

"A year and a half!?" Michael exclaimed, as if Hannah bore some personal responsibility for the inadequate systems of education for toddlers in Indiana.

To compensate, Hannah explained that she'd already made appointments to tour three of the city's independent private schools, which were the only institutions that provided full-day preschool five days a week. Michael seemed somewhat satisfied by this—she'd demonstrated she wasn't trying to sabotage the effort altogether. But Hannah couldn't help thinking that in addition to blaming her for the lack of preschools, really, Michael was berating her for the existence of the child altogether. This was arguably a fairer assignment of culpability and one for which Hannah had never, not for a single second of the last two years, ever felt regret.

"What are you doing?" Michael asked as Hannah returned her attention to her computer. He'd calmed down marginally, but his voice seemed to hold some disbelief that Hannah could be doing anything, having so wholly failed at the simple task of finding a preschool.

"Emailing the history professor at Butler," she said.

"That guy in our neighborhood?"

Hannah lifted her eyes to find her husband trying to appear disinterested, and in so trying, appearing anything but.

"No," she said. "The other one. Kate." The response was incomplete, but effective. Michael returned his attention to the television.

"Something with your exercise studio?" he asked.

"No. I told her that we'd moved into the Decker house, and she's interested in knowing more about the architect." Incomplete again. "I'm emailing her to see if she wants to meet up and talk." Not strictly true. But also, evidently not of interest to Michael, who un-paused the television.

"Sam cycles with Jeremy in some club that meets at Butler all summer long. Said the guy's a real train wreck," Michael said, his eyes still fixed on the television. "I guess his fiancée left him last summer. Took a job at another university without telling him and just up and left him at the end of the school year. Sam said he moped about it all summer long."

Moped about it, Hannah thought. Does one mope when his fiancée leaves him, when he didn't see it coming, when he arrives home one afternoon to find the person he thought he would marry just... gone? Would Michael have moped about that? Would Michael mope if he came home now and she was just... gone?

Hannah didn't ask any of these questions. Instead, she clicked "send" on her email, muttering under her breath, "Small town, big buildings."

"What?" Michael asked, his voice barely audible.

"Nothing. I'm going to bed."

"I'll be in after this episode," he said, turning his face, but not his eyes, in her direction.

THE LIGHT of the moon washing across the stairs cast shadows on Hannah's bare feet as she stepped lightly on the soft red weave of the runner. A thin white chemise blew around her calves as the chill of the night air moved through the thin fabric. Winter. It was winter, and the house held the cold.

Over the banister, Hannah could see the construction debris below: sawhorses, tools, the giant lights set atop tripods, plugged into brand new, twenty-first century outlets. The men had gone for the day. They'd be back tomorrow. But the presence of the tools without the crew somehow made the house seem even quieter, the capacity for sound, and its present absence, augmenting the silence.

Above her, at the top of the stairs, sat a bench, its yellow uphol-stery thick and curved over the armrests. Funny. She didn't remember buying it. Though maybe she had when she'd bought the chair for the study. Along the walls, photographs. Someone else's family. Not hers. She stopped at one in particular, running her fingers over the wooden frame and glass. She knew this man, his obsidian eyes staring at her, his ebony hair neatly combed in the style of men at that time.

She shivered, an involuntary and nearly imperceptible movement of her shoulders that traveled down the sides of her torso. She wrapped her arms around herself and felt her skin, bare. No wonder she was cold. And then the warmth of a blazer placed around her shoulders. Heavy. Wool. Carrying an unfamiliar scent, a spice reminiscent of black pepper, traces of citrus and pine rising above.

She turned to see a man, familiar. She knew him. His eyes, as black as the midnight expanse of the house, matching his hair, rested on her. He wore a vest over his white shirt, unbuttoned now, his tie loosened at his neck. It was the end of his day, too.

He looked past her to the photograph, and Hannah turned, following his gaze, seeing that they were one and the same, this man on the stairs standing next to her and the man in the photograph hanging on the wall. When she faced him again, she found his eyes had returned to her, and she reached up touching his mouth, the tips of her fingers pressing lightly. She'd expected her fingers to move through him —a ghost, she thought. But her touch met with the resistance of his flesh, and his hand reached for her wrist as he held her fingers to his lips, the pressure of a kiss.

Hannah heard the insinuation of a breeze between them, the house itself seeming to breathe, then she realized the movement of the air was a sigh that had escaped her own throat. He released her hand to her side but held her gaze, his eyes focused on her as the corners of his lips curved almost delicately into a smile, which she found herself returning as if in introduction.

Hi, I'm Hannah, she would have said.

The smile left his face, and his eyes traveled down to her shoulder, where, beneath the blazer, he placed a finger so very lightly under the thin spaghetti strap of her chemise, allowing the width of silk to slide down her arm. His eyes rejoined hers, his head tilting to the side as he posed his silent invitation. Hannah lifted her hand to her other shoulder in answer, sliding the strap down the other arm until the entire chemise drifted to her ankles in a pool of moonlit silk, and she stood before him in nothing but the black blazer he'd wrapped around her.

He stepped toward her, and Hannah thought she saw behind the blackness of his eyes an emotion she knew—a hopeful despair, a knowledge of disappointment and a refusal to surrender to it. He lifted a hand to her breast, his hand brushing over her as she closed her eyes against the sensation of him. She had expected, when she opened them again, that he'd be gone, vanished back into whatever liminal space he'd emerged from. But she found him there still, his hands so firmly on her body, she thought it possible he might pick her up and carry her the remainder of the steps.

But he did not.

He moved her gently to recline on the stairs, coaxing her below him, the blazer falling open around her body as he knelt between her legs.

"Andrew," she whispered, leaning back, offering herself to him. "Andrew," she said again, and his eyes flashed, the moonlight striking them as they set upon her with the act of her naming him. He dropped his mouth to her breast, and she felt his tongue, his teeth, his lips on her.

On the ceiling—she had never noticed before, not truly—the moulding formed a perfect perimeter, a small piece of crown that traced the outline of the foyer in a near perfect square. The fixture that hung from the center was not a chandelier, or not what one thought of when one thinks of a chandelier. It was a single pendant positioned at the level of the landing itself. Hannah was thinking about the fact that she had never once seen that fixture emit light, even now with electricity running to it. She had never once seen Gary's workers try to turn it on or mention to her that it should be rewired. She was thinking about this when she felt his mouth between her legs, his hands against her hips, his tongue seeking, exploring.

Her back lifted involuntarily off the stairs even as he held her hips steady, and she was so close. A little more of him and she would be there.

"Andrew," she called to him, hearing his name echo through the house, and he looked up, his dark eyes finding hers, and she was so close.

"Hey!"

Hannah blinked, trying to focus, trying to find him again in the night.

"Hey!"

"What?" she whispered into the dark. "What's happening?"

She blinked again and saw Michael above her, leaning over, nudging her shoulder rather aggressively.

"You tell me?" he said. "Who the fuck is Andrew?"

Hannah scrambled to the top of the bed, nearly head-butting Michael in the process. She pulled the sheet up over her chest, thinking she needed to cover her breasts, but realized they were covered. She was wearing her pajamas.

"I asked you who Andrew is," he said angrily, nearly yelling.

"I—I don't know what's happening," she stuttered, and truly she didn't. She was in the bungalow, Michael next to her. But she didn't want to be. She wanted to go back, and the desperation grew as the dream receded, her mind grasping at the silver light in his black eyes, and his hands holding her waist, and his mouth on her body. But the images slipped through her fingers as though she'd been grasping the fog that sometimes rolled in off the Harbor.

"Answer me, god damnit," Michael yelled.

"I—I don't know," Hannah pleaded. The dream faded, the fog burning off, leaving behind nothing but the sensation of distant warmth and safety amid present cold and confusion. "I don't know what's going on."

From the room across the hall, Hannah heard Molly begin to cry; her father's yelling had awakened her. Her father's yelling had awakened her, and she was scared, and Hannah felt panic seize her and shake her as violently as she'd been woken from the dream itself.

"You woke up Molly," she growled, connecting with that most real element of her consciousness.

"Who. Is. Andrew?" Michael asked, each word its own accusation.

"I don't know any fucking Andrew!" It was the panic speaking, the need to be released from Michael's questions so she could attend to Molly, so she could move the black wool blazer, warm around her shoulders, to the furthest corners of her mind where other forgotten dreams resided.

Michael clamped his mouth shut, shocked by both her language and her sudden ferocity, and he lifted his hands, a gesture of both his surrender and his refusal to get up to attend to his daughter. Hannah threw back the covers and got out of bed, crossing the hall to Molly's room to comfort the scared child and rock her back to sleep.

CHAPTER 17

Molly insisted on walking rather than being carried, and so up the two of them went on the lavender granite staircase of Butler University's School of Liberal Arts and Sciences, one tread at a time. Students skirted around them offering a range of salutations from annoyed huffs to delighted coos.

As they arrived on the second floor of the three-story building, Hannah moved to the side and consulted the directions Kate had texted her.

> Kate: Off the stairs, to the right, down the hall,
> room 247.

"Room 247," Hannah said under her breath as she examined the placards beside the doors along the corridor.

She felt the fatigue from the night before along with the pained silence of her interactions with Michael before he left for work that morning and attributed her inability to get her bearings to that.

"Germy," Molly said, as Jeremy approached them from the other end of the hall.

Hannah waved, grateful to see the familiar face.

"I was just coming to find you," he said, walking briskly toward her. "I thought maybe you'd gotten lost."

"It's not a very big building," Hannah observed, but then, consulting her watch, she saw she was nearly fifteen minutes late. "Oh, I'm sorry. It took us forever to get out of the house." She refrained from mentioning the conspicuous dawdling by Michael, who seemed intent on lingering about for as long as he reasonably could.

"It's totally fine," he said. "Kate is running late with a student anyway."

Hannah was relieved to hear this, having imagined the professor brushing her mahogany hair out of her celadon eyes in frustration as she waited impatiently for Hannah's tardy arrival.

Jeremy led them down the hall to a small suite of offices that belonged to Kate, Jeremy, and—given the door count—two other professors.

"We can wait for her in my office," he suggested as he ushered Hannah and Molly into the small, cramped space.

"Gertie?" Molly asked as they walked through the door. "Gertie?" She lifted her hands, palms up to denote the question.

Jeremy laughed, sitting in a chair behind a well-used wooden desk that looked like it could conceivably be as old as the building itself, which Hannah guessed, made it at least as old as the Decker house.

"Sorry Molls," Jeremy said playfully. "Can't bring the dog to work."

Molly pinched her eyebrows together, her confusion plain enough.

"Gertie can't come to work with me, honey," he explained again. "Gertie's at home."

Molly accepted the answer without further complaint, though she did little to conceal her disappointment. Hannah took off her coat, along with Molly's, and Jeremy hung them on a hook behind his door. Hannah sat at a small table in front of a window behind Jeremy's desk and removed a coloring book and crayons from her purse. Molly unenthusiastically accepted the distraction.

Next door, Kate's voice could be heard inviting a student to "drop by any time," before she leaned her head around the doorway into Jeremy's office, "You two ready?" Seeing Molly on Hannah's lap, she stepped fully into the room. "Hi Molly, sweetie," she said. "We can just meet in here." She disappeared briefly into her own office, retrieving a folder before returning to join Hannah at the table.

"So, let me be completely transparent here," Kate said rather abruptly; no one had accused her of being opaque. "I'm interested in writing something on Decker. The more I learn about him, the more I think there's something there."

Despite Kate's promise to be transparent, Hannah felt she was speaking an entirely different language. *Writing something on Decker.* What did that even mean? If Kate wanted to "write something on Decker," she should.

"But I don't want to step on anybody's toes with this. Can you tell me where you two are in your research?" Kate asked. "I'd love to collaborate."

Jeremy shifted uncomfortably in his chair as Hannah looked at him, her eyes pleading for help. A large bookcase extended nearly the entire height of the wall beside his desk, and Hannah found her eyes drifting to the shelves there—to books whose titles she'd never before heard and to photographs of people she did not know.

"Hannah, I think you said you'd pulled a few newspaper articles. And then you also have the blueprints," Jeremy prompted.

"I also met with his grandson," she volunteered. She saw Jeremy's shock at this revelation. "Not long ago," she added in an attempt to put the meeting into proximity with the more "official" research Jeremy and Kate had done. "His name is also Andrew. He didn't know much, though. Just that Eleanor's parents weren't very happy that she married Andrew. The first Andrew, I mean."

Molly, bored with her crayons already, slid off Hannah's lap and toddled over to Jeremy, seeing the selection of random objects on his desk—a highlighter, a pad of paper, pens, a computer.

"Pick you up," she said, raising her arms for Jeremy.

"Molly, honey, leave Jeremy alone." Hannah held up a green crayon, hoping to persuade her daughter back to her coloring book, but Jeremy had already reached down and lifted the child onto his lap, handing her the highlighter and a pad of paper before returning his attention immediately to Hannah.

"My niece went through that phase," he said and smiled at Molly's phrasing. "What else did Andrew say? The second Andrew."

Kate sat back in her chair, her take-charge demeanor softening.

"Really, not much. He had some family stories. I guess Eleanor's father wasn't very happy about her marrying Andrew—you both got that part right. Eleanor's mother died when she was very young, so it was just Eleanor and her father. Andrew Moore also thought that maybe Andrew had a business deal that fell through, and that's why he killed himself."

"That sounds like more than *not much*," Kate said.

"I found some photographs of all of them when they were kids and returned them to him, and he was mostly just grateful for that," Hannah explained. "He didn't really tell us much we don't already know."

"What was the deal?" Kate asked.

"What deal?"

"That he killed himself over." Kate flipped through her papers as if the answer might be found there.

"Oh. I didn't ask." Hannah bit the inside of her lip. "I should have asked that. I'm sorry. He just kind of threw it out and then moved on."

"Don't apologize. It's not a big deal," Jeremy said, though Kate's face suggested she disagreed on that point. "Did he say why none of them wanted the house?"

"Yes," Hannah said, pleased to have an opportunity to redeem herself. "He said he's the only one still in town, and he's too old for a house that big. They're actually looking to downsize." She handed Molly the crayon to go with Jeremy's highlighter.

"Did he say why the bank didn't foreclose on the house after Decker died?" Kate asked.

"That was a little weird," Hannah said, pivoting in her chair to face Kate.

"He said he never even thought about it."

"He never thought about it?" Jeremy parroted, incredulous.

"I think the bank didn't foreclose on the house because they were financially just fine," Kate said like a judge rendering a verdict.

"No. He said Andrew shot himself because he lost all his money, and then Eleanor drowned herself in her family's quarry because she couldn't get over Andrew's death," Hannah summarized.

"That doesn't really seem very likely," Kate said, and she pulled the articles on the quarries from the folder Jeremy had made for her, identical to the one he'd made for Hannah.

"I had trouble following those," Hannah admitted reluctantly.

"I did, too, so I created a chart." Kate pulled a piece of notebook paper from the folder and held it up. Jeremy slid Molly off his lap, allowing her to keep the highlighter and crayon, and she returned to Hannah, who picked her up placing her on her own lap.

"What is that?" Hannah asked.

"It's a timeline of the mergers and dissolutions of the various quarries," Jeremy explained.

"So based on this, Dailey Quarry becomes Daily Limestone Limited when it merges with The Stone Hollow Mill right around the turn of the century," Kate said, craning her neck to see the chart now in Jeremy's hands. "It remains pretty stable until the mid-1920s when it just starts buying up all the tiny quarries in Bedford. Then it merges with Stinewell Stone in Bloomington..."

"These don't really look like mergers," Jeremy said, his finger moving over the chronology plotted out by Kate. "He's just buying. He's buying all the other quarries."

"Look at the date of the last acquisition," Kate said.

"November 2, 1932," Hannah said.

"That's almost three years into the Depression," Kate said.

And two months before he died, Hannah thought.

Kate's interest lay elsewhere though. "That means the company was still profitable. Who was running it?"

"Is Walter Dailey still alive? Maybe Eleanor's running it?" Hannah said, recalling the description of the "beautiful and tenacious" woman Andrew had married.

"I don't know about that," said Kate. "A woman running a limestone quarry in Indiana in the 1920s?"

"What's this?" Jeremy asked as he lifted another article from Kate's folder. Hannah leaned toward Jeremy, and he tendered the article to her. It must have been something Kate found in her own research.

Bedford Gazette - May 26, 1925 -
Decker Breaks Ground on Family Estate
Indianapolis architect and developer Andrew
L. Decker of Decker Developers, Ltd. has
taken the first step toward building what is
sure to be a home nearly unrivaled in the
Indianapolis area. Having secured the permit
to build the 9,000 square foot, three-story
manor, Decker states he has designed what
will be his family's home and plans to
personally oversee every aspect of the
project from the corner stone to the last
roof tile.

The house will overlook the Hyde Park neighborhood of luxury estates, which Decker
Developers has been solely responsible for
designing and developing since Decker first
purchased the land more than three years
ago. Now, he has decided to make the exclusive enclave the site of his own home. Like
all of the homes in Hyde Park, we can assume
this one will prominently feature our very
own Indiana limestone. After all, what is a
Decker house without Dailey stone?

When asked, Mr. Decker commented that his
young daughter, Margaret, was the inspiration behind the house. "Meg said she wanted
a big yellow house with a big green yard.
So, I told her I'd see what I could do about
that."

Mrs. Decker suggested the inspiration may
have been more practical. "Andrew makes it a
priority for his designs to include the

What Hannah noticed immediately about the article was that it included the first photograph of Andrew she'd ever seen in which he looked unhappy, contrasting sharply with the jaunty tone of the article itself. As she examined it more closely, Andrew's discomfort announced itself in unambiguous terms. Hannah had seen photographs of him appearing contemplative, studious, joyful, even pleasantly, if intentionally, posed. But in the photograph from Kate's file, Andrew's face did not display even the slightest sign of enjoyment.

Rather, he stood at an angle, his hand clasped firmly in the hand of another man, identified in the caption as "Mayoral candidate and Marion County Treasurer, John Duvall."

Mr. Duvall was small, squat, his face round and plump. His proximity to Andrew who stood tall, his shoulders pulled back, his chin slightly lifted, accentuated the contrast between the two men. Andrew's height relative to the candidate for mayor created a challenge of proportions for the photographer, and Hannah saw that Andrew was actually positioned slightly behind Mr. Duvall, allowing Duvall the advantage of perspective that is possible in a two-dimensional medium.

While Andrew's posture was sufficient to convey his displeasure, his face was likewise stiff, one eyebrow elevated just slightly higher than the other, his jaw tight. The blacks of his eyes held what Hannah thought to be actual animosity as they reached the lens of the camera. Either oblivious or unconcerned, Mr. Duvall smiled openly, the span of his grin pushing his full cheeks back into his ears.

"Do you know who that is?" Kate asked. "The other man I mean. Obviously the one on the right is Decker."

Jeremy shook his head indicating he had no idea of the identity of the other individual in the photograph.

"That's John Duvall. He was the mayor of Indianapolis from 1926 to 1927," Kate said, her voice growing dark. "He was Klan." An explanation, if ever there was one, for the gravity of her tone.

"Jesus," Jeremy breathed, reaching for the article from Hannah's hands and examining the photograph more closely. "Where did you find this?"

"I searched Duvall. Well, I searched Stephenson first," she said, referring to the Grand Dragon of the KKK in Indiana in the 1920s. "I just figured that someone as prominent as Decker during this time might have had some run-ins with the Klan. And... he did... apparently."

"Was Andrew part of the Ku Klux Klan?" Hannah asked. The very thought of it caused her physical pain as she prayed silently, No, no, no, no.

"Absolutely not," Kate said. "Andrew's Italian and Catholic. Or if he's not Catholic, if he's Protestant either because his wife is or his father was, he's still got family who are Catholic."

Hannah was reassured by the consensus that Andrew wasn't part of the KKK, but could not, then, reconcile that with his position, so close to this individual. Though, Hannah noted, he appeared none too happy to be there.

"Who was he? Duvall?" Jeremy asked. "I mean, other than a mayor. Why would Andrew know him?"

"He was mostly a businessman," Kate said. "Before he was mayor, he was the treasurer of Marion County. But he also was one of the first commercial bankers in Indianapolis and owned a real estate firm of some kind. But he was part of that whole Klan frenzy here in the 1920s. When he ran for mayor, he had the full support of the KKK behind him, and they were a not insignificant percentage of the General Assembly, then. Something like half the legislature and thirty percent of the white men in Indiana were members of the KKK in the 1920s. The governor was Klan.

"That would have been pretty hard on someone like Decker because the Klan's primary target in the 1920s in Indiana were Catholics. Bombed their churches, marched in the streets, intimidated their people, shut down their businesses and their schools. It was the largest Klan organization in the country. Here. In Indiana. It would have been impossible for Decker to do business—at least on this scale—without interacting with them. But he doesn't look real happy about it."

Hannah tried to imagine the thoughts going through Andrew's mind as he stood in front of the camera, hand-in-hand with the Klan.

Kate continued. "So, this guy, John Duvall, he was eventually thrown out of office after it was discovered that he traded all kinds of favors in exchange for getting people to vote for him. I'd guess he told Decker that if he wanted to build his dream home and keep the permits coming on his development there, he better make nice with the Klan. Throw votes their way, keep his money in their banks. And probably above all, keep his head down." Kate looked across the space between Jeremy and herself, her expression reflecting a depth of thought.

"This is why I think he's worth writing about," Kate finally said, breaking the silence. "He's so exactly of this time here. But as I said, I feel awkward doing that because I wouldn't even know about him if it weren't for you two."

"He would've had an interesting connection to World War I, too, being a first-generation German-Italian-American in that war," Jeremy added. "I bet there were some interesting conversations around that dinner table."

"Well, Andrew wouldn't have been there to hear them. He was already in New York when the war broke out," Hannah qualified.

Jeremy inclined his head accepting this finer distinction. "Do you remember where he and his brothers were stationed?"

"The article covering his return to Indiana said his brothers died in Italy, but I don't know where Andrew was. I'd assume he went with them," Hannah said.

"That would be an interesting angle, too," Jeremy said, appearing to consult Hannah for her agreement.

"When were they drafted?" Kate asked.

"They might not have been drafted. They might have enlisted," Jeremy said, saving Hannah from having to offer yet another *I don't know*. "When the U.S. entered that war, there were whole infantries of Italian-Americans, who went and fought in Italy on behalf of the United States. Decker and his brothers might have been part of that."

"Kind of complicated if they're half German, too," Kate added to the volley of speculation. "Although, maybe not. Italy desperately needed troops. They would have occupied a strange position though, because German immigrants before World War I were seen as the 'good immigrants', while Italian immigrants were pretty disfavored. To put it lightly. Lots of nativist, xenophobic views about Italians at the time. So, *Andrew Lawrence Decker* was probably more than happy to be German for most of his life, and then all of a sudden, that's not such a good thing either."

"Well, I mean, he wasn't German or Italian. He was born here," Hannah cut in.

Jeremy looked down at the article again, and Hannah followed his gaze, noting the young man's midnight hair just visible below his cap, the bronze of his skin evident even in the black and white of the photograph.

"Yeah, maybe," he equivocated. "He's turning out to be kind of a complicated guy, Decker," Jeremy said finally.

Hannah raised her eyes from the article hoping to gauge Jeremy's meaning by some expression on his face. Finding none, she offered a soft hum of agreement. "He's always just a little bit on the outside." Her voice traveled over the words as if they might not fully belong to her. Andrew seemed to her to be so many things, and yet not quite any of them. Not quite German, not quite Italian; not quite upper class, not lower class; he was Ivy educated, but not elite; he was a Midwestern kid from a small town making his living in the city.

So many things, and yet, not quite any of them.

"It could be an interesting paper. Maybe even a book," Kate said. "But I don't want to take over your project."

"There's room for all of us to work on this together," Jeremy said. "This doesn't seem like a big deal to me. We'll all just be co-authors."

Jeremy's response assured Hannah that she too could agree to the arrangement.

"Okay, I'm going to continue to do more research, then. Unless anyone has any objections," Kate said.

"No objection here," Jeremy said. "Hannah?"

"No objection," Hannah replied, thinking she rather liked the idea of herself as a "co-author." Her grandmother would get a kick out of that.

<h1 style="text-align:center">CHAPTER 18</h1>

" I think we're just about ready for you to start making those kitchen cabinets," Gary said as he stood in the doorway of the Decker house's study. "Assuming that's something you still want to do."

Hannah had been sitting at the desk, rereading the collection of articles Jeremy's librarian had pulled, trying to identify details she might have missed before. She'd failed to closely examine the short obituary of Andrew's mother, Idalia (Filannino) Decker. Ida died in March of 1934, a little more than a year after the third of her three sons died, survived only by her daughter Mary and her granddaughter Margaret. Hannah wondered what she'd died of—the obituary didn't provide a cause of death. It actually didn't provide much of anything at all, no more than five short sentences. But Hannah assumed that at least part of what killed her had been Andrew's death. How could it not have?

On the floor to the side of the desk, Molly played with the blocks Jason and the rest of the crew had made her. She was occupied and content, but Hannah had no illusions about whether she'd be able to have Molly with her when she started working on the cabinets.

"When do you need them?" she asked.

"That's really up to you," Gary said. "You might ask one of the kids from Butler to watch her," he suggested, seeming to understand where Hannah's concern lay. "I bet you could find some kid there who'd love to earn their beer money watching that little one a few hours a week. I have to say, she's about the best baby I've ever met."

He clearly meant it as a compliment, but all Hannah could think was that her daughter, with little exception, tended not to protest no matter the situation she found herself in. There were times when Hannah worried that her daughter had come to see her position in the world as entirely tenuous—as if she'd been allowed to remain at an exclusive party to which she hadn't actually received an invitation and at which her continued presence, at least in part, stemmed from her having gone largely unnoticed.

"That's a good idea," Hanna said. She could email Kate to see if she had any students who might be interested. "Assuming I can get a sitter, when could you start?"

"I'll have Conner come in and you two can talk about that," Gary said. "He can order the materials while you're setting up a sitter."

"Sounds good," Hannah agreed.

She leaned back in the desk chair she'd purchased for the room, watching Gary as he walked back through the living room and presumably across the foyer toward the other half of the house. She'd purchased the chair from a furniture store on the far north side of the city, chosen it from among endless options, chairs in all styles and colors. She settled on a high-backed, tufted chair reminiscent of the one she'd seen in the photographs of Andrew in this study. That chair had been leather, which Hannah thought cold and drab—even in the black-and-white photograph, it appeared a dark gray. Hannah opted for an upholstery in a mustard yellow with a repeating pattern of red poppies that brought out the red of the area rug below the desk and would match the set of mustard-colored velvet drapes she'd ordered.

"Miss Hannah?" came a voice from the door. Hannah looked up to find a tall, thin man standing just outside the study.

"Yes? Conner? Come in," she said, closing the folder of articles.

"Gary sent me over to talk to you about the cabinets for the kitchen. This a good time?"

"Sure," Hannah said, suddenly aware of herself sitting behind a desk in her study, the chair rising up behind her as Conner approached and respectfully removed a tattered Purdue Boilermakers cap. He carried the plans for the kitchen rolled up in his hands and, with Hannah's invitation, stepped behind the desk, flattening them across the desktop. They included the layout of the kitchen, the angles of the walls much closer to ninety degrees than anywhere else in the house given the amount of new construction in that room. Hannah reviewed the measurements, remembering her grandfather's gentle instruction, his encouragement, the warmth of his calloused hands on hers as he corrected her.

She missed him suddenly, an urgent sensation washing over her, and she determined to call him as soon as her meeting with Conner ended. Her grandfather was hard to get ahold of these days, treating his cell phone not unlike a landline, leaving it on his dresser or the kitchen counter and checking it a couple of times a day. He didn't always return calls, never texted, and hadn't set up his voicemail. But she would try.

"Good morning, Dr. Korman," Hannah heard Jason say from the foyer, his voice interrupting both her meeting with Conner and her silent promise to her grandfather. "I'll get Gary."

"I'm not here to talk to Gary," Michael returned brusquely. "Just thought I'd drop by and bring my wife lunch."

Hannah lifted her phone off the desk, checking to see whether she'd missed a text from him; she hadn't. Moreover, it was only 11:25 a.m.—a tad early for lunch.

"Where is she?" Michael asked.

"I'm in here," Hannah called out, and before long she saw Michael walking purposefully into the room.

"It's warm in here," he said, sounding surprised as he entered the study. Hannah tipped her head toward the black rotating space heater beside of the desk.

"Is that okay for Molly to be on the floor there?" he asked.

"I'll come back later, Mrs. Korman," Conner said, but Michael stepped forward blocking the young man's movement around the desk. Michael held a paper bag in his hand; he had indeed brought lunch.

"Hi. I'm Dr. Korman. You are?" he asked, extending his hand.

"Conner," the young man said, shaking Michael's hand. "Conner Miller. I'm working on the kitchen, but I can come back."

Michael seemed satisfied enough with this introduction, though the interaction had revealed in a matter of seconds his real purpose in being there.

"What's going on with the kitchen?" Michael asked, looking from Hannah to Conner and back, inviting either to respond. He stepped aside, effectively trading places with Conner, the young man on the far side of the desk and Michael now looking over Hannah's shoulder at the plans rolled out across the desktop.

"We was just talking about Mrs. Korman's plans for making the cabinets for the kitchen," he said, the shuffling of his feet betraying his discomfort. "Gary asked me to come in here and give her the measurements and order the materials."

"You're still thinking of doing that?" Michael asked. It was impossible for Hannah to discern whether the question was prompted by curiosity or disapproval, but either way, it had been a long time since she'd updated him on anything to do with the house.

"I thought I'd get one of Kate's students from Butler to watch Molly for a couple hours a day while I worked," Hannah said, thinking Michael was less likely to refuse her with an audience present.

"That sounds like a good idea. We could use a regular babysitter anyway. Might let us get out, just you and me, once in a while," he said, a comment Hannah thought was not for the benefit of the audience but reflected his authentic approval of her plan. She felt herself relax, though only momentarily.

"What's this?" Michael asked, running his hand over the back of the desk chair.

"It's the desk chair we talked about," she said.

"This isn't what we talked about," he objected with a thin note of disgust. Conner cleared his throat nervously. He'd already tried to excuse himself twice and been told to stay.

"It's got flowers on it," Michael said, the disgust even more prominent.

"It's pretty," Hannah said pleasantly.

"I don't want my study to be *pretty*."

It was strange to think of the study as his. This was only the second or third time he'd ever stepped foot in it. But she didn't have time to argue with his description as he continued. "And I asked for something sleek, something contemporary, something that would support my back. God. What has gotten into you lately? I can't even trust you to buy a chair. What the fuck even is this?"

Hannah looked to Molly, who had been mouthing a half-circle-shaped block but had stopped abruptly at the sound of her father's rising voice.

"Whoa," Conner said. By the look of it, the utterance had been somewhat involuntary, but having started down this road, he seemed committed to the journey. "I know I shouldn't say nothing, but you shouldn't talk to Miss Hannah that way."

Michael faced the young man, his eyes narrowing on him. Hannah watched in silent dread as Conner straightened himself to his full height, splatters of white spackle giving his jeans a 1990s retro, acid-washed appearance. He put his cap back on his head, lifting it just an inch, the repositioning making his eyes more visible as he broadened his shoulders.

"Go get Gary," Michael snapped at Conner.

"Gladly," the young man said, evidently figuring it mattered little at this point what words were exchanged between the two of them. He pivoted to walk out of the room.

"Hey, Conner?" Michael said, and Conner paused, turning his head to the side, his back still to Michael. "Is Andrew here today?"

Hannah felt the room fall away around her, the walls blurring, her feet seeming to come unmoored from the floor before she ricocheted back to earth.

"Michael..." she said, though even to herself the voice sounded far away, as if it came from outside the room, outside the house.

"Who?" Conner asked, turning fully around, his face warped with confusion.

"Never mind," Michael said. "Get Gary."

IN THE END, Gary refused to fire Conner. His crew was his crew, he said, and Conner was part of it. Michael made a point of reminding Gary who was actually paying for the project, and Gary calmly thanked Michael for the job and reminded him that staying on target for a July finish meant keeping his crew—all of them—working. Michael eventually backed down, with an instruction to Hannah to "return the fucking chair" and to Gary to "keep his fucking guys in line." Then he left the paper bag—lunch—on the desk, on top of the plans for the kitchen cabinets, and returned to work.

When the dust settled, Conner returned to the study, out of necessity—the team needed the plans back. Hannah was sitting in the high-back tufted mustard-yellow chair with the red poppy upholstery.

"I'm sorry to bother you. I—we need the plans," he said.

"Of course," Hannah said, lifting her elbows, knowing he could see she'd been crying. Her mascara had mixed with her tears forming watercolor tracks of charcoal on her cheeks, which she'd tried with only minimal success to wipe away.

"I think the chair is pretty, Miss Hannah," he said, keeping his eyes down as he rolled up the plans. "It looks good in this room."

"Conner," Hannah heard Gary call sharply from the living room.

"Coming," the young man returned as he walked out of the room and back toward the kitchen.

Hannah picked up her phone and searched her contacts for her grandfather's phone number. She listened as the phone rang. Twice. Three times. A fourth. After the fifth ring, the ubiquitous woman's voice spoke, "The caller you are trying to reach has a voicemail box that has not been set up..."

Hannah hung up before the woman could complete the instructions. She would try him again tomorrow.

☙❧

"I TRIED to call my grandfather this morning," Hannah said, still feeling a bit bewildered at how very much she wanted to talk to him.

"Yeah? How is he?" Jeremy asked. Hannah could feel him examining her but kept her eyes straight ahead, watching the toddler and the dog who were, it seemed, walking each other.

Upon joining up with Jeremy and Gertie, Molly had decided she had no interest in being wheeled through the neighborhood in her Chicco chariot. She much preferred to walk like the grownups. And like Gertie, who admittedly was not a grownup, but seemed to enjoy some of their privileges. Hannah had lifted the child out of the stroller and set her on the ground where she and Gertie wandered ahead until the length of Gertie's leash limited their distance.

"I couldn't reach him," Hannah said. "And he refuses to set up his voicemail, so I couldn't leave a message."

"That's frustrating. Did you need to talk to him about something specific?" Jeremy asked.

"I wanted to tell him that I'm going to be making the cabinets for the kitchen in the Decker house. He's a cabinetmaker and a woodworker, and I thought he'd think it was cool."

"Did he teach you how to do that, then? When you lived with them? With your grandparents?" Jeremy asked.

"Yeah," she said, smiling half-heartedly. Up ahead, Molly lost her balance and fell—her snowsuit restricting her movement and making her clumsy. Gertie stopped, nosing at her chest in encouragement. Molly pushed Gertie's nose aside and managed to right herself, using the dog's back as a convenient balance.

"I'd love to see what you make," Jeremy said, and he sounded sincere.

"I moved in with them when I was twelve," Hannah said, though she hadn't been asked.

"I think I knew that," Jeremy replied, though she was fairly confident she'd never told him. There was so much she hadn't told him and so much she wanted to.

"It was either them or foster care," she said, stealing a glance in his direction. She saw the light bobbing of his head. He looked neither surprised at the disclosure nor repulsed by it.

"Do you want to tell me what happened?" he asked.

She felt like she could tell him. They were friends.

"My dad broke my arm," she said. "When I was twelve. He got mad at me, and he broke my arm."

It was the most complete version of that story she'd told to anyone other than Michael. She could have recalled that specific rage in incremental detail if she'd been asked. She could have recounted what had happened from second to second, from the moment she'd tripped over her shoe, accidentally scuffing the freshly painted living room wall with her backpack, to the sound of her arm—snap—as it broke in her father's hand, and the wave of nausea that followed with the pain. But no one had ever asked for that depth of detail, and she had a nearly constant desire both to tell everyone she met about that event, and to hide it deep within her so that no one would ever know.

When she'd told Michael the same short summary she'd told Jeremy, his eyes had grown large with horror, and he'd responded decisively, "I'm glad they took you out of that house. I'd hate to think what could've happened to you if you'd stayed." That he'd said that was how Hannah knew he loved her and that he'd be a good father.

Jeremy said nothing, his eyes focused straight ahead of them, but his hand found hers, and he pulled it between them as he wove his gloved fingers between hers, holding tight. And then finally, he said, "I'm so sorry that happened to you, Hannah. I'm so sorry."

Hannah knew she should remove her hand from Jeremy's for any number of reasons, including that having only one hand on the stroller made it hard to steer. But she didn't, and his thumb brushed over the back of her glove before he pulled away and tucked his hand into the pocket of his coat.

"That must have been hard," he said as she returned her grip on the stroller.

"It's gotten harder for me," she said. "Since I had Molly. Harder to understand. I thought it would get easier. But it got harder."

"Because you can't imagine doing something like that to her?"

"I can't imagine letting someone do something like that to her."

Jeremy stopped again and faced her, his expression suddenly tense. "Are you worried someone might?" he asked, his voice as tight as a bow drawn.

"No," she said, facing him as well. "No. But I worry sometimes. I worry that I want more than someone who won't. And then I feel ungrateful. I have so much. So much more than I ever thought I'd have."

"What did you think you'd have?" he asked gently.

Hannah looked ahead at Gertie and Molly trundling along the road. "I mean... nothing."

"Hannah," Jeremy said, shaking his head. "I wish—"

Without warning, Jeremy's hand shot out of his pocket with the force of the leash as Gertie let loose a single, explosive bark. The sound reverberated off the leafless trees and was quickly followed by another bark. Gertie lunged at Molly, her teeth clamping around the front of her snowsuit, knocking the small child over. Molly immediately started crying, a loud howl of fear and, Hannah suspected, pain as her head hit the pavement.

Jeremy and Hannah both ran ahead trying to separate the dog from the child, but Gertie turned toward them, baring her teeth, growling. She'd at least let go of Molly's snowsuit, and Hannah had expected Molly to run to her. Instead, Molly called out loudly, "NAKE! NAKE!"

The word took Hannah just a moment too long to translate, as it was followed almost immediately by Jeremy's expletive, "Son of a bitch!"

Gertie then lunged in the direction of Jeremy's legs, and Hannah saw the long tan and umber creature attached to his ankle. Jeremy reached down, grabbing the snake around the middle and quickly whipped it against the side of a tree as Gertie continued barking.

An older woman, a neighbor Hannah had not yet met, burst from her house and ran frantically across her lawn toward them. She picked up Molly as Hannah turned toward Jeremy.

"A copperhead," he said over the sounds of Molly howling and Gertie barking, and he withered to the ground, sitting on the damp cold of the roadway.

"Owie," Molly said, closing her eyes tight, and Hannah wasn't sure whether she meant the sight of Jeremy, who very clearly had an owie, or herself, the goose-egg from her fall to the pavement already announcing itself through the wisps of her hair

"I'm calling 911," the woman said.

Hannah reached for Molly, who reached for the side of her head, voicing her "owie" again. "Molly needs to go to the hospital, too," Hannah said, unsure how hard her daughter had fallen.

❧

IN THE EMERGENCY DEPARTMENT OF THE CHILDREN'S HOSPITAL, Hannah lay on a hospital bed, her body wrapped around Molly's, eyes closed but not asleep. Her thoughts were focused on Jeremy, who had been taken to the adult trauma hospital on the other side of the academic health center's campus, when she heard Michael say her name.

"We're waiting for the radiologist," she whispered as he entered the bay.

He walked slowly over to the bed, obviously ill-at-ease from the argument they'd had that morning. And here she was, lying on a hospital bed with their daughter, absolutely bedraggled, exhausted, and overwhelmed beyond repair. Michael knelt by the side of the bed and kissed first Hannah's forehead, then Molly's. Molly's eyes opened briefly, then closed with disinterest when she saw who it was.

"What happened?" he whispered.

"Nake," Molly replied, not opening her eyes.

"What?" Michael asked, unable to translate.

"A snake. A copperhead. We were walking around the neighborhood, and Molly saw a snake, and it scared her, and she fell backwards and hit her head on the pavement. She was crying hard enough that I thought we should go to the hospital."

"A copperhead?" Michael asked. "At this time of year?"

Hannah shrugged. "Maybe he was confused."

Michael chuckled and took Hannah's hand in his, bringing it to his lips.

"Mrs. Korman?" a voice called quietly from the back of the bay.

"Yes?" Hannah replied, trying to see over Michael's crouched figure.

Michael stood and extended his hand. "Hi. I'm Dr. Korman," he said, placing a slight emphasis on the "doctor."

The woman, who introduced herself as Dr. Leland, the ER

attending physician, seemed relatively unimpressed with Michael's credentialed introduction, but she shook his hand anyway.

"Radiology has okayed you for discharge. It's just a bad bump. Keep ice on it and give her Motrin if she seems to be in pain. Are you driving them home?" she asked, addressing Michael.

"Yes, but I have to go to the house and get my wife's SUV. For the car seat," he said. Hannah thought she saw a flash of actual shame move across his face, a realization of some sort.

"We've still got to get her discharge instructions printed out and some paperwork signed," Dr. Leland said. "If you want to go trade out cars or whatever, you have some time to do that."

Hannah waited in the emergency room bay with Molly until Michael returned from the Decker house.

That weekend, Michael made another trip. To Target. Where he bought a five-point-harness car seat and installed it in his car.

CHAPTER 19

More than a week passed before Hannah worked up the nerve to knock on Jeremy's door. As she stood on his porch, Molly's hand in her own, she could hear his television. But when she heard his gruff voice—"Go lie down, Gertie!"—she knew he hadn't missed their walk by accident or injury. He hadn't lost track of time, hadn't forgotten, hadn't had something else come up. He had chosen not to go. She set the basket on the doorstep, took Molly's hand in hers again, and returned to the Decker house.

The basket was not a pre-manufactured, saran-wrapped gift basket of jams and crackers and sausages of the variety that Debbie had gifted to her. Rather, it contained a selection of things Hannah herself had picked out, and which had some meaning to her or to Jeremy or to the both of them: a pair of wool socks she'd seen him wear; a Wonder Woman collar for Gertie—the dog had probably saved Molly's life; a copy of the new Chaplin biography—she suspected he already had it, but this one was a gift from her; a box of peanut butter cookies from Insomnia Cookies; and a DVD of *Breaking Away*, even though she had no idea whether he owned a DVD player and suspected that, like most people, he could probably stream the movie if he had any interest in watching it.

She'd included a "Get Well Soon" card—the most appropriate card she could find given the dearth of "Recover Quickly From Your Snake Bite" cards offered at Target. She'd agonized over what to write, spending most of Tuesday with her pen hovering over the cardstock only to have the words refuse to come. She'd set her pen down, walked out into the Decker house foyer, talked to the workers, and returned to the study, only to try and fail again. Ultimately, she'd signed her name. "Hannah K." And left it at that.

When she drove past his house on her way out of the neighborhood that afternoon, the basket was no longer sitting on the front step, and she assumed he'd brought it inside. When the following Monday came and went and Jeremy and Gertie again were absent, Hannah grasped what had happened. Jeremy was her friend. But there were defined boundaries in such friendships, and for months, they'd both been stepping up to that line, seeing which of them, if either, would step over first. He'd seen it, too, she thought. And had stepped back.

She walked her two laps around the neighborhood's familiar loop and waited for Molly to fall asleep. Then she placed the child's stroller in the study of the Decker house, turned on the baby monitor, climbed the stairs to the third floor, sat down in the small closet of one of the north-facing bedrooms, and wept.

❦

"I THINK I've found a sitter for you," Kate said as she sat on the bench at the exercise studio and slid her boots on. "One of our majors said she nannies in the summer, doesn't have time for a full-time job during the school year, but would love a gig that was like six hours a week or so. Sounds perfect, I think?"

Hannah nodded. "When can she start?"

"I don't know. She seemed really excited. Can I just give her your contact info and you can work that out?"

"Oh, sure. Absolutely."

"Everything else going okay?" Kate asked.

"Sure," Hannah said. She suspected she was not terribly convincing.

"I heard what happened to Jeremy," Kate said quietly, though not quietly enough, as Laura perked up beside her.

"What happened to Jeremy?" Laura asked as she zipped up her coat.

"He got bitten by a copperhead over by his house," Kate said, and Hannah could tell that Kate knew substantially more about the events of that afternoon than she'd chosen to share with Laura.

"A copperhead? This time of year?" Laura asked.

"Yeah," Kate replied. "His doctor said the snake was probably very confused."

Hannah offered a chuff and then stopped immediately when both Kate and Laura paused their conversation obviously expecting her to explain what she could possibly have found humorous about the incident.

"Sorry, I literally said that same thing to Michael. Maybe the snake was confused."

Laura's eyes twitched. "You already heard about it?" she asked.

"The whole neighborhood is talking about it," Hannah said, despite the fact that the neighbor who came running out of her house to call 911 was the only person in the neighborhood, other than Jeremy, that Hannah had yet met. The reference to neighborhood gossip, though, had satisfied Laura—a supremely believable explanation from her perspective, it would seem.

"I'd stick around and talk, but I'm the math parent in Jacob's classroom today." Laura waved quickly and headed for the stairs.

"Hannah," Kate said with Laura safely out of earshot. "Be careful there. If that's what you want, do that. But don't kind of do it," she said.

Hannah's hands began to tremble, making it hard for her to tie the laces of her sneakers and requiring her to start over as she lost the loop.

"I don't know what you mean," she said, her pitch artificially high and breathy, revealing she knew exactly what Kate meant.

"Okay," Kate said, not pushing the issue.

❧

KATE'S STUDENT, Emory, was a dream. A junior and a member of the tennis team, she had almost no free time during the week, except three hours after class on Tuesdays and Thursdays before practice. This didn't leave enough time for her to accept the kinds of jobs her classmates held—working retail or waiting tables. But she had a car, and she loved kids, and six hours a week worked perfectly for both her and Hannah. This schedule did require Hannah to change her routine slightly. But as her friendship with Jeremy unraveled and her work on the cabinets in the kitchen could only be done on Tuesday and Thursday afternoons, Hannah adjusted to Tuesdays, Thursdays, and Fridays at the Decker house.

Hannah found that the work on the cabinets occupied her mind and her heart, both of which had spent too much time in flux since she'd moved to Indianapolis. The crew seemed to treat her differently as she produced the boxes, one after the other, then the doors and drawers that accompanied. They had initially approached her with trepidation, probably assuming they'd end up having to redo the cabinets and, therefore, Gary's indulgence of her request would delay the project and increase their workload. After she'd made the first cabinet, the trepidation evaporated.

"She's every bit as good as any of the custom cabinetmakers I've seen," she overheard one of Gary's workers tell him. And of course she was; she'd been apprenticed by one.

After this, the crew happily adopted her; she was one of their own. Or close. She'd been listening to the men in her house for the past several months and had no illusions that when she joined them in the kitchen, they kept their penchant for four-letter expletives to a minimum. But they relaxed their conversations around her, talking about kids and wives and girlfriends, shows they streamed, games they'd watched, tales of jobs they'd enjoyed and, naturally, ones they had not. Hannah found herself surrounded by men who reminded her of her grandfather and of her brother. And if they weren't a complete salve to her various wounds, they helped.

It was in the third week of this work that Hannah received a text from Kate:

Kate: Coffee to talk about Decker?

Hannah: Yes!

They met on a Tuesday afternoon at the cafe attached to Butler's bookstore and campus cafeteria, a single limestone building constructed right around the time Margaret Decker married Gerald Moore.

"I've hit a complete roadblock," Kate said as she sat across the table from Hannah, the familiar manila folder that held her research on Decker sitting in front of her. Hannah had brought hers as well, along with her laptop.

Around them, students moved through the small cafe, talking, giggling, texting, studying. The next classes, Kate explained, started at 1:00, and the traffic through the campus coffeeshop would lighten at that point. Until then, Hannah found herself straining to hear Kate over the din of voices at tables next to her, in the line at the front of the shop, and among the constant stream of students moving through the coffeeshop.

"I was thinking of going to St. Joseph's cemetery," Hannah said. "I don't really know what I expect to find though—"

"No, that's a good idea. I feel like, with this guy, you never know what you're going to find. Are you thinking of going soon?"

"I was going to go tomorrow afternoon."

"I'm teaching then. Can you shoot me an email when you get back?" Kate asked, taking a bite of a ham and cheese croissant.

"Sure," Hannah agreed.

"I will say, I've combed the newspapers and the genealogical records, and there's just nothing else about him out there. The Indiana Historical Society's heard of him, but they don't have anything—though they said they'd be interested in anything we find. Have you taken those blueprints over, yet?"

"No," Hannah said, feeling slightly guilty.

"Don't feel bad. It's not like they've got an exhibit ready to go or something. They're just going to be archived and then sit in a storage room until they can figure out what to do with them. I'll tell you though, what I've got on Decker, what I've found so far, it doesn't really... hold together, you know?" Kate said this clasping her hands tightly, her fingers interlocking.

"How do you mean?" Hannah asked. She felt like Andrew "held together" just fine and suspected that people like Kate were just unaccustomed to the way people like Andrew had to be so many things, so many people all at the same time. Such an existence led to contradictions. Or appeared to from the outside.

"I just mean, I don't really understand who controlled the quarry in that relationship. Who held the purse strings?"

"Why?" Hannah asked, unable to find the connection between Andrew "holding together" and Andrew "holding the purse strings."

"Well, the quarry continued to operate into the 1970s," Kate said, pulling out her timeline, which had been carefully updated. She'd taped a second sheet of paper to the first, continuing the saga of the quarries.

"This means two things to me," she went on. "The first is that the Deckers didn't lose their shirts in 1929. Or 1933, for that matter."

"Then why did he shoot himself?" Hannah asked, a question that had plagued her since she'd first seen Andrew Decker's photo from the depths of a brown cardboard box in her attic. If she thought about the question a bit more, she might have settled on a different phrasing— less "Why did he?" and more "How could he?"

In any case, Kate had thoughts. "I don't know why he did it, but it doesn't look like it was because he lost all his money or whatever other mythologizing this family has contrived."

"What's the second thing?" Hannah asked, resigning herself to the irresolvability of the first question.

"I think Eleanor controlled Dailey Limestone or some part of it. Have you found anything else at the house? Any other documents? Letters? Maybe business contracts or something?"

Hannah thought about all the photographs she'd found and about how she'd returned them to Andrew Moore and gotten his description of his family. She thought about how Kate probably would have viewed those photographs with a much more strategic eye and would have known to ask much more insightful questions of Andrew Moore. She realized that even these short months later, she herself would have asked very different questions given another opportunity.

"I really only have the blueprints. But Kate, he did stop building even if he didn't stop designing. You can see from the neighborhood that he stopped building. That had to have had a financial impact on him. And Andrew Moore was clear: a deal fell through, and he killed himself," Hannah said.

"Maybe," Kate replied, dropping her gaze to her chart of quarry acquisitions and consolidations.

Hannah scanned the coffee shop. Kate had been right; as they approached 1:00, the room emptied, and the previous chatter of students reduced to not much more than a murmur. Hannah found herself looking up every time she heard the whoosh of air that accompanied the door opening. At first, she didn't understand why her attention was so easily called to so ordinary a sound, but slowly she realized that each time, she expected it to be accompanied by Jeremy. He'd come walking through the coffee shop, see the two of them, smile, sit down, talk, catch up.

"I mean, no," Kate went on, pulling Hannah's attention back to their conversation. "I understand why he stopped building in 1929: because people stopped buying and couldn't get residential loans. My grandfather was an attorney at Chicago Title during the Great Depression, and it put him out of business. He moved to southern Illinois and tried to take up farming. Anyway, not what we're here to discuss. I'm just saying, if the grandson's story is that Decker lost his fortune in the Depression and that by 1933, he was so destitute that he shot himself —" her voice had increased in volume as she argued her case, and a couple of students at the table next to them turned in shock at the reference to the man's death. "Well, I need a whole lot more information in order to agree with that," Kate said, bringing her volume back down.

"Isn't it possible he was ashamed? His wife's business survived, and his didn't? Particularly for someone… like him, who'd worked so hard, and then it all came crashing down. He was just so destroyed by that. Maybe." She said this with the image of him held in her mind, his eyes as they'd appeared in her dreams, hopeful and despairing, sharp and full of sorrow.

"Maybe," Kate said. But the creases at the corners of her eyes, the set of her jaw, spoke of doubt.

CHAPTER 20

When Hannah said she wasn't sure what she expected to find at St. Joseph's Cemetery, this wasn't entirely true. As she approached the plot that she'd cross-matched with the cemetery's grid, she expected to find at least two things. The first was a family burial site—Andrew, Eleanor, and Margaret. The second could not be so easily articulated.

Hannah didn't believe in ghosts or visions or spirits walking the earth. Or she didn't believe in them in any more fervent a way than most people—thinking that maybe unknowable forces moved on a plane not completely accessible to the living, only occasionally perceivable by us. She did believe in God and in Heaven, even though she hadn't been to church in years and couldn't have said what religion most closely described her. She also wasn't sure whether she believed there was a Hell, but she kind of hoped there was, just so there'd be no chance of running into Jack Burke in the afterlife.

Despite her flexible view of the barriers between the living and the dead, as Hannah walked through St. Joseph Cemetery, observing the names of the German Catholics buried there, she did think, or perhaps not think, but hope—and it was a hope that stood against her better judgment—but she did hope that when she found Andrew's grave, something there would speak to her, that she'd feel a presence—his—and that she would have, in a way, met him.

She brought flowers. It seemed like the thing one should do when visiting a grave, and she'd brought them for Margaret, Andrew, and Eleanor. She imagined that Margaret's grave probably received regular attention; her children were still living. But Hannah thought likely not a single person currently living on this planet had ever met Andrew or Eleanor, and their graves might reflect this.

As she approached the Decker family plot, she realized that neither of her expectations would be met.

Three markers, flush with the grass, occupied the space directly below the large limestone cross on which the single, family name, DECKER, had been carved in relief. Directly below the imposing light gray angles of the cross was Andrew's grave. And it did not speak to Hannah, nor did she feel his presence there. Indeed, what she felt was his profound and permanent absence, an indisputable, incontestable finality.

ANDREW LAWRENCE DECKER
28 SEPTEMBER 1889 – 12 JANUARY 1933
FATHER HUSBAND BROTHER SON

His body lay under there, Hannah thought. Under her feet, the tangible remains of his person. The confirmation of his once-existence. There. Below. She knelt on the ground, feeling the cold wet of the earth seep through the knees of her jeans, and placed the bouquet below the marker. She heard herself then, the catch in her throat, followed by the soft, sad, stuttered sob as the tears fell from her eyes, disappearing into the stone marker, already damp from the late-winter air.

How she missed him. How she *had* missed him. How had *she* missed him?

Shoot me an email and let me know what you find, Hannah heard Kate's voice in her ear. What could she say? She'd found that he was dead.

The tears continued to fall from Hannah's eyes, and the straight, etched lines of Andrew's recorded life and his recorded death blurred before her. She wiped the back of her hand under her nose, sniffling and feeling small and silly for doing so. And then she shifted her weight to view the marker to his left.

MARGARET MARY DECKER MOORE
22 FEBRUARY 1923 - 7 JUNE 2014
BELOVED MOTHER WIFE AND DAUGHTER.

Hannah lay the bouquet against this marker, as well, offering a silent "Thank you" to the woman for taking such good care of the Decker house and promising to care for it equally well now that it had passed into her possession. She turned then to the marker on Andrew's right, lifting the back of her hand to wipe the remaining tears from her cheeks and laying the flowers below the marker.

ROSE IDALIA DECKER
3 OCTOBER - 4 OCTOBER 1920

Hannah blinked, her eyesight clearing even as her comprehension became clouded. She recalled Jeremy's blue-inked notation on the bottom of Andrew's and Eleanor's newspaper engagement announcement: *Pregnant?*

Yes, it would seem.

Hannah stood, her knees aching from the hard earth as she straightened them beneath her. To the right of Rose's marker lay the marker of a man who had evidently died in 1938, and while Hannah had no doubt that he was loved and missed by his family every bit as much as Andrew, Margaret, and Rose, he was not, in fact, part of the Decker family. More specifically, he was not Eleanor, who by all appearances, was missing.

Hannah walked to the back of the cross and found, to her surprise, Henry, Idalia, Francis, Joseph, and Mary. It had not occurred to her that Andrew's parents, brothers, and sister would also be buried on this plot, and it had never occurred to her that Eleanor would not be. The strangeness of this was underscored as Hannah emerged from the other side of the cross, having walked a complete circle to see that

Gerald Curtis Moore was buried to the left of his wife Margaret, someone having decided that in his repose, he should be with his wife, and she with her father.

❧

"SHE'S BURIED WITH THE DAILEYS," Kate said, turning from her computer to face Hannah. "I mean, she's the last Dailey, so it's a small plot, but she's there with her mother and father."

They sat in Kate's office, a Thursday morning. Molly watched a mystery-solving cartoon dog on her tablet, and Hannah had just shown Kate the photographs of the Decker family's graves she'd taken the day before. Kate had done a quick search of public records to find the burial site for Eleanor Alice Dailey Decker, born 1893. It had taken a couple of minutes, but she'd found the location: Crown Hill Cemetery. Just a short drive from the Decker house.

"What should we make of the fact that she's not buried with Andrew?" Hannah asked. "Especially if she loved him so much, she drowned herself rather than live without him."

Kate lifted her eyes to the water stain on the ceiling above her desk, its faint brown outline resembling an old, faded treasure map. No "x" on the ceiling, though, only cracked plaster.

"I don't know," she replied. "She couldn't have been buried in St. Joseph's. She wasn't Catholic. I'll tell you, I'm more struck by the fact that Margaret isn't buried with her mother."

Hannah reflected on this. Although the thought of her daughter's death brought about a surge of nausea and, even in the hypothetical, made her feel nothing short of panic, she did hope that when the time came that Molly left this world, she would do so long after her mother and be buried as close as possible to her. There were arrangements that, in the absence of this, Hannah could imagine— Molly buried with her husband's family, for example, as Gerald Moore had been buried with Margaret. But to be buried with Michael's family rather than with Hannah—this she could not imagine.

"I don't think that surprises me," Hannah said, recalling the photograph she'd seen of Andrew holding Margaret, the way he radiated absolute delight with her in his arms.

"It's touching really," Kate said, her usual clipped speech subdued with sentimentality. "He's buried there between his two daughters." She paused, shifting the photograph of Eleanor's grave up and down on her computer, watching the headstone shoot up to the top of the screen and then dragging it back into view.

"Germy!" Molly exclaimed suddenly, jumping out of her chair and bolting for the door.

Kate leaned precariously over the edge of her chair, trying to look around the corner of her door.

"Hey Molls. What are you doing here? Where's your mom?" Hannah heard Jeremy ask. She found herself leaning, not unlike Kate, precariously to the side, trying to see into the hallway. Before Hannah could succeed in tipping the chair over, Jeremy materialized inside Kate's doorway, Molly in his arms. Hannah smiled, a friendly, broad greeting, which vanished as Jeremy pressed his lips together in a hard, thin line, then averted his eyes in favor of Kate.

"Perfect timing," Kate said, evidently unaware of the dynamic between her two friends. "Hannah and I were just going through our latest pull of research on Decker. I think I've hit a wall, I was telling Hannah on Tuesday, and she drove down to St. Joseph's cemetery yesterday and checked out the Decker family's burial plot. Turned out you were right about the pregnancy back in 1920. They had a daughter who lived about two days. So, I'm trying to figure out if we're ready to start writing. I'm not really sure if we have enough quite yet—" she seemed prepared to go on when Jeremy stopped her.

"Kate. Hey. It sounds like you guys are doing some really good work here, but I think I'm going to step back from this project. I've got to get my tenure stuff turned in by July, and I'm not sure this work fits very well within my research agenda," he explained, setting Molly down on the chair she'd previously been sitting in.

"Oh," Kate said, sounding thoroughly taken aback. "Huh. Well, I know you've got your plate full. Let us know if you want to jump back in."

"Sure thing," he said agreeably, backing out of the office. "Good to see you again, Hannah," he added with a formality that seemed previously foreign to them.

"You, too, Jeremy," Hannah said, mimicking his tone despite her sense that she didn't quite know what his tone was. He offered another tightlipped smile before leaving Kate's office, and Hannah heard the latch on his office door make a barely audible click as he shut her out.

Kate pursed her lips and said, almost as if bringing Hannah into her confidence, "I'm on his tenure committee. He has to know I wouldn't encourage him to work on a project that I thought wouldn't strengthen his tenure case." And then the confusion fell out of her face as she looked more intently across the short distance between Hannah and herself.

Hannah recalled Kate's words from several weeks earlier. *Don't kind of do that*, she'd said. It was evident enough that one of them had decided not to.

CHAPTER 21

Michael arrived home fifteen minutes later than usual, stepping into the kitchen from the garage and setting a bouquet of flowers on the counter behind Hannah. An impromptu gift, Hannah could not identify any notable occasion for the gesture. He kissed her quickly on the cheek.

"I stopped at The Bee's Knees on the way home," he said, referring to a florist close to downtown. "I thought these might brighten your mood."

She struggled to find any words that would be adequately responsive. So much more than just her mood had changed over the past several months. And even if this were a very belated attempt to make up for his explosion in front of Gary's crew, flowers were hardly enough.

She settled on, "Thanks," and opened a cabinet to find a vase.

"I miss you," Michael said.

She had a feeling she knew what he meant. Even before his confrontation with her at the Decker house, she'd felt herself drifting away from him. He had to have felt it, too.

"How was work?" she asked, her face still and calm, her eyes focused on something beyond him, as if she could see through to the other side of him. Or maybe just wished she could.

"Good. Great, really. Thanks for asking." He sounded authentically grateful to her for her inquiry, and she felt suddenly sad for him, for them both. "How's the house? How are your cabinets?"

"Good. Almost done."

"Wow! Good for you. I'll tell you, I wasn't sure—" he paused, stopping himself, but she knew what he wasn't sure about. He wasn't sure she could do it. "What I mean is... It just seemed like a really big job, and I didn't know if you could do something like that without Robert or Mason."

"Mason doesn't do woodworking," she said flatly.

"Right." Michael took off his coat and set it across the back of a kitchen chair. "Do you remember that story you told me? That guy who wanted a kitchen island, but he had a galley kitchen with no logical place to put an island? But he threw such a fit, you and Robert gave him one, and then he had to pay you again to uninstall it when he couldn't get his refrigerator door all the way open?"

Hannah laughed, and it seemed she was laughing at two memories —the work she and her grandfather had done for the man and the joy she'd had sharing that story with Michael, seeing that he'd thought it truly funny. She'd assumed the exchanges between that man and her grandfather would fall into the "you had to be there" category, but Michael had laughed at the story and told her that he admired the noble life she'd had in South Carolina, how her grandparents had raised her, the way her grandfather taught her his trade. That was years ago now, and Hannah would have supposed he'd forgotten.

"You should set up an Etsy shop or something. You're really good," he said, though he hadn't seen the cabinets, so had no conceivable way of knowing whether she was "really good."

"Etsy?"

"Yeah. Sam's wife makes jewelry and sells it on there." When she didn't respond, he added, "It's a website."

"I know what it is," Hannah said. "Maybe I'll look into that." She placed the flowers one at a time into the tall glass vase she'd selected from the cupboard.

"Everyone at work is really impressed with what we've been doing on that house. I didn't realize, but it is a really historic house. There aren't many mansions left in the city proper that haven't been converted to offices or apartment buildings." He sounded like he was repeating information he'd heard from someone else. Sam, Hannah assumed. Maybe Debbie. "I know I complained about it at first, but I think it's going to end up being an exceptionally fortuitous investment." Sam again.

"I'm glad you feel that way now," she said.

He moved slowly across the kitchen, wrapping an arm around her waist as she stood back regarding the bouquet of flowers arranged in the vase. He rested his chin on her shoulder, watching as she readjusted a few of the stems.

She turned in his arms, facing him.

"You smell like sawdust," he murmured. "Sawdust and shampoo, and a little sweat. Were you working at the house today?" he asked.

"Yes," she said, feathering her fingers through his hair. His hands were warm on her body through her shirt. It had been his, an old Oxford that he'd intended to throw out.

"Did you think of me wearing this shirt all day?" he asked.

"Yes," she lied.

His fingers toyed with the button below her collar, posing a question. She answered, her fingers brushing his to the side as she slid the button through, opening the shirt further. Michael worked at the remaining buttons until he'd reached the end of the shirt and could spread it open before him. He lifted her onto the counter behind her and leaned forward, kissing the thin skin over her sternum, his cheeks brushing the sides of her breasts. She recalled his fascination with her breasts when she'd been pregnant. "Marvelous" was the word he used to describe them.

"If I could live inside this body, I would," he said, running the flat palms of his hands over her chest. "You look incredible, these days," he gushed.

"These days," Hannah repeated, much preferring the movements of his hands to those of his mouth.

"I'm sorry. I'm trying to tell you you're beautiful. Your body is incredible. I think you are incredible. You're the most beautiful woman I've ever seen." His eyes were earnest and full of admiration, and she struggled to reconcile the sentiment of his overture with its effect. But he was trying. He was trying with the flowers, and the kisses, and the words. She should try, too.

"Where's Molly?" he asked as her fingers slid under his chin, lifting his lips to hers.

"She's in the family room playing with the activity center your parents got her and watching Wild Kratts," Hannah said between kisses.

"There is no part of that sentence that makes any sense to me, but I take it Molly is occupied?" Michael tugged at the button on Hannah's jeans making his intention unmistakable.

"What? Here?" Hannah asked, her eyes darting around the kitchen.

"Let's be adventurous. Why not?" he asked as if it were rhetorical, as if there weren't a litany of reasons why not.

Hannah allowed him to tug her jeans down until they fell to the floor under her feet, then he unbelted and unbuttoned his own trousers, allowing them to fall with his underwear. She wrapped her legs around his waist, and tilted her head back until it rested lightly on the cabinet door behind her, and she found that, with her eyes closed, much like the dark of night, with her eyes closed, he could be anyone.

❧

"THEY LOOK GOOD, HANNAH," Gary said. "I couldn't have hired someone to do it better."

Hannah beamed broadly at the compliment and held her phone up to snap a picture, quickly texting it to both of her grandparents and Mason.

"Have you ever thought of setting up an actual business, an LLC or something?" Gary said, running his hand over the smooth cream-colored enamel of one of the base cabinets.

"No," Hannah demurred. "I can make the cabinets, but I don't know anything about running a business."

"Well, if you're interested, I'd be happy to pull you in on some of our kitchen renos," he offered.

"Maybe," Hannah said, finding a spot over Gary's shoulder to focus her attention.

"If you ever change your mind, you let me know," Gary said. "This reminds me though. I think we're going to start on the owners' suite, and I wanted to talk to you about the closets. Do you have a minute?"

As it turned out, Hannah had more than a minute; she had more than an hour. She didn't need to relieve Emory until 3:30, and it was only 2:00.

She walked with Gary up to the second floor. Portions of the wall were still open as wiring, plumbing, and ductwork were installed, and their shoes left prints in the dust on the floorboards.

"About these closets," Gary began as they entered the bedroom.

Eleanor Decker had been right when she'd commented that Andrew built his homes with every modern convenience available at the time, and this included the 1920s version of a walk-in closet—meaning it was physically possible for one to walk into it. Hardly larger than a coat closet by contemporary standards, the owners' suite of the Decker house included two such closets, one between the bedroom and the corresponding bathroom, and the other between the suite and the staircase. His and hers, Hannah thought, wondering which one had been *his*.

Overlooking no detail, each closet included a built-in dresser fitted against the inside right opposite a set of ornately carved hooks. The inclusion of a built-in dresser was consistent throughout the closets in the house, or most of them. Some of the smaller guest rooms lacked this amenity, and only the slightly larger north-facing closets in the attic contained them. However, special attention had been paid to the dressers in the owners' suite closets, each constructed of finely sanded and stained tigerwood. The pulls fanned out into an exquisite brass lily, which concealed the screw fastener beneath.

Although the closet that shared a wall with the staircase had a solid back, the river-sand mortar giving that wall its characteristic texture, the other closet contained a door leading into a modest ensuite bath-room—one sink, one toilet, one tub.

"Those Fritz Brothers plans basically knock all this out," Gary said. "They turn the bedroom on the other side of this into a combo walk-in closet and a much larger ensuite bathroom."

Hannah recalled that from her own review of the plans.

"So, I had an idea," Gary continued. "I thought, maybe you might want to take this dresser apart, and then when we build out the bathroom, you could rebuild the dresser in there, use it for towel storage or whatnot. The wood is just beautiful. We could design the whole bathroom around it, with the lilies and the tigerwood. I figured you might know how to pull it apart and then put it back together when the time comes."

It was a brilliant idea, and Hannah guessed probably not all that complicated. The hardest part would be getting the box out of the wall, which would depend on how Andrew's cabinetmaker had affixed it. But she thought it could be done.

⁂

"You have to press the microphone, Robert," Hannah heard her grandmother say with pronounced exasperation. This was followed by the sound of the phone's microphone brushing up against something, probably a shirt sleeve or a pair of jeans, as her grandfather sorted out how to put the phone on speaker. Hannah leaned back in the tufted mustard-yellow chair of the study, smiling.

"Are you there, Hannah?" her grandfather asked.

"Yeah, Grandpa. I'm here. Can you hear me?"

"I can hear her!" her grandfather said, sounding equally surprised and pleased with himself.

"Well, talk to her then," her grandmother instructed.

"I got your pictures," he said. "Did you make those?"

"I sure did. Just like you showed me," she said.

"You sure did," he said, once again sounding rather pleased with himself.

"Don't try to look at the pictures while you talk to her. You're going to hang up on her," Hannah's grandmother warned.

"Hi, Grandma," Hannah said, as if she were calling to the other side of a room they were all in.

"Hi, baby girl. How are you?"

"I'm good. How are you?"

"Oh, you know. It looks like you've got quite a house there in Indianapolis," she said.

"I think it will be. When we're done with it."

"We'll have to come up and see it when it's done," Hannah's grandmother said.

Hannah nose began to sting, a sharpness that preceded tears, as she thought about how wonderful it would be to have her grandparents visit and how incredibly unlikely it was that they ever would. "I would love that. Or I could visit you. *We* could. Michael and Molly and I."

"I want to see that house, though," her grandfather said, and she could almost see him adjusting his posture in his chair, sitting up, eyes bright with curiosity. "I want to see all the things you're doing to it. Can you send me more pictures?"

"Absolutely."

Hannah updated them on Molly—her new words, her new friends, Chloe and Cora—and Hannah had made some friends, too, she wanted them to know. And Michael's job was going well; they were taking a trip to London this summer.

"How exciting," Annis said.

"Take pictures," Robert said.

There was a pause, neither side really knowing what to say next, what to talk about. Hannah found herself wishing her grandparents were the sort of "old people" caricatured on television and in movies, people who inventoried every organ system, every minor ache and pain, the increasingly frequent doctors' appointments and prescriptions. At least then, there'd be something to keep them on the phone. Annis Kemp would never, though. A far cry from a southern debutante, Hannah's grandmother still wouldn't have lowered herself to the level of people who bemoaned "getting old" or remarked on the effect of various foods on one's aging digestive system.

Hannah could recall a church pitch-in they'd gone to when Hannah was in high school. A woman there, while shoveling spoons full of potato salad into her mouth and talking through the thickness of the macerated potato and mayonnaise, lamented, "I'll pay the price for these onions later tonight, I expect."

And Annis Kemp had replied, "I suppose we'll all pay the price for your description of it now," setting her own fork down on her plate in disgust.

Now, as her grandmother's silence expanded in all directions around her, Hannah wished she could ask: What hurts, and what makes it better? And is the pain worse now or has it lessened with time? But Hannah's grandmother was a woman who'd once been nearly as tall as Hannah herself, and whose hair had once been a fiery red, the echoes of which just barely reached Molly, and the Kemps did not talk of such things.

"Hey, Mason said he heard from Mom a few months ago," Hannah said, instead.

"How *is* Mason," Hannah's grandfather asked, refusing to acknowledge the reference to his daughter.

"Fine," Hannah replied. "Building houses and fly fishing. I think I'm going to go out to Montana this summer and visit him. With Michael and Molly."

"Will you take pictures and send them?" Hannah's grandfather asked. "It sure would be nice to see you two together."

"Absolutely," Hannah replied.

"Listen, we have to get going," her grandfather said, though he offered no reason why, and it seemed unlikely his schedule was all that full.

"Okay. I understand."

"We love you, baby girl," Hannah's grandmother said from what seemed to be very far away.

"I love you both, too," Hannah said.

She ended the call and watched as her cell phone's screen faded to black. She tapped the face and dialed Mason. No answer. It was the middle of the day for him. She could see him, though, his dark blond hair sticking out from under the mesh of whatever lost-and-found baseball cap he currently wore, his jeans, like those of the men in her house now, marked with spackle and paint and the brown smudges of fingers that had spent the day steadying nails and screws.

Hannah: Miss you big brother.

No reply.

CHAPTER 22

As it turned out, it hadn't taken much to disassemble the dresser in the owners' suite closets. Andrew's cabinetmaker had relied on the tension of the dressers' rails to lock the structures into the wall. He'd then caulked the sides to create a seamless built-in but had not resorted to the crude modern practice of using epoxy to super-glue the wood to the wall. Piece by piece, the dresser slid out, as Hannah carefully removed the nails, brackets, and dovetail joints that held it together.

The removal of the base of the first dresser provided Hannah her greatest reward, revealing a small handful of items which, at some point in the life of the house and of this singular chest of drawers, had slipped through the drawers, pushed against the back, and slid through the century down to the floor beneath. A black plastic comb, which she assumed had belonged to Mr. Moore. And then a sock and a cufflink that both appeared older somehow. The thread of the navy sock carried a lack of uniformity typical of darning. The gold cufflink's face was square with mother-of-pearl inset.

His dresser, then.

She carefully labeled the parts and moved them to one of the guest rooms for safekeeping. The sock and cufflink would be kept in a more private location.

Hannah descended the stairs to the kitchen. That entire side of the first floor was nearly complete, and she marveled at how just a few months before, she'd stood in this space and doubted it would ever be possible to reconstruct what Fritz Brothers had so wholly demolished.

"I'm going to go do some work in the study," Hannah said, seeing Gary and Jason comparing stains for the family room floor.

"About that," Gary said and looked to Jason, who picked up where Gary left off. They seemed hesitant to broach the topic but forged ahead.

"It's time for us to run the electricity, internet, and heating to that room. And we're going to have to get into that wall between the living room and the study—the one that holds the bookcases. I know it's important to you to keep the built-ins intact as much as possible. So, Gary and I have roughed out a plan. You got a second?"

They walked into the study where Jason detailed the necessary work.

"Do you think you can disassemble those shelves and put them back together," he asked as he and Hannah stood next to the desk, staring at the wall opposite. Two built-in oak bookshelves extended floor to ceiling on either side of a large fireplace with a breathtaking burnt-red tile surround. Every inch of the wall—floor to ceiling, doorway to corner—was occupied by either fireplace or bookshelf. For this reason, it would be one of the more complicated parts of the renovation.

"Probably," Hannah said, eyeing the bookcases, trying to determine how they'd been affixed to the wall behind them. "I won't know till I start. But I need to contact the library about these books. When do you want to start?"

"Well," Jason said, adjusting his hat, "I mean, we could start as soon as the books and cabinets are gone." Hannah grasped his meaning; they hoped to start today.

"I'll call the library now," she said.

THE RESPONSE HADN'T BEEN what she'd anticipated. Leslie, the librarian in charge of "donations", requested the books be boxed and brought to her so that she could go through them and determine which ones if any the library would accept. Leslie could either toss the rest in a giant dumpster behind the library or return them to Hannah to be dealt with by way of a yard sale or thrift store. Having received her marching orders, Hannah started the laborious task of boxing the books as soon as she ended the call. Gary's team decided to use that time to begin the demolition of the corresponding bedroom wall upstairs. The second phase of the renovation was officially underway.

Hannah hadn't closely examined the books in the study previously, though her eye had been drawn, as one might expect, to the shelves themselves. Each bookcase was composed of a lower cabinet with two leaded glass doors and five shelves above. Both cabinets were empty; whatever they'd once held had been disposed of either by Margaret, her children, or Fritz Brothers. But the books above had apparently been deemed too much trouble to remove. Having spoken with Leslie-in-donations, Hannah had a suspicion as to why.

On the bottom shelf rested a set of encyclopedias of the kind Hannah vaguely recalled from old television commercials. She couldn't remember what it cost to purchase an entire set, but assumed it involved some unknown number of installments of $19.95. Obsolete, now, with the internet, the whole set likely valued at less than a single installment.

A large dictionary and several Civil War history books also crowded the lowest shelf of the case. Hannah set them aside thinking they might be of interest to Kate, and then suddenly curious, opened the front flap of one. The name Gerald Moore had been printed in black felt-tip on the inside cover. The senior Mr. Moore was a Civil War buff, it would seem, or maybe a professor like Jeremy. In all their research on Andrew and Eleanor, Hannah and Kate hadn't extended their investigations to the next generation, though the operations of the Dailey's quarries into the 1970s indicated the Moores had continued their family's interest in limestone at least to some extent. Hannah texted a handful of photographs of the Civil War books to Kate and was met with a kind:

Kate: Thanks. I actually have most of those already.

Into the box and to the library, Hannah thought.

She then turned her attention to the shelves above.

Books by the yard, she thought of the books that spanned the remaining shelves. Their muted colors added more vibrancy to the room than she'd given them credit for, and the study seemed to dim as she pulled them from their shelves revealing the dark wood of the back of the shelf. The books themselves—both paperback and hardcovers—appeared all of an era, as if the pages had made a pact to traverse the years together, aging in a uniformed yellow, acquiring a similar dry brittleness. There were, of course, titles she recognized. *The Jungle Book, The Adventures of Huckleberry Finn, David Copperfield, A Farewell to Arms.* Books she'd read in high school. Other titles were less familiar. *An American Tragedy, Babbit, The Beautiful and the Damned, The Enormous Room, The Glimpses of the Moon.*

Hannah opened the front flaps to find the familiar signature of Andrew Decker on some, though not all, of the books. Andrew liked fiction, it would appear and, as she flipped through the pages, reading a paragraph from one, a couple of sentences from another, she found herself once again standing in a space distinctly inhabited by him. The words of the books ran through her mind as they must have run through Andrew's, the tips of her fingers brushed over pages that had once felt the brush of Andrew's fingers. The realness of his experience, a necessity—his mind necessarily held these words, these stories—draped over her as she set the books carefully in the cardboard boxes at her feet. As if she weren't the one holding the marker, the box was labeled "Andrew's Books" and set back from those that would be donated.

The cabinet that flanked the other side of the fireplace, like the boxes of photographs from the attic, seemed to have been arranged chronologically. The pages just slightly less yellowed, slightly less brittle, the covers of the books harkening to the decades that followed Andrew. Spy thrillers, sci-fi, political suspense, romance, Hannah flipped through the books, but barely needed confirmation to know they'd never been held in Andrew's hands. She packed them carefully in another box, cleverly labeled "Moore Books."

All in all, it had taken her no more than an hour to complete the task, far less than she'd thought. At the conclusion, she turned her attention to the bookcase Jason said would need to be disassembled, at least temporarily. Hannah removed each of the shelves, which lifted out of their positions easily enough. While there were plenty of ways in which Margaret's refusal to update the house had frustrated the current renovation, that she hadn't painted over the bookshelves eased the process of removing them. Hannah labeled each piece and set it against Andrew's desk behind her.

With the shelves removed, she could easily see the puzzle Andrew's cabinetmaker had constructed for her. The shelf supports were uncomplicated, stained and sanded one-by-twos doweled into the sides of the bookcase. The dowels, too, had been sanded and stained, made nearly —but not quite—invisible. With an X-acto knife and a supreme amount of patience, Hannah successfully loosened the seams and removed the shelf supports, working from the top of the case down to the cabinet.

At the cabinet top, Hannah noted the thin strip of quarter-round set into the shelf, a nice touch, much more aesthetically pleasing than a simple ninety-degree seam. She traced the X-acto knife along the back edge of the cabinet but found that the quarter-round required much less coaxing than the one-by-twos above and pulled away from the shelf's backing with little more than the weight of the knife itself. As she labeled and set the piece behind her, she saw concealed beneath not the seam of the cabinet meeting the panel behind, but a set of small brass hinges.

The top of the cabinet lifts, Hannah thought. She immediately attempted to do so only to find that the side trim secured the top in place. This was little worry, as all three pieces seemed designed for easy removal. The dowels holding them in place were loose; the only thing truly securing them to the back of the case was the tension provided where the three pieces met in the ninety-degree angles of the case itself. With the trim removed, she effortlessly lifted the top of the cabinet revealing the shallow storage compartment below.

Hannah glanced furtively around the room, almost expecting to find she was being monitored, that she'd somehow been "found out." But no one was there, and the only things behind her were Andrew's desk and the pieces of the cabinet she'd thus far pulled apart. She took her phone from her pocket, pointed it into the shallow space below and took a picture.

Hannah: Found a few things that might interest you.

Kate: When can we meet?

⁂

HANNAH CLIMBED the familiar purple granite stairs to Kate's office. She'd walked the short distance from the bungalow to the campus after Emory arrived, enjoying the way the more recent weather had started offering the early promises of spring. The walk had also helped to soothe some of Hannah's nerves, which had been nearly uncontainable since that Tuesday. Rounding the corner into the cluster of four offices that housed Kate's, Hannah saw that Jeremy's door was closed. A thin whisper of disappointment passed through her as she speculated that he'd been "warned" of her arrival and had closed his door in anticipation. The solid, dark-stained walnut refused to give up its secrets as Hannah heard Kate calling to her enthusiastically from the office next door.

Hannah pushed down her thoughts of Jeremy, taking a seat in the chair that accompanied the small table behind Kate's desk, and retrieved an accordion file from her bag.

"Eleanor wasn't running the quarries," Hannah said, starting from the end. "Andrew was. And he was good at it."

"What?" Kate said. She rolled her chair over to the table and waiting as Hannah slowly pulled document after document from her folder.

"I've organized these," Hannah said, feeling a confidence completely foreign to her. "I've got business records, correspondence from his attorney, two wills, contracts for the purchase and sale of quarries, contracts for the purchase and sale of land in the neighborhood, contracts for the sale of limestone, and Kate, he had fifteen thousand dollars in cash in there," she said, breathless as she set the papers in organized stacks on the table. "I didn't bring that though."

"Jesus," Kate muttered.

The two sat in silence, staring at the yellowed papers, the black ink, the various fading seals of notaries and government offices. Kate spun her chair to her laptop quickly typing, then spun back to Hannah, her eyes wide.

"Fifteen thousand dollars is more than three hundred and fifty thousand dollars in today's cash," she said.

"Why did Andrew have three hundred and fifty thousand dollars stored in a bookcase in his house?" Hannah asked.

"I don't know. Maybe he saw the banks collapsing around him and thought his money was safer at home. Maybe he was tired of banking with the Klan," Kate speculated.

"I think he thought Eleanor was going to leave him," Hannah said. "And he wanted to make sure she didn't take all of the money with her."

"What makes you say that?" Kate asked, bewildered.

Hannah had already constructed a narrative based on her own review of the materials. Kate might as well have been walking into a ninety-minute movie eighty minutes in.

"Hey Kate, do you mind keeping it down a touch," came a voice from around the corner, and Jeremy stepped into the doorway looking mildly annoyed.

"Oh, Hannah. I didn't know you were dropping by," he said, smoothing the front of his shirt.

"You have to see what she found, Jeremy. Take a look at all of this," Kate said, quickly adding, "Sorry we were being loud. Were you working on your tenure stuff?"

Jeremy didn't answer, already drawn to the collection of documents that sat on the table before Hannah.

"What is all this?" he asked as he gingerly lifted the stack of letters, then set them back down.

"Nearly every single thing you could want to know about Decker's finances from about—" Kate opened the ledger quickly checking the date "—1925 to the day he died."

Jeremy puffed out a breath of air. "Where'd you find this?" he asked, finally making eye contact with Hannah.

"It was inside a fireproof lockbox in a cabinet in the study. Like inside it. He had the cabinet built with a false top, and when I was taking it apart so Gary could install the wiring and stuff behind it, I realized it lifted up. The box was inside with the key still in the lock and then all this was inside that."

"I wonder what else that house is hiding," Jeremy said, though he seemed to be talking mostly to himself. "I'd be tempted to pull apart every built-in in the place after this."

"Take a look at what she's found, Jeremy. What else could there be?"

Hannah thought of the cufflink and the sock. There might be other things.

"Why didn't he put it in a bank? Like in a safe deposit box. Or even in a safe in his house?" Jeremy asked.

"He might not have been very fond of the banks. There were lots of reasons in 1933 not to rely on them," Kate offered. Jeremy bobbed his head from side to side as if these were passable, but not totally satisfying explanations.

"I also think it was important to him that this stuff was hidden," Hannah said.

Kate and Jeremy both turned to her expectantly, waiting for her to say more.

"I've never found a safe in the house," she went on. "Maybe there was one at one time, but if he'd put all this stuff in a safe, Eleanor would've known it existed. There's a lot here he wouldn't have wanted her to know about."

Jeremy moved to sit in the chair across from Hannah.

"Eleanor was leaving Andrew. Their marriage was falling apart. In fact—" and in her words, in the in fact, Hannah claimed an air of authority when it came to Andrew. She knew him better than anyone. Or at least anyone living. She resumed. "I don't think he killed himself because he was broke. You can look at these documents. He was not broke. He was barely even struggling. I think he killed himself because Eleanor broke his heart."

The look on Kate's face spoke to her disapproval of the sentimentalization of his final act. She required evidence of such a saccharine assertion. However, Jeremy's expression, the subtle tilt of his head, the softening of the creases around his eyes which had intently fixed on the stacks of paper in front of Hannah, indicated he had less trouble believing the explanation.

Hannah decided to start from the beginning.

The first relevant document chronologically was correspondence to Andrew from his attorney, a man by the name of Mr. David Harper, Esq. Although Hannah couldn't know how the two had become acquainted, the documents suggested a long relationship conceivably spanning the entire length of Andrew's adult life in Indiana. Further, Harper acted as more than just an attorney to Andrew. He provided guidance on business and personal matters and frequently, given the complexity of Andrew's marriage, matters that occupied both spheres simultaneously. Such was made evident in one of his earliest letters to Andrew, dated approximately one week before the newspaper announcement of Andrew's engagement to Eleanor. That letter advised Andrew on how to maintain his own financial autonomy in light of Walter Dailey's insistence that Andrew "not derive any financial benefit" from his marriage to Walter's daughter.

"Andrew Moore said Eleanor's parents were not happy about her marriage to Andrew Decker. Reading between the lines here, it's pretty clear her father thought Andrew was marrying Eleanor for her money." She lifted her eyes to Jeremy. "In retrospect, it seems he was probably marrying her because she was pregnant."

"He might have just loved her. I don't know why that's so hard to believe," Jeremy said.

"Either way," Kate said, without elaboration.

Hannah filled in. "Either way, Andrew had his own assets." Hannah recalled Andrew Moore's description of the nature of that in-law relationship. "In this letter, Harper's warning Andrew not to be distracted by Walter's treatment of him and that he needs to protect 'his own not insubstantial assets'." She allowed the air-quotes to reference the language used in Harper's letter.

Harper's letter cautioned Andrew that although "the limestone craze" would eventually come to an end and the Daileys' stream of income would be reduced to a drip, Andrew's skills as an architect and his growing proficiency in residential development would never be obsolete. If the Daileys wanted to keep assets separate, so much the better from the perspective of Andrew's attorney.

"Wow, that's some amazingly bad advice," Jeremy commented with a chuckle.

Kate did not join him. She appeared to have suddenly grown serious as the features of Decker's life began coming into focus in a rather unexpected way. "He's writing this in—when? 1920?" She took the letter from Hannah and examined the date. "Nine and a half years before the Great Depression. Not bad advice for the time."

"And it ended up—I mean not on purpose—but it ended up working out because Andrew and the Daileys kept their finances separate. At first, anyway," Hannah said, picking up a brown leather business ledger and handing it to Kate. "Andrew essentially treated his wife's family's business like a subcontractor. He purchased their materials and used them when he built his houses. But he had no ownership interest in it. And neither did she, technically."

Hannah continued as Jeremy sat back in the chair listening. She felt different—different than she'd felt even a month before when she'd struggled to explain her childhood, when she'd bristled at the mention of Andrew's social class, of his limited mobility. She sat upright now, her hands moving around the table as she referenced one document or another, enlivened by the unfolding details of his life.

"So, it looks like it took a little while for Andrew to get his footing after moving back to Indiana," Hannah went on. "When he and Eleanor married, he was working for Matson, that architecture firm that's mentioned in the article about his return to Indiana. But in 1921, Harper helped him establish Decker Developers and that's when he purchased the farmland from Karl Hyde." She handed the Operating Agreement for Decker Developers, Ltd. to Kate. "According to this, Andrew let Mr. Hyde stay on in his family's farmhouse at no cost or rent until his death.

Mr. Hyde was almost in foreclosure and had been worried that the bank would take his farm and turn him out into the streets. But Andrew purchased the land from him and allowed him to just stay there."

"That was nice of him," Jeremy said, pouting out his bottom lip.

"It was more than nice," said Kate as she skimmed the purchase agreement that Harper had drawn up. "He got a steal on the land in exchange for it. He paid for all of it in cash. I bet he borrowed against the land to get his business off the ground."

"I don't know if he did or not, but he's pretty conservative when he eventually starts building." Hannah handed over a stack of sales contracts to Kate, who handed half of them to Jeremy, the two of them flipping through the pages with her. The contracts demonstrated the restraint of a man who, in the midst of the roaring twenties, merely purred. He began at a pace of about one house per year, fully custom homes for each of his clients. After the first couple of years, he increased the pace only slightly to three or four houses per year. This explained the lines of demarcation in the neighborhood, with the fifteen original homes all of the same era—1922 to 1929—and the remaining homes built after 1945, some well after.

"He also contracted out his services as an architect. So, he was making money on top of the neighborhood construction by drafting plans for private clients in other up-and-coming areas," Hannah explained as she strained to see the contracts over the span of the table —not that she had any real doubt as to what they said.

"Is Eleanor designing houses, too?" Kate held up one of the contracts, flipped back to a page that seemed to itemize costs for services provided by Eleanor Decker.

"I don't quite understand that," Hannah admitted, not feeling the insecurity she so often felt with such admissions. "She's definitely doing something. She's a named partner in the Operating Agreement for Decker Developers, and she's in almost every sales contract for the houses in the neighborhood."

"Where does the quarry come in?" Kate asked, setting the Operating Agreement down on the table in front of her.

"It's there the whole time," Hannah said. "They use Dailey limestone on literally every single thing they build. And a lot of things they don't."

"They?" Jeremy questioned.

"I guess I'm just thinking Eleanor must've been involved in all of this in some way. Her name is all over the place. At least on Andrew's stuff. Her father seems to have a pretty tight grip on the limestone company."

"Doesn't look like he was very good at that," Jeremy piped up. He held yet another letter from David Harper, this one from 1926. "Says here, Decker offered Harper's services to Dailey because Dailey was trying to buy some enormous quarry down in Bloomington. But Dailey turned him down." Jeremy pulled the correspondence back under his eyes. "Harper says no hard feelings, but he's obviously worried. Thinks Dailey is being reckless."

"How so?" Kate asked, reaching for the correspondence.

"He thinks there's too much unquarried limestone down there, that new quarries are opening faster than Dailey can purchase the old ones. The new quarries are going to drive down the price of the stone," Jeremy said.

"He gives him the same advice in 1928 and tells Decker to keep his distance." Hannah picked up another letter.

"I guess we can deduce that Dailey didn't listen?" Kate asked.

"Looks that way," said Jeremy after a brief pause.

"He regrets it, though," Hannah cut in. "Look."

Of the many documents stored in the lockbox was a single piece of correspondence from Walter Dailey to Andrew Decker shortly after Decker's fortieth birthday. 1929—weeks before the crash that would mark the beginning of the Great Depression. He'd misjudged the man, Walter said. Failed to recognize in him the material of a solid and savvy businessman, whose counsel—and counselor—he'd have been wise to heed over the years. Walter Dailey also had some rather choice words for his daughter about whom he expressed regret that she had not developed "a sense of industry in proportion to her sense of entitlement."

"Damn," Kate said. "That's harsh."

"It gets worse," Hannah said. "He tells Andrew he's leaving the quarry to *him*. And then *he does*."

"He owned the whole goddamn thing," Kate said. "He owned the land; he owned the housing development; he owned his own architecture firm; and he owned the quarry. He owned everything. At least for a little while." This last modification was necessary to account for the few short years Andrew lived after his father-in-law's death.

"So, Eleanor owns half of Decker Developers," Jeremy said, his fingers flipping through the pages now disordered on the tabletop. "She never gets the quarry, though? It's *her family's* quarry." His voice registered Hannah's own disbelief at the fate of Dailey Limestone Limited.

"It would have been pretty unheard of for a woman to own a business like that at the time, let alone in this state," Kate said. "It's frankly astonishing that she's a partner in Decker's business, and an active one by the looks of it." She lifted a contract that bore Eleanor's initials: "EDD" on several lines and her signature at the bottom.

"Still, I bet she was pissed," Jeremy added.

"Pissed enough to leave him, it looks like," Hannah agreed, and she pulled out a Petition for Divorce and set it on the table.

"Who filed first?" Kate asked, grabbing the document while the pages still drifted toward the table.

"Eleanor," Hannah said. "She was leaving him. The best I can piece it together from what we've got here, Andrew took over Dailey's quarry operation after Walter died in '29. Harper drew up another Operating Agreement that gave Eleanor half of the quarry—pretty much the same deal they'd set up with the development—and Andrew and Harper began the process of purchasing the smaller quarries around them. This was all after the Depression had started, and Harper was telling Andrew 'It's only going to get worse.' So, Andrew backs off residential development and consolidates the quarries, which seem to be more resilient. And he's got his little cadre of clients. Like, he's selling stone to this guy Simmons who's still building houses over in Meridian-Kessler."

"He's selling limestone outside the state, too," Kate interrupted, paging through the ledger. "Universities, other state government buildings. He's finding low-risk purchasers. It's on a smaller scale than pre-Depression, but he's keeping it going." Kate picked up a contract with Empire State, Inc. "Look at that," she said. "There's Dailey stone on the Empire State Building."

"I wondered if that was what I thought it was," Hannah said.

"Seems to be," Kate replied and set the contract back down. "You know the quarry where they mined the stone for the Empire State Building is so deep and so wide you could put the Empire State Building in it?"

"Is that where Eleanor drowned herself?" Jeremy asked.

"No. It wouldn't have been filled with water then. They were still mining in it. Probably an old quarry that wasn't active anymore. And those increased throughout the Depression," Kate said.

"The article I have doesn't say which quarry. Just that it was one of her family's quarries," Hannah added. "So, all of this confirms what you said a while ago, Kate," Hannah concluded. "He wasn't ruined in 1933. He was fine."

"Well, not totally," Jeremy said. He'd found a purchase agreement, the word "CANCELED" stamped across the front page.

"Yeah, he had a couple of deals fall through that seemed pretty big. Two right before the crash and then that one." She tipped her forehead in Jeremy's direction. "That cancellation is dated January 9, 1933."

"Right before he killed himself," Kate said. "That must be the deal Andrew Moore told you about. I'm not seeing anything here that suggests he was heartbroken, though," Kate said. "And those were some pretty harsh words about Eleanor by her father. Would he have said that if he didn't think Decker would agree? And Decker doesn't strike me as a dumb man. If his wife was... as described, did he really not know?"

"I think people have the capacity to look past an awful lot when they're in love," Jeremy said absently. The room grew quiet again.

"It's the last letter from Harper to Andrew before he died," Hannah said, addressing Kate's inquiry and lifting the thin paper, its black font aged nearly to purple. "Harper thought she was having an affair."

Hannah cleared her throat and read from the letter:

19 December 1932

Dear Andrew:

I write to you concerning a most sensitive subject and it brings me no joy to call your attention to this matter. Three days ago, I saw Mrs. Decker exit the office of Mr. Murray with Mr. Edward Lehmann of Nashville. I did not see you in their company and understand that at this time you were in Bedford at the mill and so would not, yourself, have had occasion to be meeting with Mr. Lehmann. I cannot profess to have seen any exchange between the two that would be considered improper, other than a certain air about them that suggested affection.

I beg you, do not misunderstand me. I do not intend to injure Mrs. Decker's reputation with gossip, but rather, to advise you that any association with Mr. Lehmann should be discouraged. My colleagues in Nashville inform me his name is entirely unfamiliar to them, they count his business dealings among their clients at zero. I am compelled to express my deep concern that the man intends to exploit Mrs. Decker's affections at your financial expense. It is my sincere recommendation, not solely as your counsel, but as your friend, that you warn Mrs. Decker of his emerging troubling reputation, and that you admonish her to cease any further association with him immediately.

I remain, as always, your confidant and colleague.

Very truly yours,

David J. Harper, Esq.

Kate was already at her computer typing in the man's name before Hannah had even finished reading the letter. "Nothing," she said as she swiveled her chair back toward Jeremy and Hannah.

"It sounds like it was an alias," Jeremy suggested, suddenly sounding dejected.

Hannah set the letter down on the table, and Jeremy picked it up, reading it to himself.

"What's wrong?" she asked.

"It's just depressing," he said, clearly finding it all to be self-evident, and Hannah supposed it was.

"That she was cheating on him?" Kate asked.

"More than that," Jeremy said. "Just everything he lost. His brothers, his first child, and then his wife. I think I liked it better when all he'd lost was his money. By January 10th, his wife was having an affair, he'd essentially bankrupted his own business and only had hers to lean on, which must have been quite the ego boost, she's filed for divorce, planning to leave him for whoever this Lehmann guy is—"

"It does kind of explain it though," Hannah said. "I mean, why he would be driven to... do what he did."

"Are we sure he killed himself?" Jeremy asked. His face had grown pale even in the short time he'd been in Kate's office, and his eyes had a forlorn appearance that Hannah herself had when thinking about Andrew's death: that the tragedy of it was almost too much for her.

"Like what? He... ran off and joined the circus, or... what else would have happened to him?" Kate asked.

"He didn't run off and join the circus," Hannah interrupted. She was working with the edges of her words now, trying to be sensitive to the fact that although Andrew had been fully human to her for several months now, he was just becoming so for Jeremy. Hannah had begun with grief and transitioned to curiosity, as if the only thing that could bring her comfort was knowledge, an understanding of him. For Jeremy, he'd moved in reverse, his knowledge and understanding bringing him grief.

"He changed his will three days before he killed himself," Hannah pulled that document from the pile noting the signature page and the date. 9 January 1933. "It's just a copy, but he leaves every single asset he has in trust to Margaret. He provides a one hundred dollar per month allowance to Eleanor and stipulates that she can live in the house for the remainder of her life. But she only gets those things if she doesn't contest the will. Then he makes his sister, Mary, trustee."

Kate spun back to her computer. "He left his wife twenty-eight thousand dollars a year to live on. In today's money, I mean. What's the poverty rate for one person?"

"Twenty-five something, I think," Jeremy mumbled. "But she already had her half of the businesses." He paused, once again thumbing through the pages of the contracts, letters, the petition for divorce. "Why didn't anyone notice that the whole financial ruin thing was nonsense? Like, obviously it's nonsense," Jeremy asked.

"I don't know. Maybe they thought it was indelicate to point out that he killed himself because his marriage was about to fall apart," Kate speculated. "Look at the lengths his attorney goes to avoid outright saying, 'Your wife is fucking someone else.' And then once a story takes hold in a community—in a family—that's it. That's the story. And people just keep telling it, and they stop asking whether it could even possibly be true."

They sat quietly, each staring at the pile of papers on the table. The floorboard radiator kicked on with a decisive rattle. Hannah recalled a comment by Michael—months ago now—something about Jeremy moping around after his fiancée left him at the end of the previous school year. As Hannah observed the way Jeremy received the details of the final few weeks of Andrew's life, she thought, even more than she had at the time, that Jeremy probably had not "moped" when his fiancée left him. She guessed, rather, that he'd been devastated. As one would be when his heart is broken.

CHAPTER 23

"Hey where were you? I drove by the house, and Jason said you haven't been there since Tuesday," Michael asked.

Hannah had just walked through the door of the bungalow expecting to find Emory, books spread out on top of the coffee table, highlighting, annotating, typing into her laptop.

She felt completely dazed from her meeting with Jeremy and Kate. Jeremy's question about whether they were sure Andrew had died by suicide had caused her to begin questioning whether they could be sure Eleanor had. She'd died two years later, still a widow. If she'd been having an affair with Lehmann, she hadn't married him, and he'd disappeared entirely after Andrew's death.

"What are you doing home?" she asked Michael, as she hung her coat in the closest. She consulted her watch and saw that it was just before 3:30 in the afternoon. "Is Molly awake?" If Molly slept past 3:00, she'd be hard to put down at bedtime.

"Doesn't look that way," Michael said, a hint of sarcasm in his voice.

Hannah climbed the stairs heading to her daughter's bedroom, and Michael followed.

"Where were you," he asked again as Hannah opened the bedroom door.

"Wake up, baby girl," Hannah cooed, walking toward the crib. "I was meeting with Kate at Butler," she replied.

Molly stirred in the crib. She'd been sleeping with her knees tucked under her, her little rump high in the air. She rolled to the side with a heavy *plop* as she woke from her too-long nap.

"What did you need to meet with Kate about?" he asked as Hannah lifted Molly out of the crib and carried her into the light of the hallway, then down the stairs and out into the living room.

Molly opened her mouth wide, releasing a yawn. Then, as if to create balance, she closed her eyes tight against the brightness of the room.

"We've been doing research on the architect of the Decker house. I told you about this already," Hannah said. She watched Michael attempt to connect with what was evidently his vague memory of their conversation from several months ago. He'd been trying to watch something on TV at the time.

"Still?" he asked.

"What do you mean, *still?*"

"I just mean how much can there be on the guy?"

Even if Hannah had known where to begin with such a question, she wouldn't have bothered. Not with Michael.

"Yeah. It's been hard to find stuff," she said and set Molly down on the floor. Michael leaned back into himself as he crossed his arms over his chest. Hannah could see him measuring her, calculating something.

"What's it for?" he asked, accusation driving the question.

"What's what for?"

"The research. If you find out all you want to know about him, what are you going to do with it?"

"Kate wants to write a book or something, and I want to add it to my blog." She walked toward the kitchen, trying to be nonchalant, but wondering if Michael had seen, by any chance, if he'd been driving by at just the right time, had he seen Jeremy walk her to the edge of the campus, parting ways with her only when she reached the crosswalk that led away from the university and into the neighborhood beyond.

"Your what?" Michael asked.

"My blog. Debbie said I should keep a blog about the house reno. So, I started one. I haven't published it yet," she said.

"Can I see it?" Michael asked. Again, Hannah was struck by the absence of curiosity from someone who seemed to be seeking so very much information.

"Sure," she said and pulled her laptop from her bag hanging on the hooks next to the kitchen door. She opened the computer and logged into the blog she'd been keeping since she'd decided the house was hers, as Gary put it. The latest entry included pictures of the cabinets she'd made along with pictures she'd used for inspiration, drawings and photographs of 1920s kitchens, as well as a "before" picture of the demo'ed kitchen from the listing photos.

"Looks good," Michael commented. While he said this as he scrolled through the "Kitchen" page, Hannah thought it wasn't so much the blog that looked good to Michael, as her explanation for where she'd been and how she'd been spending her time.

❧

Hannah didn't recognize the number on her phone, but she recognized the area code—the same area code that corresponded with Mason's most recent cell phone number. When she answered the phone, however, she wasn't greeted by the deep voice of her older brother, which had grown even deeper over the years as his Marlboro Reds obliterated his larynx. The smooth voice on the other end of the line sounded somehow younger, simultaneously more vibrant and more dower.

"Hello," the man said. "Is this Hannah Burke?"

"Korman," she said, sitting forward on the couch in the bungalow. Something in the man's voice seemed to require her complete attention.

"Are you Mason Kemp's sister?" he asked.

"Who is this?" Hannah returned with an unnatural edge borrowed from Michael.

"This is Dr. Damon Thomas. I'm a Fellow at Regional Intermountain Hospital. Can you confirm that you are Mason Kemp's sister?"

The tone of the man's voice was professional and courteous, but with a sheen of condescension.

"A fellow *what*?" Hannah asked.

"A Fellow in Critical Care. I'm a physician."

"Oh," Hannah said. Her eyes drifted to Molly, who was marching a family of plastic dinosaurs along the floor at Hannah's feet. "Yes, I'm Mason's sister."

"Are you somewhere we can talk? Do you have a minute?"

Hannah watched as the lines between the slats of oak on the floor began to move, swerving and curving under her feet, prefiguring the changed shape she sensed her world was about to take.

"Ms. Burke—"

"Hannah."

"Hannah, your brother is a patient in our hospital right now." He paused allowing for some acknowledgment, but Hannah could offer none. "We've had a lot of trouble locating family for him."

"I'm his sister," Hannah said, though she wasn't sure who had required clarification of that fact.

"Yes. Thank you for picking up. I'm glad we were able to reach you," said Dr. Damon Thomas, Critical Care Fellow at Regional Intermountain Hospital. "Does Mason have any other family we should reach out to?"

"For what?" Hannah asked, then reconsidered her answer. "I don't know his father's name. And I don't have contact information for our mother. I think Mason has her most recent contact information. You could ask him."

"We can't ask him right now—" Dr. Thomas's voice became unintelligible. He'd put his hand over the phone, mumbling to someone in the background. "—his sister in Indianapolis," he said, putting the phone back to his mouth while still speaking to someone other than Hannah.

"Yes. I'm Mason's sister," Hannah said again.

"Ms. Bur—Hannah. Would it be possible for you to come out here? To the hospital? We'd like to speak with you in person."

Who are you talking to? Michael mouthed as he came into the living room from the office.

Hannah didn't respond. She looked down at Molly who now had the head of a stegosaurus in her mouth. A line of drool connected her chin to her sweater. Molars.

"I don't know if I can do that," Hannah said. "Could you—Could I speak with him, please? With Mason?"

"That's not possible right now, Hannah," Dr. Thomas said.

Who are you talking to? Michael mouthed again.

"Sometimes he forgets to pay his cellphone bill," she said almost hopefully.

"Hannah," Dr. Thomas said. "Your brother has—he was found this morning at his home."

Was found. Hannah heard the words. *By whom? Why were they looking for him?*

"We prefer to discuss these things in person. But they couldn't wake him up—"

"Who?" Hannah asked, struggling to picture the scene in her head and absolutely unable to do so.

"Your brother," he said as if there were no other possible person they could be speaking of, and there wasn't, but this wasn't the answer to the question Hannah had asked.

"Who couldn't wake him up?"

"Oh. The people who found him." This, as it turned out, didn't clarify things for Hannah either. He paused before he continued, perhaps waiting to see if Hannah had any questions about the people who found him. She did not.

Michael sat heavily in the chair next to the couch, his brows creased. He leaned forward, craning his neck as though there were a chance he'd be able to hear some of what was being said.

"Hannah, your brother has suffered a drug overdose," Dr. Thomas said, opting to get to the point.

"What? I don't understand." Hannah felt blunted. They must have called the wrong person. Her brother was painting houses. And fishing. And hiking on the weekends in Wyoming at Yellowstone. She had the keychain to prove it.

"This happens here a lot—"

"A lot?"

"It looks like he thought he was shooting up heroin, but it was fentanyl. Did you know your brother struggled with substance use disorder?" Dr. Thomas asked.

Substance use disorder. What was that? That sounded made up. It sounded like words people strung together to make something sound like something it was not. Either way, the answer was no.

"Mrs. Burke?"

"Hannah."

WHO ARE YOU TALKING TO? Michael was whispering, but his expression screamed. Hannah switched the phone to speaker.

"Hannah. When they found your brother, he wasn't breathing very well. We don't know for how long. He's at the hospital now. We've had a lot of trouble finding you or anyone else in his family. What is your mother's name?"

"Fiona. Fiona Kemp."

"Hannah. We don't think your brother is going to get better," Dr. Thomas said.

"Better from what?"

"During the time he was having trouble breathing, his brain was very severely damaged. We don't think he's ever going to wake up, Hannah."

"Fuck," Michael breathed.

"Is someone else there?" Dr. Thomas asked.

"My husband, Michael," Hannah said. "Is he—I don't understand. Is he dead?" she asked. The word 'dead' floated out into the room like a poltergeist.

"No, he's not dead," Dr. Thomas said. "But he doesn't open his eyes. He can't breathe on his own. He has a tube to help him breathe. He doesn't respond to our voices. And we don't think he will get better from this. Is there—would it be possible for you to come here? To the hospital, I mean. It would help if you were here in person."

Hannah looked at Michael, who'd grown pale, the lines around his mouth lengthening and drawing his face down into his jaw. He nodded to her without hesitation.

"Yes. Yes. I can come."

"How quickly can you get here?"

"I'll get her on a plane tomorrow," Michael volunteered with authority.

Hannah spun toward him, her face awash in terror at his phrasing. He *would* put her on a plane tomorrow. He would make all of the arrangements. He would secure the hotel—and a nice one, too. He would make sure a car waited for her at the airport. He would text her daily to check on her and see how things were going. He would watch Molly while she was gone, or his parents and Emory would.

But she would go alone.

"I can't take off work. There's too much to do with the Basingstoke transition," he said after she got off the phone. "I have to be absolutely focused on preparing for that. No distractions. And Molly shouldn't be exposed to something like this anyway," he argued, though Hannah thought it remote at best that concern for Molly drove any part of Michael's decision-making. The way he returned her glare told her he would not be persuaded, though.

Molly. She needed a bath. Her bedtime was in half an hour. She would have trouble falling asleep. She'd napped too long during the day. Because Emory had been sent away by Michael, who did not know his daughter well enough to know she shouldn't nap past 3:00 in the afternoon.

"I hate you," Hannah said, staring at Michael from her seat on the couch.

"What?" Michael sputtered. His cheeks pinched up in confusion, as if the squint they brought to his eyes had some property of clarification.

"I hate you," she repeated. In some ways, it had just occurred to her.

His eyes searched hers, part inquiry, part challenge. She didn't blink.

"You're in shock. I'll make your travel arrangements," he said.

Hannah got up from the couch and walked to the kitchen, grabbing her coat from the hook by the kitchen door and her keys from the bowl next to it. At the sound of the jingle of her keys, Michael launched out of his chair and followed her into the kitchen.

"Where are you going?" he demanded.

"I left my driver's license at the Decker house," she said. "Gary needed it for a permit request, and I forgot to put it back in my wallet."

"You shouldn't be driving when you're like this," he said. "And Molly needs a bath, and it's almost her bedtime."

"Then give her a fucking bath and put her to bed, Michael," Hannah said. "I need my driver's license to get on the plane tomorrow." And she walked out the door, leaving Michael in stunned silence.

HANNAH DROVE up the long gravel drive to the Decker house and parked in the small horseshoe at the front steps. It looked different in the dark, and she realized she'd never seen it this late at night. Although it was wired now, electricity running to modern outlets and light fixtures, the windows met her with their symmetry of blackness, nothing behind them but the infinite vacuum of space.

She walked into the foyer and through the living room into the study. The pieces of the disassembled cabinet leaned against the front of Andrew's desk, waiting to be fitted back together, a jigsaw puzzle of oak. The wall had been opened, a jagged wound in the mortar that extended from floor to ceiling. Silver ductwork gleamed in the scant moonlight that sliced through the room. Hannah paused in the living room on her way back to the foyer. The sideboard. The green velvet couch. The tables next to it. She ran her fingers over the back of the couch as she walked toward the foyer, toward the wide, imposing stairs of the front hall.

She glided gracefully, avoiding the clip-clop of her shoes on the tile and grateful for the runner on the stairs, though she couldn't explain why she felt the need to be quiet; she was the only person in the house. She caressed the banister as she went, as she usually did, thinking it was as close to holding his hand as she could get. In the dark, she imagined him with her, placing a dark, heavy, wool blazer around her shoulders, the scent of citrus and black pepper enveloping her. He'd walk a step behind her, chivalrous, in case she slipped or tripped. He'd catch her. She could almost hear his feet—the creak in the step fourth from the top.

Someone should really fix that, Andrew.

He knew.

At the top, she looked toward the owners' suite. From the hallway, it looked much as it must have the last time Andrew slept in it. Hannah thought there had necessarily been a last day that he walked across the threshold into that room, removed the strict, unforgiving cotton and wool threads from his body. He'd have crawled into his bed, sliding beneath the sheets and blankets, and slept and dreamt and awoken for the last time.

At the top of the stairs, she followed the length of the corridor until she reached the stairs to the third floor. She didn't know how much time Andrew spent in the attic of his home, but she suspected not much. He'd have no reason to. Like her travels to Montana, she'd make this trip alone.

She entered one of the north-facing bedrooms—the one Molly used to nap in before Emory started working for them—and went to the closet. She pulled the bottom drawer from the dresser built into the side of the closet, a luxury for the time. With the drawer removed, she pried up the solid oak board that comprised the bottom of the dresser and shined the flashlight of her phone down into the area below. She then opened the flap of her bag and pulled the accordion folder out, the papers, documents, and letters carefully arranged. She placed the papers into the black metal lockbox that rested against the floor, satisfied that it would be concealed under the base of the dresser. Then, she gazed down at the collection of photographs, copies made, just a few—their wedding portrait, a photograph with Margaret, he and his brothers—all hidden safe from even the remotest chance of Michael's discovery.

Finally, she lifted out Andrew's photograph still in its frame—the one from 1929, from his study, the one with his hands folded casually in his lap and his eyes looking so directly at Hannah, she thought it possible he occasionally moved within the photograph, his body somehow still living within the four corners of the frame. She placed the photograph in her bag. Then she replaced the board and the drawer, and closed the door to the closet, and the door to the bedroom, and the door to the house, and returned to her car.

CHAPTER 24

The room was neither ecru nor eggshell. It wasn't the color of
cabinets. It was the color of walls that had been painted too
many times to fully conceal the colors beneath. A thin sliver
along one edge of the ceiling exposed the dull paint as a mask, hiding
what had, at one time, been walls of sky blue—the color of a sky
without a single cloud, without a bird, without the pointed green tips
of leaves reaching up. A sky without life. The scuffs on the wall gave
the room its color, a yellow-gray as the fluorescent lights of the ceiling
reflected off the laminate wood of the conference room table.

They were all glad to see her. They said so. They were so happy she
could make it. They didn't like to think of Mason being alone "at a
time like this."

Had she been able to get in touch with her mother?

No. She didn't know she was supposed to try.

Had she been to Mason's trailer out by the river?

No. She didn't know he owned a trailer, and she came directly from
the airport.

They used small words to explain it all to her. Like she was a child.
She knew the reason they used the small words rather than the real
words was because they thought she was stupid. Because they assumed

the family of people who died of drug overdoses in trailers out by rivers must not be very smart. And because when they found her brother, he had a needle in his arm, and that wasn't very smart, they thought, to put a needle in your arm.

"Mrs. Korman?" a man was saying. He sounded like Dr. Thomas, but was not. He was someone else who also didn't think Mason was going to get better. She couldn't remember his name. He wore his badge on a black lanyard that extended below the edge of the table.

"Mrs. Korman?" he said again. He was addressing her.

She'd forgotten that was her name. Her name was Hannah. Sometimes it was Hannah Banana, though probably not anymore.

"Mrs. Korman? Do you understand what we're saying?" the man asked.

They were waiting for her answer.

"You're saying he's not going to wake up." She understood they were saying more than this. She understood they were asking for her permission.

"He taught me to drive," she said, and they looked at her blankly.

They didn't understand. They wanted to make sure she understood, but they didn't understand. It had been a big deal. She was living with her grandparents, and Mason came to Clover to visit. He was twenty-three, and Hannah didn't even know he'd left Boston. After she left Boston, she somehow imagined that everyone there had stayed precisely as they were, but of course they hadn't. That's why she now couldn't find their mother. It turned out Mason had been living in Georgia, so it was "easy enough" to drive up to South Carolina. He slept on the couch for a week, and Annis and Robert loved him in their own quiet way, feeding him more than any man could eat, asking about his life in Georgia. Did he have a girl, their grandfather asked. Where was he working, their grandmother asked.

He answered these questions and others, but more importantly, he realized Hannah had turned sixteen and that she should be getting a driver's license. He took her to a road so old and unused it amounted to not much more than two lines of dirt separated by some very determined grass. And that is why, when she'd arrived that morning at the airport's car rental, and the reservation that Michael had made for a luxury SUV was not available, she knew how to drive the manual transmission, the "stick", which was all they had left.

"Yes," she said, looking across the conference table. "He wouldn't want this. He wouldn't want to be like this."

"You understand that when we turn off the breathing machine, he will die?"

Hannah nodded. She had no trouble understanding that when they turned off the breathing machine, Mason would die. The trouble was that she simply could not conceive of it.

"We will make sure he doesn't suffer," Not-Dr-Thomas said, and Hannah thought it was a little too late for someone like him to suddenly worry that Mason Kemp might be suffering.

A woman led her out of the conference room and down a hall where the melody of distorted blips and beeps became the music of a macabre circus in which her brother was... what would he be... an animal trainer, she thought, and she'd be a trapezist flying through the air. But as she rounded the corner into his room, she saw he was missing his black top hat, and she wasn't wearing her sequined leotard, and as Not-Dr-Thomas and the woman who accompanied him moved around the room, the *PPUUUshhhht PPUUUshhht blip beep, blip beep* quieted to a *HUUUsssshhhh*.

Hannah crawled onto the bed, looking down the length of the white sheet at her brother's long, nimble legs that did not move, and she lay her cheek against his broad, firm chest that did not move, and Hannah thought, he was loved. He was so loved. She couldn't imagine the despair that took him from her when for his whole life, for every day of it, for every sliver of every minute, he had been loved. By her.

❧

HANNAH DROVE up the dirt road to the address the hospital had given her, the address where Mason had "been found" the previous morning. They'd told Hannah, as they handed her a sheet of paper—a copy of a copy of a copy, its print so distorted Hannah could have been viewing it through the bottom of a water glass—that everything she needed to know about funeral homes and burials in Bozeman was contained on that sheet. She'd found it ironic that the group which had so many recommendations to make about the end of Mason's life seemed suddenly to have no real idea how to begin his death. She'd finally gone with "the one most people around here use." And the funeral home told her she should get Mason—or his body anyway—something to wear. For his funeral. And for the unspecified term thereafter.

Now, she sat in the Honda, facing what was apparently Mason's trailer and thought, *There is nothing here that will work.*

She didn't need to go inside to know that. She could tell from the way the door hung open—whoever had found Mason hadn't closed it after themselves. She could tell by the oven range under the window and the thin layer of snow covering the cooktop. Someone at some point had strung a set of multi-colored Christmas lights across the front of the trailer, but they weren't twinkling, and as Hannah followed the length of green rope to the end of the trailer, she saw the prongs of the plug limply hanging, the lights, not their illumination, having evidently been the entire objective of the decor.

She could go inside, she thought. There would be things that belonged to him there. But even that seemed beside the point. There would be things that belonged to him, but that didn't *go with him*, that didn't fit with her memory of him, that went with someone who "was found", but not with her brother. There was nothing of him there.

Hannah put the car in reverse, listening to the kazoo hum of the manual transmission as she backed down to the end of the dirt road where she could turn the car without risking the hazards of snow drifts.

In town, she found a mall. She purchased a suit from one of two department stores that anchored the mall. She had his height and his shirt size, and guessed the rest, and what did it matter anyway. It was a gray suit, charcoal, flannel, as if he might get cold. She also purchased a light blue oxford and a burgundy tie that he would wear for eternity.

By the time she returned to the hotel, after purchasing the suit, dropping it off at the funeral home, and eating dinner, it was nearly 10:00 Indianapolis time. Long after Molly had gone to bed. Or should have gone to bed. She pulled the Honda into a parking space outside the hotel and texted Michael.

Hannah: How is everything going?

Michael: Fine. How are you holding up? Want to talk?

Hannah: I'm fine. I'm going to go to bed. Talk tomorrow.

Michael: My mom says she can only stay for the week. When do you think you'll be back?

Hannah: Before then.

Michael: Before when?

Hannah: Before a week.

Michael: Can you be more specific?

Hannah: No.

Michael: Is there a special toy or something that Molly uses at night. A teddy bear or something?

This last text indicated there'd been difficulty in getting Molly to sleep. Hannah assumed the difficulty was not related to the absence of a teddy bear—though Molly did have a giraffe she liked—and had more to do with the absence of Molly's mother. This reminded Hannah of the absence of her own mother, for years now, and how the hospital was "pretty sure" they could "track her down" with just the little bit of information Hannah had given them. Hannah struggled to comprehend how it was that the hospital could track down Fiona Kemp in a matter of days, while Hannah hadn't been able to locate her in years. This left Hannah to conclude that for the past several years, maybe three, maybe more, it wasn't so much that Hannah couldn't track her mother down, as that she really hadn't cared to try.

❧

THE STARCHED WHITE sheets of the hotel room greeted Hannah as she crawled into bed and lay her head down on the pillow, punching it lightly, trying to negotiate space for herself. On the table next to the bed, she set her watch and her phone, and the photograph of Andrew, positioned to face her, his eyes bright, his smile warm and kind. She felt that her eyelids contained the small lead weights of a fishing lure, pulling down, down, and then bobbing back up, each time Andrew coming back into view, his eyes still on her.

She reached up and turned out the lamp on the table, and the room became shrouded. Her eyes grew heavy and stopped their bobbing, the lids resting, closed, veiling darkness within the darkness. The sheets around her held heaviness, a warmth cloaking her not in cotton, but in comfort, with his arm resting across her side, pulling her to him until her back met his chest, and his knees curved into the bend of her own, and she slept wrapped in him.

❧

HANNAH COULDN'T IMAGINE how her mother had managed to afford the ticket or the black suit she'd arrived in, but she had and in time for Mason's funeral at which she was one of two in attendance. The minister was a stranger, but kind enough to offer the graveside service. Surprised as she was by her mother's presence at Mason's funeral, she was equally surprised by her mother's appearance.

The intervening years hadn't treated Fiona Kemp well, though Hannah wondered whether her memory of their last meeting wasn't completely accurate. Fiona was only twenty-five years older than Hannah, but it could have been fifty. There was no mistaking the two as family, the crisp blue of Fiona's eyes, her height, the blonde hair—even if from a bottle. But that resemblance could be teased apart, a difference in similarity. The two women had so clearly inhabited wholly different realms of the world, Hannah struggled to believe they could possibly ever have known each other.

Where Hannah's hair was smooth, layered into a soft frame around her face, Fiona's hair stopped below her shoulders, the ends in need of a trim, the color so aggressively monochromatic it could have been painted by a child. The lines of her face were etched deep, not merely with grief, but with the unforgiving erosion of life's many hardships. Fine creases around her lips suggested years of puckering around a cigarette. Her frame was as thin as Hannah's, but Hannah guessed her mother's "svelte" figure was the result of empty pantries, not expensive exercise classes.

The minister offered his commendation. "Acknowledge, we humbly pray, a sheep of your own fold, a lamb of your own flock, a sinner of your own redeeming. Receive him into the arms of your mercy, into the blessed rest of everlasting peace, and into the glorious company of the saints in light."

A sinner of your own redeeming. Hannah objected to this. Mason was not a sinner. She couldn't imagine he'd ever done anything in this world that would qualify him for the reductionist moniker of "sinner." But the minister recited the words with the end of one meeting up with the beginning of the next as though he didn't have time for the spaces between.

As he continued, Hannah felt her knees buckle beneath her, and she lifted her face toward the wide expanse of the blue, Montana sky, and her mouth opened as she screamed into the heavens her grief and rage and emptiness. And then it seemed, she had not done those things. Her brother had died, and the earth had opened beneath his casket, ready to swallow him, and she stood motionless across from her mother, and the minister, and the casket as the tears tipped over the edges of her eyes and fell silently down her cheeks to the ground.

"Did you know?" Fiona asked as they sat across from each other at the Maggiano's in the mall where, just two days before, Hannah had purchased Mason the best suit he'd ever worn.

"Did I know what?" Hannah asked.

"That he had a problem?" Fiona clarified without accusation. The suggestion wasn't that Hannah knew and should have done something, or that she hadn't known and should have.

"No. I had no idea."

"Me neither," Fiona said. "How are you?" she asked when Hannah remained silent.

"My brother's dead."

"I mean, in Boston. How are you? How are you and Michael?" Her mother's voice was airy, a bit of a rasp, but it had a certain quality to it in the face of Hannah's growing animosity. Like still water being poured into fine crystal.

"I'm not in Boston. I'm in Indianapolis."

"Oh. When did that happen?" Her register raised, her voice floating. She could have been asking when a neighbor had gotten a new car.

"October. Where's Dad?"

"He's in Jacksonville. He couldn't come. His health's not so good these days. He's—" she paused, looking over the table at her daughter, her mouth almost flinching as she searched for the words. "He's dying, Hannah. The doctors found a tumor in his throat, and they said they can remove it, but it'll grow back."

Fiona dropped her eyes to the plate of lasagna in front of her. Hannah watched as a bead of condensation dripped down the side of her water glass, moving in fits and starts until it was finally absorbed into the white tablecloth, no sign left of its long journey to the table.

"Good," Hannah said. "I hope it hurts like hell."

With a jerk of her head, Fiona's eyes met Hannah's across the table.

"You don't sound like yourself," she said.

Hannah didn't feel like herself. "How would you know?" she asked and watched as Fiona's face collapsed in shame. Hannah had wounded her, and she wondered, *Is this power? Is this what it's like to have power?*

"When I was little," Fiona began, "all I ever wanted to be when I grew up was a mom. I loved kids. I babysat every kid in the neighborhood. I played with dolls long past the age when it was probably okay to be playing with dolls." She hummed a note of humor at this, and Hannah could see she'd remembered something specific that she wasn't prepared to share. "I just wanted to be a mom. And then it turned out, I wasn't so good at that, I guess. It's hard to be a mom. Or a good one anyway. Maybe when you have your own kids you'll understand."

Hannah stared at the woman across from her. The story was feeble, a few lines to explain expanses too wide to bridge, and the woman appeared too frail to traverse even short distances.

"I have a daughter," Hannah said, and Fiona's face crumbled further. "She's two. Her name is Molly."

Fiona silenced, blinking against the increasing glassiness of her eyes. "It's too late, isn't it," she said after a couple of seconds, her face becoming reconstituted, her eyes finding a place to rest their gaze. "I'm too late."

❧

MICHAEL DROVE SILENTLY along the highway, the night sky passing as Hannah stared out the passenger side window of the car.

"Emory is with Molly. My parents had to head back to Boston this morning," he said. They were the first words he'd spoken since collecting her baggage and asking her how her flight was. She'd said it was fine.

A semi drove too close to the side of the car, and Michael swerved into the lane next to him. He muttered half a curse under his breath but stopped himself from completing it.

"How was the funeral?" he asked.

"Fine." In the reflection of her window, she saw him steal a glance at her.

"Do you need to go back out? For his belongings or anything?"

"He doesn't have any belongings."

Michael placed a hand on Hannah's knee.

"Did you get a sense of how long he'd been using?" He exited the highway, and the garish lights of the city's big box district exploded in front of them.

"No."

"Did they say how he even got to this point? People don't just start shooting up heroin?"

"He got hurt. At work." The energy needed to explain the steps between a work injury and Mason *being found* evaporated before Hannah could regurgitate the chronology the social worker had gleaned from Mason's medical records—the woman had taken time with Hannah, had explained to her things Hannah both desperately wanted to know and now wished she could forget.

"Well," Michael said, his eyes focused on the road, "they don't prescribe heroin for work injuries, and I'm assuming he didn't think he was shooting up Advil."

The black of the night and the white of the streetlights and the reds and oranges of the big box marquees moved in slow motion across Hannah's field of vision as she faced Michael. He swiveled his head quickly, then returned his eyes to the road.

"What?" he asked.

She took his arm by the wrist, lifted his hand from her knee, and placed it on the armrest between them.

CHAPTER 25

"Hi Hannah, dear." Gary stood in front of her, his hands on his hips. His eyes matched the tone of his voice—reverent and respectful. "Mr. Korman came by and told us about your brother. We're just so sorry."

Hannah put Molly on the floor, and the little girl headed for the study, familiar with the routine that had developed when they went to the Decker house. Her blocks were in there, and now, in just the week that Hannah had been gone, heat filled the room, too. For as much of Hannah's life as was recognizable to her, she could have been gone for years, but for the continuity of Molly's appearance. The house, having tipped past the worst of the renovation, was now on the mend, as it were. Large scars marked the walls where portions had been removed to install ductwork, conduit, and plumbing, and had since been patched. Even the smell of the house had changed, the fine powder of sawed wood and mortar replaced by the sharper scents of primer, wood stain, and industrial cleansers. They'd crested the mountain and commenced the descent down the other side.

Jason walked into the foyer, and Conner followed shortly after. Both wore Gary's same reserved expression.

"I'm so sorry to hear about your brother, Hannah," Jason said, echoing Gary.

"It's okay," she said in a tone she might have used had one of them spilled something on the carpet and apologized for the mess.

"I suspect it's not," Gary replied, and Hannah lifted her eyes to see the man, his orange golf shirt washed far too many times, faded at the sleeves and around the buttons.

"That fentanyl's awful shit," Conner added. "My cousin died of that down in Austin, Indiana."

Hannah saw Jason shoot him a silent warning, and Conner dropped his head down examining the lines of grout in the foyer's floor.

"It *is* awful," Hannah agreed, and Conner's shoulders relaxed. He peered up meaningful, his eyes finding hers. They knew each other, she thought. Not like they'd met before, which they obviously had; she'd known him for months now. But like she suddenly recognized him and had just now remembered where she knew him from.

"Well, we're going to be working mostly upstairs today on that owners' suite. You let us know if you need anything," Gary said as much to Conner and Jason as to Hannah.

"Thanks, Gary," Hannah said, and she joined Molly in the study.

❧

As HANNAH and Molly re-acclimated to the house after the week away, Hannah saw that indeed, the mountain had been crested. The kitchen was complete, with walls wanting for paint, but no other work remaining to be done there. With the continued progress of the plumbing and electrical work, the first floor now had a functioning bathroom, situated conveniently off the kitchen and family room. Hannah wandered the Decker house and saw that it fast approached the point where one might turn to the fun of light fixtures, area rugs, window treatments, fabric swatches, and paint samples, those final touches that make a house one's own.

But as Hannah removed the bottom drawer and lifted the panel from the bottom of the dresser in the closet of the north-facing bedroom, and carefully returned the photograph of Andrew to the shallow cavern below, she found she had little energy for such pursuits.

Staying true to her established practice, Hannah returned to the bungalow for lunch before deciding to spend the rest of her afternoon at the Decker house reassembling the cabinet in the study during Molly's nap time.

"You going on your walk, Miss Hannah?" Conner asked as Hannah backed the stroller over the steps of the portico down to the driveway. The gravel had been replaced with small tan pebbles while she was away.

"Yes," she replied evenly, watching as Conner shifted uncomfortably in the foyer, his eyes drifting toward the clouds overhead.

"What is it, Conner?" Hannah asked, unable to conceal her irritation at being held up.

"Conner?" Jason called from the depths of the house before he could respond to her. He offered a closed-mouth smile before turning back to the house, leaving Hannah to her walk.

The neighborhood hadn't changed in the week she'd been gone. The houses were the same, the pavement still with its familiar gray-black. If Hannah concentrated, she could even see the random stones and twigs along the side of the road just as they'd been for months now. Nothing had changed. And yet, everything had. She pushed the stroller along the road, making the solitary walk with only her memories serving as companions. A drop rolled down her cheek, and she reached a finger up, trying to decipher its origin.

She stopped, seeing that the familiar Midwestern gray had given way, the thick, heavy navy of twilight had decided to make an early afternoon appearance, and she realized too late that this wasn't twilight, but storm clouds. The sky opened suddenly, though if she thought about it, it had been growing progressively darker as she'd made her first lap around the neighborhood. The first drops hit her nose and forehead and cheeks mixing with the tears there. But the storm soon adopted an intention, and the large drops turned to unrelenting sheets of rain that matted her hair to her forehead and saturated her coat as she stood in the middle of the road.

"Hannah!" a voice called. She followed its direction and saw that she'd stopped directly in front of Jeremy's house. Its light blue door thrown open, he stood looking at her, his face contorted with worry. Had she meant to stop there? She hadn't realized. Or she didn't think she had.

"Hannah! What are you doing?" he called again. But she couldn't answer him with her lips gulping at the water as it poured off her head and cheeks into her mouth.

Jeremy ran toward her, across his lawn, his eyes squinting, his body bent as if he could somehow dodge the buckets of rain, even as they turned his blue t-shirt nearly black and drenched the thick brown waves of his hair. He reached her and posed his question again. "What are you doing out here?"

"Walking," she said, the words hollow.

"Come inside," he insisted significantly more loudly than he needed to. There was no thunder to yell over, only the sound of the rain slapping against the pavement and rooftops. He didn't wait for her to respond, but picked up the stroller by the footrest and the handle and carried it, complete with Molly sleeping deep under the blankets, into his house. Hannah followed close behind. He set the stroller in the dining room and pulled a set of French doors closed before returning to Hannah, who stood dripping on the rug in the living room.

He removed his socks, soaking wet and caked with enough early spring mud that Hannah thought she would have to buy him a new pair to replace the ones he held; they could not be salvaged.

"Here. Give me your coat," he said in a low whisper, and Hannah was unsure whether his attention to his volume was intended to prevent Molly from waking, or to prevent Hannah from shattering, splintering into a million shards of porcelain, which she felt she might do at any minute irrespective of the volume of his voice.

Hannah handed him her coat, and he hung it over the back of a chair in the kitchen where it dripped persistently onto the tile floor.

"I'll get you a towel," he offered in a strangely perfunctory manner. He jogged up the stairs and returned some moments later wearing a dry t-shirt and carrying a navy-blue towel which he handed her. She took it from his outstretched hand but made no movement toward drying herself.

"Hannah, are you okay?" he asked, his worry for her announcing itself in the tightness of his voice and the angle of his head. "What's going on with you?"

She raised her head, facing him and saw the single deep crevice between his eyebrows.

"My brother died," she said numbly, the tears continuing to fall down her cheeks even without her acknowledging them.

"Oh my God, Hannah. Oh my God. I'm so sorry. When did this happen?" He took the towel from her hands and brought it to her forehead, drying her face and pushing the matted hair back from her eyes and cheeks.

"Last week. That's why I was gone," she said, though she had no idea if he'd noticed she was gone.

"That's awful. I'm so sorry. Let's sit down. I'll get you some water," he said and started walking toward the kitchen.

Hannah followed behind him through the narrow passageway between the staircase and the living room. Without knowing quite why she did it, or from where she got the courage, Hannah reached forward taking Jeremy's hand in hers. He startled at her fingers against his and stopped walking, turning toward her. His eyes cast down at their clasped hands, and he slid his fingers fully around hers, his thumb brushing the back of her hand. He met her gaze then, as she brought his hand to her lips, placing a kiss against the ridge of his knuckles.

His expression was difficult to read. She saw in it a look of wanting she knew well from other men, from Michael himself. But that hunger was restrained by something she didn't recognize as he canted his head nearly imperceptibly in the shadow cast by the staircase.

"Hannah," he whispered, his eyes full of the ache of remorse. "Hannah, I don't understand what you want from me." His voice reached her as something between a whisper and a plea, and he lifted a finger, tucking a loose strand of wet hair behind her ear, his eyes following the work of his fingers there.

"I don't know," she said, tears falling as if in competition with the torrent outside. "I feel like I can talk to you. I liked our walks together." She knew how silly it sounded, even though it was true.

"I liked our walks, too," he said, and took his hand from hers reaching toward her cheek, the pad of his thumb brushing away the tears.

Hannah leaned into his palm, feeling its soft warmth against her face. She could see in the clench of his jaw, in the way he removed his hand, bringing it to rest against the waist of his jeans, that he was trying to decide. And at some length and with pronounced difficulty, he did and stepped back from her. His eyes grew larger as her tears continued to fall, as her grief deepened at the loss of her brother, at the loss of her mother, and, as she saw, as Jeremy dropped his head, shaking it back and forth, at the loss of this man. This was over. Whatever it had been, it was over.

"I think I'm really messed up, Jeremy," she said, smoothing her sweater across her abdomen.

"Let's get your coat," he said, ignoring her comment. "I'll drive you home."

"You can't. You don't have a car seat. I'll walk," she said and turned, looking out the window of his living room to see that the rain—as if endorsing her good decision to leave—had stopped.

"I'll walk you, then," he said.

He retrieved her coat from the kitchen, and they walked back to the gates of the Decker house where Jeremy told her good-bye, and Hannah thought, in fact she was absolutely positive, that he meant it.

CHAPTER 26

"The blue room" had been given its name on the day Hannah and Michael moved into the Decker house, when the couple had developed various short-hands to direct the movers where to take boxes and furniture. On the east end of the house was the owners' suite, Molly's bedroom next to it, and "the blue room"—an additional bedroom that faced the front of the house, a large bow window extending out in line with the breakfast room below. Although the sunlight that radiated into the south-facing room was unparalleled in much of the rest of the house, it was decided that Molly should take the north-facing bedroom across the hall. Slightly smaller, its protection from the sun might make sleep easier for her.

Hannah moved a bedroom set from the attic down into the blue room, and while she had no way to know whether Andrew had ever rested his head against the flower inlay of the honey and cherry colored headboard, she liked to think he had. She liked to think he'd propped a white cotton pillow on its end and leaned back, perhaps reading *An American Tragedy* or *The Constant Nymph*, books which bore his signature, and which Hannah had taken to reading, imagining that to have her hands touch the pages and her eyes pass over the print, was to touch some part of the world he had touched, to see the world as he had seen it.

She sat on the edge of the bed and allowed her hand to brush slowly over the curve of the footboard. She was quite sure this had been Andrew's and Eleanor's bed. It really had to have been. It was the right age, but too large for the guest rooms in the west end of the house, and too formal for young Margaret. There was no way to know when it had been relegated to the attic, but Hannah assumed that much like Michael, someone in the Moore family had decided the bed wasn't fashionable—too old and by modern standards, too small—and stored it away.

Michael thought it unsuitable in nearly every conceivable way—too small, too old, and "used," a term he'd spoken with the air of someone who next might have lifted the bed by his index finger and thumb, holding the odious furniture out from his body like a dirty sock to be disposed of as promptly as possible. Hannah had placed the bed just back from the bow window, which allowed her to hang long panels of blue and yellow silk from the windows framing the headboard.

In the month they'd been living in the house, Hannah had resisted the urge to sleep in the room, sensing that Michael remained suspicious of her, of her distance from him, her complete lack of interest in his ever more infrequent attempts at intimacy. He'd taken to working longer hours, coming home later and later into the evening until at least once a week, he came home after Hannah herself had gone to bed.

On such nights, Hannah thought, really, it shouldn't matter if she retired to the blue room, slept in the "used" bed, and read yet another of Andrew's paperbacks. She resisted the urge, though, suspecting that Michael would perceive the act as further separation and although the word "divorce" had drifted in and out of her mind, Hannah couldn't bear the thought. The failure, the collapse, the disruption and chaos, the child without a father.

They'd moved in before the house was completely finished. Gary had assured them this wouldn't be a problem, and it was much preferable to extending the lease on the bungalow. The work remaining on the Decker house included the reconfiguration of the guest rooms over the dining room, kitchen, and family room, as well as the third-floor renovation, but it was otherwise ready to be lived in.

A week before moving into the house, Hannah met with the architect Gary recommended for purposes of designing the third floor. Christine Scrift was as Gary had described her, perfectly suited to the project. As Hannah outlined the study area, the bedrooms, the bathroom, the play area, Christine took enthusiastic notes, smiling with each word Hannah offered. But her blueprints were all of that project that had been completed, with Gary suggesting they wait until the second floor was completed before moving to the third. That project had been postponed a month to give Hannah and Michael a chance to settle into the rest of the house, removing items from storage, attending to some of the landscaping, developing a punch list as they noted small things that required attention—a piece of trim that hadn't been painted, a loose faucet in Molly's bathroom.

Hannah heard the doorbell below and rose from the bed, jogging quickly along the corridor and down the stairs, hoping to reach the door before the visitor assumed no one was home. As she pulled the large wooden door back, she saw that it was Patricia, the neighbor who'd come to her assistance when Hannah, Molly, and Jeremy encountered the copperhead all those months ago.

"I'm sorry, I hope you don't mind me dropping by like this," Patricia said, stepping into the foyer without waiting to be invited. "Your phone numbers aren't in the neighborhood directory yet, so I couldn't call." Without pausing, she continued. "Wow, you have really cleaned this old place up. We honestly didn't know what was going to happen to it. We—I mean, the neighborhood—we thought maybe they'd eventually just tear it down, and we were worried about what would go up in its place, you know? But we were just so pleased when we heard a young family bought the house. We knew it was going to mean a lot of strangers in the neighborhood, a lot of trucks and noise, you know, but I think we were all just more than happy to make that sacrifice if it meant this old house wouldn't be torn down. I knew Margaret. Did you know that? I moved into this neighborhood with Carl when we first married back in '82, and Gerald had just died, but

Margaret and I, we had a few conversations over the years, and she'd just be so pleased. So pleased to see all this."

Hannah found herself standing in the foyer of her home, blinking in disbelief, trying to follow the various chicanes of Patricia's conversation as the woman finally concluded her narrative with: "So anyway, we thought maybe you and Michael would like to host this year's Founder's Picnic. It's in June."

"I'm sorry," Hannah said, trying to catch up. "Did you say you knew Margaret?"

Patricia looked at her with confusion, then allowed the scowl on her face to relax as she unabashedly surveyed the foyer and the stairs up to the second-floor landing, then craned her neck so as to glimpse the living room.

"Close the door, dear. You'll let in flies," Patricia said.

Hannah obeyed, giving the front door an affectionate shoulder to encourage its full closure.

"Where's your little one?" Patricia asked, now craning her neck in the opposite direction, toward the dining room and kitchen.

"She's playing in the family room," Hannah said. "I was just putting some things away upstairs and then we were going to eat lunch."

"Oh, that sounds lovely. Thank you," Patricia said, and Hannah realized she'd unwittingly invited the woman to a meal.

Resigning herself to the momentum that had been established for her, Hannah directed Patricia to follow her through the dining room and have a seat in the breakfast room while Hannah prepared turkey sandwiches and fruit salad for herself, Molly, and their guest.

"I take it your husband is at work?" Patricia asked as Hannah sat Molly in her booster seat.

"Yes. He works for Rue in research and development."

Patricia nodded, her theory evidently confirmed, and took a bite of her sandwich. Hannah put half a sandwich, a sliced apple, and a sippy cup of milk on Molly's tray.

"Do you still take your walks with Jeremy? I haven't seen him join you in, gosh, more than a couple of months now." Her attempt to sound casual and friendly had the paradoxical effect of emphasizing her pursuit of gossip, and Hannah was aware, for the first time, of how much the neighborhood knew about things she'd never intended to share: the history of this house, the details of her renovation, the frequent absence of her husband. And her friendship with Jeremy.

"I think he got busy with the end of the semester," Hannah said, trying to sound disinterested. "And, I don't know, maybe he went on vacation for the summer."

"No," Patricia said, pocketing part of her sandwich in her cheek so she could respond. "He's home. I see him out there gardening almost every day. Don't you? When you go on your walks?"

"No," said Hannah. She decided that for purposes of this conversation, she would employ a model of discretion her grandmother had taught her. "We must not be out at the same time."

Patricia let the silence linger. But Hannah's tone had changed, and Patricia would have to adapt accordingly. "Hmm. Well. In any case, we think it'd be lovely if this year's picnic could be at the house of the founder himself," she said with a wide smile.

"Um. When is it?" Hannah stumbled.

"June 18th. We always celebrate on the third Sunday of June. Even though Decker purchased the land on a Thursday." She took another bite of her sandwich.

"I'll have to talk to Michael and see whether that's something he's interested in."

Apparently thinking the deal had been made, Patricia prattled on about how the invitation would go out in the next neighborhood newsletter, how the event was a pitch-in, but the hosts were responsible for providing drinks, and did Hannah think that was something she could do? Patricia also commented that many of the neighborhood's residents would be curious about the work that had been done inside the house, so Hannah might want to put down some plastic runners to prevent dirt being tracked into her house as the neighbors took a look-see. Patricia proceeded with suggestions related to everything from what kinds of drinks "the neighborhood" generally enjoyed, to thinly veiled guilt trips that after all the inconveniences "the neighborhood" had suffered during construction, Hannah and Michael should be generous in allowing access to their house and "try not to keep too many of the doors upstairs closed."

Hannah interrupted her with a return to an earlier topic. "You said you were friends with Margaret?"

"Well, I don't know if I'd say we were friends," Patricia responded. "She was an odd one, Margaret. Though I can't blame her, I guess, with what happened to her." She looked up at Hannah, raising her eyebrows in such a way that Hannah thought Patricia really hoped Hannah didn't know, and she could reveal the tragic end of Andrew's and Eleanor's lives with a dramatic flair only she was capable of.

"Yes, I know," Hannah said, articulating each word individually in order to convey that she did not view the suicides of Margaret's parents with the same zeal Patricia evidently did.

"Do you know why Margaret decided to continue living here, with all its history," Hannah asked.

Patricia sat back in her chair and wiped her mouth lightly on her napkin. "Like I said. Margaret was odd. She had the largest house in the neighborhood and never hosted the Founder's Picnic a single time. A celebration for her own father, and she wouldn't host it."

"Did she come to it?" Hannah asked. She saw no connection between her question and Patricia's response, but was curious, nonetheless.

"Oh yeah, she came to it. Just refused to host it. And her aunt never came. Not a single time. Now that woman was really a piece of work. Refused to speak to anyone in the neighborhood. 'Course I only knew her for a couple of years before she died, too."

"You knew Mary Decker?" Hannah asked. Molly, who was long overdue for her nap, stopped fidgeting and turned her attention to her mother.

Patricia, too, had caught the whiff of something in Hannah's interest, and her eyes narrowed. "I don't think anyone knew Mary Decker, except Margaret. I knew *of* her. But she did not socialize. Not like you, being so generous with your home and your time," she added.

Hannah realized she hadn't closely inspected Mary's grave marker and had no idea when she died. The late 1980s it would appear, but having been appointed the executor of Andrew's estate, she'd stayed in the house well past the time an executor was necessary. She'd lived longer than Margaret's husband.

"Are you okay?" Patricia asked.

Hannah closed her mouth, trying once again to feign disinterest. It was too late, though. Hannah had revealed herself as in possession of significantly more information about the Deckers than Patricia.

"I'm fine. It just never occurred to me that Mary Decker would have lived so long."

"Eighty-nine years old when she died," Patricia said. "I hope I have a run that long."

Hannah stood and removed Molly from her booster seat, allowing the child to meander back to the family room.

"I think they stayed here," Hannah began, focusing on a corner where the wall met the ceiling over the table, "I think they stayed here because they loved him." She allowed the bold sentimentality, folding her arms across her chest. She began walking toward the threshold of the breakfast room, an indisputable indication that it was time for Patricia to take her leave. Not being utterly—though admittedly fairly close to—devoid of manners, Patricia stood as well, leaving her plate on the table, and joined Hannah as she strolled back to the foyer.

"I think they both loved him," Hannah continued. "I think he was a good and kind man, who loved his family above anything else, and he adored Margaret. And when he died, this house was all they had left of him. And they couldn't stand the thought of letting it go." Hannah opened the door for Patricia. It was time for her to go. "And in holding onto it so tight, in trying to keep every little thing just as he'd left it, they almost destroyed it."

Patricia lingered in the doorway, not ready to depart. She'd probably hoped Hannah would give her a private tour—the first in the neighborhood to see the renovated Decker house. But no invitation was forthcoming, and Patricia found herself as she'd been an hour before: leaving Hannah with little choice but to close the door lest the flies get in.

"I think she killed him," Patricia said suddenly as Hannah reached to shut the door. "Mary. I think Mary saw her brother sitting up on this big hill in his big mansion, with all his money, and she convinced him to change his will and then she killed him. And she killed Eleanor, too. Worked out pretty well for her, I'd say."

The accusation reached Hannah as if it had been delivered by fist. She felt sick, not just at the thought of Andrew's own sister taking his life, but at the enthusiastic meanness with which Patricia had offered the hypothesis about a woman she'd never met and a family she apparently could only describe as "odd"—whom she resented largely for their lack of participation in neighborhood picnics. Hannah wondered if it wasn't so much that Patricia thought Mary had killed Andrew, as that she secretly hoped she had.

"Thanks for dropping by," Hannah said coolly.

Patricia shrugged and turned to go before calling over her shoulder, "Make sure Jeremy comes to the picnic. My niece is going to be there, and Jeremy hasn't come to a single neighborhood event since that Erika left him."

Hannah closed the door behind her and returned to the family room.

"Nap time, baby girl," she said as she picked up her daughter, climbed the kitchen stairs, and placed Molly in her crib. She closed the blinds and kissed Molly's forehead before backing out of the room and shutting the door behind her.

On the third floor, she pulled up the bottom panel of the dresser and reached for the stack of photographs. She paused, examining the photograph of Andrew from his wedding day, his young, angular face simultaneously softer and more defined than it would be just nine years later. Her purpose lay adjacent to this, though, and she flipped through the copies of the photos until she found the photograph she'd been looking for. Eleanor and her wedding party, Mary in attendance. Hannah tried to see her, see past the faded black and white of the photo, past Mary's youth, into her eyes. Had she been capable of something so horrifying as what Patricia had described?

Hannah returned to the portrait of Andrew and Eleanor, tracing her finger over the line of his dark hair, nearly black given the limited range of color in the photograph, and then placed the stack back against the floor, lifting the framed picture of Andrew out instead. She leaned back against the wall and closed her eyes, feeling the weight of the photograph in her lap.

As her head rested on the wall behind her, she thought, just faintly, she could feel Andrew's head in her lap, the weight of it. She sat on the green velvet sofa in the living room, and he'd come to her, laying across the cushions, closing his eyes, finding comfort under her touch. She would have brushed his hair off his forehead, as she knew it sometimes fell out of place, random strands of ebony, or so the photographs she'd seen suggested. She might have unbuttoned the top one or two buttons of his dress shirt, allowing her hand to rest against the warmth of his chest. He would have accepted her invitation. He would have encouraged her hand further.

Without warning, her mind pulled, almost violently it seemed, to the image of him standing next to the drafting table in the study mere months before his life would end. She saw the plans on the table, the plans he was working on then and had nearly completed, his signature still missing from the bottom corner. He was working. He was working up until the day he died. He was drafting and planning and purchasing and selling. He was playing with his daughter and reading paperbacks that he tucked ever more tightly between the shelves of his carefully constructed bookcase. He was saving money and stowing it away in a secret compartment in his study in case Eleanor left him, planning, preparing. Looking forward.

Hannah put the photograph back and replaced the dresser panel and drawer, jogging quickly down the two flights of stairs to the study. Sun poured in through the southern window across the reds and yellows and blues of the rug. She was grateful Michael hadn't taken complete dominion over the study. Although his computer sat atop Andrew's desk, he'd allowed the chair to stay, and Hannah couldn't recall a single time since they'd moved in that Michael had turned on the computer. It seemed he wanted the room to be his but had no intention of making use of it.

Hannah had carefully rebuilt the cabinet, preserving the hidden storage compartment after moving the items to the dresser in the attic with the rest of her trove of treasures. The tubes with Andrew's blueprints remained where she'd set them—tucked in between the shelves and books of the bookcase. Michael hadn't even noticed them.

She pulled the five tubes down and set aside the two she and Jeremy had already inspected. She opened the first of the remaining three, finding that it contained not a new blueprint, but the original plans for the Decker house, his original draft, his signature in the bottom right-hand corner, a testament to the house she'd altered but, as Patricia commented, prevented from falling into ruin. Hannah thought briefly that she'd frame the draft and hang it in the foyer.

Opening the second tube, Hannah removed the rolled paper and saw immediately the horror of Andrew's last moments. The plan, residential, a house, not as large as those he was building before the crash, strangely modern even for the time, and unfinished, his signature absent. And across the length of the paper, in brown, the color having oxidized with time: blood.

Hannah rushed to open the door to the terrace as the bile rose in her throat. Stepping out into the sunlight, she vomited over the railing into the grass. She lifted her face to the sun, working to catch her breath, fighting the unwelcome images that assaulted her mind. Among them, pervasive, unrelenting, from beginning to end, a reordering of the events of Andrew's death, a reassembling of the room in that disastrous last moment.

She returned to the study, seeing the room as if for the first time, as it had been when it belonged to Andrew. His desk floating in the center, his chair tucked in behind it, facing the fireplace and his books and the hidden compartment within the cabinet. His drafting table positioned just back from the French doors leading out to the terrace, making use of the southern sun exposure and, in warmer months, on days like today, allowing a breeze in if one opened those doors, as Hannah had.

She walked over to the desk and ran her fingertips across the grain, thinking once again of Gary's words at their first meeting: Decker had sat down at this desk in his study and shot himself. She'd imagined that scene, compulsively replaying it as though she'd witnessed it herself, as though she'd been there, the way his body would have fallen forward, collapsing on the desk as she'd seen in movies. Or perhaps he'd have slumped to the side, draping over the arm of the chair. She lifted her eyes to the wall behind the desk, allowing for the unimaginable horror that could have been depicted there depending on the circumstances of the last seconds of his life.

It had always struck her as strange, though, the complete absence of any sign of that violence. No hint of tragedy on the desk, no wear to the varnish from someone's endeavors—after his body had been "delivered to the coroner" as the article stated—to wipe away what of him had been left behind there.

She looked down at her feet, at the rug beneath them with its cheerful tufts. She stepped back and crouched down, peeling up the corner of the rug closest to edge of the desk. It was heavy, retaining much of the dust of the construction. She'd vacuumed it repeatedly but hadn't yet had any of the rugs professionally cleaned, thinking it made more sense to do that after all the construction had concluded. Her hands trembled so badly the entire corner flapped back at her with a loud clap against the floor before she finally managed a more controlled second attempt.

It occurred to her there was probably a process undertaken in a room that had seen such a tragedy as this one. There were practicalities, indelicate matters that required attention. One hundred years later, a room might hold those histories without any physical remnant of them. Inspection might reveal nothing.

She allowed the corner of the rug to flap back once more, a faint perimeter of dust marking the edge of the corner she'd disturbed. She scanned the length of the rug; the fringe had long ago worn away. She found herself standing at the edge in the space that might once have been occupied by Andrew's drafting table, and she peered back at the French doors, imagining the room with the table still there. The doors hung open, looking out on the front lawn, a view entirely unobstructed by anything but the limestone railing and balusters of the terrace.

Hannah crouched to the floor again, this time bringing her hands to the center edge of the rug, the weight of it greater as she rolled the entire width back. Scooting her knees along the dusty floor, she rolled the rug to the edge of the desk. And there she saw it. A Rorschach shadow, old and faded from some distant attempt to scrub it clean, uneven against the reddish stain of the hardwood floor.

She twisted her body, examining the view behind her again, the light spilling in across her back, Andrew's desk a solid wall of oak in front of her.

She heard Gary's voice again: *He sat down one afternoon at the desk in that study and shot himself.*

But it seemed he had not. And Hannah stood, releasing the rug, watching as it unfurled like a party blower on New Year's Eve until it lay flat against the floor, and her mind bent and twisted and contorted around the impossibility of what she'd been told.

CHAPTER 27

"How are you holding up?" Kate asked, as she and Hannah stood just outside the exercise studio.

Hannah shrugged. Even being asked caused her nose to tickle and the tears to sting behind her eyes. When Kate wrapped an arm around her shoulder and pulled Hannah into her side—an attempt to avoid some of the sweatier parts of her body post-workout—Hannah melted.

"Oh, friend," Kate said as Hannah sniffled into Kate's shoulder. Laura joined them, wrapping her arms around Hannah and Kate and leaning her head against Hannah's back.

"I'm glad you've started coming again," Kate said. "I was worried when you stayed away so long."

"We're so glad you're back, Hannah," Susan said, stepping out from behind the desk where she'd been updating the studio's social media posts. "We're so sorry for your loss."

"Thank you," Hannah said.

The other women moved around the slowly growing group, not quite close enough to Hannah to join the hug, but also treating the situation with reverence.

"I'm so sorry, Hannah," some of the women whispered as they walked past her, placing a light hand on her shoulder or gently rubbing a small circle in the center of her back.

"Let us know if there's anything we can do," said another woman, who attended classes on the weekends.

Hannah let go of Kate and stood to her full height, taking a deep breath, blinking away new tears and attending to the existing ones with the backs of her hands. She walked to the playroom and picked Molly up.

"No be sad, Mama," Molly said. She touched a small finger to Hannah's wet cheek as Hannah lifted her into her arms.

Laura held tight to Hannah's side, as if afraid to leave her alone. "Should we get coffee?"

Kate nodded her agreement. "Hubbard and Cravens?"

"Do you want to come over and see the house? We can have coffee there, and Chloe can play with Molly," Hannah suggested, thinking that if the conversation turned sad, she'd rather not be in a public place. Hannah shifted her weight to make it easier to balance Molly, who at two and a half, looked easily on pace to match her mother's height.

"Yeah, why don't we just follow you there," Kate suggested.

KATE AND LAURA oohed-and-ahhed over the house, and rightfully so; what had been accomplished there really did astound. Although neither had seen the house before its renovation, Hannah had told them it required updating in nearly every possible way. Now, Hannah admitted some pride in the part she'd played in the transformation, and Laura, like Gary, suggested that Hannah should offer her cabinet-making skills for hire.

"I had an interesting conversation with one of the neighbors last week," Hannah said as she set down three large mugs of coffee on the table in the breakfast room. "She knew Margaret Moore. And Mary Decker, Andrew's sister."

This caught Kate's attention, and she pulled her lips back from her coffee mug, maintaining the shape they'd taken in anticipation of her first sip.

"I meant to tell you earlier but... I... I didn't know how to."

Hannah hadn't seen Kate or Laura since she'd returned from Montana. Her initial absence from them had been inadvertent—partially the paralyzing grief over her brother's death. But then that combined with the shame she felt at what had happened between Jeremy and herself and the possibility that Jeremy would have confided in Kate, or even if he hadn't, that somehow Kate would know. Having failed to respond to the handful of text messages from Kate, Hannah found that the longer she stayed away, the harder it was to return. Then, she and Michael had moved into the Decker house and that had occupied her time, as had meetings with Gary and the architect who would work on the third floor. Eventually, Hannah realized it had been nearly two-and-a-half months since she'd seen her friends. With some effort at courage, she'd forced herself back to the exercise studio.

"She knew Mary?" Kate asked, following the same worn path Hannah's inquiry had tread.

"Yes. And she had some interesting thoughts."

"Who's Andrew," Laura asked.

"Decker," Kate said. "Andrew Decker. The architect who built this house. We've been doing research on him for a few months now."

"Oh, fun!" Laura said.

"She—my neighbor—she said she thought Andrew had been murdered." Hannah stomach turned over as she spoke the words.

"By Mary?" Kate asked, her voice dragging over the name in a tone that was equal parts disbelief and disgust at the very idea.

"Well, that's considerably less fun," Laura said.

"I don't know how we'd ever prove that," Kate said. "I haven't done much research on Mary—any, really. But I would imagine we could google the hell out of her and only come up with her obituary. Sounds like she was pretty reclusive."

"I would be too if I were living my entire life worried that people thought I'd killed my brother," Laura said.

A distinct unease fell over the three women. There seemed to be something about the discussion of Andrew's death that tacitly centered Mason's. No one really seemed sure what remained to be said about that, though probably what could be said was that there were no words.

Hannah detailed her strange conversation with Patricia, and her own suspicion, now fully a conviction, that Andrew had been murdered.

"I'm not comfortable with this speculation," Kate said, the tension in her face matching the tension in her voice. "There is literally nothing to suggest that Mary did something like that. There's nothing to suggest anyone did something like that."

"I don't think he killed himself," Hannah said. It was at least the third time she'd said it since they'd sat down together. "He was standing when he shot himself, Kate."

Laura, whose mug had been traveling toward her lips at steady intervals, stopped mid-sip. "He shot himself in this house?" She glanced in the direction of the family room, as if such an event a century ago nevertheless required assurances that the current occupants of the house were safe.

"In the study," Hannah said.

"Did you know that when you bought it?" Laura whispered the question, though there was little risk of anyone overhearing and no indication it would matter if anyone did.

"No. I guess a murder has to be disclosed to a buyer, but not a suicide," Hannah said.

"Well, that would be one reason to lie about how he died, I guess," Laura remarked, an observation that hadn't occurred to Hannah.

"What makes you think he was standing?" Kate asked. The words seemed to find their way into the room against her better judgment.

"Do you want to... see?" Hannah asked both of the women.

Kate nodded silently and set her coffee mug on the table. Hannah glanced at Laura—a wordless invitation.

"I do not," Laura said without hesitation. "I will stay here and keep an eye on Molly and Chloe. You two can go... do that."

Kate followed Hannah to the study where Hannah showed her the blueprints explaining her theory that Andrew had been standing at his drafting table working when he died, rather than sitting at his desk. As Hannah rolled the plans out flat against the top of Andrew's desk, Kate brought her fingers to her lips, an obvious effort to maintain her composure.

"Oh my God," she breathed.

The nausea and panic returned to Hannah, starting in the center of her belly, then rising to the small divot at the base of her throat. She swallowed forcefully but couldn't control the trembling of her hands.

Kate placed her palm over the back of Hannah's hand. "Are you okay?" she asked.

Hannah couldn't even begin to think how such a question might be answered. "I need to show you the floor," she said. The word "need" operated in so unadulterated a way, she could have been referring to her need for water or food.

"Okay," Kate said, removing her hand from Hannah's and stepping back from the desk.

Hannah grasped the long edge of the rug and slowly rolled it until the underside of it reached the desk. Anxiety moved through her like a static only her veins could hear as she worried there might be nothing there, that she'd imagined it all. But as the rug cleared the floor, it revealed the light watercolor outline concealed beneath.

Kate gazed down, bringing her fingers to her lips again. She lifted her eyes to the desk, then dropped them back to the floor. "Well, he definitely didn't die at his desk," she said, as she stepped back.

Hannah released the rug and it slowly rolled back over the floor, moving the air beneath it with a hush. "Who shoots themself while standing up?" she asked.

Kate gazed down at the rug, the edge of her thumbnail making its way between her front teeth. "I don't know how much we can make of the last-minute thought process of someone who took his own life," she said, finally, her tone low and solemn.

"I don't think he did," the assertion made now for a fourth time.

"Hannah," Kate said, her voice a peace offering. "I don't think you want him to have. Which is not the same thing as him not having done so. And I can understand why. It's very disturbing to think that someone could reach a point where they didn't want to live anymore. And I admit that the family's story about why he did it doesn't hold up to much scrutiny. But ours does: that he thought his wife was going to leave him and that he'd lost so much already. Hannah, she'd filed for divorce. Someone might be inclined to take their own life because of that." She offered the summary with obvious caution, her eyes never leaving Hannah's.

"It's infinitely more probable that Decker would be devastated to learn that his wife was divorcing him for another man, and that he'd end his life because of it, than that his sister would trick him into changing his will and then kill him. I mean, his attorney telling him that Eleanor was cheating on him—that's what made him change his will."

"She's just a nosey neighbor," Kate continued as Hannah grew increasingly more distressed. "She fancies herself the neighborhood know-it-all and traffics in gossip and speculation."

"Maybe," Hannah said. She ran her hand over the blueprint laid out on the desk, realizing too late that she'd run her hand over the smear of blood, the brown arch extending up, then sliding down and off the edge of the page, obscuring the faded ink of Andrew's signature. She brought her hand quickly to her side, wiping it on her pants and immediately felt silly for doing so—there was nothing to wipe off. But her eyes fell to the title of the plan. She hadn't noticed it before, covered in part by the brown stain against the white, the ink smeared: Decker Cove. Beverly Shores, IN.

"Look," Hannah said, directing Kate to the title of the plan. "It's a vacation home. A getaway. In Beverly Shores."

The blueprint depicted a modest three-bedroom home, a strangely modern plan with the second floor staggered over the first through nothing more than a single staircase. It evoked an almost mid-century architecture—remarkable given the time period in which he'd drafted it.

"I bet the cash was for this project," Hannah said.

"That is absolutely wild speculation, Hannah," Kate replied.

But Hannah suspected that if she'd pushed further, Kate would have admitted to at least some persuasion. How could she not? At the beginning of the worst year of the Great Depression, Andrew Decker was preparing to build a vacation home on Lake Michigan. Doing so with cash was in keeping with how incredibly conservative he'd been with the rest of his projects. It was also *not* in keeping with a man so despondent he would end his life while standing over that very plan.

CHAPTER 28

Hannah lay in bed listening to the owl that had made its home in the trees outside the Decker house. Molly had been put to bed hours ago, and Hannah had stayed up well into the evening not so much to welcome her husband home as to talk with him about several matters that required his attention. But the hour had grown late, and the sun had dropped below the horizon, and she'd gone to bed alone.

It had been days since she and Michael had sat together and talked, longer still since they'd done anything more than that. She'd stopped trying to guess when he might be home, his hours had become so erratic, but this was, she thought, the latest he'd stayed away, still gone at 1:12 a.m.

In the month that they'd lived in the house, Hannah had acclimated to its various creaks and groans. The way the wind blew over the chimney caps, the way the joints of the walls settled at night, expanding during the heat of the day, then giving way to the relative cool of the evening.

She liked the sounds of the house, a song only a very small number of people could claim to know, among them Andrew and herself. In the dark, the melody gave rise to his presence, the groan of a joist was

Andrew walking up the stairs after a late night in the study below spent pouring over the large rolls of paper that held his next idea, his next project, his dreams for the future.

His foot came down on the fourth step from the top, which always offered a protest at being of service. He climbed each tread with effort, slowly, pulling his blazer off, loosening his tie, his hair already out of sorts, the dark strands falling across his forehead as he rounded the corner into this room, as he peeled the layers of clothes from himself, hanging them in a closet or armoire, laying them across a chair, as he climbed between the sheets of the bed, offering his tired body to her.

She pulled him to her, weary but enlivened, the warmth of him reaching her before his body did, and she could see him hovering over her, his dark eyes finding hers in what little light the bedroom held at this late hour.

"What are you doing still awake?" he asked, not much louder than the sheets as they shifted under his weight and around his body.

"I waited up for you," Hannah replied. "I was hoping you would come to me."

He smelled strange, not as she remembered him, not like black pepper and citrus, sharp and clean and light as she breathed him in. But like musk and soap and detergent.

"Hannah," he said. "I want you."

"I want you, too," she replied, reaching for him, aching to feel the weight of him on her.

"Let me go brush my teeth. I'll be right back." The words reached her like they'd been spoken in another language.

"What?" she asked, confused as she fought her way back to the surface.

She saw, then. It wasn't him, and she shrank back, her body repelled despite having pulled him to her just seconds before, her disappointment announcing itself even in the dark.

"What is it?" he asked, no longer whispering. "What's going on with you?"

"Am I asleep?" she asked, knowing she was not.

"No. But this marriage is a nightmare," Michael said, and he rolled out of bed, grabbed a throw from the reading chair, and left the room to spend the night elsewhere.

❧

THEY SAT across the table from each other in the breakfast room, not speaking. Hannah could remember only the vaguest features of what had happened the night before. She was fairly confident she hadn't said his name; she wasn't *that* confused. Her head had cleared quickly as she heard Michael's voice where she'd expected Andrew's. Not that she knew what Andrew's voice sounded like. But she thought that if she ever heard it, it would be the sort of voice that could only have been his. In any case, the voice that had spoken to her last night had been Michael's.

"I'm sorry about last night," Hannah said.

"I am, too," he said with a touch of irony.

"Why were you home so late?"

She assumed he was probably having an affair. Having been repeatedly rebuffed by her, he'd found someone else to tell him his work was important and to listen to his endless anecdotes about the very clever people who weren't her. It wouldn't be hard for him to replace her. Approaching fifty, in the zenith of a successful career, he could offer an awful lot to someone looking for a very narrow set of qualities.

There had been times over the past month or so, as his hours became more unpredictable and stretched later and later into the evening, that Hannah hoped maybe he was having an affair. That he would leave her and relieve her of the responsibility of being the one who ended their marriage. Or at least, in its official capacity. Then, the thought having announced itself, Hannah would feel a flood of panic, sometimes so much so that it stopped her, gripping her around the ribs, claiming the air in her lungs, and she'd gasp and gulp and try to force the air in again, as she thought about where she might go and where Molly might go and who would ever love her.

For Michael's part, when he did come home, he never smelled of alcohol, or smoke, or the sweet scent of time intimately spent with another woman. He smelled as he had when he left the house, if a bit staler. On the weekends and evenings when he was home, the tell-tale signs of hushed phone calls taken in another room or texts quickly read and deleted didn't interrupt their day. If the marriage failed, it would fail because of her.

"Are you worried I'm having an affair," he asked, setting his coffee mug on the table with enough care that it almost didn't make a sound against the wood.

"I'm... no. I don't think you're having an affair—"

"Would you care if I were," he challenged.

"Yes. Of course I would," she replied honestly.

"Well. At least there's that. I'm not having an affair. But I do need to talk to you."

"Okay," she said. She set the spoon she'd been using to stir her coffee on the table. Michael looked around furtively until he saw a receipt from something Hannah had recently purchased for the house, and he slid it under the spoon.

"We're moving to London," he announced. "Well, not exactly London. Basingstoke."

"What?" Hannah coughed, the coffee in her mouth having "gone down the wrong pipe" as Mason used to say.

"I'm being transferred to the Basingstoke office." He took another sip of his coffee.

"I—I don't understand. How long have you known?" She could feel the blood draining from her face as the reality of what he'd said set in.

"I've suspected for quite a while. But the announcement came a couple weeks ago."

"What about—" she looked around the breakfast room with its large bay window.

"I talked to Debbie last week. She said with the work we've done on this place, it'll sell before she even puts it on the market. I guess I have to thank you for finding this place, and for Gary, and, well, for the work you did on it, too. Debbie says we'll make a killing when we sell it." He was smiling, beaming, really.

"I—I don't want to go," she said not with indecision, but with dread.

"What do you mean you don't want to go? Why on earth would you want to stay in fucking Indiana? We've had nothing but trouble since we moved here. Just one disaster after the next. You and I..." his voice softened, his eyes searching hers. "Hannah, this marriage is in about as bad a shape as it's ever been. We... you could use a fresh start."

"A fresh start," she echoed.

"And I'm going to be making so much money." He laughed, leaning back in his chair. "I mean, jump on the listings because, my dear, you can absolutely buy another mansion."

Hannah fell silent as the bits and pieces of the past several months began to fall into place. He'd known. He'd known for months. He'd known it was a possibility since they moved, and that it was a near certainty since, well... his response to the quotes. No big deal. It's what he'd expected. He'd known since then. All the work she'd done, all the time she'd spent, he'd seen all of it as nothing more than an increase in the return on his investment.

"I don't want to go," she repeated.

"Well, I don't know what you think you're going to do. You're not staying here. I'm not paying for two separate households just because you've decided—inexplicably—that Indiana is your home. Not when you could be living in England. Not when I'm living in England."

Hannah felt numb. She wanted to argue with him but couldn't form the words.

"Did you need to talk to me about something, too?" he asked, the matter of their next residence evidently having been adequately decided.

"A picnic. The neighborhood wants to have a picnic."

Michael looked at her blankly, and Hannah knew he hadn't the slightest idea what she was talking about.

"Every year there's a picnic in honor of the founding of the neighborhood. It's in June. The neighborhood wants to have it at our house this year."

"Great. We'll treat it like an open house then. Maybe I can ask Debbie to print up some stuff ahead of time." Michael got up and walked his mug into the kitchen, setting it on the counter next to the sink.

Hannah stared out the window of the breakfast room across the front lawn of the Decker house. At some distance, she thought she saw the shadow of a man, ebony hair, tall, the sleeves of his white shirt rolled up just below his elbows as he stood surveying the neighborhood, *his* neighborhood, below. He turned looking behind him, finding her through the window of the breakfast room, sitting at the table, the mug of coffee cooling in front of her. And before she could tell him she was sorry—sorry for ripping out the walls of his bedroom, and the tile of his bathroom, for disassembling the spaces he stored his secrets, and for abandoning him and his house and his neighborhood—he'd disappeared into the trees beyond and was gone.

CHAPTER 29

She wasn't sure what the point was. Why even bother with the renovation of the guest rooms? But Michael had been firm that he wanted the house done. Completed. All work finished. Well, not the attic. They wouldn't get to that. But the first two floors should be ready to start showing when they listed the house in October. Hannah felt it, too. A commitment not to Michael, but to Andrew, to finish the work she'd started on his home and to do so with love. He'd built the house with love—she was sure of that—and for as long as it stood—which, predictions were, would be a good, long time given the materials of its construction—it would have been renovated with love, with care and attention to the hopes and dreams that had been born there. And those that had died there, too.

Gary had taped up large, plastic tarps covering the end of the hallway on which the guest rooms were located and stated that he'd begin the process of demo and reconstruction as soon as Hannah removed the dressers from the closets. There were only two, and with Emory back in the service of the Kormans for some of the summer, Hannah estimated it would take her less than two days to do it—one dresser each day.

It was the first dresser though, that held the letters. As Hannah pulled apart the individual components, she'd eventually reached the bottom panel, the piece of wood on which the last drawer slid into place and under which, in the attic, Hannah had created her own secret compartment. The panel lifted all too easily, modified to do so, as Hannah had modified the dresser in the attic. Below it, against the floor, surrounded by dust and the contractured body of a long-departed wolf spider lay a stack of letters, yellowed by time, and crisp to the touch, held together with nothing more than a thin piece of twine. Hannah flipped through the envelopes, perhaps fifteen in total, and all but three were to Eleanor from a Mr. Edward Lehmann. The three that weren't from Mr. Lehmann were from Eleanor, addressed to him and returned as undeliverable.

❧

July 5, 1931

Dear Mrs. Decker,

It is with the utmost restraint that I send this note of gratitude for your conversation last evening. I have found myself in the hours since, unable to concentrate on the matters of my daily life—a situation of some conse-quence as my daily life requires significant concentration. I seem only able to think of your voice, the soft delicate melody of your laughter, the brief touch of your hand to mine. I have resigned myself that these small exchanges are all I might ever know of you and that they alone will have to suffice for the remainder of my life.

How little that which thou deniest me is.

With admiration,

Edward J. Lehmann

September 3, 1931

Dearest Eleanor,

I am cast out as an Israelite in the desert, lost, wandering, aching for manna, aching for you. Please write. Tell me when I may see you again. I am meeting with clients in Chicago next week with plans to acquire a hotel there. Please tell me you'll be waiting for me when I return.

But thou, contracted to thine own bright eyes, Feed'st thy light's flame with self-substantial fuel, Making a famine where abundance lies.

With greatest longing,

Edward

September 10, 1931

Dearest Eleanor,

I write to you from Chicago, a most exciting city. My heart will always be in Nashville, though if you are with me, I would call any home my own. Chicago offers numerous opportunities to expand my acquisitions. The hotel, which I am told I will own by week's end, is fourteen stories high! With the assistance of my regular investors, we plan to refurbish it and make it one of the jewels of Chicago. I must tell you, sweet Ellie, that all

I can think of as I walk through these halls is how you feel against me, your breath, your hands, your lips. I desire these things as one desires the air one breathes. I feel I cannot continue without you. These endless meetings with pompous men who would look down on me save I have more money than the lot of them combined – I cannot bear them. I wish only to have you near, to lay with your body against mine, to hear my name spoken with your lips. I am lost. I will leave word when I have returned.

With longing,

Edward

December 22, 1931

Dearest Eleanor,

I have received your most recent letter and am met with an explosion of emotions I can scarcely describe. Confusion, betrayal, fear, grief. I have believed us to be of one mind. I had felt until meeting you that I would never find one who, like I, reached beyond the narrow boundaries of this world, seeking to create the world anew. I thought I had found that person in you. But you tell me you do not mean to leave with me to New York.

If I allow the memories of us to return, to assault me with the nearness of you to me, I recall our earthly bodies still feverish with love, our spirits bound as if our union itself were divine. Your promises then were hollow. You intended nothing more than to use me for your own bodily gratification while I, myself thought you aspired to leave this provincial life, to leave this man who fails to recognize the strength of your vision, who would keep you in a small world, with nothing to offer but his own small dreams.

You have deceived me. You have no intention to leave. You indulged fantasy when I spoke of a future. You engaged in frivolity when I spoke of enterprise. This must be good-bye.

Edward J. Lehmann

January 11, 1932

Dearest Eleanor,

The weather has turned cold, and I am cold with it, left without the warmth of your touch. Have you no compassion for me, no love? Can you deny what we have shared? I fear my business must take me to New York in the new year and I ask beg you to join me. I understand your obligations, to your husband, to your daughter, to your businesses. I assure you, your businesses can be managed from New York. Indeed, it may well be wise to assign management of such a large operation to my attorneys as you and I will have much to keep us busy as we acclimate to life in New York. But I could do none of this without you. I could bear it not were I forced to endure the mindless prattling of mindless men without you by my side.

We must meet. I must see you. My time in Indianapolis is coming to a close, and I must have an answer. I cannot live in such purgatory.

Then why, lovely girl, should we lose all these blisses?

That mortal's a fool who such happiness misses;
So smile acquiescence, and give me thy hand,
With love-looking eyes, and with voice sweetly bland.

With hope, anticipation, and love,

Edward

❦

March 14, 1932
Dearest Eleanor,

I hesitate to write this letter. But the distance from you has made the heart fonder. Indeed, my heart has been broken. I find I simply cannot live without you. My arms ache for you as if I have lost a limb. I regret I was not kinder at our last meeting and would ask only that you should meet with me again that I might explain my love for you and my confusion at your circumstance.

I had not realized your father's deception, your

husband the thief. That your father should deprive you of your birthright as your husband played his accomplice, no woman should be expected to endure such. It is understandable why one should desire a divorce under such circumstances, such betrayal, but I would counsel no haste. Divorce will grant you none of what you desire and may deprive you of well more than mere birthright. The circles of society in New York are cloistered and would be impenetrable to a woman carrying such a mark.

Much must be resolved, understood, weighed, considered and, naturally, balanced against the love we have for each other. We must meet.

Yours with deepest love,

Edward

March 25, 1932

Dear sweet Eleanor,

I have received your most recent letter and am pained by the distress I read in your words. I would give all my wealth to be there for your comfort. Yet it seems I only cause you pain. Would I be so selfless as to continue tormenting you with my presence, a constant reminder of what we had but cannot have. I stand above looking down at a maze constructed for us by this cruel world and by each turn, I confront yet another impenetrable wall.

I must return to Chicago and from there to New York. I have no further business in Indianapolis, and my continued presence risks attention to ourselves that we would be strained to refute. Could I stand before the accusation that I love you and deny that it is true? And what of Andrew? He must suspect. If your description of your distance, your fidelity to me, is accurate, surely, he must know.

What I do, I do for you, my Ellie. I cannot risk your safety, your reputation, your future, for the sake of my own selfish heart. I fear I must, absolutely, say good-bye.

With greatest sorrow,

Edward

April 8, 1932

Dearest Eleanor,

I have received your most recent correspondence, and I must beg you, please, do not contact me again. Love has made your heart sick—as is mine—but I fear it obscures the clarity of sound thinking. You speak of hatred for your husband, but this cannot be. Hatred, Eleanor, poisons good judgment, and destroys oneself while destroying the other. You must leave me to your memories. We had a most extraordinary experience of which many live a lifetime in deprivation. There must be no further contact. You must return to your life.

EJL

❧

June 25, 1932

Do not write to this address. You risk too much. You must be patient. I will send word.

EJL

❧

December 2, 1932,

Yes, my love.
EJL

❧

October 14, 1933
My Edward,

I write to you in desperation. Where have you gone? Is what they say true? Have I been deceived and in such deception been made a villain. I believed our love to be true. I believed our dreams merely delayed. And, yet, you are nowhere to be found. You must come for me. I cannot be without you.

My love forever,

    Eleanor

❧

March 30, 1934

I fear I am losing my mind, Edward, and I cannot live like this. I fear I have been stupid and gullible, earning every condemnation my father had for me in his final years. It was never me you loved. I was taken by your words, your promises of a life beyond this bleak stone state. But it was not I, you sought. Please write to me. Tell me I am wrong!

I didn't know, of course, that Andrew left his interests to Margaret. As I didn't know all that my father left to Andrew. It seems I am always the last to know. And what am I to do now? Every day, I walk the rooms of the house he built, and look across the table at his face in that of my daughter, and I am HAUNTED! His voice is everywhere, his blood still on the floor. Oh God!! I cannot bear it. Please Edward. Please, prove my fears unfounded and I will spend my life at your side, your love, your wife.

Your eternal,

    Eleanor

❧

December 20, 1934

My Dear Eleanor,

I am so sorry not to have written earlier. I have just come back from New York where I hope to establish a home for us. My business partners tell me the opportunities for property acquisition are unparalleled there. I must meet with you to discuss this new situation. Please meet me at the old Bedford quarry on January 12. With the new year, we will have a new start and leave all of this ugly business behind. Margaret is in good hands with Mary and with Andrew's estate. We can finally start a life together.

Yours,

Edward

CHAPTER 30

Hannah watched closely as Kate read through the letters, then read through them again, hoping she might glean from the lines on Kate's face, the minute changes in her expression, some hint of what their next step should be.

"So, not Mary, then," Kate said, finally looking up.

"Not Mary."

"Lehmann?" Kate asked.

"Not clear," Hannah replied.

Kate knit her brows together in contemplation as she looked out the window of Hannah's kitchen across the side lawn of the Decker house. "You found all of these under a dresser upstairs?"

"Sort of built into the dresser. They were in a compartment under the bottom drawer. Like the cabinet compartment in the study."

"What's your theory?" Kate asked.

Hannah worried her lower lip between her teeth, the accusation resting heavy in her chest. "Edward or Eleanor or both of them murdered Andrew, probably imagining that his estate would pass to his wife. When it came out that Andrew's will left everything to Margaret, Lehmann left Eleanor. He had no use for her. But then he started to get worried that because he'd left her, she'd go to the police and turn him in. So, he lured her out to the quarry one night and pushed her in."

Kate was still nodding her head well after Hannah had stopped talking. "That's a lot of speculation based on not many words," she said finally.

"What's your theory?" Hannah asked.

"Fuck," Kate sighed into the table. Not exactly a theory, though an answer of sorts. She looked up just in time to see Hannah's confusion.

"What do we do with this?"

"What do you mean?" Hannah asked, her confusion genuine.

Having entered the house just eight months earlier, in the time since, she'd uncovered any number of documents that disrupted the prevailing theory of Andrew's death and possibly Eleanor's, too. Hannah recalled Jeremy's distress at learning that Andrew may have died by suicide not because he lost his business, but because he lost the love his life. It seemed even that was no longer certain.

"I want us to give this some very serious thought—who do we tell, and what are the consequences?" Kate said, her expression almost grave. "Right now, Andrew's family has this historically indexed and quasi-romantic story of his and Eleanor's deaths. And it's tragic, but it's also kind of beautiful. If we come forward with this, that's gone. And what it's replaced with is this story of infidelity, murder, petty social envy, a woman who was ready to leave her young daughter for a con man, a man who essentially stole his wife's inheritance. Would you want to know all that if these were your grandparents? Would you want everyone to?"

Hannah leaned back in her chair and lifted her gaze to the ceiling. Constructed of drywall not mortar, newly painted, flawless, a brilliant white. Her thoughts wandered to her brother, to Mason, to the stories she'd one day tell Molly about her uncle. Those stories would likely evolve in their complexity as Molly grew older, but Hannah couldn't say, as she sat across from her friend, as she considered the life of Andrew Decker, as she considered the life of Mason Kemp, whether she'd tell her daughter that Mason had been found with a needle in his arm.

"You see?" Kate asked.

Hannah nodded. "It's the truth, though," she said, with a conspicuous lack of confidence. "Or we're pretty sure it's the truth."

"If we were even just one more generation removed, I wouldn't worry so much about this. And if we really had some definitive proof. I'll stipulate that Eleanor was having an affair. Also, she was obviously planning to leave Decker because he stole her inheritance—"

"He didn't steal the quarries. Walter left them to him, and Andrew made her a partner in that business," Hannah interrupted.

"Well, but—"

"Walter thought Andrew would be better at running them than Eleanor and look at all this." Hannah gestured at the pile of letters on the table. "He was right. If he'd left it to Eleanor, she'd have turned it over to Lehmann, some con man she met six months earlier."

"Fair point," Kate conceded. "Though if he'd left it to Eleanor, Andrew probably would've died at a nice old age, like his sister. But it does get at what my issue here is. Still so much conjecture. And real damage to be done to that family."

Hannah heard the front door open, and Gary call out his usual "Hallowww."

"In the kitchen," Hannah called back. Having heard the voice, Molly toddled in from the family room beaming up at her old friend.

"Hey pumpkin," Gary said to Molly as he walked into the kitchen.

"I not a pu-kin," Molly said.

"You're not?" Gary replied in mock confusion. "What are you, then?"

"Molly!"

"So you are," he said.

Hannah introduced Kate, then observed Gary as he spied the pile of papers on the kitchen island.

"What's all this?" he asked.

Kate and Hannah exchanged a glance, an unspoken *Are we going to tell him?* passing between them.

"We found some letters in a dresser in the guest room," Hannah said. "They um—they make it look like Andrew might've been murdered, and—maybe Eleanor... I don't know. It's not clear."

Kate adjusted her posture in her seat, leaving Hannah with the impression that Kate would have answered the unspoken question: *No, we are not going to tell him.* But Gary's face remained placid, the news reaching him as if he'd expected it all along.

"Lotta secrets in this house, I'd guess," he said, tapping one of the letters with the tip of his index finger. "So, the guys are going to come by today and get started on that guest room corridor. I know Mr. Korman wanted it done before that picnic y'all are hosting, and if we start today, I think we can get that accomplished. That okay with you?"

"Yeah. Sounds good," Hannah replied.

Gary offered a quick "thanks" and excused himself with promises to return after lunch to start the work.

Hannah heard the front door close, followed shortly by Gary's truck pulling around the house and down the drive. There was no risk he'd overhear, and yet she felt the need to keep her critique hushed. "That was weird. He just completely ignored what I said."

"That's Indiana," Kate said. "He didn't want to know, and he's not interested in talking about it. And I'm guessing, if Gary doesn't want to know, Andrew Moore definitely doesn't want to."

CHAPTER 31

Debbie was the first to arrive. As requested, she'd brought a stack of pamphlets about the house: The Decker House.

Hannah paged through the glossy, over-exposed photographs of the rooms she'd nearly called her own. Her throat ached with sadness as her eyes fell upon the blue room, the beautiful oak and cherry bedroom set that would stay with the house. She thought about the next owner, the next person, who would trail their hand along the smooth, dark banister of the staircase, who would one day discover the Rorschach shadow under the rug in the study. In an instant, she perfectly comprehended why Margaret had never sold the house, why she'd lived there each and every day of her life, refusing to move even after marriage, after being widowed, as her children grew up and moved away.

Would the next owner understand? Would they care for and love this home as Andrew had, as Margaret had, and as Hannah had—if only transiently? Or would they convert it to a bed and breakfast, rip out walls, tear out built-ins, "modernize," "update"? Would they paint every piece of trim white and every wall gray, as was the fashion?

Or perhaps they, too, would become transfixed by the architect who'd built it, wanting to know everything about him until they felt him next to them at every turn, a step behind on the stairs, a shadow among the trees on the hill down to the neighborhood. Would he visit them in their dreams, and keep them company when they felt alone?

Encouraging the open-house purpose of the picnic, Michael had agreed with Debbie—and incidentally with Patricia—that the second floor should be made available to people who wished to tour the house. Doors should remain open, clutter put away, personal items stowed. And what did it matter, they'd have to pack them soon anyway? Might as well pack them now and put them in the attic. Suddenly, Hannah could picture exactly how the three boxes of photographs must have made their way up to the storage room, locked behind the door, forgotten. An accident by the family.

"I can't get over this transformation," Debbie gushed, believing she'd paid Hannah a compliment.

Hannah just nodded as Michael accepted the comment with an enthusiastic thank you.

Hannah turned the pamphlet over in her hand. Debbie's contact information was contained on the back with a note that all "serious offers" would be entertained. Michael had explained that in the absence of comparable properties, Debbie was employing a strategy of not providing a listing price and seeing what came in. This would also maximize the number of searches the house appeared in.

Hannah put the pamphlet back on the table. "I'm going to go set things up outside," she said, picking Molly up and propping her on her hip.

Debbie offered Michael a sympathetic smile. He must have told her about some of his *difficulties* with his wife of late.

Outside, Molly raced over to the play set Debbie had suggested would make the house look more family-friendly, less foreboding. Hannah felt guilty imagining that Molly must think of the giant structure as her reward for all of her patience with the cold months indoors, when really it was just another way to market the house, for Hannah to break her promise to both Molly and Andrew in one fell swoop.

They'd rented picnic tables and chairs, and Michael had borrowed a cornhole set from Sam. Purdue University versus Indiana University.

"Not sure I care about either of these teams, but whatever," he'd said when he removed it from the trunk of his car.

They'd had the front yard professionally landscaped prior to moving in, but the shrubs were still small and appeared outsized by the house, little green punctuation marks at the foot of the three floors of yellow brick.

Patricia was the first of the neighbors to arrive, but not by much. Soon, the rest of the neighbors assembled on the front lawn as if they'd been waiting years for this event, and maybe they had been. Each brought a dish to share, the Midwestern pitch-in: half-cobs of corn, bar-b-que, rhubarb pie, potato salad, corn bread.

Michael did the grilling, a talent Hannah hadn't known he possessed. The neighbors milled about talking to each other, gesturing vaguely at the house, largely ignoring Hannah and Michael, now irrelevant, their temporary status making them hardly worth the energy of getting to know. Hannah watched as the neighbors disappeared into the foyer, then re-emerged half an hour later, some with one of Debbie's pamphlets; they were going to be part of the "serious offers" solicited by the enthusiastic real estate agent.

Strangers, all of them, Hannah thought. Or almost all of them. The sun shone a vibrant orange by the time Jeremy and Gertie meandered slowly up the drive. Hannah saw them from her position next to the play set. She asked one of the middle-school-aged neighborhood kids to watch Molly while she went to say hello. It had been three full months since Hannah had last had a conversation of substance with Jeremy.

"Hi," Hannah said, unable to hide the nervous quaver in her voice.

"Hi, Hannah. How have you been?" The formality was back, an unwelcome plus-one to the party.

"Okay," she said. "I'm glad you could make it."

"Well, I understand you're moving, and I wanted to make sure I got a chance to say good-bye." He said this as if there were a possibility he might be mistaken, but it was all straightforward enough. She was moving; this was good-bye.

"Yeah," she said sadly and watched as his eyes narrowed nearly imperceptibly.

"You don't seem happy about that."

"Well, it's probably for the best," she replied.

"Is it?" He seemed emboldened, examining every movement in her face as she received his challenge.

Hannah bent down and cupped Gertie's jowls offering an exaggerated, "Hi, puppy," in a movement that allowed her to avoid Jeremy's eyes and his challenge. She stood back up in time to see him redirect his focus to the area behind her, and she turned just as Michael approached, hand outstretched.

"Hello, Professor," he said jovially, and shook Jeremy's hand just a touch more aggressively than the situation called for.

"Michael. Good to see you again," Jeremy replied. The formality. It was grating.

"It's been... what... since Halloween?"

"Something like that," Jeremy said, his eyes flitting to Hannah's for just a second.

"Come on and grab a plate, and I'll show you around the house. A personal tour," Michael said, placing an arm around Jeremy's shoulder as if the two were old chums. As if their entire acquaintance weren't a single Halloween party eight months earlier.

"GER-TEE!!"

Hannah spun around just in time to see Molly running from the play set toward Jeremy and Gertie. Gertie, having heard the voice of her old companion, tugged on the leash, catching Jeremy wholly off-guard and pulling herself free of him. The dog ran toward the toddler, and Hannah saw the look of absolute terror on Michael's face as he naturally assumed his daughter was about to be mauled by a Rottweiler. It was hard to imagine Michael could have been more surprised, but he clearly was as Molly wrapped her arms around Gertie's neck and the dog returned the affection with enthusiastic licks to Molly's beaming face.

Jeremy, Michael, and Hannah ran over to the two old friends, and Jeremy reclaimed the leash that had dragged across the yard.

"Ger-tee, Ger-tee. Silly dog," Molly said. She looked up at her father, then pointed to the dog, "Ger-tee," she introduced. Molly then recognized Gertie's owner and with a smile nearly as bright as the early evening sun, offered a further enthusiastic, "Germy!"

"Hey there, Molly," Jeremy replied, awkwardly.

"You went 'way. Where?" Molly asked, furrowing her brow purposefully.

"Just been busy," he said, tucking his hands into the pockets of his shorts, the leash slipping up over his wrist.

"Pick you up?" Molly invited, lifting her arms toward Jeremy.

Michael leaned over slowly and picked his daughter up. She seemed displeased and reached toward Jeremy, but Michael held her out to Hannah, indicating his wife should take their daughter.

"I think we're going to have to postpone that house tour for another time," he said as Hannah took Molly into her arms. "I'd say it's time for Molly to go to bed, wouldn't you?" Michael addressed Hannah but didn't take his eyes from Jeremy.

"I really just came to say good-bye," Jeremy offered.

"Good idea," Michael growled.

"Michael!" Hannah said.

"Go inside, Hannah. It's Molly's bedtime," Michael instructed, and he turned away from Jeremy to look at her. "Go. Inside."

Hannah allowed her eyes to travel to Jeremy, who offered her a single nod that she should do as Michael had asked, and Hannah turned toward the house, sensing that Jeremy wasn't the only of her neighbors now watching her.

CHAPTER 32

Hannah jumped involuntarily as she heard Michael enter the bedroom. She stood at the dresser, pulling her pajamas from the top drawer. The last of the guests had finally departed, and Molly had been asleep for close to an hour. Hannah had spent much of the evening at the window of her bedroom, looking down on the party in the front yard of the house that was almost hers and watching as Michael held court, Jeremy long gone, the neighbors accepting the explanation that Hannah had to put their young daughter to bed.

She stepped out of her shorts and t-shirt and into the worn cotton of her pajamas. Her hands shook as she lifted the shirt over her head and brought it down over her shoulders.

"So. Jeremy." Michael enunciated the words as if they had a physical weight to them and sat, dejected, on the edge of the bed.

Hannah turned from the dresser, facing him. He seemed small, the events of the evening having reduced him somehow. Or maybe he'd always been that small, and Hannah had never dared really to look at him. But his shoulders slumped forward, his eyes focused on some intricate weave of the rug that extended out from under their bed.

"There's nothing going on between Jeremy and me," Hannah said, her voice wavering just a bit. "We sometimes take our walks at the same time. After lunch. When I'm trying to get Molly down for a nap."

Michael's eyes searched hers, and Hannah could see that he truly wanted to believe her, but couldn't bring himself to, and why should he. It was so incomplete a truth as to be false.

"I don't understand what's happened here," he said. "I've given you everything you asked for." His gaze arced with intentionality from one side of the room to the other, his point made: this house.

"Are you leaving me?" he asked when she didn't respond. Truly, he sounded desperate. Hannah recalled his comments about Jeremy "moping" and thought, *No, Michael would not mope.*

"What about Molly?" he continued, the itemization of his concerns giving Hannah the distinct impression that his affections had evolved over the past several months in ways she hadn't anticipated or noticed. Though, hers had, as well.

"Is that why you want to stay here in Indiana? To be with Jeremy?" he asked, his hands folded in his lap.

"No," Hannah said, honestly. "I'm not... Jeremy and I aren't... We didn't do anything."

"Are you coming with me to Basingstoke?" he asked, refusing to accept her description of her interactions with Jeremy.

Hannah took a deep breath and looked past Michael out into the hall at the top of the staircase visible beyond the bedroom door.

"No," she said. "I'm not."

Michael nodded, his resigned expression suggesting he'd expected that to be her answer. "Can you explain this to me?" He sounded almost childlike. "If it's not Jeremy, what is it? What's happened?"

"I just—" Hannah searched for the words. "I want more... than this."

"More than a fucking mansion?" he asked, his petulance returning.

Hannah shrank back.

"I'm sorry. I'm sorry," he said, recalibrating, offering his hands upward in a gesture of surrender. "What can I do? What do you need?"

Hannah tilted her head to the side, her eyes meeting his. She wondered how long this person had been inside of him, how long had he been capable of being this, and why had he never been so before? In all the years they'd been together, Hannah couldn't recall a single time he'd asked her what she needed, nor really appeared ever to have given it any thought. And now it was far too late.

He looked directly at her, his eyes full of the anticipation of loss, and Hannah saw his age, the way a slight shadow demarcated the translucent skin beneath his eyes, the way the line of his jaw had softened over the years ever so slightly.

"I think—" she began and stopped. She felt a strange need to protect him. "I don't think you can give me what I need. I don't think you're capable of it."

"Capable of what?" he demanded.

"Of being someone who doesn't make me feel like they've done me a favor by loving me," she said.

"Is that what you get from Jeremy?" he asked.

"I'm not having an affair with Jeremy!" Hannah exploded.

"I don't believe you." He stood from the bed, then, having weighed his next move, and added, "People like you don't leave people like me unless you have someone else to run to."

Hannah bobbed in response to the comment, as if the insult had struck her physically. "People like me."

The words rippled out like rings of pond water after the disturbance of a stone. He'd said it with the intent to injure her, but he believed it, too, and that cut deepest.

Hannah began walking toward the door. "I'm going to sleep in the blue room."

"Hannah—" Michael pleaded. "I'm sorry. I didn't mean it."

"You did mean it," she replied calmly. "And I'm going to sleep in the blue room."

She walked past him and closed the door, allowing the latch to slide reluctantly but decisively into place as she left him alone in their bedroom.

The hour of the night and the angle of the moon left the hall veiled in darkness, but Hannah had spent enough time in the house that she could feel her way along the corridor toward the stairs to the attic. She'd travelled the path countless times, and although some things in the house had changed since they'd bought it, the number of steps from the top of the main staircase to the small baluster of the stairs to the third floor remained constant. The railing under her palm and the suggestion of Andrew's hand under her own guided her up the stairs to the unrenovated, roughed and scuffed walls of the third floor.

She crossed the attic, entering one of the north-facing bedrooms, and closed the door behind her. In the closet, she pulled the bottom drawer and panel from the dresser, picking up the photograph of Andrew that lay safely stowed beneath. She sat, leaning back against the closet wall and held him to her chest, breathing in and out, feeling her heartbeat steady. She closed her eyes seeing the images of him in the light that bloomed behind her lids, the way his eyes, bright and alive, looked directly at her, telling her it would be okay; it would all be okay. She exhaled again as the warmth of his black wool blazer fell around her shoulders. It would be okay.

And then she heard him. Michael. He opened the door and peered around the frame, making out the outline of Hannah's figure on the floor of the closet.

"What the fuck are you doing?" he asked, crossing the room. "What is that?" He nodded toward the photograph, then reached down to take it from Hannah's hands, evidently imagining she would voluntarily relinquish it. As Michael reached for it a second time and she gripped it to her chest curling in on herself, Michael used a foot against her thigh and his arms against her arms, and pried her open like a clam, grabbing the photograph she held to her center like a pearl.

It was dark in the room, darker still in the closet, and he stepped back to see what the frame contained. Undoubtedly, he'd thought it would contain a photograph of Jeremy, and as Hannah emerged from the closet demanding that he "Give it back. It's mine. Give it back," she saw the expression on his face transition slowly from confusion, to comprehension, to disgust.

"The fuck is this?" he asked.

"Nothing. Give it back!" she said, her voice elevating with desperation. She'd risen from the floor, effectively standing over Molly's bedroom. The only things muffling their voices were the joists of the attic floor and whatever jazz age insulation had been placed between them.

Michael froze, only his eyes moving as he looked from the photograph to his wife and then back at the photograph.

"Andrew," he whispered as Hannah saw the pieces fall into place for him. "This is Andrew."

"Give it back," she said again, the plea almost aspirational.

"He's dead, Hannah. You're in love with a dead man?" He showed her the photo, sounding truly concerned. Then, having apparently entertained the matter with more depth, he revised his assessment. "This is fucking crazy," he said, his lip curling in repulsion.

"Michael. You just... You don't understand."

"No. You're certifiable," he continued, propelling the words from his mouth with increasing force. "You belong in a fucking psych hospital. I should have you committed, take Molly, and move the fuck on."

Hannah froze. Something about the threat, its specificity, the vitriol with which it was made, caused her to believe him, made her believe that he'd do it. He would have her committed. He would divorce her and leave her in some kind of institution, padded walls, drooling patients, small white cups of pastel-colored pills.

"That's... that's not true," she said. "I'm not crazy."

"The fuck you aren't," he said and threw the photograph toward the space under the dresser in the closet.

Hannah tried to catch it, but in the dark and with his unexpected movement, she missed, and the glass shattered against the hardwood floor. She ran over to the dresser, knelt before the photograph trying to pull the exposed paper from the shards of glass. Immediately, she felt the sting against her fingertips, followed by the wet drops of blood sliding down her slender fingers as she pulled them back.

"I'm going to bed," Michael said, his voice not much more than a whisper. He began backing out of the room in a manner that spoke to his fear of her, afraid to turn his back on her, unsure what someone as *crazy* as she might do next.

"I'm not crazy," Hannah sobbed, wiping her tears with the backs of her hands.

"I have to work tomorrow. But when I get home, you and I are going to have a talk about exactly what help you need and what that means for your moving with Molly and me to Basingstoke."

She heard his footsteps recede in the attic hallway, then down the treads of the attic staircase. After a couple of minutes, in the distance of the house, a door closed.

It hardly mattered at this point, but Hannah replaced the base of the dresser and slid the bottom drawer into place. Standing up, she brushed her pajamas as if brushing off dust. Or shame. As she rounded the stairs onto the second floor, she saw that the hall light was off, and their bedroom door was closed. No light illuminated the crack under the door.

The house was silent, and despite the warmth of the June day, Hannah was cold. She walked to the hall bathroom and rinsed her fingers, less damage done there than she'd thought, but blood still had gotten on her pajama shirt and on the towel as she blotted her hands dry.

She walked across the hall into the blue room, closing the door behind her, and curled up in the bed. Michael had been right, every word he'd uttered had been accurate. She was crazy. She had lost her mind. She'd fallen in love with a dead man. And even now with the threat of divorce and psych hospitals looming, the dream of him was so powerful, so necessary for her that she thought truly, she didn't mind being crazy. She preferred it to the brutal cruelty of sanity.

Outside the window, she could hear the wind move through the branches of the trees around the house. They groaned with the effort of their swaying as the wind tried and failed to carry them away. She wondered if Andrew had lain in this bed listening to such night noises. And if sometimes it was possible that he did still.

Hannah placed the palms of her hands together and tucked them under her chin. She closed her eyes, hoping sleep would find her.

And then he was there.

She felt the weight of him against her back, spooned in, his knees tucked neatly behind hers under the crisp sheets of his bed, his arm draped across her chest. She knew it was him, the dimensions of him fitting around her like she'd been made for him, the gold of his wedding band glinting off the faint, silver light of the moon as it sneaked in around the edges of the drapes.

"Andrew," she whispered, reaching for his hand. It was warm in hers as she brought it between her breasts tucking it there with her own. She could feel his breath against her, his exhalation shifting the strands of hair at her neck. She couldn't recall letting go of his hand, but she must have because it moved the hair back from her neck, exposing the skin beneath, and then his lips replaced his hand, the brush of them beneath her ear, the sharp lightness of his teeth as he brought her earlobe into his mouth.

Hannah sighed against him, tilting her hips back to meet his. She reached a hand up and found his hair, her fingers sliding between the strands as he continued to kiss her neck. His thumb traced the waistband of her pajamas, and she inhaled reflexively as his fingers feathered at her navel. Then his hand, finding the hem of her shirt instead, moved over her ribs to her breast. He cupped first one, finding her nipple with a delicate brush, and then the other, mirroring his attention.

Hannah pulled her shirt over her head and, dropping it to the floor, rolled to her back, Andrew's mouth already kissing the tops of her breasts, her sternum, then pulling her nipple between his teeth. She arched under him and raked her fingers through the ebony strands of his hair, her hands finding his chest and back bare, his shoulders strong, defined as he held the weight of his body over hers.

He nudged her legs to the side, resting his hips between her thighs, the pressure of him against her, hard and ready, the tension in his back under her fingers shifted minutely as his mouth moved over her body, unhurried, merely sampling her. Hannah reached down and removed her shorts, tossing them in the pile with her shirt as Andrew's lips brushed over her hip bones, first one and then the other, and then his fingers slipped, slowly and purposefully between her legs, his mouth brushing across the space below her navel, making a path lower and lower, still.

She heard her voice call out for him as his tongue joined his fingers, and his other hand held her waist, holding her still, his tongue working until she was panting with how much she needed him.

"Andrew, please," she called to him, but he would not release her, not yet. And then she felt it, radiating out of the center of her body, down her legs, into her chest. And for a moment she was lost, with only the strength of his hand on her hip.

She had not fully caught her breath when she felt his teeth against the insides of her thighs and she was pulling at his shoulders to bring him to her, but he would not be rushed, his mouth moving slowly, stopping to kiss her navel, her ribs, her breasts.

And then he was there above her, gazing down at her, his hair disheveled from his earlier efforts and from Hannah's fingers, which had left the strands at odd angles. His eyes bore down into her, deep seas of sapphire under the thick black of his lashes. He moved a hand down her body, lifting her thigh against his hip, never taking his eyes from hers, as he entered her, his lips to hers, his mouth firm and warm against her own. His teeth pulled and nipped, and his mouth covered her mouth, and she opened beneath him, her tongue finding his as he moved inside her. The length of him was almost too much, but he pulled away leaving her desperate again for the entirety of him, needing him to be almost too much again and again. She was becoming someone else, hungry, desperate, and he met her with every movement of his body.

He rolled her over to straddle him and brought his hands to her waist, moving her atop him, his eyes closed, his mouth parted as her body moved with his, the force of his grip on her hips letting her know he was close. She leaned toward him, her lips finding his, finding that he was hungry, too, as his hands trailed the length of her back and threaded into her hair pulling her to him, seeking something deeper and deeper inside her as she crashed down over him.

His eyes opened as his breath moved, quick and fierce, and Hannah met his gaze, seeing the tension in his jaw, the sinew of his shoulders, his hands grasping for her, pulling them together again as he trembled under her, and she fell with him calling to him and he held to her. His body tensed and then relaxed, and Hannah dropped her head to his shoulder, draping her body over his. She could protect him, she could keep him safe from the evils of the world he had inhabited, and he could do the same for her and the two of them, they could live here, in this space and be safe.

She turned her face inward, burying herself in his neck, in the scent of black pepper and citrus, her lips brushing over the light fluttering of his heartbeat as it began to calm, his hands, soft and warm, running up and down her back. She could feel his breath against her shoulder. And then against her ear, in the dark, she heard him.

"Hannah."

And he was still.

CHAPTER 33

The alarm on her phone woke her, alerting her that it was time to rise and get ready for her exercise class. She laughed wryly. *Yes, better not miss my workout.*

She hadn't closed the blinds in the room the night before, and the early daylight shone in across the bed, across the floor where her clothes lay in a heap. She rolled to her side, examining the bed beside her. Evidence of her insanity, she hoped she'd find him there, sleeping, still, his breath heavy and regular, his eyes moving behind his lids as he dreamt of her. But he was gone. He'd visited and left, and while the sheets twisted and tangled around her, Andrew was not within them.

"Mama!" Hannah heard Molly call from across the hall. "Mama. Come."

Hannah threw on her pajamas and walked into the hall. The door to the master bedroom was open, but the room was empty, the bed made, Michael gone. Hannah pondered briefly, feeling somehow distant from all that had occurred the night before, whether Michael had gone to work or whether he had gone instead to do whatever it is one does when he wants to have his insane wife committed. She hardly knew what those steps were, but Michael had seemed intent on completing them. And who could blame him?

She pulled Molly from her crib and dressed her and then thought, wherever Michael went, she didn't want to be home when he returned.

✦

Kate and Laura smiled weakly as Hannah took her place between them at the front of the room. One look at her reflection in the mirrors told her all she needed to know about the effect of the previous day's events on her. She'd pulled her hair into a ponytail, but wisps of it refused to be contained and flew at random from the sides and top of her head. Her face was blotchy, her eyes red from crying. And whatever else she'd done last night. Although she knew the moves well and had developed significant strength by this point, her arms and legs shook as she attempted to hold the isometric positions typical of the class.

She could see both Kate and Laura inviting eye contact but kept her focus straight ahead. Jennifer glided slowly between the two rows of women, and even she seemed to pause, if only briefly, catching sight of Hannah, evaluating her, then moving on.

As class came to a close, they adopted their pose of meditation, shevasena. Hannah turned her palms upward. She wanted to feel safe. She tried to close her eyes, but the white-gray textured tiles of the ceiling remained in her field of vision. She felt the dampness of her tears as they slid down the sides of her face into her hair, though she couldn't pinpoint when exactly she'd started to cry.

Then, across the narrow space between them, she felt the warmth of Kate's hand in hers, holding to her, and then Laura's hand, the steadiness of their bodies against the trembling of her own. Their assurances against her doubt.

The women around her began to stir, to rise and clean their spaces and move toward the cubbies outside the room and toward whatever plans they had for the rest of their day. But Laura and Kate remained still, and Hannah turned her head meeting Kate's eyes.

"Friend," Kate whispered. "Let's go back to my house. You shouldn't be alone right now." On her other side, Laura's hand squeezed lightly.

It seemed Kate and Laura collected her piece by piece, holding her as one holds the broken shards of a beautiful vase as they walked into Kate's house, Laura on one side with Chloe, Kate on the other, Hannah and Molly in the center. Steve was on his way out the door to work when they arrived, but his movements slowed, then stopped as he saw the women and two young children approaching the front steps.

"I can be late," he whispered to Kate and followed them back into the house. They walked slowly to the kitchen and took seats around the table in the bright, sunny breakfast nook.

"I'll take Molly and Chloe to the playroom," Steve said, setting his keys on the kitchen island along with his messenger bag. The two little girls followed Kate's husband down the stairs to the playroom in the basement, and Kate and Laura turned to Hannah, taking her hands in theirs again.

"Your brother?" Kate asked.

Hannah stared straight ahead at the bowl of oranges in the center of the table. She shook her head, and the tears started anew, tracking down her cheeks and falling to her gray tank top, marking small, charcoal polka dots.

"Michael?" Laura asked.

Hannah turned, her face confirming Laura's suspicion.

"What did he do?" Laura asked, ready for battle.

"It's what I did," Hannah whispered.

"I doubt it," Laura replied.

Hannah caught Kate's *take it easy* look directed at Laura.

"I think—" Hannah began, "I think I'm going crazy." She thumbed at the placemat in front of her.

"Did he tell you you were crazy?" Laura asked.

"Yes. But he's not wrong," Hannah said.

"I can promise you he is," Laura said.

"What happened?" Kate invited.

Hannah told them everything. She told them about Jack Burke and Fiona Kemp, about Michael and the wedding and the hotel bar where they met, about how she'd loved him once, or she thought she had, and he'd loved her once, or he sort of had. She told them about the picnic and Jeremy and how Michael was wrong about Jeremy, but almost not. And then she told them about Andrew, about the photographs she'd found and the way she felt him with her always, about the way she saw him in the house, and heard him in the silence there, about how he visited her and made love to her, and how she didn't mind if she was crazy if it meant that she could keep him, and she thought she could endure almost anything, but not the loss of Andrew. And so, when Michael told her he was going to have her committed, she thought the only things that upset her about that were that he was going to take away Molly, and the pills were going to take away Andrew, and so she'd be better but worse.

The women sat in silence as Hannah unraveled before them. Steve appeared in the kitchen and set the kettle on, then returned to the basement.

"You're not crazy; you're lonely," Kate said, running her thumb over the back of Hannah's hand.

"And I'm also guessing your ACE score is off the fucking charts," Laura added.

"What's an ACE score?" Hannah asked.

"It's hard to explain. It measures trauma. It's like a golf score; lower is better," Laura replied.

"Do you think I need to be committed?"

"No," Kate said without hesitation. "I don't even know what that means. *To be committed?* Like to be sent to a hospital? No, you don't need that. You need a really good therapist and a divorce lawyer."

"But I'm in love with him," Hannah whispered. "I'm in love with someone who's dead."

"No, Hannah. You aren't," Kate said gently. "You are in love with a dream, a dream of someone who is kind and smart and who loves you, and who, from the pictures, was pretty easy on the eyes. But you don't know Andrew Decker. You don't have any idea what he was like. You don't know what his favorite song was or his favorite color. You don't know what he looked like when he slept, or whether he snored. You don't know if he was good in bed or selfish and inattentive. You don't know if he talked with his mouth full or was the kind of guy to fart in bed and then flap the covers."

Hannah laughed at this, and Laura smiled.

"You aren't in love with him, Hannah. You want something you don't have. You want something that isn't even all that extraordinary. And you aren't crazy for wanting it."

The kettle whistled loudly, and Steve returned from the basement, pouring three mugs of hot water, which he set on the table along with a box of Darjeeling tea. He ran a hand lightly over the span of Kate's shoulders, then disappeared once again.

"You aren't going to be committed. That's not even how that works," Kate said, smiling kindly at her friend. "You and Molly can stay here, and Steve will get you a lawyer from his firm that you can talk to. You aren't crazy."

Later that morning, after they drank their tea and Steve kissed Kate on the cheek and left for work, Laura and Chloe returned home with instructions to Hannah to let her know if she needed anything. Kate, Molly, and Hannah then drove to the Decker house, where Hannah packed one suitcase for herself and one for Molly while Kate waited in the car for them. Then Hannah called Michael at work and let him know that she and Molly would not be coming back to the Decker house.

CHAPTER 34

The room was lightless. Hannah had missed dinner. Downstairs, the front door closed. She hadn't heard it open, but the sound as it closed created a sucking noise that reached her even behind the door of the bedroom. She could hear the voices downstairs, too, and some of the words, from where she lay under the quilt that Kate's mother had made when Kate was awarded her doctorate.

"... don't think I should stay," a man said at a volume that could be heard but suggested he didn't want to be.

Not Michael. He'd already tried to visit and been refused. He hadn't handled it well. She could tell by the way Kate had said, "Steve's walking him to his car."

That was two weeks ago, and at first, Hannah thought she had this in her. But then, she'd met with the attorney at Steve's firm, and the profound finality of it all—her failure—descended over her. She said she'd call when she was ready to file. She had two unread emails from the lawyer on her phone.

Below, a small voice, high, excited, unintelligible. Molly's. A pang shot through her, and she rolled to her side, folding in on herself, pulling the quilt up under her chin. She closed her eyes—like a child. *If I can't see it, it's not there.*

"Thanks... trip... airport." Steve's voice.

The door opened, then closed again. *Sloosh.*

The voices below reached her, wordless. Molly, Steve, Kate's kids. Receding as they moved out into some part of the house where voices were less inclined to travel up the stairs to the guest room. "Hannah?" It was Kate through the door, the rap of her knuckles making it a duet. "Hannah, there's someone here to see you."

Hannah felt herself fold farther into the quilt. She pictured Michael's face and almost found relief in that. He would tell her enough of this; time to come home. And she'd get in his car with Molly, and this would all be over. But she could picture nothing after that. Her mind did not expand into the Decker house, into her bedroom, into her bed with Michael next to her.

The door squeaked open, and the light from the hall cast a single bar of gold through the room, cutting a narrow rectangle of vivid green and blue on the rug.

The door closed again, and Hannah was no longer alone.

"Hannah, dear?"

Hannah rolled to her side, trying to make out the figure in the dark.

"Hannah." Weight on the edge of her bed.

"Grandma."

"Oh, baby girl."

"Grandma, you're here."

"I'm here."

"Grandma. It hurts. It hurts."

"I know. I know, baby girl. It hurts like hell."

❦

"No, no, no, no, no, no!" Molly stomped her feet, creating an impressive echo throughout the foyer of the Decker house.

"It's okay, Molly," Hannah coaxed. "It's just for the weekend."

"We're going to the zoo. Doesn't that sound like fun?" Michael asked, with ill-fitting and artificial exuberance.

Molly lay down on the floor, chest-to-tile. "Nooooooo!!!" she howled.

"I—I can't do this," Michael said, looking to Hannah with absolute terror behind his eyes. "What am I supposed to do? People will think I kidnapped her."

"She's just not—" Hannah stopped. She was prepared to say, "used to you," which was true.

Imagining that all they needed was some time away from each other, Michael had gone alone to Basingstoke. He'd found an apartment, alone. And he'd purchased enough furniture to make it hospitable, alone. He'd made his dinners and eaten them, alone. And he'd called Hannah weekly, leaving messages that when she felt up to it, he was ready for her—for them—to join him. And then he'd left texts. He missed her. He had a home ready for them. The schools were better than in Indiana. He'd found an apartment across from a park. Finally, Hannah answered the phone and told him. She would be filing for divorce at the end of the week.

She couldn't see him crying and had never seen him cry during their marriage so had no notion of what had been his state on the other end of the phone. But he returned to Indianapolis a week later, accepted service and subsequently signed the divorce papers without much fuss. Hannah's attorney told her he'd briefly toyed with the notion of fighting her on the house, but that hadn't lasted long. There'd also been some talk about his seeking full physical custody of Molly, a prospect that now seemed laughable considering his daughter's response to the agreed upon visitation schedule of every-other-weekend.

"She doesn't like me," Michael said.

"She doesn't really know you, Michael," Hannah said.

Molly quieted as she sensed she'd be getting her way, and Hannah leaned over and picked her up off the floor. She rested her head on Hannah's shoulder, shuddering from the efforts of her tantrum.

"Why don't you join us for dinner?" Hannah suggested. "Why don't we start there?"

"Yeah, okay," Michael agreed. He placed his coat in the closet and followed Hannah across the foyer into the breakfast room.

"I made a casserole," she said.

"Jesus, you are a Hoosier," Michael said, then immediately corrected. "Sorry. I mean, it smells delicious."

Molly, realizing that the tide had turned fully in her favor, allowed herself to be placed in her booster seat, and Hannah set a spaghetti casserole on the table. Michael went to the kitchen and pulled an extra plate from the cupboard, adding a place setting for himself.

"How's Gary?" he asked once they were seated.

"He's good. He gave me two more jobs south of here, so that's keeping me busy." Hannah scooped some of the casserole onto her plate. "Molly, use your fork," she said, as Molly lifted a fist full of food to her mouth. The little girl scowled her dissent but picked up the small fork next to her plate.

"Any interesting galley kitchens?" Michael asked, with a chuckle.

"No," Hannah said, returning a smile. "The houses are older than that."

She felt the faint prick of disappointment as she realized suddenly that the story of the island in the galley kitchen was not Michael's favorite story about her time with her grandparents; it was the only story he knew. There were others that were better, and she wasn't sure whether she'd never told them to him, or whether she had, once, and he'd forgotten.

They ate in silence for a few minutes longer, both pretending to focus on Molly, as if she might need something, until she eventually threw her hands in the air.

"All done!" she announced with the confidence of someone who might receive a medal for the accomplishment.

"You can get down," Hannah said, and Molly slid from her seat. Hannah got up and walked with Molly to the kitchen. She pulled a dishrag from the sink, wiping Molly's hands which she'd surreptitiously relied on to some extent during dinner. Then Molly made her way to the family room where she'd play until bedtime.

"You still take your after-lunch walks?" Michael asked as Hannah returned to the table. She cocked her head to the side and frowned as she regarded him, disappointed in the transparent motivation behind his question. He'd never believed her. Even after she told him everything. It seemed unfathomable to him that Jeremy would have refused her, would have walked her to her house without so much as a peck on the cheek.

"I haven't seen Jeremy in months," she said.

"I mean—I couldn't stop you. We're not married. You can take walks with whoever you want," he said, trying so very hard to sound casual.

"Just the same. Our schedules must not overlap anymore," she said.

Michael set his napkin next to his plate. "I guess it's expecting too much to think she'd come with me to Boston for Thanksgiving." He gazed purposefully toward the family room.

"You're actually supposed to have her for Christmas. I'm taking her to Clover for Thanksgiving. You want to take her to Boston for Christmas?" The thought of not seeing Molly on Christmas landed in Hannah's gut like an anvil.

"I don't know how I could," Michael said. "I don't see this resolving itself before then."

"Things don't resolve themselves, Michael. You have to spend time with her."

Michael exhaled and scanned the breakfast room. "They did a nice job," he said. "*You* did a nice job."

"I didn't do anything in this room," Hannah demurred.

"Maybe not this room," he agreed with some evident reluctance.

"It's too big for us. We only use five rooms in the entire house, and two of those are bedrooms."

Michael gazed at her, wide-eyed.

"What?"

"You sound like you're thinking of selling," he said.

"Don't worry. I'll let you know when I do. I know you have to consent to the sale, too," she said, feeling defensive.

"No. That's not what I mean," Michael said. "It just never occurred to me that you'd ever want to sell this place."

"It really doesn't make very much sense for us," she said a little sadly.

"Where would you go? Would you stay here? In Indianapolis?"

"Oh yeah," she said. "I think just some place smaller."

Michael nodded. "Do you want me to reach out to Debbie?"

"Not yet. Let's get through the holidays."

HANNAH STEPPED out of her car and pulled the collar of her coat up around her ears. The parking lot was plowed, and large hills of ice and snow lined the perimeter of one side, creating a shortage of spaces at the Indiana Historical Society. She'd gotten one of the few that remained. She recognized Michael's car and hoped she wasn't the last to arrive.

Her fears were put to rest as she walked through the doors of the conference room to see Michael, Kate, and Carrie—the Executive Director of the Indiana Historical Society.

"The Moores are running late," Carrie said as Hannah found a seat around the large conference room table. "Weather."

"Someone's supposed to come from The Society of Architectural Historians, too," Hannah said.

"They're attending by Zoom," Carrie said. "Chicago got hit worse than we did."

"Jeremy's running behind, as well," Kate added, setting her phone down—the message from him had just come through. She stole a glance at Hannah, who tried to appear disinterested in that piece of information, but assumed the act wasn't persuasive.

It had been impossible to avoid Jeremy over the past year and a half —they'd lived quite literally down the street from each other for much of that time. But they'd done their damnedest, managing to limit their interactions to the occasional-if-unavoidable "Hello." "Good to see you again." "Good-bye." And then, six months ago, she and Molly moved, and even in their small town with the big buildings, Hannah and Jeremy did not cross paths.

"You can always count on Indiana to deliver the most inconvenient weather," Carrie said.

Banal small talk to pass the time. The storm had been impressive, though. Thirty-six hours earlier, a previously mild, if rainy, winter dumped ten inches of snow on the ground, then dropped the temperature to an impressive eight degrees Fahrenheit. Then, just for good measure, it delivered another three inches of snow.

"Well, you know what they say," Kate said. "If you don't like the weather…"

"Stick around; it'll change," Hannah volunteered.

Michael smiled in her direction.

"Sorry, I'm late," Jeremy said from the door behind Hannah. "I swear to God, this city refuses to learn how to do winter." He unwrapped a scarf from his neck.

"Cleveland," Kate said to Carrie, as she pointed to Jeremy.

"Santa Monica," Carrie said, pointing to herself.

"Oooooh," the room offered in unison.

The arrival of the three Moore children interrupted the small talk and completed the room, and The Society of Architectural Historians was brought online.

"Alright. The plan is for the purchase of the house by IHS and SAH, for purposes of creating a museum about the architect Andrew Decker and his wife Eleanor Dailey Decker," Carrie said, beginning the meeting with an air of officiality. Hannah half expected her to hammer a gavel on the table. Instead, she passed around an agenda.

In accordance with the agenda, Hannah detailed the items she had in her possession, including some of the original furniture from Andrew's time in the house, along with his books, several of his original signed blueprints, and a number of important documents that assisted in establishing the chronology of the man's life.

"And we'll be clarifying that he was murdered, rather than that he died by suicide. Correct?" Carrie asked, her question intended, it seemed, for the Moores, though it was Kate, Jeremy, and Hannah, who so firmly and convincingly argued for this correction.

"About that," Andrew Moore said, his gaze sliding in the direction of his sister Nancy, whom Hannah thought did bear a striking resemblance to her mother. "I don't know what the rules are on something like this. And we're all in agreement that our grandfather was murdered. He didn't kill himself." Craig and Nancy both nodded their agreement. "But we don't feel comfortable pointing fingers. Seems to us *the who* of it all is pretty undetermined." His eyes met Hannah's, seeking her agreement.

She sympathized and felt her loyalties to the Moores announce themselves; she understood the weight one carried as the custodian of another's legacy. Still, she didn't think it seemed undetermined. The only things Hannah couldn't determine were the finer details. Who pulled the trigger? How did they get in the study without Andrew noticing? Questions to which she'd reconciled herself never having the answers.

Carrie saved Hannah from having to weigh in on the matter. "I agree that it's not actually clear what happened in that study on January 12th, 1933. I'm confident he did not die by suicide. But I also agree there is real harm to be done in suggesting the identity of a murderer in a case that was closed one hundred years ago. I mean, if I'm understanding correctly, his sister was a suspect for a short time."

"Aunt Mary absolutely did not kill him," Nancy said. "That is simply not possible. If she could have stepped in front of that bullet, she would have."

Craig and Andrew offered a single synchronized nod of their heads. *That matter is settled*, it said.

"We do run into this issue from time to time when dealing with families connected to our exhibits," Carrie said. "The fact that an exhibit—or even an entire museum—is created to honor someone's life doesn't necessitate that every detail be told about that life."

Jeremy raised his hand to speak.

"You don't have to raise your hand," Carrie said, smiling flirtatiously.

"Yeah, you're tenured now. You get to just interrupt and hold forth," Kate added.

"Congratulations!" Hannah offered, the first words she'd spoken to him in months.

"Thanks," he returned, then addressed Carrie. "I feel fairly confident that Edward Lehmann murdered Decker. Especially since he disappeared afterwards and never returned to the Midwest. His name doesn't show up in a single historical record that I can find, so I'm pretty sure it was an alias. What I'm unclear on, is the role of Eleanor —or anyone else, for that matter—and that gives me pause."

"We can just say something general. That his death was thought a suicide at the time, but that evidence discovered years later suggests an intruder shot him," Carrie suggested. "I mean, Lehmann was definitely intruding."

The Moores huddled together, their three foreheads nearly touching. "We're comfortable with that," Andrew said, addressing the full group again. "But we don't want the love letters or Harper's December '32 correspondence included in the exhibits."

"Tom, what are your thoughts?" Carrie asked the 2-D image on Zoom.

"That would mean emphasizing his contributions to architecture and her connection to the history of the quarries, and doing that over any personal biography, which is fine with us. That's what we're interested in anyway."

"Michael, any concerns?" Carrie asked.

"None," he said. "I'll be honest. I have no interest in this museum. I'm only here because, at least for now, I own half of that house."

Carrie appeared surprised by the sharp tone of Michael's retort but recovered quickly and continued outlining the steps forward—the plans for the acquisition of the house, several ideas for exhibits within it, a timeline confirmed, and potential funding, both public and private.

The meeting adjourned with Andrew Moore, Hannah, Jeremy, and Kate offering to serve as the first members of the museum's Board of Directors.

"You want to grab a coffee?" Kate asked Hannah as people collected their coats and hats at the conclusion of the meeting.

"Maybe another time," Hannah said. "I think I might take a walk along the canal. Clear my head. This has been a lot to take in. I'll text you, later?"

"Sounds perfect," Kate said. The two women exchanged a hug, and Hannah started packing up her belongings. Before long, she and Michael were the only two in the boardroom.

"I think you made the right decision," Michael said.

Hannah evaluated him, seeking to determine what ulterior motives might be at work in his enthusiasm for selling the Decker house, essentially making it impossible for anyone to live in it ever again. She found no malevolence lurking behind his eyes, though.

"You're right that it's too big a house for just two people," he said, the qualification seemingly aimed directly at her suspicion of him.

"I think his grandchildren are happy, too," she said.

"You really think his wife's lover killed him?" he asked. He'd received a bolus of the architect's biography when Hannah came to him with the idea of selling the house for purposes of establishing a museum.

"I don't know," Hannah said honestly. She could still hear Jeremy's confidence from just thirty minutes before. "I know he didn't kill himself. And I think Margaret Decker knew that, too. I just think that was a lot easier of a story to tell than jealousy, and affairs, and con-artists, and all that. And then once Eleanor died, I imagine no one really felt like there was much to be gained from pointing a finger in *her* direction."

Michael bobbed his head from side to side in consideration of her arguments. "I suppose," he said and buttoned the last button on his coat. "Well, enjoy your walk." He offered Hannah a quick peck to the cheek, a strange, awkward farewell, before walking out into the hallway and out to his car.

Hannah lingered in the quiet of the boardroom. Carrie had left the documents on the center of the table, evidently planning to come back and retrieve them later. Among the photographs the Moores had contributed were many Hannah had never seen before, those that hadn't been left behind in the house, that had been kept with the family and brought out for purposes of the exhibits Carrie had described.

Hannah gazed down at the handful that sat on top: Andrew with his high school basketball team in 1906; Andrew sleeping in the solarium, a book resting on his thigh; Margaret playing with the daughter of a boarder the Deckers had taken on during the Depression; Eleanor sitting in one of the guest rooms she'd turned into an office for herself. Hannah brushed a hand over the top of the photographs, each of them memorializing some aspect of Andrew's life she could never possibly know.

She left the boardroom, allowing the door to close behind her, and walked out of the brick and limestone building, a plume of white vapor preceding her as she stepped into the frigid air. She felt strangely at ease, as if she'd safely delivered Andrew Decker into the hands of those who loved him, to whom he belonged, and thus, she could finally say good-bye.

She crossed the parking lot, her attention focused on her feet for fear of slipping on snow or the newly formed ice. As she reached her car, she saw Jeremy leaning against the back of his Honda. He had his black quilted coat pulled tight around him, a knit cap snug over his ears. His nose and cheeks were pink from the time he'd spent outside in the cold.

He stood, tucking his hands nervously into his pocket as Hannah came closer.

"Hi," he said.

"Hi."

"I heard you say you were going to take a walk."

CHAPTER 35

Hannah angled her face up to the sun, which cut through the bright green of the trees, warming her cheeks and shoulders. It had been uncharacteristically warm so far that June. The black asphalt of the road had absorbed the heat of the day, and Hannah could feel it radiating through the bottoms of her sandals. Up ahead, Molly pedaled with determination, her small bike rocking back and forth between the two training wheels. Beside the bike, Gertie trotted, probably displeased with the pace, but unwilling to leave her human's side. Jeremy walked next to Hannah, one hand holding hers, the other holding Gertie's leash.

"We talked about Mason, today," Hannah said, still facing the sun.

"Those days are always hard. How are you holding up?" Jeremy asked.

"Okay, I guess. It gets easier every time we talk about him."

Jeremy let go of Hannah's hand and brushed a loose strand of hair out of her face, tucking it behind her ear. She smiled at him meekly, and he brought his lips to her temple, placing a delicate kiss there.

"She thinks I should let my mom come visit for Christmas this year. What do you think?"

"If you feel ready to see her again. You might suggest she stay at a hotel," he said, offering a compromise of sorts.

"You don't think that would be weird? What would I tell her?" Hannah asked.

"That you'd like to see her, but want to take things slowly," he said, smiling at their inside joke. This had been Hannah's bold request to Jeremy eighteen months earlier in the parking lot of the Indiana Historical Society. I'd like to start seeing you, but I want to take things slowly.

And so, they'd resumed their walks, finding a pace that worked for them both.

"I'll take the drinks up to the house if you want to take Molly home," Jeremy said, handing Hannah Gertie's leash. From the foot of the hill, Hannah could see the tables and chairs, the white tent already erected in anticipation of the picnic that weekend. She hadn't resided in the home for some time now, but retained a key with the blessing of both the Moores and the proprietors of the Decker-Dailey History Museum that now owned the property.

"Thanks," Hannah said, handing Jeremy her keys, grateful she would not have to haul the heavy cooler up the long, now-paved driveway.

He kissed her softly on the cheek, lingering for only a couple of seconds—there would be time for more kisses later—then started climbing the hill, the cooler rolling behind him. Hannah paused for a minute watching him, the yellow bricks of the house fixed and unmoving before her, then she continued on around the loop with Molly and Gertie until they reached the yellow Cape Cod with the blue door and well-tended gardens.

"I'm going to watch TV," Molly said as she climbed up on the couch once they were inside the house.

"Okay, baby girl. We'll have dinner when Jeremy gets back."

"Okay," Molly said, already distracted by Gertie who climbed clumsily onto the couch and nosed her way under Molly's arm.

Hannah passed through the living room and into the kitchen. It was warm, but there was a breeze outside. She opened the back door letting the summer air flow through the screen door into the kitchen, carrying the scent of cut grass and summer sun with it.

Tomorrow, they'd host the Founder's Picnic. They'd offer drinks for the neighbors who would bring bar-b-que and cornbread and potato salad and rhubarb pie. But tonight, they'd have dinner together in the kitchen, and then they'd sit in the living room and talk until it was time for Molly to go to bed. Later, they'd go to bed themselves, and Jeremy would pull her to him, his body warm under the cool sheets, and in the dark of the room, she wouldn't be able to see him, but she would hear his voice, and feel his hands and his lips, and she'd know it was Jeremy and that he loved her.

As for Andrew, he didn't visit anymore, but he'd always be there in the house he'd built. He'd been happy there, and sad. He'd raised one daughter and mourned another. He'd slept, and breathed, and laughed, and cried. He'd made love and lost it and been both joyful and lonely. These were the things Hannah sometimes thought as she walked through the corridors of the museum, as she adjusted a small item of Andrew's or Eleanor's in one of the exhibit rooms. That Andrew had been, at one time, completely and totally of this world and that she was still, in some ways, sad that he no longer was, and that his time here had been so abrupt, so short.

But mostly, now, Hannah thought that she was of this world, and that she'd been happy and sad, loved and been loved, slept and breathed, and laughed, and cried, she'd made love and lost it, been both joyful and lonely. And while many of those she loved were no longer here, their time abrupt and short, hers was not. And she stood at the screen door facing the backyard of her home with Jeremy, turned her palms upward, open to possibilities, closed her eyes, and breathed.

DISCUSSION QUESTIONS

Below are several questions that may assist in framing your book club conversation.

1. The Prologue of *Load Bearing* is told from the point of view of the Kormans' realtor, Debbie, who simultaneously shows the Decker house to the Kormans and the Kormans to the reader. Why do you you think the author chose to open the story this way?

2. There are several important metaphors contained in the book that (hopefully) deepen the reader's connection to the characters and their story. Some of those include, the Decker house, Hannah's skill at cabinet-making, and the title of the book itself. What do these things represent and what do they tell us about the characters in the story?

3. How does the author make use of space to define and guide Hannah's journey? How does space shape our own world? Are there spaces in this book and in our lives that are privileged, disvalued, gendered?

4. What is it about Andrew Decker that draws Hannah to him? In what ways are Hannah and Andrew similar to and different from each other? Does Hannah admire Andrew? Is she merely physically attracted to him?

5. When Mason dies, Hannah reaches a crisis point. What is it

about her relationship with Mason that makes his death so hard for her? They hardly ever saw each other, communicated inconsistently by phone and text, and their conversations seem relatively short and superficial. Were they "close"?

6. Although *Load Bearing* is women's fiction (centering Hannah's story), there are several very important men in this novel, and they are all quite different from each other. How do Michael, Mason, Hannah's grandfather, Jeremy, Gary, Connor, Jason, Jack, and, of course Andrew Decker, represent masculine qualities that are either supportive and/or destructive for Hannah? Are these men (any of them) "good men"? What makes them good or not?

7. As Hannah learns more about Andrew Decker's marriage to Eleanor Dailey, she learns that her original impression of the Deckers is far from accurate. Why do you think the author wrote the Decker marriage as so deeply flawed (and ultimately broken)? Does this strengthen or weaken the overall story? Would it have been better to have the Deckers truly be "a couple for the ages" as Andrew Moore describes them? Would having a marriage to aspire to have helped Hannah fix her marriage with Michael?

8. How does this novel raise questions about the allocation of power within a marriage? How *is* power allocated in the Korman marriage? In what ways is power unequal?

9. Jane Hartsock is a Midwestern author, and this novel is set in the Midwest. In what ways is the novel itself *Midwestern*? How do you see Midwestern culture and norms represented? How might this story be different if it were set in New York City or Denver, Colorado?

10. At the end of the novel, Hannah tells Laura and Kate that she thinks she's crazy. They tell her she's not; she's just lonely. Are they right?

11. What role do Laura and Kate play in protecting and healing Hannah? What does this say about the importance of women's friendships?

12. In the scene in the blue room after the Founders Day Party, is Hannah fantasizing, dreaming, experiencing psychosis, or does Andrew Decker's ghost actually visit her?

AFTERWORD

Whenever I read a piece of historical fiction, I am always left feeling a little disoriented. I often read historical fiction to learn about history but come away uncertain what was history and what was fiction. The purpose of this Afterward is to assist in differentiating the two. Further, because one of the purposes of this novel is hopefully to inspire some curiosity about the history of Indiana, I provide additional resources if one wishes to explore more deeply.

Nearly all of the people portrayed in this novel are fictional. The Kormans, Kemps, and Burkes are not real people, and are not based on real people. The Deckers and Daileys, and Andrew, Eleanor, and Margaret Decker in particular, are not real people and are not even loosely based on anyone who ever lived (as far as I know). The Decker house is an amalgam of several city mansions existing in Indianapolis, the histories of which I have intentionally not investigated because I did not want to, even accidentally, approximate a specific home, neighborhood, architect, or builder.

The quarries and mills are similarly constructed—an amalgam of many, many quarries that existed in Bloomington and Bedford in the first half of the twentieth century. Although I have done considerably more research into those quarries so that they could provide (hopefully) an accurate backdrop for this story, Dailey Limestone, Ltd. is not based on any single quarry. Indiana limestone built every structure referenced in this novel (and quite a few that weren't), and its dominance from 1922-1932 as noted in this novel produced significant wealth for the owners of the quarries and mills, the towns in which they were located, and the lives of the individuals who worked in them.

There are other aspects of this story that are more closely connected to real settings. Butler University is a real university, though Kate and Jeremy are not based on any specific professor there. The fitness studio Laura, Kate, and Hannah frequent is based on Barre Ripple Studio in Broad Ripple. Hubbard & Cravens is my step-dad's favorite coffee shop. And Meridian-Kessler is a lovely and very real neighborhood in Indianapolis. Hyde Park is not.

John Duvall was indeed the mayor of Indianapolis from 1926-1927. His biography, including his connection to the Ku Klux Klan, is accurately reflected in this novel. Likewise, the influence, behavior, and membership of the Ku Klux Klan in Indiana is accurately portrayed here to the best of my knowledge.

With respect to the history of Italian immigration as it relates to Indiana's quarries and mills, it is true that twenty Italian men immigrated to Indiana in 1882 approximately ten years after the unification of Italy (1871) for the express purpose of working in the limestone quarries here. They were specifically hired by David Reed of Reed Quarry, which is located in Bloomington, not Bedford.

This same period of time saw an increase in the number of Catholic German immigrants, hence St. Joseph's Catholic German cemetery in which Andrew Decker and his family are buried. Dr. Henry Decker's experience as a physician, as described by Jeremy, is also accurate for his time and location in Indiana.

As a final matter, I have not read Melania Trump's "autobiography," nor do I intend to. After all, which Melania is it the autobiography of? I did like her coat on inauguration day, though.

BIBLIOGRAPHY

The following resources were relied on in the drafting of this novel:

Patrizia Audenino, "The Paths of the Trade: Italian Stonemasons in the United States." The International Migration Review. 20, no. 4 (1986): 779-795

Sarah Bowman. "The surprising Indiana origins of the Pentagon, Empire State Building and more landmarks." IndyStar. February 1, 2022.

Robert C. Brown. "The Indianapolis Mayoralty Cases." Indiana Law Journal. 4, no. 3 (1928): 194-199.

Kurt Christian. "Vintage photos illustrate vital role of Indiana limestone in U.S. History." The Times-Mail January 31, 2016.

Hattie Clark. "Artists on a Limestone Canvas: From tablets of Indiana bedrock, cutters and carvers sculpt the pillars, cornices, and facades of some of the nation's most famous buildings." The Christian Science Monitor. August 4, 1987.

James J. Divita. "The Indiana Churches and the Italian Immigrant 1890-1935." U.S. Catholic Historian. 6, no. 4 (1987): 325-349.

Bethany Emenhiser. "The Street that Limestone Built: A walk through the Vinegar Hill National Register District." The Herald Times. June 17, 2017.

Fragrantica. "Blenheim Bouquet Penhaligon's: for men." Url: https://www.fragrantica.com/perfume/Penhaligon-s/Blenheim-Bouquet-3940.html

History. "Italy in WWI." Url: https://www.history.co.uk/italy-in-wwi

Indiana University Bloomington. Building a Nation: Indiana Limestone Photograph Collection. Images Collection Online. Url: https://webapp1.dlib.indiana.edu/images/splash.htm?scope=images/VAC5094

J.P. Leake. "Health Hazards from the Use of the Air Hammer in Cutting Indiana Limestone." Public Health Reports (1896-1970). 33, no. 12 (1918): 379-393.

James H. Madison. The Ku Klux Klan In The Heartland. Bloomington: Indiana University Press, 2020.

BIBLIOGRAPHY

Monroe County Public Library. Indiana Bedrock: Limestone Industry TIMELINE. url: https://mcpl.info/sites/default/files/Timeline.pdf

Andrea Neal. "Indiana at 200: The Fame of Indiana Limestone" Greensburg Daily News. July 24, 2014.

Clay W. Stuckey. "Origins of the Indiana Limestone Company." 2nd Ed. 2016.

Fiorello B. Ventresco. "Loyalty and Dissent: Italian Reservists in America During World War I." Italian Americana. 4, no. 1 (1978): 92-122.

William Clayton Wilkinson Jr. "Memories of The Ku Klux Klan in One Indiana Town." Indiana Magazine of History. 102, no. 4 (2006): 339-354.

Sara Wittmeyer. "Preserved Quarry is a Lesson in History." Indiana Public Media July 13, 2015. Url: https://indianapublicmedia.org/news/preserved-quarry-lesson-indiana-history.php

Katja Wüstenbecker, "German-Americans during World War I." Immigrant Entrepreneurship 1720 to the Present. Url: https://www.immigrantentrepreneurship.org/entries/german-americans-during-world-war-i/

ACKNOWLEDGMENTS

In 2020, at the height of the pandemic, a good friend asked whether I ever write any fiction. It was an off-handed question related to the fact that I have a background in creative writing but write almost exclusively academically. I said no and made a joke about how I might consider starting given Freud's theory that writers of fiction are neurotics seeking to escape reality; there was a lot one might want to escape in 2020. I wrote rather frenetically, and most of it was not very good. But it had been a while (years, in fact) since I'd exercised that part of my brain, and in that time, it had atrophied significantly.

I finally came to the idea for this book when I was developing a course on health in Indiana and wanted to include the history of Indiana's limestone quarries. In light of the roundabout way I came to the subject for this novel and my own age at rediscovering fiction-writing, there are a number of people I wish to thank:

Thank you to my first-readers of this novel, Silja Koivuniemi and Michelle Mates, whose suggestions, honest feedback, and encouragement were invaluable.

I owe an enormous debt of gratitude to my extraordinary writing group, Mid-World Arts, for their serious attention and for their incredibly detailed suggestions and frankly, instruction in fiction writing. An extra thank you to Michael Murray for reading the whole damn thing, cover to cover, and providing helpful thoughts and suggestions along the way.

Sincere thanks also goes to the readers of my penultimate revision: Melody Chu, Isabelle Felix, Gifford MacShane, Sara Miller, and Amy Turner and, of course, to Erik Ives, who asked the question "Do you ever write fiction?"

To my Marshmallow Peelers, Emily Beckman and Katy Head, thank you for patiently and lovingly reading and painstakingly critiquing other things I wrote as I reacquainted myself with a voice I hadn't used in nearly half my life. And thank you for cheering me on at every turn of this strange journey. You will forever be inextricably intertwined with any fiction writing I do, as will the memories of our time spent bundled around fire pits, comforts to each other while the pandemic raged.

Thank you to my family—particularly my father who taught me to read and my mother who taught me to write and to my children, who are readers and writers themselves.

Finally, thank you to my husband Steve, impossibly steady and enduringly supportive. This is not the first time I've come to you saying, "I think I'm gonna..." and followed that up with a project that would take years. The response is always the same: "Okay. Cool." I know you asked me to marry you for your birthday, but you are the gift.

ABOUT THE AUTHOR

Jane Hartsock is a Hoosier by birth and by choice. She resides in Indianapolis, Indiana with her husband, their two children, and one poorly-behaved but well-intentioned Irish Terrier. She is a Bioethicist and a Medical Humanities professor, as well as a member of the board of the Good Trouble Coalition, a health justice and health advocacy organization that works to improve the health of Hoosiers.

If you enjoyed this book, please consider leaving a review on Amazon or Goodreads.

You can reach Jane on her website: https://janehartsock.com/ or connect with her on social media to discuss books she's read and how much coffee she's consumed: